Wolf's Den

The Ballad of
Tul'ran the Sword

Book the Fourth

Dale William Fedorchuk

E'thriel Publishing

AN E'THRIEL PUBLISHING BOOK

CALGARY

The Series

Other novels in the *Tul'ran* series by
Dale William Fedorchuk

The Ballad of Tul'ran the Sword

A Time, and Times, and Half a Time

Abandon Hope

Wolf's Den

When the Stars Fall

Escape and Evade

The Sacrifice

Ichor (coming soon)

All available in paperback, hardcover, and Kindle e-book editions from Amazon worldwide.

My novels are works of fiction that were not created from Artificial Intelligence programs. These words are mine. I give Jesus Christ credit for my abilities and for inspiring my writing. None of the words in my books came from a machine.

Please enjoy them.

The Copyright

The Acknowledgments

Dedicated, as always, to El Shaddai, who inspired it.

Second, to my beautiful, patient, loving, and kind wife, Anika. In this fourth book, I've chosen to honor a part of her heritage by incorporating the Ojibwe or Anishinaabe people into the novel. I am truly blessed by the gift of Anika in my life.

Third, to my beta reading group, who read the drafts and provided helpful insight, encouragement, and proposals: Anika Fedorchuk, Mike Bennett, Payton Goller, and Kendell Anquist.

I published this novel for Payton's 15th birthday. Happy Birthday, my dear niece. I wish you many more.

I am indebted to John MacArthur, who wrote *The MacArthur New Testament Commentary, Revelation 1-11* and *Revelation 12-22*. His books gave me a deep insight into the Tribulation period and what we can expect. If you're interested in the study of end times, I highly recommend his works. I also derived information from David Jeremiah's book, *Answers to Your Questions about Heaven*.

I authored this novel before August 2023. Since then, some distressing events in the world have paralleled scenes in my novels. If you find yourself distressed by current events, I encourage you to go to davidjeremiah.org for answers from a biblical scholar. If you read this novel after the Rapture, his site will tell you what comes next.

The Tales

The Cast

Tul'ran az Nostrom Tul'ran the Sword,	Born in 2037 BC, he became a famed warrior after Gutian renegades murdered his family and God assigned him as one of His Judges for the era before the time of Abraham.
Erianne de mi Corazon, Lady az Nostrom	Born in 2067 AD, Erianne became a Time Historian for the Time Travel Initiative. After a fractious introduction, she and Tul'ran fell in love and married.
Quil'ton az Peregos, Lamek Davis, "Mick" Lam'ek az Peregos	Davis, a retired Navy SEAL, joined TTI as a Protector. He became lost in time in 2025 BC and assumed the identity of Quil'ton az Peregos.
Omarosa of the Wastelands	The mother of two daughters, Innanu and Anatu.
Ro'gun az Peregos, Bondsman az Nostrom	Innanu's husband, and a Mesopotamian warrior bound to both Tul'ran and Quil'ton's House.
Dr. Heather Wu, PhD	A brilliant Programmer, one of many who programmed the time and spatial coordinates for the Navigation Coins used by TTI's Time Historians.

Darian Ostrowski, Darian O.	A former Controller for the Order of Purity, a terrorist organization run by Satan, she sacrificed her life to save Tul'ran on the World of Hope.
Dr. Johan Weinstein, PhD	A brilliant physicist who became a Time Historian to restore his family's honor by trying to kill Adolph Hitler. He married Gwynver'insa and stayed on the World of Hope after Tul'ran and Erianne left.
Gwynver'insa	A prophet of God and now the Empress of the liberated planet of Spes, the World of Hope.
Major Coventry Quarterlaine	A retired U.S. Marine seconded to TTI as a troubleshooter.
Dr. Michael Sullivan, MD, "Sully"	Davis's former teammate on the SEAL Teams, now a physician specialist.
Jeannie Sullivan	Sully's wife and a skilled trauma nurse.
Marjatta Korhonen	The Administrator of TTI, who reports only to the Supreme Global Leader.
Erasmus Hart	Head of Special Projects Division, a clandestine arm of TTI that reports directly to Korhonen.

Dr. Payton Dumont, MD	A trauma surgeon employed by TTI on Atlantis.
Malchus Contradeum	The Antichrist, who died and had his body indwelt by Satan.
Jezebel Brandt	Contradeum's former Executive Assistant and now Satan's slave-bride.
G'shnet'el	Formerly an angel of Heaven who fell with Lucifer and became one of Satan's chief lieutenants in Hell. He rules in the Abyss over unjudged souls.
E'thriel	Formerly an angel of Heaven who fell with Lucifer, before Tul'ran and Erianne helped to redeem him.
Evo, She Who Was Not	Created as the first woman on the planet Everhome, she grew to resent God and seeks to destroy Him.
Princess Wenonah Bearspaw	The hereditary ruler of the Nine Tribes of Ma'ilingan Waazh, the world known as Wolf's Den.
Baamewaawaagizhigokwe	Princess Wenonah's mother and the leader of the Tribes of Women on Ma'ilingan Waazh.
Chief Eric Ravenclaw	The Chief of the Tribes of Men on Ma'ilingan Waazh.

Nicholas Ravenclaw	The Chief's son and future leader of the Tribes of Men.
Aakwaadizi ("Dizi")	A sentient Wolf, which speaks telepathically with humans and is a weapon for the Tribes of Men.
Miikawaadad ("Miikaw")	A sentient Mountain Lion, which speaks telepathically with humans, and is a weapon for the Tribes of Women.

A Taste of Things to Come

Wolf's Den, 175th Year of Winter,
16,000 light years from Earth

Terror.

Terror tasted different in the mind than in other senses. The Hunter sniffed the wind, though his thought sense was far superior to his smell sense. The Den called him home from his long patrol, unexpectedly, and the route he took had been an unusual one. He had stumbled on the woman quite by accident. She shouldn't have been here, either.

The Hunter lay on his belly, not even feeling the snow. It was cold, but his long patrols accustomed him to the cold. This made him an invaluable asset to the Den because very few could hunt when the temperatures dipped this low.

His prey impressed him. After his mind contacted hers, she shielded her thoughts and pulled away from him into non-thought. It took considerable effort to enter the non-thought and hide behind its shield.

He wondered where she was going. There were no settlements this far north; the conditions didn't allow it.

He raised his nose to sniff the air again, and this time caught a ripe scent suggestive of many days of travel. He rose from the ground and scanned the snow in the scent's direction.

There.

Slight indentations, though carefully concealed, showed a path away from him, still going north. How intriguing. He again heard the call to return home, but didn't answer. Stealth was paramount against such wily prey; it wouldn't do to advertise his presence.

Another flash of terror. It was delicious on his mind and his mouth watered. It had been a while since he'd eaten human flesh. The taste, he remembered, was luxurious. Home could wait. He'd sample this one's flesh first.

It was difficult to track his prey. She was slow and cautious, picking places to rest which was not immediately discernible to his keen eye. The wind had shifted and now blew at her back, which disappointed him. Funny how the weather sometimes tried to spoil a perfect hunt. It didn't matter. He'd kill her soon enough.

He looked to the sky, gauging the path of the sun. It would be dark soon and the advantage would be his. She knew he was tracking her; he was sure of it.

Given such knowledge, she'd be loath to start a fire. Once the temperature dropped, if she didn't have shelter, she'd freeze. He licked his lips. Even a frozen woman's flesh was delicious.

The trail she left took a sudden turn into a large cleft in the mountain. He shook his head. Foolish, very foolish. He could see the sheer walls of the canyon. They'd give her no escape. The end of the canyon trapped her; she'd have to double back. Straight into his stomach. He yawned and his stomach growled. He had followed this prey for hours now, and the canyon walls were getting tighter. Just as he abandoned caution and ran after her, the path took a sharp turn.

He skidded to a halt, astonished. The trail ended at a sheer rock face. He could see her footsteps in front of the face of the rock. She couldn't have climbed it; there were no foot or hand holds. He stepped up to the rock and scratched at its surface. He sniffed it a few times before reaching out with his tongue to lick it. Solid rock.

He could no longer sense her thoughts or her scent on the wind. Angry, he walked away, but the memory of the taste of her terror lingered on his mind. He saw the footprints of rabbits near the path. They would be an easy kill and would sustain him if he waited. Somehow, she eluded him, but there was only one way out of the canyon.

He'd wait until she crawled out of her hole and then he'd sink his teeth into her flesh.

CHAPTER THE FIRST:
HOMECOMING QUEEN

Spes Deserit, in the Year of Our Fight 2375
Mission Day 46... the Day of Armageddon

Death.

The most feared face in human history has never belonged to the current tyrant of the day, or a narcissistic terrorist, or a famous entertainer with the morals of an alley cat and the conscience of a snake.

No, the most feared face has always been whatever caricature exists in a person's mind belonging to the specter holding the sickle ending his or her life.

Great philosophers opine death is the end of all things, a blank oblivion into which the soul disappears; of the person, nothing remains except the memories left behind, be they good or bad. Others posit death as being the reincarnation of life into something or someone else, or a place to do penance while awaiting salvation.

To Darian Angelic Ostrowski, who never thought of death as anything other than a source of soul-curdling fear, it was a new form of reality for which she hadn't prepared and for which she wasn't ready.

Darian felt the strength of E'thriel's arm as her guardian angel cradled her shoulders. On her other side, the power of her Lord flowed in currents from His body and massaged her from shoulders to shoes. The sun, revealed for the first time in hundreds of years on Spes Deserit, shone warmly upon her face. She felt more alive, more complete than ever in her life.

Except she was dead.

Her body, kneeling in front of her, braced to the ground by the spear empaling her heart and protruding out of her chest, was enough to convince even her most cynical side.

She watched as a conveyance lumbered from a maw near the entranceway to the Hall of the Ancestors. It was dusty, but seemed to be well-powered as it rode on a band of magnetic energy. It was a half-sled, not having an upper shell or canopy covering the sides like the train which brought her back to her friends. The walls of the conveyance came up just below the chest of a tall person.

Darian bit her lower lip as the man she claimed as a brother in her dying breath grimly marched to the waiting conveyance, his large right hand gripping the hilt of Bloodwing the Blade so tightly the knuckles glowed white.

Tul'ran had changed. She'd seen anger and grief mill around the muscles of his face as he'd stared at her skewered body until blue-colored energy rose from the surface of Bloodwing and plunged into his arm. Darian had stiffened, expecting the energy of uncreation to dissolve Tul'ran where he stood.

Fascinated, she watched as the Blade's quantum state physically changed the man she'd both feared and admired into... something else.

Tul'ran's eyes glowed a brilliant blue, and the copious muscles of his body writhed like serpents under his clothing and armor. His face darkened, shadows growing duskier under the ridges of his eyebrows and cheekbones. He had left on his face the streak of blood where her fingertips had touched him, a war painting of her life's essence running vertically down his cheekbone under his left eye to the edge of his mouth.

Whatever Tul'ran had been, he was no longer just a man. Something else now owned his body, and it terrified her. The Sword Himself jumped onto the conveyance, and it sped away. He hadn't looked back, didn't wave farewell, or acknowledge the scene behind him.

Tul'ran had become Death, and he was about to wreak havoc on the world. Darian shuddered. She'd asked him to avenge her, but now she had no desire to see what he'd do to affect her revenge.

She shifted her gaze to where her body laid in Erianne's arms as Erianne sat on the grass, cradling her tenderly and sobbing. Erianne had pulled the spear out of Darian from the front and cast it aside, screaming as the shaft came out of her corpse, covered in blood and gore. Erianne had sat back, pulling Darian's bloodied corpse onto her chest and shoulders, having no concern about the body fluids seeping into her leather armor, and wailed.

Gwynver'insa had disappeared, but came back with four attendants and a litter. The Empress kneeled beside Erianne and wrapped her arms around the taller woman's shoulders, her gentle voice shaking.

"You must let her go, sister. We must take her down into the Hall to wash her body and make her ready for the last rite of passage to her eternal home."

Erianne dropped her face onto Darian's head and moaned.

"I can't, sister. I can't let her go. We didn't do right by her, Gwyn. We should've gone back for her, ripped her out of Abaddon's arms, and brought her with us. She was part of our group and we abandoned her, and now she's dead!"

Gwynver'insa dropped her forehead onto Erianne's hair, as tears cascaded from her large blue eyes while the other woman sobbed.

"Yes, but she came back to us, Erianne. Wherever she went after we left, she found Yahweh and gave Him her soul. She rests in peace, sister. Get up, my love, and help me carry her home. We must prepare her for the Last Passage."

Darian felt tears roll down her cheeks and looked at Jesus, wonderment in her eyes.

"They're grieving for me?"

Jesus's smiled glowed on His face.

"Of course, they're grieving for you. This was once a world where people loved quickly, but deeply.

Someone could know you for a half day and by the evening meal adopt you as if you sprung from their loins. Erianne's heart has always been a carefully concealed wellspring of love for people; especially those who had been maltreated or ill-loved. Gwynver'insa and Erianne may not have known you for long, but they love you as they would love their closest sibling."

Darian took a long breath of newly cleansed air into her lungs.

"I promised Gwyn I'd be there at her wedding, Lord. It was the first time in my life I looked forward to anything. It was the one promise I'd hoped to keep."

The Lord turned Darian by the shoulders so she could see and feel the warmth of love emanating from His face in waves.

"There are many mysteries as it concerns Heaven and the life after this one. Once you have passed into the next life, We will give you an eternal body. It is one so complete in perfection, you would appear to someone in the life you left behind as a god. Once you have crossed over, Darian, you cannot come back."

Jesus's eyes twinkled.

"Of course, there are always exceptions to every rule and my Father and I do make the rules."

Darian laughed and hugged her Lord.

"Can we talk about Gwyn's wedding?"

Jesus grinned.

"We can, but not at this moment. Do you want to stay and watch what happens in this world? Or are you ready to transcend to the next?"

Darian thought about His question as she watched Gwynver'insa and Erianne lovingly wrapping a thin sheet around her body, covering everything except for her face. It was strange how at peace her face looked.

An attendant went to pick up Darian's feet to lift her onto the litter, but stopped, startled, as he found Gwynver'insa's small hand tightly clenched around his throat.

"Touch my sister and you die!" Gwynver'insa said, pain and sorrow turning the words into a hiss. She pushed the gaping attendant away and turned to meet Erianne's startled gaze.

"Only kin must carry Darian's body where it is to go for cleansing. It is the way of the People. Even if it were just me, instead of my tall, strong sister at my side, I would put Darian across my shoulders and carry her into the Hall. Until we have bathed and clothed her, Erianne, a stranger must not touch her."

Johan came ripping out of the doors to the Hall of the Ancestors just then, his eyes wild and breath coming out in gasps. He stopped, wide-eyed, as he saw Darian lying on the ground, and the blood drained from his face.

"How?" he asked, his throat barely squeezing out the word.

Gwynver'insa went to him and folded herself into his arms, crushing herself into his chest.

"It's my fault, Johan. As soon as I heard the sun had come out for the first time in hundreds of years, I raced outside, heedless of my personal safety. Tul'ran, Darian, and Erianne chased after me. Tul'ran and I were the first ones out the door. I, oblivious to danger, laughed and twirled under the sun, while an android sent by a Combatant advanced on Tul'ran's back to kill him. Darian pushed Tul'ran away from the attack and put herself in the path of the android's spear. Tul'ran reacted immediately and destroyed the android, but it was too late for Darian."

Johan's face tightened hard, his lips drawing into a rigid line.

"Androids! Combatants! Damn them to the lowest depths of Hell!"

Gwynver'insa squeezed his torso again.

"Gently, Johan. There is no shame in grieving, my love. Your pain displaces your tears into anger, and your rage cannot help us."

When Johan looked down at her, his voice softened, but the stiffness never left his face.

"She didn't die because of you, Gwyn. She's gone because I left her behind. I tossed her away like a used sheet and now she lies dead under one."

Erianne took a firm step forward and seized both of their stares with her brittle green eyes.

"Don't do that! Don't take away Darian's courage and sacrifice by taking responsibility for her death! She could have yelled, stayed in place, or frozen while the attack happened. Instead, she deliberately put herself in harm's way to save my husband. We shall honor her for her sacrifice and give her the hero's death she so richly deserves. We will *not* appropriate her bravery by making her the weak sister and taking accountability for her actions!"

Gwynver'insa bit her lip at the harshness of the response, and Johan nodded slowly.

"You're right. Darian wouldn't have wanted us to blame ourselves. She was too tough to play the victim." He looked around the area opposite the massive doors. "Where's Tul'ran?"

Erianne's face lost some of its fierceness and she gaze off into the direction into which the conveyance was long gone.

"My husband transcended manhood and humanity when Darian sacrificed herself for him. He has become a Fury, a Destroyer, a Berserker, and he rides to bring war in its most lethal form to the Combatants."

A grim smile crossed Johan's lips.

"Then they're already dead. Good riddance."

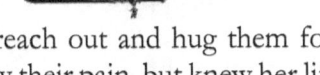

Darian wanted to reach out and hug them for one last time, touched by their pain, but knew her life was done and all such chances passed. She turned to Jesus, head bowed.

"I can't watch anymore, Lord. I saw what Tul'ran and Erianne did to the Gutians in the Massacre of the Gap. We saw what Bloodwing did to him minutes ago. I'm no longer the person who bathed in the blood of others and rejoiced in its flow. I'm ready to go home."

Jesus's smile, she thought, was one of the most beautiful things in the universe.

"Go with E'thriel," He said. "I must stay and watch, for Tul'ran is about to undergo his greatest trial and he may need my Voice in his ear before this day is done."

Darian bowed deeply, turned, and grabbed E'thriel's arm.

"C'mon, E'thriel. You're going to give me flying lessons before this day is done."

E'thriel laughed and guided her to take a step forward.

"By your command, your Royal Highness."

They took a step. Darian hadn't known what to expect. A long journey through time and space; a guided tour of the universe as they made their way to Heaven? Perhaps they would travel through a long, cold, winding wormhole, like their trip to Bethlehem?

With God, it was so much easier and gentler. She lifted her foot from Spes Deserit and dropped it onto a gleaming floor in the Kingdom of Heaven.

Her mouth dropped. The floor was smooth gold, with tall, thick agate pillars raised in a sky filled with a gentle snowy light. She and E'thriel were the only two in a corridor leading to a massive set of bronze doors.

Her second surprise was her attire. She'd been wearing the same clothing after her death as she had before the spear plunged into her back. Now, she dressed in a full-length, fully sleeved light gray shift, which conformed to her body without clinging.

Darian looked at E'thriel and quirked an eyebrow. He'd become grave, his face stoic, as if he steeled himself for an ordeal to come. She was going to say something, but he nudged her forward to the double doors.

When the doors opened, the scene before her made her stomach drop to her toes.

Jesus sat on a throne so white it made her eyes hurt. He did not look the same as the Man she just left. His face was gaunt and gray, and the scars on His wrists and feet were bright red. She had to rip her face away from Him. With no hint from E'thriel, she sunk to her knees; her face turning as white as the marble surrounding her.

"Darian, look at Me."

Darian started crying as she reluctantly tore her eyes from the floor and stared at His robe.

It was black and red, like arterial blood. Multiple squares made up His coat, but they weren't squares of cloth. They were small videos, each depicting a scene from her life when she tortured and killed others, had sexual intercourse out of wedlock, cursed, slandered God, and worshipped Satan. It was the vilest and most degrading thing she'd ever seen. It was the embodiment of a sinful life. Her life. The robe held every sin she'd committed, and her Saviour wore it instead of her. Darian wanted to throw up, and sank lower to the floor, moaning.

"Darian," Jesus said, in His tender voice. "Look at Me."

Reluctantly, filled with self-hatred and loathing, Darian forced herself to look upward into His eyes.

"E'thriel," He said, His voice a stern command, while He held her gaze. "Does this child's name appear in the Lamb's Book of Life?"

Darian tore her eyes away from the Lord, and the hideous robe she ought to have been wearing. E'thriel had moved to a massive book supported by two bronze pillars. The Author gilded the pages of the book in gold, and they glittered as the massive angel turned the pages, slowly. The cover of the book looked like they made it of white lambskin, but veins of gold shot through it. A title appeared on the outside cover made of raised gold metallic letters.

For long, tense minutes, everyone remained still as her guardian angel leafed through the pages of the Book. Finally, E'thriel paused on a page, ran his finger down the left side, then looked up with a broad smile.

"Yes, Lord, the name of Darian Angelica Ostrowski appears in the Lamb's Book of Life."

A tsunami of relief washed through Darian.

She didn't know exactly what it meant, but if it was important to the Lord, then it was important to her. Jesus stood up, and Darian stiffened. He unclasped the gruesome robe clinging to His body like a disease and flung it upwards. A bright flash of light exploded in her eyes.

When the sparkles in her vision cleared, she saw the robe back in her Savior's arms and it had become a beautiful, brilliant white. Jesus, now dressed in gleaming clean clothes, walked to Darian and draped the transformed robe around her shoulders.

"Darian, My blood and tears have washed away your sin. Your faith in Me has kept your name from being blotted from My Book of Life. My Father and I do not just forgive your sins; We have cast them as far away from Us as the east is from the west. Stand up, daughter."

Darian rose shakily to her feet. The light gray gown adorning her body had also changed into a brilliant white smock. Jesus held the cleansed robe to allow her to slip her shaking arms into the gloriously soft sleeves. The hood of the robe stretched halfway down her back. It was luxurious beyond anything she'd felt against her skin.

Jesus guided her to a smaller throne beside His.

Still shaking, she sat down, half expecting the marble throne to be as hard as, well, a rock. To her surprise, it felt as if she sank into a deep, silk-covered cushion.

No longer ashen with pain and sorrow, Jesus's skin glowed with power and exuberant health. His robes had transfigured into an appearance one could only describe as dazzling. He gestured to a wall in front of them, which lit up with new video projections.

"Darian, every human is required to give an account of their lives before they enter the Kingdom of Heaven. We will now review your life together."

Darian drew a long, ragged breath.

"This is going to be ugly, Lord. Do we have to?"

A knowing look crossed His face.

"I have forgiven you your sins," He reminded her, gently. "We will review your life in the light of My Grace."

Darian settled back into the back of her throne, determined to steel herself against what she knew was coming. It started well. She watched in awe as the Holy Spirit reached into her mother's womb and touched Darian at conception, giving her an eternal soul. She viewed her birth and was quick to note the differences in the atmosphere from what she expected. There was no celebration of an exhausted mother and a relieved father. Instead, a smug look passed between them as if they'd just accomplished phase one of a mission.

For the first twelve years, her life was a whirlwind

of childish activity. She trembled with delight when her father presented her with a horse for her sixth birthday. She remembered Rembrandt well; he was her only source of friendship and companionship as she grew up. Rare was the day when she was not walking, riding, feeding, cleaning, or just lying on the neck of her horse as they napped in a meadow on a warm summer day.

Her parents were extraordinarily wealthy. Darian's bedroom was the size of a middle-income earner's house. Every toy she desired was in her room the next morning. Her maids bathed her, dressed her, and played with her whatever game she commanded. She was a Princess, and she ruled her domain with the casual disdain royalty sometimes confers upon the poor people who must serve them.

Then she turned thirteen.

Darian's stomach clenched as she expected to see the vile debauchery her parents plunged her into when she came of age to have her menstrual cycle. She reached out and grasped Jesus's left arm, unmindful of the impropriety flowing from a servant clenching the limb of her King without permission. He didn't so much as flinch.

"Lord, do we have to watch this?"

Jesus laid His right hand over hers and drew her eyes to His.

"Darian, you do not sit in judgment of your parents, and we are not here to cause you pain. You will see nothing of the evil foisted upon you. Be at peace, daughter."

Darian settled back. True to His word, none of the remaining scenes had any of her parents' sexually vile conduct and the abuses of her body.

Only wonderful moments flitted across the screen. It showed times when Darian exhibited kindness, acts of charity, and love. She watched as she met Claude and fell into a whirlwind of love and romance, but the sequence ended before Satan tortured her and she abandoned Claude. Johan danced in front of her like a marionette, trying to keep her from pulling the trigger on Tul'ran and Erianne, and she laughed aloud.

The scenes from her life rolled by until the Android plunged the spear into her back, and then it was done. Darian shook her head, feeling drained. With the removal of the scenes having within them acts of evil, whether perpetrated by herself or others against her, the story of her young life was brutally short. There were delightful scenes, but they were few and far apart.

One such scene lingered in her mind. It was the day, just after she turned fifteen, she found an abandoned orange kitten and brought him home to nurse back to health. She'd called him D'Artagnan and loved him until the day Satan ripped her out of her parents' arms. Her hand tightened on Jesus's sleeve again.

"Lord, whatever became of D'Artagnan? Except, don't tell me if it's horrible!"

A loud purr sounded in her left ear, and she just about leaped off the throne. Darian squealed as a large, orange, long-haired cat carefully jumped off the arm of the throne and climbed onto her lap. Tears gushed out of her eyes as she scooped the feline up with both arms and wrapped him around her face. She held him there for a few minutes, sobbing. When she put him back onto her lap, he shook himself indignantly before starting the laborious process of cleaning her cooties off his luxurious fur. Darian laughed, wiping at her tears with her right hand.

"I didn't know animals went to Heaven."

Jesus's eyes reflected her joy.

"Not all do, but We recreate those cherished by Our children on Earth to become their companions again in Paradise. You will find Rembrandt stabled at your home, eager to run with you on his back again."

Darian giggled as her left hand messed up the places D'Artagnan was trying to clean with his raspy pink tongue.

"Thank you, Lord," she said. "You have blessed me beyond imagining."

Jesus washed her tears away from her right cheekbone with His left hand.

"My darling daughter, you've barely begun to experience the blessing and joy of Heaven. You are going to have a welcoming party fitting for a homecoming queen. However, your party will have to wait for a short time. Before then, you have some urgent preparations to make."

Curiosity lifted her eyebrows and Darian half-shook her head.

"Preparations, Lord? Are we going somewhere?"

His smile was like a searchlight stabbing across tumultuous waves on a moonless ocean, casting happiness and hope on turbulent waters.

"How would you like to officiate at a wedding?"

CHAPTER THE SECOND:
"PARTING IS SUCH
SWEET SORROW"

Spes, the World of Hope, in the Year of Our Peace 0001
Mission Day 95 ... 47 days after Darian's funeral

It was the third day of the marriage celebration between Johan, newly installed Emperor Consort, and Gwynver'insa, Empress of the World. Tul'ran stepped outside for a breath of fresh air, the moon glowing in the sky above him. Gwynver'insa had graciously created a bench for them to sit on and enjoy the view of the universe. Tul'ran loved Spes's night sky. He and Erianne came up here often to sit beneath the stars, tease each other, and snuggle. He would miss this world when it came time to leave.

A figure stepped out of the gloom and sat beside him under the emerald moon. Tul'ran tried to rise, but the man put a hand on his shoulder.

"To what do I owe this honor, El Shaddai?"

The Lord smiled.

"Is it not enough to say I wish to enjoy the company of one of My favorite sons beneath the sky of My creation?"

Tul'ran laughed softly.

"Were I not your Judge, the bearer of a sword giving me infinite destructive powers, I'd fully believe it." He cast a glance at Jesus's face. "How did you know, Lord, I wouldn't succumb to temptation and take on the mantle of a god?"

"I didn't," Jesus said, His voice solemn. "The choice was yours, Tul'ran. I gave you every reason to choose Me and My path, but until you declined the power, I didn't know which way your decisions would take you."

Tul'ran drew a sharp breath.

"Was it not a terrible risk to take, Lord?"

Jesus smiled.

"It was. It is the risk We have taken with every human being since the day We created Adam and Eve. Since the day We created every version of Adam and Eve in the Universe. We didn't create humans to be robots, obeying Our every whim. The Father and I wanted companions, friends, people who would walk with Us through eternity."

Tul'ran looked over the fields in front of him. Gwynver'insa had already created crops and orchards for her people. Soon, she would cover the entire world with fields, trees, lakes, and streams. Many creatures would walk the land and swim in the planet's waters.

She and Johan discussed a new system of governance to include some small measures for population control. Both learned the lessons from the history of Spes Deserit and were loath to repeat the mistakes leading to the barren soil stripped bare after Tul'ran leveled the world.

"And when You have fully enjoyed the company of one of Your favorite sons, El Shaddai, what then?"

Jesus gestured upwards into the stars.

"We are unraveling the influence of evil in the universe, Tul'ran, with your help and the help of your fearsome bride. While We have focused Our efforts on the planet of your birth, My son, there are many places in the cosmos needing the Prince and Princess of Death. Go to the Crystalline Wall with the Nine. We will send you out on our next assignment."

They sat in silence for a moment. Tul'ran looked over at his Savior and smiled.

"Yes, but not tonight, right, Lord?"

Jesus laughed and settled back onto the bench. Gwynver'insa had constructed it to be very comfortable. He might have to take the design back to Heaven with Him.

"Yes, My son, not tonight. When you are ready to leave this place, take the Nine to the Garden and I will meet you there. Look, here comes your Lady."

Erianne glided over and took one knee in front of her King.

"Lord. Do I interrupt?"

Jesus slid over on the bench to give her room to sit with her husband.

"You do not. I was just telling Tul'ran your time here must soon end."

Erianne lifted Tul'ran's arm and snuggled into the

crook where arm met shoulder.

"Excellent. Another mission. I hate to say it, but I'm getting a little bored."

Tul'ran's eyebrows sought escape from his forehead, and Jesus's laughter boomed into the night. He stood up and stretched before turning to face them.

"You have done well, my Judges. I can give you a few more weeks of sanctuary before I make life more exciting for you. Enjoy the view, and the harmony, while you can."

He was gone.

A husband and his wife sat quietly beneath a beautiful night sky, while a comet raced through the cosmos far away, framed by the brilliance of a tapestry of stars, webbed by the gossamer strands of nebulae, through which plunged an emerald-green moon. Behind the massive doors behind them, they could hear laughter and revelry as the People celebrated the marriage of their Empress. Somewhere birds, created by the bride for this occasion, cooed and sang their arias.

Soon, they'd leave, but not tonight.

Tonight was for the moon and the stars, and the love burning in their hearts as their lips met under the joy-filled eyes of their loved ones in Heaven.

Spes, the world of Hope, in the Year of Our Peace 0001
Mission Day 96

Empress Gwynver'insa, the First of Her Line, stretched to the full length of her short frame and grinned at her table companions.

It was just the four of them, herself, Johan, Erianne, and Tul'ran, and she reveled in the peace of their company. She ought to have felt exhausted after three days of marriage celebration, but she was too exhilarated to notice the demands fatigue placed on her body.

"Truly, it is a joy to be married," she said, dropping her eyelashes as she gazed with appreciation at her husband.

Johan had the courtesy to blush, as Tul'ran and Erianne grinned at him.

"Truly, it is a joy to be married to you," he said, striving to not be awkward.

Gwynver'insa giggled and then cast a mock glare at her Warriors.

"Yahweh has whispered into my heart; you are to leave us soon. Have we so quickly lost flavor on your lips that you would flee at war's end?"

Erianne smiled languidly.

"Your Imperial Majesty, behold my husband, who lays like a limp noodle at my side. Three days have we fully celebrated and never once drawn our swords. Why, only this morning I heard him speak of starting a farm and raising horses. If we stay any longer, I fear he will remove his armor, walk about shirtless and in house pants, and look for seeds to plant. Nay, I must remove him and quickly, before Tul'ran the Sword becomes Tul'ran the Bored."

Tul'ran shook his head at her, grinning, as the others roared their laughter.

"Ever the tease, my love. Your mischievousness deserves its own ballad. Gwynver'insa, my regal sister, you know how much Erianne and I love you.

El Shaddai sets our feet on the path of war on another planet where the citizens cry to their Lord for redemption. We can stay awhile longer, but not longer than a while."

The Empress nodded soberly.

"I hear you, milord brother. We, the People of Spes, owe you and your bride a great debt. This world will never forget the exploits bringing us to the end of the Multi-Millennial Fight. Before you go, though, I have tasks for you to fulfill to give us a chance to keep the peace your forces of arms mastered. Can you abide with us long enough for the completion of those tasks?"

"Of course, sister," Erianne said, stretching out her long legs and leaning against her husband's heavily muscled chest. "Name our duties, Empress."

Gwynver'insa rose, walked over to Erianne, and dropped to snuggle under the taller woman's right arm.

"Erianne, I so enjoyed my time riding Darkshadow and Destiny's Edge; I intend my first animal creation to be horses. I have fallen deeply in love with those you brought to this world. Second, you must train the Princess Darian Guard to make them fully efficient before you leave. Third, Tul'ran, you must train me in using a sword. While it is my deepest desire to never see violence fall upon this world, again, I shall prepare against it with my Guard and the force of my arm."

Erianne pulled the little Empress into her side and kissed the top of her forehead.

"By your command."

The next day, Erianne and Gwynver'insa stood in a meadow just outside the massive doors of the Hall of Everlasting Joy. The Empress dressed in the armor she created for herself in the Garden on the day she first met Erianne and Tul'ran. She looked like an elf dressed in leathers, and Erianne thought she was adorable. Gwynver'insa beamed up at her taller sister.

"Please describe a horse I could create suitable for an Empress."

Erianne thought about it for a moment, sifting through the history lessons in her mind. In her time, horses were rare and only enjoyed by the extremely wealthy. An image flickered in her head, and she grinned. A perfect horse for an Empress.

"You must create the Akhal-Teke horse for yourself. It is among the oldest horse breeds in the world from which I originate. People originally bred them for strength and agility, resulting in a horse elegant and exotic in appearance. The Akhal-Teke have excellent bones and gleaming coats. Because of the glossy sheen of their coats and their frequent golden colouring, we know them as the 'Golden Horse.' You will love this horse, I promise."

Erianne described every attribute of the Akhal-Teke horse, while Gwynver'insa clapped her hands with delight. The horse she created was a masterpiece. To Erianne's surprise, Gwynver'insa named her horse 'Erianne's Promise.' She constructed an elaborate reddish-brown saddle, inlaid with gold and platinum designs, worthy to be sat upon by an Empress.

"Now," she said to Erianne once she made

Erianne's Promise, "I shall fashion a horse suitable for my husband, the Emperor Consort. What design do you have for him?"

Erianne bit her lip to keep from laughing, remembering Johan and Darian bouncing up and down in their saddles as they rode through the desert to El Shaddai's Oasis. Johan was tall, but she could choose a horse fifteen hands high to provide a more comfortable ride than the large mares he rode in the desert.

"I would have you create for him the Haflinger horse. The Haflinger is a small but elegant horse that people in my world developed by mixing many species, notably Tyrolean ponies and Arabian horses. It has a polished head, broad chest, and sloped shoulders. A Haflinger's body is chestnut, but the mane and tail are flaxen, giving it a lovely and unusual contrast."

The Empress took Erianne's detailed instructions and created a horse smaller than hers, but one wondrous in his beauty. Erianne watched again, with awe, as Gwynver'insa closed her eyes and sketched arcane symbols in the air. The air in front of her shimmered, wavered as if uncertain of its loose composition, and then solidified into another stunning equine.

"Truly, sister, I am in awe of your gift from El Shaddai, allowing you to craft substance from thought. Are you sure you will be safe when we leave?"

Gwynver'insa folded herself back into Erianne's arms.

"Will you not spend the next few weeks training

my new Guard? Will the Sword Himself not instruct me in those weeks in fighting with a sword? You will have secured me to the best of your abilities. My people are tired of war, Erianne. They are grateful for my gift and understand I use it to better their world. If anyone tried to rise and bend me to their avarice, the People would tear them apart. No, I do not fear for my safety. My people are thirsty for the peace I offer them."

Erianne sighed.

"I hope you are right, sister. It would kill me should harm befall you."

Gwynver'insa pulled away and smiled. She reached up to touch Erianne's cheek.

"I love you, too. Now, shall we show my husband his wedding gift?"

She and Erianne walked the horses to Johan's favorite garden, where they found him muddling through the mathematics of an ancient physics text. Gwynver'insa bowed to her much taller husband and presented the Haflinger horse to him. He was so choked up he couldn't speak for a full minute. Finally, he swallowed and bowed deeply to his wife.

"My darling wife, this horse is a treasure. I thank you from the bottom of my heart."

Gwynver'insa did as always when joy consumed her: she stretched out her arms and danced three pirouettes under the crystal-clear blue sky.

"I am so pleased. What will you name him, Johan?"

Johan side glanced Erianne and fought to keep a straight expression on his face.

"One man made an enormous difference in my

choice of vocation. His view of the universe transcended his time and impressed people like me multiple generations after his death. Though you may not understand the reference, my love, I shall name my horse 'Einstein.'"

Erianne rolled her eyes.

"Of course you will."

Tul'ran chose the moment to walk up to them, leading Darkshadow and Destiny's Edge, both of which were saddled and ready for exercise. The time they spent in the Garden with El Shaddai had left the warhorses with more fat on their bodies than the Sword Himself liked. His eyebrows flew to the top of his forehead when he saw the two equines on whom the other three lavished love and praise.

"Long have I roamed the desert of my world and yet never have I seen such beautiful horses as these. Truly, sister, you have outdone yourself. Much of what you have made has stunned me with its beauty, but these are the pinnacle of your creations."

Gwynver'insa ran up to him and leaped into his arms for a bear hug.

"Thank you, brother," she said, her eyes shining. "Your soul-thought brings my heart joy."

Erianne was still having a tough time with the changes in her husband's physical appearance. When she met him, he was four inches shorter than her and had long, thick, black hair. He was still a heavily muscled man, but his brief tenure as Tul'ran the Uncreator had changed him physically.

Now he was as tall as she and his hair was as white as snow, except for a band of black hair circling his head like a halo or a simple crown. She walked up and kissed him.

"How now, covenant-husband? Do we ride?"

Tul'ran smiled, the joy of his love for her shining in his eyes.

"We ride, Princess of Death, for our horses can barely walk, so rotund are their bellies."

Erianne clapped her hands together in an imitation of Gwynver'insa.

"Excellent! Come, Johan, come Gwynver'insa, mount your four-legged creations. Let your people see our joy. Race you to the meadow!"

Spes, the world of Hope, in the Year of Our Peace 0001
Mission Day 127

It was time. They all knew it, though none desired the heartache to come. Tul'ran and Erianne prepared for their departure even as they trained the Princess Darian Guard and put Gwynver'insa and Johan through the paces of sword training. Johan had resisted at first, claiming an exemption given he was a scientist and not a fighter. His wife gently put down one tiny foot, and he joined the hours of sweat and tormented muscles.

The morning of their departure found them outside of the Hall, with Gwynver'insa struggling to keep her face untwisted as she stood before Erianne.

"Sister, this morning tears rained down from my eyes as I awoke to the day beginning the journey leading to you leaving me. I need to know, beloved sister; will I see you again?"

Erianne took Gwynver'insa's smaller hands into hers and looked deeply into the tiny woman's large blue eyes.

"My darling sister, I covenant with you thusly: Tul'ran and I shall return. Years may pass before the event, but I will plead with El Shaddai to return us to Spes before our life's end, so we may once more rejoice in your company. I make this promise to you as if we spilled blood between us."

Gwynver'insa pulled Erianne into a long hug, and Erianne kissed her on the top of her forehead. Erianne pulled back and stared at the Empress with a serious look.

"Provided, of course, my husband and I survive the next mission laid out before us."

Gwynver'insa snorted.

"To whom do you speak, sister? Have I not seen you and Tul'ran dance death in the Judgment Seat, your arms, legs, and blades a blur? Did I not witness Tul'ran the Uncreator go out against this world to wage war against the Twelve in my name and bring back victory? You prophesied, Erianne, the Combatants would kneel at my feet and beg for mercy, which they did. I tell you the truth, if there is a force in the universe capable of withstanding you and your husband, I would rather not know it. The thought of such a thing would make my heart fail."

Erianne pulled Gwynver'insa into another hug.

Neither had met a force greater than Tul'ran, but they would.

After they disengaged, Gwynver'insa wiped her tears and smiled through them.

"At least I will not shame myself as we ride to the Garden." She rubbed her small bottom. "I have not forgotten the bruise on my backside after I first fell off Erianne's Promise."

The first day they rode together, Erianne challenged her compatriots to a race. Race, the Empress did, into a stand of newly created trees, the boughs of one of which dropped her onto her backside. While horrified at first, they had a good laugh once she assured them she was unharmed.

"Your advisers were very unhappy with us, Gwyn," Erianne said. "I was afraid they were going to force us into the Judgement Seat for putting your life in jeopardy."

Gwynver'insa lifted her chin high.

"I am the Empress of the World and you are the Heroes of Spes. They would rue the day if they tried."

Johan and Tul'ran brought up their horses. Tul'ran and Erianne had put Darkshadow and Destiny's Edge through their paces in the last thirty days, and both looked sleek and ready for war. The departure of the stallion and beautiful mare would leave many young hearts broken. Even during their training, Tul'ran and Erianne delighted in giving children rides on the two warhorses.

The Empress of Spes, the First of Her Line, mounted Erianne's Promise and took her place beside her husband, Emperor Consort Johan. They led the way from the Hall, with Tul'ran and Erianne riding Darkshadow and Destiny's Edge behind them. Third in the procession was the Princess Darian Guard, carrying the unit's banner, a tipped golden crown hanging from the point of an upright silver spear on a field of blood red.

Between the two ranks of female soldiers of the

Princess Darian Guard marched the Nine remaining Combatants, their necks and wrists chained to one another. The Guard treated them kindly and gave them frequent stops to refresh themselves and have a rest. No one had spoken to them harshly since their capture, nor did any of the People evidence anger when dealing with the Nine. The People pitied the Nine, for they were to be exiled from a world the People believed their Empress would make more amazing than ever it had been.

As Gwynver'insa rode away from the Hall of Everlasting Joy, a tide of humanity piled through the massive wood doors like ants leaving a hill. To the surprise of the Empress and her party, the People were determined to make the long march to the Crystalline Wall to honour their liberators one last time. Everyone came. All one hundred forty-four thousand survivors of the Multi-Millennial Fight left the Hall of Everlasting Joy to make the five-day trek to the entrance of the Garden.

The procession was long and snaked through trees shading, with large, deciduous leaves, the path upon which they trod. A wind caressed the leaves of the trees, like lovers will, gently, then rising in a rush, before settling again. Birds played on the wind currents, adding their song to the symphony of the wind and the leaves and the trees. The air smelled fresh and hinted at a promise of a spring not seen by the land for so many years; everyone had all but forgotten the glory of it.

The rising sun splayed over the immense line of people walking and singing along the road to the Crystalline Wall. They marveled at the fields, trees, and fruit their Empress created for them, with Johan's detailed descriptions, before the dawn of each day.

They didn't have the variety of meals offered by the Food Makers, but they didn't care. Each bite of fresh fruit, each taste of fresh berries, each morsel of fresh vegetables was a treasure for the pallet and a joy for their souls. It reminded them the age-long war was finally over. Soon, they would grow crops and raise livestock with their own hands and delightfully share them with others.

Erianne had made a recording of all one hundred and fifty verses of the Ballad of Tul'ran the Sword and presented it to a singer loved by the People. The singer crafted it into a Spesian melody and added thirteen new verses about the Battle for Spes Deserit. By the time the procession started their journey, all the People knew the Ballad by heart. It gave them boundless joy, and gave Tul'ran a megadose of embarrassment, to sing the Ballad at least once on each day of their journey.

It was a festival in motion. Children ran along the sides of the procession, tagging each other, and giggling as they tried to escape from one another's clutches. Men and women walked along offering refreshments and snacks to the massive crowd of people, who walked faster and slower, blending in with one another, as they found new conversations to join. The procession looked like a brook splashing over large stones in the water, pulsating as people merged in and out of the march to laugh and sing and talk.

The People of Spes would talk about the exodus

for the next five thousand years.

On the first night, Gwynver'insa called a council under the brilliant gleam of the green moon.

"Have you consulted with El Shaddai on the destination of the Nine?" she asked, settling back into the chest of her husband as they sat around a fire.

Erianne smacked Tul'ran's shoulder. He had stretched out under his cloak, his head on her thighs as he stared at the millions of stars above them.

"Do you see how it is done, lazy husband? Johan sets his back against a tree, providing warmth and support for his wife's form, while my husband's massive head chokes the blood supply to my legs."

Tul'ran turned to look at Johan, who was grinning. Johan loved when the two of them sparred.

"I would do the same, milady wife, but it has been a full day of riding beneath a warm sun. How often have I seen you pinch your nose and make bleating sounds like a goat when my exertions have left its sheen upon my skin?"

She smacked him again, this time a little harder.

"Never, that's how many times! I swear, Tul'ran, your capacity to exaggerate rivals your balladeers."

Tul'ran grinned.

"Was it not you, milady wife, who taught my Ballad to the People? You had every chance to shave embellishment from the lyrics and present the truth to them. Why, even now they could sing the Ballad of Tul'ran the Titmouse, who vanquished foes with bodily odor instead of steel!"

Erianne glared at the top of his forehead as Gwyn and Johan laughed their delight.

"This trip ain't over yet. Milord husband," she translated for Gwyn's benefit, "I do not see the end to this path and I have the Empress's singers under my sway. The Legend of the Titmouse may yet thrive."

After she finished giggling, Gwynver'insa took their attention back to her question.

"I would not have you take the Nine to our moon. While Yahweh informs me it is a wondrous place, with more than enough capacity to sustain life, I am concerned they will somehow find the means to wage war again. I would not have them destroy our moon, or bring the Fight back here. If not there, where shall you take them?"

Erianne answered, while finger combing Tul'ran's long white hair.

"El Shaddai spoke into our minds not two days ago. He told us of a world He created much larger than yours. On it is one vast island of vegetation and fresh waters. He composed the rest of the planet of sand, with the occasional oasis strategically situated here and there to give them a path around the world. The temperature is always moderate, and they will not have to live under harsh conditions. It is a place set in the far reaches of the cosmos. No humans live anywhere near it."

Tul'ran shifted his head, taking the pressure off Erianne's thighs.

"They will have everything they need to thrive. If they work together, they will populate the planet and bend it to their benefit. Should they choose, after a time, to continue their conflict, they will empty the world of humans. The choice will be theirs and no innocents will die from their foolishness. If they so choose, they can have a relationship with El Shaddai and He will teach them from His knowledge and wisdom. It will not be a prison if they regard it as an opportunity. They will not be back here again."

Gwynver'insa sighed.

"To be separated from their home world is a harsh punishment, I know, but I could not consign them to death. Everyone deserves a chance at forgiveness and to walk away from their misdeeds. I cannot trust them to never infect the People again. I thank you for taking them far from here, and wish the journey did not need undertaking."

Tul'ran sat up and unrolled the sheepskin he always carried with him on Darkshadow. He looked at Erianne slyly.

"The last time we laid on this roll, you favored me with a kiss. Shall we reprise the scenario?"

Both her eyebrows rose on her gorgeous face.

"Milord husband, how kind of you to draw my attention to the memory! As I recall, I first kissed you after you put a blade to my throat and threatened to kill me. I most certainly do not wish to reprise the scenario."

Gwynver'insa bolted upright, her eyes huge.

"What?! I must have that tale!"

Tul'ran and Erianne took turns telling it, each account becoming more outrageous than the other, as they passed the blame back and forth for the 'misunderstanding', as Tul'ran called it, leading to Erianne fainting onto the desert floor.

By the time they finished, all four were holding their sides; they were laughing so hard. Later, as they snuggled under Tul'ran's cloak on the sheepskin roll, Erianne leaned over to give Tul'ran a long, soft kiss.

"As terrifying as the day was, milord husband, I would gladly live it again to have this chance to be in your arms."

His eyes softened, and he smiled.

"I give you my oath, beloved wife, on the blood we have spilled between us; I will never again raise a blade to you or utter a threat of harm. You know of the duress I was under then, which convinced me you were my enemy. I'd die before I would hurt you."

Erianne snuggled into his muscular chest and let her eyes drift up to the stars.

"I know. Because I'd kill you if you tried."

She drifted off to sleep, with the rumble of his chuckle resonating in her ears.

Four days later, Gwynver'insa called a halt before the incredibly high Crystalline Wall, a living barrier made up of sentient trees. They were the only living things, other than the People, to survive the Fight. Their intelligence permitted them to seek sources of nutrients deep underground. Being made of a translucent green and blue indestructible crystal, the trees did not need light and water to survive. Their defences were enormously powerful electrical currents, which they used to fend off Combatants and their war machines throughout history.

After several futile attempts to destroy the Crystallines, the Combatants pursued Abaddon for the methods by which the Combatants could destroy the Crystalline Wall. Abaddon refused to give it to them. He knew Yahweh created the Wall to protect the Garden within and considered divulging the knowledge to be a betrayal.

When one Combatant became too insistent in his demands for a solution for the destruction of the Crystalline Wall, Abaddon drew his angelic sword in a blur of motion and cut the combatant in two, vertically, from his head down through his groin. He then had a courier deliver an organ or piece of flesh to each of the remaining Combatants as a warning. It angered the Combatants, but they never challenged Abaddon on that, or any other issue, again.

Johan slipped off his horse, sighing with gratitude, and stretched out a hand to assist his wife in dismounting Erianne's Promise. The Empress walked up to the Crystalline Wall and placed her left hand over her heart. With her right hand, she raised her sceptre and gently tapped it against the extensive glassy surface. A sound, like glass chimes tinkling in a gentle wind, came from high above them and transmuted into words.

"Who comes?"

Gwynver'insa took a step back and extended both arms back and out, as if to incorporate the entire population behind her.

"We are the People of Spes. For millennia, war burdened us, our numbers thinned to near extinction. We cried out to Yahweh, the Lord our God, and begged for mercy and redemption. He sent to us these warriors, Tul'ran az Nostrom, the Sword Himself, Prince of Death, the Uncreator, and his matchless wife, Erianne az Nostrom, Princess of Death, the Tamer of Gods. Together, they broke the backs of our enemies, rendered still the cannons that shattered our nights and our lives, and released peace from its cage. Behind us stand the Nine, the last remnants of the Combatants who laid this world to waste. We beseech you, open your gates to the Warriors of the Empress Gwynver'insa, the First of Her Line, so they may take the Nine through to a new world where we exile them for the rest of their lives."

Silence descended. No one dared to move, for fear of making a sound. Even the wind stopped, as if frightened to disturb the majestic contemplation of the Crystallines. The answer came in a symphony of glass chimes.

"Long have we awaited this day. Once more shall there be peace between the Crystallines and the People. Enter, Tul'ran. Enter, Erianne. Bring with you the Nine. Take them far from here into exile. Never again shall there be a war on Spes, the World of Hope."

The Wall before them, which had appeared as smooth and solid as polished glass, parted into individual trees. They shuffled to one side and divided in the middle, a symphony of tinkling and chiming that left the People enchanted.

Erianne and Tul'ran dismounted from their horses, looping the reins over their long noses and dropping them to the ground. Both horses were so well trained, they wouldn't move without a command from their masters. Darkshadow dropped his muzzle to the grass and took a large mouthful.

Ever the opportunist.

Of one accord, Tul'ran and Erianne approached

Gwynver'insa and kneeled before her on one knee, heads bowed. The Empress raised her hand, and the entire multitude froze as if made of stone.

"You should know, Warriors of the Empress Gwynver'insa, of the impact you have had on this world and how we will remember you. From this day forward, I shall rename the months of our calendar as follows. The day I proclaimed our Redemption and the cessation of the Fight shall be the first day of the month I now name 'Revelation.' It was on that day I revealed myself to the world as its Empress and introduced you as our redeemers. The remaining eleven months I now name in this order: 'Sacrifice', 'Darian', 'Tul'ran', 'Erianne', 'Johan', 'E'thriel', 'Bloodwing', 'Darkshadow', 'Destiny's Edge', 'Prophecy', and 'Fulfillment.'"

"On this, the sixth day in the month of Darian, I must perform the saddest duty of my life. I must take your request and rule upon it. How may I serve you, Warriors of the Empress?"

"Your Imperial Majesty," Erianne said, her voice muffled by the tightness of her throat, "we seek your leave to depart this world, taking with us your enemies, with our word to you we shall place them in exile where they will never again threaten your peace."

Tears streamed down Gwynver'insa's cheeks.

"My beloved brother and sister, you break my heart. Though I have known you for what feels like seconds in my long life, I love you more than I have loved any other person. Go with my blessing. Return with my joy."

Gwynver'insa lifted Erianne's head and kissed her

on both cheeks. She did the same with Tul'ran.

They rose and Johan stepped forward.

"Tul'ran and Erianne, I'm truly sorry to see you go. No matter what we've been through, I've always had confidence in your ability to keep me safe. Godspeed, my friends."

Erianne grasped his extended right arm at the forearm.

"Are you sure you're going to be okay, Johan? You're millions of light-years from home and you'll never see Earth or your loved ones again."

Johan smiled and cast a glance at Gwynver'insa before he replied.

"Everyone on Earth thinks I'm dead. I have all the love I need here. Besides, Gwynver'insa told me you've promised to come back. I'm already planning the celebration of your return."

Tul'ran grasped his right arm.

"You have my respect, Johan. Keep well. Both of you are now the salvation of this world. If ever you find yourself in desperate circumstances, lift a prayer to El Shaddai. We will come to your aid in fury, teeth bared, and swords raised."

Johan laughed softly.

"If that's not a deterrent to our future foes, nothing will be."

There was nothing more to do or to say. The four of them had spent the last four nights under Spes's beautiful starry skies, talking about how much they meant to each other. They laughed over their stumbles and cried as they recounted their losses.

They proved to one another family is more than blood. It can be the resolute choice to recognize a like spirit and bring them into the fold of family, a bond sometimes deeper than shared genes.

Tul'ran gathered up the chains binding the Nine and wrapped them around his left arm. He led Darkshadow and the Nine through the opening in the Wall, his back stiff and straight. Erianne turned and faced Johan, the People, and the Empress, who was still quietly crying.

She drew Caligo with a flourish and held her angelic sword high in the air; the sunlight glinting off the silver blade and gold inlays.

"People of Spes, we, the Warriors of the Empress Gwynver'insa, salute you!"

The crowd roared their response, one hundred and forty-four thousand and two voices screaming their farewells with such emotion it left a lead fist in her chest and tears in her eyes. She turned her horse's head and followed her husband into the Garden.

For possibly the last time, the Crystallines closed behind her, and they left Spes, the World of Hope, behind.

CHAPTER THE THIRD: DISCOVERY

The Abyss, May 11, 2099
Two days before Satan inhabits the Antichrist's body

Satan and G'shnet'el roared with laughter as they watched Contradeum press the red-hot iron into his belly button. The human's screams were sweet music to the ears of the Prince of Evil. Contradeum, still shrieking, dropped the iron and fell to the ground in a fetal position. The agony was so intense, tears streamed from his eyes, and he sobbed like a little child.

"Why?" He asked, moaning through the intense pain. "I served you and I worshipped you. Why would do this to me? I brought people to you who gave you their souls!"

Satan reached down and curled his claws into Contradeum's hair, viciously yanking him to his knees.

"You dare question me?"

Satan drove a fist into the human's stomach, right on the burned spot, expelling the air from Malchus's lungs in a violent whoosh.

"I'm greater than you could ever be. God created me to lead worship to Him, to stand above all the angels and ensure their respect and devotion to Him. I served Him for more than hundreds of thousands of your years. The angels revered me like I was God. All I wanted was the place at His left Hand I deserved. I was the most beautiful of all his Creation until Eve came along. God didn't need humans to reign with Him. He had Me! Me, you stinking, wretched piece of meat! Do you want to know why I torture you? I loathe you. You and your kind took my place!"

Just as Contradeum was catching his breath, Satan kneed him savagely in the face, shattering and displacing all the bones in his forehead and cheeks. It was a blow capable of killing a mortal man, but Contradeum was no longer mortal. White fiery flames of pain licked at the edges of his sanity, but they would diminish. His body was immortal, which meant it would heal itself, quickly and painfully, to be ready for the next dance with agony.

Contradeum didn't have time to feel sorry for himself. Trying to survive the torment was all he could do then. Later, he would come to fully grasp the stupidity of serving Satan and believing his lies.

Later is most often too late.

"When he recovers," Satan told G'shnet'el, "immerse him in a vat of molten bronze. He always wanted to be idolized, so let's turn him into an idol. A living bronze statute of Malchus Contradeum,

Supreme Global Leader of the Government of Democracy. After he recovers from the casting, reheat the bronze every three hours until it's hot enough to scorch his flesh to blackness. After he endures his torment for a time, we'll cut him loose with lasers. I have many plans for him, and all of them will be delicious. I'm going down into Hell for a short while. Keep Contradeum entertained."

G'shnet'el returned his master's sickening grin and slashed his whip across Contradeum's back, ripping up blood, flesh, and bone. Torture gave him a sadistic, almost sexual pleasure. Fresh souls were always so much fun. They screamed, begged, pleaded, and cried out for a God Who would no longer listen to their petitions.

Eventually, they would get so used to the constant pain, they would barely react to his sadistic ministrations. G'shnet'el loved the daily imports of fresh souls into the Abyss and into Hell. They kept him from being bored.

The best part was they could have avoided all this pain just by accepting Jesus Christ as their Savior. One simple choice and no eternal torment. It was all so delicious.

A troubling thought momentarily flitted across G'shnet'el's mind. When the Holy Spirit brought Abaddon back to the Abyss, He warned G'shnet'el He would judge him for the way he and the other fallen angels treated humans in the afterlife. The warning had bothered him for a long time, but the lure of human pain was too much. Their pain was the most precious of narcotics. Grinning sadistically, he ripped another lash into Contradeum's back.

The eternal torment would be worth it.

G'shnet'el was wrong, but he didn't know it yet.

Satan flew down into the depths of the home of the unsaved dead. He needed some information, and he had to have it before he took Contradeum's flesh as his own. Once he wore human flesh, he could no longer come here because it wouldn't be possible to rip himself out of the human body. It didn't matter. He intended to escape his prophesied eternal damnation in the Lake of Fire. If all went well, he would flee to another planet in the cosmos and rule it as his own. He would never come back here again.

The Evil One stopped before a row of millions of caves circling the planet called Hell. It was scorching hot.

He found the cave he needed and walked in. There were no doors on the caves or bars; they weren't necessary. No one escaped from the pit.

Anchored to the wall in the cave was a young man about six feet tall. His back was broad; he had a brawny chest tapering down to a small waist. His head was full of light brown hair. The man had a hooked nose bordered by two sunken, dull blue eyes sitting over cheekbones thrust over a thin-lipped mouth. His chin and jaw were square, and a full beard hid them both.

Satan noted with interest no one had tortured the man recently. His healed body looked firm; insolence and hatred glowed in the man's eyes.

"What do you want, demon? Have I not suffered enough for my alleged 'sins'?" The man spat. "Let me down off this wall and we'll see how well you would do in a fair fight."

Satan's lips curled in a demonic mimicry of a smile.

"Like how well you fought against the Gutians who cut off your testicles and blinded your eyes? Such a fight you put up that day, Al'ran az Nostrom!"

Al'ran screamed and tried to rip the manacles out of the rock wall, striving to free his arms and legs to attack his tormentor.

"Don't speak to me of that day, foul beast! They took me unawares! It was three against one! I could have bested any of them."

"My, my, Al'ran, what an intriguing thought. Yes, I think I will let you and the four Gutians who attacked you be our evening entertainment. You will fight in the arena against them and prove your worth in battle. Excellent idea!"

Some of the color left Al'ran's face.

"They're here? Those barbarians are here? Did you send them to this place?"

Satan was enjoying himself.

"No, Al'ran, mighty orchard keeper, tender of swine. The same boy who killed you took his vengeance upon them and sent their souls to Hell with twenty of their brothers."

Rage flared in Al'ran's eyes.

"Tul'ran! Are you telling me the cowardly little excrement who killed me also ended the lives of four and twenty barbarians? Impossible!" Al'ran paused. "Wait, is he here, too?" A sneer curled on his lips. "I would like to have a word with my son if he's here."

Satan walked over to Al'ran and raised both hands over the chained man's face. He asserted light pressure with his thumbs over Al'ran's eyes.

"That's the problem, Al'ran. He's not here. Correction, he was here some time ago and left with four souls." Satan bore down with his thumbs, and Al'ran screamed. "Can you imagine my distress, Al'ran az Nostrom? Your very son invaded my domain, intimidated my Gatekeeper, corrupted one of my angels, and left with four souls who deserve to be where you are now." Al'ran's screams intensified unbearably as the Evil One pressed down hard enough to pop his eyes out of their sockets. Satan ripped out both bulging eyes and shoved them into Al'ran's mouth to gag him.

"What's the matter, big man? Hate being blind? Your eyes will grow back. Swallow your eyes, Al'ran, as I would have you swallow your pride."

When Al'ran refused to comply, Satan took a knife out of his belt and sawed a line across Al'ran's belly, spilling his guts onto the hot rock wall. Al'ran tried to scream, but choked on his eyeballs and finally swallowed them. Satan stepped back and waited for Al'ran's body to heal, enjoying the taste of the man's screeches. After a long while, the healing process ended, and Satan stepped forward.

"No," Al'ran shrieked, "no more. Please! I beg of you! What do you want? I'll give you anything! Anything at all!"

"Of course you will," Satan purred, as he ran the knife's edge along Al'ran's cheek, drawing blood. "Tell me, Al'ran, did your son come to visit you while he jauntily strode through my kingdom as if he ruled it and not I?"

Al'ran's body went limp against the manacles shackling him to the wall.

"No," he said, his voice a husky whisper. "The ungrateful little pissant. He put me in this place and couldn't even bring himself to come and apologize or take me from here. I wish he were here. I would like to see what he could do against me as an unfettered whole man."

"Al'ran, Al'ran, such bitterness. He's your son. Do you truly wish him here with you in the infernal regions of eternity?"

Al'ran glared at Satan, the intensity of his hatred palpable in the confines of the cage.

"Truly. And gladly."

Satan punched Al'ran in the stomach and waited until his lungs filled with air again.

"Then tell me where he would go to hide from me, Al'ran. Where could I find your sweet little boy so I can bring him here, where he belongs?"

The knowledge glowed in Al'ran's mind as if it were a recent memory.

"Gilgesh. You'll likely find him in Gilgesh. I sent him there to be trained by Quil'ton az Peregos. If Tul'ran's not there, Quil'ton will know where to find him."

Satan's fists were a blur as he punched Al'ran's face repeatedly until it was a bloody pulp and the former orchard keeper barely clung to consciousness.

"Such a good father," Satan sneered. "Thank you for your cooperation."

He left the cave and flew back up to the Abyss. With G'shnet'el, he watched over Contradeum's futile attempts to resist being lowered into a vat of boiling bronze by three fallen angels.

The Evil One laughed, enjoying Contradeum's shrieks and protestations. His screams ended once Contradeum was fully immersed and liquid bronze filled his lungs. The entertainment was over for now.

Satan clapped his hand on G'shnet'el's shoulder.

"I have a task for you."

Atlantis, May 13, 2099 AD, after the indwelling

Mick, Heather, Jeannie, and Sully sat in Mick's quarters, numbly watching the Antichrist's usurpation of the world's religions and the destruction unleashed by his declaration. His statement rendered invalid every law based on some form of religious teaching and the people embraced the new destructive chaos passionately.

"Is this the end of the world?" Jeannie said, tears streaming down her face.

Davis shook his head.

"No, we're only halfway through the Tribulation. According to what I've been reading, the next three-and-a-half years are going to be Hell on earth. It will be the stuff of nightmares."

"What kind of nightmares?" Jeannie asked.

Davis retrieved his personal device and opened a file.

"For starters, listen to these words. Everything I've read suggests this is coming next:

> I looked when He broke the sixth seal, and there was a great earthquake; and the sun became black as sackcloth made of hair, and the whole moon became like blood; and the stars of the sky fell to the earth, as a fig tree

casts its unripe figs when shaken by a great wind. The sky was split apart like a scroll when it is rolled up, and every mountain and island were moved out of their places. Then the kings of the earth and the great men and the commanders and the rich and the strong and every slave and free man hid themselves in the caves and among the rocks of the mountains; and they said to the mountains and to the rocks, 'Fall on us and hide us from the presence of Him who sits on the throne, and from the wrath of the Lamb; for the great day of their wrath has come, and who is able to stand?"

Davis searched the faces of his friends.

"What I just read to you is from the Holy Bible, in the book called Revelation. Chapter six, verses twelve through seventeen, if you want to read it yourself. We may not understand all of it yet, but you can count on one thing. We're in for it now."

Sully took a deep breath.

"So, what's our exit strategy?"

Davis looked at him dumbly.

"What do you mean?"

Sully reached out and squeezed Davis's shoulder.

"Come on, Mick. How long have we known each other? No matter who was Team Leader, we always knew we could count on you to pull us out when things got FUBAR. Well, it sure looks to me like things are FUBAR now." He gestured to the three-dimensional holographic display of global riots hovering at the front of the room. "It won't take long for the unrest to come here. We need a plan, Master

Chief, and we need it now."

Davis shook his head glumly.

"I don't know what to tell you, Sully. Where do we go? This world has become a microscopic place. What's happening out there is going to come here, probably sooner than later. I'm open to suggestions."

"Why do we have to go to a place?" Heather asked in a timid voice.

"Explain," Jeannie said.

Heather opened her palms where two God Coins glistened under the ambient light.

"We could go to a when and leave all this behind."

Davis could see Jeannie and Sully perk up. He hated to be the bucket of ice water drenching the spark of hope.

"We pulled up the Time Scepter, Heather. The quantum bubble back to Mesopotamia is gone. We couldn't go back if we wanted to."

Heather pursed her lips.

"Who brought the Scepter back, Mick?"

He frowned.

"I thought Coventry brought it back."

"Coventry had a lot of things on the go, and I offered to carry the Time Scepter. After she handed me the case, the two of you left the IP to gather the MetaMaterials. I removed the Scepter and hid it in the canyon wall, and covered it with MetaMaterials canvass. I couldn't bear the thought of never seeing our Mesopotamian family again. The case I came back with is empty. I carried it to the storage room. No one was going to stop the last Programmer from performing her duties. That's how I got away with locking up an empty case."

Jeannie's eyes lit up.

"Then we're safe? We can escape all this by going back in time?"

"Whoa," Davis said, holding up his hands. "Let's rein this one in for a second. If we go back and stay there, we could cause a temporal loop or a rift. We would take ourselves out of this timeline completely. Can you tell us, Heather, we won't cause a time disruption?"

Wu shook her head, frustrated.

"I don't know, Mick. Look at all the garbage the terrorists pulled by going back and forth to the same IP without causing a temporal distortion. It's like the timeline is a living thing. If you unsettle it, it pushes back. We can't go into the future. How do we know the four of us didn't disappear forever tonight?"

Sully rubbed his forehead.

"So, if we escape to the past, we could fulfill our present destiny of disappearing from the timeline by escaping to the past? How does it make sense? Isn't it the very definition of a temporal loop? I'm not saying we shouldn't do it, but we need to think this through carefully."

There was a knock on the door, and Davis held up one finger.

"Hold that thought," he said as he crossed over to the entryway. His quarters didn't have the fancy door access system once enjoyed by the Programmers. It was just a door and didn't show him who was on the other side. Not that it mattered. They no longer had enemies in the present.

Davis swung the door open and froze.

Erasmus Hart stood on the other side with a large caliber handgun pointed a couple of feet away from Davis's head. Beads of sweat formed above Hart's eyebrows, and he looked stressed. The hand holding the gun trembled slightly, but Hart kept the muzzle directed at Davis's forehead. Hart's eyes were wild and kept darting from the Master Chief's face to over his shoulder into the quarters. When he spoke, his voice shook.

"I'm here to ask you a question, Mr. Davis. Your life depends on the answer. Are you a Christian?"

Davis stayed still, but his mind was racing. Hart had been a police officer; it would be hard to disarm him. He stood far enough away to prevent Davis from tearing the gun out of his hands, but close enough he wouldn't miss his shot. Davis's eyes narrowed, ignoring the muzzle of the gun that looked like the size of a fire hose. If Hart was here to arrest him, why was he alone? Hart knew Davis was a SEAL and a Protector. He wasn't stupid. He should have had a team with him, and a quick survey of the area showed Hart didn't have one. Davis took a deep breath. Time to roll the dice again.

"Yes, Mr. Hart, I'm a Christian."

Erasmus Hart stared at him wildly for a moment, then he pulled the gun away from Davis's face and set the safety. He tucked the gun into a shoulder holster and nodded.

"Then I need to speak to you, Mr. Davis. Right now. Can I come in?"

Davis's heart was pounding as relief fluttered through his mind.

"You certainly have an interesting way of getting

an invitation. C'mon in."

Davis stepped aside and Hart quickly walked into the room. The other three occupants stared at him with enormous eyes. Hart nodded at them, sweat beading on his forehead.

"I'm sorry for scaring you. I really am. This is a dangerous situation, and I needed someone to talk to. Someone I could trust."

Davis walked in behind Hart and gestured to a chair.

"Have a seat, Mr. Hart. I guess I don't have to tell you consorting with Christians could get you killed?"

"I'm already a dead man, Mr. Davis."

Heather saw that the older man's hands were shaking.

"Mr. Hart, can I get you a cup of tea? You look distressed. I have a chamomile tea, which might help a little."

Hart nodded, looking sheepish.

"Please, Dr. Wu, call me Ras. Yes, I would very much like a cup of tea. I apologize to all of you for barging in at gunpoint. I had nowhere else to go."

Sully shifted in his chair.

"As a matter of curiosity, Ras, what were you going to do if Mick said he wasn't a Christian?"

Hart shifted uncomfortably, beads of sweat trickling down the sides of his face.

"I would've apologized for the intrusion and said I was following up on a lead."

"Then why put a gun in his face at all?" Jeannie asked.

"Ma'am, I don't blame you for being angry. I needed to know the strength of Davis's conviction.

I'm not a Christian, although I'm looking at it hard right now. While I grew up in a Christian home and many members of my family were of the faith, they all disappeared during the Second Cataclysm. I've been drifting along with every explanation the government has offered for the Second Cataclysm and ignoring the truth. Until now."

Heather came back with the tea and offered it to their guest. He took it and the teacup rattled in the saucer as he tried to still the shaking of his hands.

"What's happened now, making you consider becoming the target of everyone out there who wants to torture Christians to death?"

Hart took the tea and blew on it before putting it to his mouth. The lines around his eyes tightened.

"Have any of you seen Korhonen since she came back from Rome?"

The other four looked at each other and shook their heads.

"No," Davis answered. "We knew she stayed until Contradeum woke up from the dead and a few days afterwards. I didn't even know she was back."

Hart's hands shook again.

"Yeah, she's back. At least her body is."

Sully cocked his head at the Special Projects Team Lead.

"What do you mean? Is she dead?"

Hart licked his lips.

"The woman who's sitting in the Administrator's office isn't Marjatta Korhonen. Oh, she looks the same and has the same voice, but the essence of her is gone. She's acting like she joined a cult or something. All she does is smile, with a dreamy look on her face, and talk about how beautiful Contradeum is. You won't believe this, but I caught her signing some forms with the name 'Mrs. Marjatta Contradeum.' She says she's his slave-bride."

"Slave-bride!" Heather exclaimed. "Marjatta Korhonen? She'd cut her own throat before she called herself someone's slave-bride!"

Hart pursed his lips.

"I know, right? She also has this weird tattoo on the underside of her wrists. On her left wrist, in red ink, is a tattoo of a dove holding a bloody arrow. Her right wrist has a tattoo of the Latin numbers VI, VI, VI, with each number at the pointed edge of a triangle containing an eye with rays around the edges. When she puts her wrists together, the dove sits within the triangle. She told me everyone was going to have to get the triangle tattoo soon to buy and sell everything, including food. Apparently, the tattoo on her left wrist identifies her as one of Contradeum's brides. I'm telling you, people, the woman I knew no longer lives in her body."

Davis extended a hand and grasped Hart's shoulder. He could feel it shaking under his palm.

"Hey, easy, Ras. We believe you. Is getting the tattoo freaking you out?"

Hart shook his head.

"No, my new orders are freaking me out. Contradeum has a burr in his bonnet about some guy named Tul'ran az Nostrom somewhere in Antiquity. The same era you were in, Master Chief." He noticed Heather and Davis had stiffened when he mentioned Tul'ran's name. "Do you two know him?"

"No," Davis said, his mind firing, "But we've

heard of him. He has a reputation for being a dangerous man to have as an enemy. His body count is high. Most people try to avoid him as much as possible. Why does Contradeum care about some warrior who died over four thousand years ago?"

Hart shrugged.

"Beats the hell out of me. Here's the kicker. He told Korhonen to put a team together, go back to Antiquity, find Tul'ran az Nostrom, and kill him. She told me she thought it was a wonderful idea. Korhonen! This is the woman who turned herself inside out to avoid the slightest anomaly. Now she's signing a warrant for the death of a man in the past, which we have no right to do, and she's gunning for his wife, too. I saw the orders. She's sending you out on this mission, Master Chief. All four of you."

Heather's eyebrow pointed elegantly upwards on her face.

"I thought she wanted me close to home since I'm the only Programmer left?"

Hart shrugged.

"This is what I'm saying, Dr. Wu. The Marjatta I knew would never commit you to this mission. Apparently, Contradeum knows the two of you spent eight months in Antiquity together. You programmed your way back without an AI. If you take a long time to find this Nostrom guy, you might have to program new coordinates to return. That's why you must go. TTI is finished, Dr. Wu. Marjatta said there'd be no new time missions, and she smiled when she said it. We're all to serve Contradeum now and he wants everyone present on Earth to worship him."

Sully shifted in his chair and shared a glance with Jeannie.

"So why are me and my wife going?"

Hart grimaced.

"You're a doctor and she's a trauma nurse. For your mission to be a success, Contradeum wants you to extract and bring back a chunk of Nostrom's spinal column. He wants to mount it on his desk or something stupid like that. Quarterlaine is going with you. Five on the team, four short of optimal. Korhonen will give you ninety days in Antiquity to complete your mission. After that, she'll issue a forced recall. If you come back empty-handed, they'll interrogate you for why your mission failed. They're going to use drugs on you. The first question they're going to ask is whether you're Christians."

Davis had been watching Hart closely as he told the story.

"You want to come with us, don't you?"

Hart jerked as if Davis had slapped him.

"How'd you know?"

Davis smiled.

"Body language. How desperately you gained our attention. Why are you so afraid to stay here, Ras?"

Hart rubbed his face and sighed.

"I'm the one who put you in Sylvia Oslo's hands when you first transitioned back. We were incredibly careful to stage your fake arrest in case we missed blanking a holo feed. Apparently, we weren't careful enough. Someone saw a security feed and pushed it up the chain. Now Korhonen is asking questions about the feed. One of my friends told her it might be a time slip, or an aberrant anomaly, but I don't think she's buying it. Eventually she's going to find out I was behind it and then it's going to get ugly."

Sully nodded, understanding dawning.

"You want us to save your butt by asking Korhonen to take you as one of our Protectors?"

Hart had the decency to blush.

"I know it's self-serving. I really am leaning towards developing a Christian faith. There's a better chance of surviving to make the decision if I'm with you."

Davis sat back in his chair and looked at Hart, leaving his face carefully empty. His instincts were poking the back of his head with skeletal fingers and screaming 'no'. He and the three people in this world to whom he was closest were now exposed. If he believed Hart, they limited their exposure to the man sitting in the chair in front of them. Or not. Either way, the present was more dangerous to them than the past.

He knew they'd never succeed in a mission to bring back Tul'ran's proof of death. The famed warrior had disappeared from the timeline, and probably the entire planet. Davis tossed off the worry. Looking too far into the future was the best way to self-defeat.

Davis glanced over at Sully, who was looking at him expectantly. Sully gave him a subtle nod. They had served together a long time and knew how each other thought. His look said, 'one evolution at a time.' The phrase helped many a SEAL survive BUD/S. Davis turned to Hart.

"I think it would help the mission if we had a seasoned officer with us. Once we get our official orders from Korhonen, we'll ask her to add you to the team."

Hart looked relieved and jumped to his feet.

"Thank you! You don't know how much this means to me. I'll leave you alone. Sorry again for busting in at gunpoint. I'll wait to hear from the Administrator."

He bowed awkwardly and made his way to the door, Davis following him. After Hart left, Davis secured the door and listened for any sounds in the hallway outside. He went back to the group, who were sitting like birds on a wire.

Heather got up and walked over to hug him.

"I was so worried when that idiot shoved a gun in your face. Are you okay, Mick?"

Davis's lips turned up, the bare ghost of a smile on his somber face.

"I'm a little shaken up. It's never fun having a gun pointed at your head." He side glanced at Sully, who turned a delicate shade of red. "Worse, though, is knowing Hart identified us as Christians. His knowledge puts us in grave danger."

"So why bring him with us?" Jeannie asked, still upset with Hart's use of a firearm to get Davis's attention.

Sully answered her.

"You know the old saying, honey. Keep your friends close and your enemies closer. We're going to have to watch our sixes, Mick. Hart was all kinds of nervous, dancing on the chair like a tick on the head of a hot pin. There's some truth in what he says, but I'm not sure how much of it was true. Do you think they have Coventry figured as a Christian?"

Davis shook his head.

"Not sure. We need to let her know, subtly, that the four of us are exposed. If she isn't, they might trust her and will probably task her to kill us if this op goes south. Jeannie, you'll need to contact Coventry. Bring her into Sickbay on some pretext and find a way of getting word to her. Do it so you won't get recorded on a holo feed. We should expect we're now under continuous surveillance. Heather, you need to look at our God Coins again. Hart mentioned a forced recall. Something tells me they've found a way to bring us back, even if we're not ready to return. I don't know how much time we have to prepare, but the sooner we get started on some contingency planning, the better off we'll be. Let's call it a night, okay? Our stress levels are going to climb a little over the next few days."

Sully and Jeannie rose, and they all hugged good night. After the Sullivans left, Heather and Davis collapsed on the couch. He could feel waves of emotions flowing from her as she snuggled under his arm.

"Are we doing the right thing, Mick? Bringing Hart with us feels like carrying a poisonous snake in one hand and a mouse in the other."

He smiled at her analogy.

"We trust God on this one, Heather. I've been dancing at the far edges of my comfort zone since I joined TTI. If TTI orders us to go on a manhunt for Tul'ran, we'll have to go. This makes no sense. As far as Contradeum knows, Tul'ran's been dead for millennia. Why go back to make sure he dies? With any luck, we can figure out what to do when we get back to our village. At least we can see the kids again. I hope they're okay. Have you followed them on the timeline?"

A tear leaked from Heather's face.

"They don't exist in history, Mick. There's no record of them anywhere, other than our memories. I didn't tell you this, but I brought back their DNA samples. I ran a gene trace and couldn't find their DNA in the world's recorded gene pool. Of course, the pool records aren't perfect, and history may not have recorded their descendants. All I can tell you is from what I remember of them. We might go back, and they might be dead."

A pang struck Davis's heart. They tried to set up their little family as best they could, but it might've been for nothing. He sighed. He loved people who died thousands of years before he was born. The wonder of it always pulled at his brain, making him worried about a psychological schism.

There was nothing normal about time travel.

After Hart left Davis's quarters, he wasted no time getting to Korhonen's office. He closed the door and waited for her to acknowledge him. She looked up from the main screen on her desk and smiled, her eyes glazed.

"Did they go for it?"

Hart swallowed twice.

"Davis said as soon as you task the mission, he'll file a request to add me to it."

Her smile widened. She looked like she'd been smoking drugs. The dreamlike quality of her eyes suggested a euphoric state far beyond anything Hart had ever seen.

"Excellent, excellent. This is the second time I've saved you, Hart. The first time you failed me by not making sure Wu was dead. I forgave you for your clumsiness; it turned out to be a fortunate error. The second mistake, well, I should've executed you for your second mistake. You collaborated with an enemy of the state when you put Davis and Wu in the water to meet Oslo. Had you not cooperated with my investigation, you'd have been swimming with the sharks. Or did you forget?"

———†———

Hart shuddered. How could he forget how he 'cooperated'? She had his own people take him into custody after she came back from Rome. They brought him into her office in chains after beating his body with rubber stanchions. It was surreal; he kneeled on the floor struggling to breathe with bruised ribs and she sat there with her stupid smile on her face.

Her face never changed as she had played the holo of Davis and Wu appearing on the Lens, surrounded by armed personnel outfitted in black from head to toe. They escorted Davis and Wu to the escape terminal and sealed them into a pod. The pod launched off the island and streaked down to the ocean. The scene shifted as long scanners picked up the diver exiting the water and entering the life pod. Minutes later, the diver emerged from the pod and dropped back into the ocean.

The display shifted back to the security team re-entering the Emergence Field. Hart saw a figure dressed in MetaMaterials exit a side door and have a brief discussion with the Team Leader. Seconds later, they all dispersed.

The stoned smile never left Korhonen's face the entire time.

"The mistake you made, Hart, was in failing to scrub your DNA from the MetaMaterials suit. We scanned every suit in storage, which took a long time. Every suit has a history file. When we found your DNA on a suit, we downloaded the history file and matched it to the date and time on the holo feed of Davis and Wu returning. The man who stepped out of the shadows was you, Mr. Hart. Do you wish to deny it? If you do, I'll convene a formal inquiry."

Hart had felt sick to his stomach. A formal inquiry. A court martial where the sentence upon conviction was death. His death.

"What do you want from me, Administrator?"

Korhonen had nodded pleasantly to one guard, who slammed a rubber truncheon into Hart's kidneys. He doubled over in agony. Her smile never wavered.

"My dear Mr. Hart, you have disappointed me in the past, but this! This is treason. The diver was none other than former Regional Supervisor Oslo, who launched a nuclear missile from the submarine transporting her to Atlantis. The same missile burned Babylon to the ground and took out the world's food supply. We could lay all the world's starvation on your shoulders, you know. Your failure to notify me of her contact with you was solely responsible for her being in the wrong place at the wrong time. What do you say about that, Hart?"

When he didn't answer fast enough, the guard hit

him again. Lights danced in Hart's eyes as pain lanced through his body in waves.

"I didn't... I didn't know they were going to launch a missile. Swear it. Firing on Babylon wasn't part of the plan."

Korhonen removed her shoe and lifted his chin with her toes. She'd painted her toenails red, he noticed, wondering why he'd find the observation important. The light in her eyes was different. They glowed with malice, as if she found his pain delicious.

"What was the plan, Hart? Answer faster if you want to avoid more pain."

"She just wanted a meeting with Wu and Davis," he babbled, as quickly as he could get the words out of his mouth. "That's all. She didn't tell me what it was about, just that she wanted a face-to-face with them before you and Contradeum got your hooks into them."

She surprised him by kicking him in the face with the ball of her foot, causing blood to gush out of his nose as lights danced behind his eyeballs.

"You will not speak of our god in such a disrespectful way," she hissed. "You must refer to him as the Supreme God of the Earth and couch your words with humility."

"I'm sorry," he mumbled, watching the blood dripping from his nose onto the floor. Korhonen rubbed her big toe in his blood, and painted lines on his face with it.

"You'll be sorry, Hart, if the Supreme God of the Earth ever hears you talk like that. You're lucky he's a gracious god. Open your mouth. Good. Now suck the blood off my toe. You can do better, Hart. Make it nice and clean. Good boy."

Hart gagged as she took her toe out of his mouth, the taste of blood making him nauseous.

"What do you want from me?"

Korhonen slipped her foot back in her shoe, her face still locked in the languid look Hart despised.

"What makes you think I want something from you?"

Hart spat blood out of his mouth.

"You could've put a bullet in my brain and dumped me into the ocean. That's what you did to Wood. Do you remember the little incident of Wood's murder which I covered up for you?"

The guard slammed the truncheon into his back, and pain exploded in his brain.

"Hart, you traitorous weasel, such a nasty thing to say! There's no record of me killing someone. None. Such foul and baseless accusations. You'll do anything to save your pathetic skin, won't you? I'd gladly execute a traitorous simp like you. Our gracious Supreme God of the Earth has other plans."

Korhonen walked around her desk and sat in her plush leather chair. She activated a screen and the images of Davis and Wu hung in mid-air.

"Behold, our intrepid explorers. Lost in Antiquity until we recovered them. They saved a lot of lives when they came back. We need them to do one more mission. Two people from Antiquity somehow disrupted *his* plans and disrespected the Supreme God of the Earth. Can you imagine their impertinence? Someone gave *him* the names of Tul'ran az Nostrom and Erianne az Nostrom. We need to send Davis and Wu back into Antiquity and search for these two people. You'll go with them. Once they find these two characters, you'll kill them and bring back proof of death."

Hart looked at her dully.

"I'm a cop, not a hit man."

The truncheon exploded into his back, and he doubled over in agony.

"No, Hart, you're a dead man. If you want to keep breathing, you'll do whatever I tell you to do. I'm telling you to take a trip and kill two people. Are you good with it, Hart, or do we need to explore alternative options?"

His tongue felt swollen, and the coppery taste of blood lingered in his mouth.

"They'll never take me with them. How will I explain why I have to go? I'm not a Traveler."

Her smile became dreamier.

"I don't know. Come up with something, you little weasel. Be creative. Just get on their team."

———————✦———————

He got on the Team. Hart shuddered again. They beat him even after he said he would comply. He urinated blood for a full day after he 'cooperated'. During his recovery, he put together a plan to approach Davis and Wu.

The results of which he had just briefed the Administrator.

Korhonen noticed the look on his face.

"How did you get them to agree?"

Hart kept his emotions from his face.

"I did what you said, Administrator. I got creative by telling them I was running because I was afraid of being caught for helping them meet with Oslo. They bought it. I'm in."

Korhonen played with her hair as she stared at the large holo of Contradeum sitting on the wall normally portraying the ocean. This holo had him riding a horse through ocean surf and he was shirtless. She seemed to have forgotten about her suggestions about how he might infiltrate Davis's Team. Hart suspected where her mind was and lunged away from the gutter.

"Good, good. Draft the orders, Hart. Task Major Quarterlaine to accompany them and brief her. If Davis and Wu can't find these people, bring them back here. If they refuse to come back, kill Davis and torture Wu until she cooperates. Try not to kill her. She's still the only Programmer we have left. Now get out."

As Hart backed away from her desk, Korhonen spread her legs wide as she continued to stare at Contradeum's image. Hart tore his eyes away as her right hand drifted downwards. He couldn't watch her descent to madness any longer and was grateful he was leaving Atlantis.

He already decided he wouldn't be coming back.

The pills he was going to pack would make sure of it.

CHAPTER THE FOURTH: ROCK 'N' ROLL

Atlantis, May 30, 2099 AD... seventeen days after Satan takes possession of the Antichrist's body, midway through the Tribulation

The Earth trembled. It pulsed as if it had a heartbeat.

Since the early 1960s, when recording devices were sophisticated enough to register the tremors, the earth shook exactly every twenty-six seconds. Every twenty-six seconds, seismologists on multiple continents record a measurable blip on their detectors. The source of the pulse came from a part of the Gulf of Guinea called the Bight of Bonny. Some say the pulse's origin point is close to a volcano on the island of Sao Tome in the Bight of Bonny.

Almost one hundred and forty years later, the shaking worsened. The tremors popped up anywhere the seismic plates ground against one another.

To make matters worse, under the surface of the Earth lay a vast, interconnected cauldron of magma waiting to vent its anger upon the living and the soon-to-be dead.

Mick Davis watched the most recent newscast on the growing seismic events and furrowed his brows. Over fourteen hundred earthquakes in Iceland alone. Similar numbers of increasing temblors around the globe. He remembered the prophecy he read out of the Bible to his Team on May 13 and it carved worry lines into his forehead.

Davis and his Team spent the last two and some weeks putting together an excursion package to Mesopotamia in 2005 BC while anxiously watching the holo news feeds. Besides the casts about seismic activity, the feeds gleefully showed people hunting down and killing Christians, then tying them to the hoods of their vehicles like trophies and driving around like madmen.

Looting calmed down because there was nothing left to loot. Buildings with carved out doors and windows littered the cities, devoid of anything useful and sometimes charred with fire set by frustrated, hungry people.

Angry climate-change protesters marched wherever they could get a few people together and some attention from roaming holo cameras. They blamed the earthquakes and the uptick in volcanic activities on the world's failure to regulate climate change, while ignoring the devastating effects nuclear war had had on the planet, and every prediction in the Bible.

The rest of the feed focused on pleasure in every

hedonistic, demonic, and sadistic form. Narcissism, already a problem before the Tribulation, bloomed into a normal human state. Only the need to satisfy one's deepest, darkest desires occupied people's senses twenty-four hours a day.

Activity in TTI had sped up to a frantic pace, but supplies were short, and they were suffering from a lack of leadership. Marjatta Korhonen was still living in la-la land, and the Team saw her rarely. Davis was itching to get back into the past. A big earthquake was coming, and Mick Davis didn't want to be on the planet when it hit. At least not in this location in the time stream.

Heather walked into the living room just as the holocaster, who appeared to be sitting on their couch and sipping a cup of hot liquid, concluded his summary. She shook her head as the image faded from view.

"Holo technology has become a little too real. I swear I could've walked up and taken the mug out of his hand."

Davis turned to look at her, admiring how she looked in her light blue tunic. Mesopotamian fashion suited her.

"You look lovely. How does the outfit feel?"

Heather's lips twisted.

"It's a little tight for my liking. I guess men in Ur wanted women to have nothing to hide. Why do I have to look sexy in the middle of the desert?"

Davis eyed her up and down with exaggeration for effect.

"You do look sexy, but I can't speak to the fashion of the day. Erianne's the Historian in the family. She would give you a better answer than I ever could. I wonder how the kids are doing?"

It was Heather's turn to laugh.

"The kids? You're barely older than Tul'ran, and Erianne isn't far behind him. They're hardly kids."

Davis folded Heather into his arms.

"You had to be there when Tul'ran walked up to my hutch at twelve years old. Darkshadow was so huge by comparison, Tul'ran looked like a carrot hanging from the horse's teeth. I decided to adopt him the second I saw that scrawny little kid. No matter what we look like now, or how old he is, he'll always be my son."

Heather snuggled into his chest.

"I'm sure they're fine. He *is* Tul'ran the Sword. How do you feel about our orders to find him and kill him?"

Davis grunted and pulled away from her.

"We'll never find him. I'm certain of it. Even if we do, no one on this Team has the capability of killing my son, especially with that wildcat of a wife at his back. Whoever signed our orders has been smoking crack."

Heather left the living room area and dropped a nondescript bag at the entrance to their room, with Davis at her heels. They piled at the door the last of their personal effects, at least those they could take with them to Antiquity.

"I'm not sure if Marjatta's smoking crack, but she's definitely not herself."

Davis reached down, lifted his backpack, and slung it over his shoulders.

"Even since she came back from Rome, she acts

like she's high all the time. I'm ready to slap her insipid smile right off her face."

Heather reached up to adjust the straps on his backpack and tapped him on the shoulder.

"Don't let Hart hear you talking about Korhonen like that. He's her eyes and ears on this mission; best not to forget it. Do you believe what he said about wanting to become a Christian?"

Davis helped Heather sling her pack across her slender shoulders. He adjusted the straps and checked to make sure the pack wouldn't bounce against her lower spine.

"Not for a second. It was a sloppy attempt to get inside our group. He still thinks too much like a cop. If he asks about Jesus, of course we'll tell him what he needs to know, but don't hold your breath. Erasmus Hart is in this for Korhonen."

Wu expelled a rush of breath.

"I feel so frustrated. These missions are hard enough without having to guess when he's going to slip a knife into our collective spines."

Both froze when the door chimed. They exchanged looks, wondering if their room was under surveillance and Security overheard their treasonous comments. Davis opened the door slowly to find Sully waiting for them with furrowed eyebrows.

"What's taking you two so long? We're on the ramp in five mikes. What's with the sour looks?"

Davis stepped out of their room, leading Heather by her left hand.

"Nothing, man. We're just tripping out on a little paranoia. You and Jeannie ready?"

Sully stepped in with them as they walked at a

quick pace to the Emergence Room. The hallways of the building teemed with people scurrying to complete last-minute tasks before they transitioned.

"Yup. She's on the Lens already, excited as all get-out about her first Time Transfer. I've made sure both of us took anti-nausea meds after you told us about your last transition to Mesopotamia."

Heather grimaced as her stomach twisted at the memory. A rapid calculation, coupled with a pitching lifeboat, warped the translation, and made her very sick. Rarely, the Lens translated environmental kinetic energy into the transition parameters. It was easy to program out. All you needed was time.

"It's going to be a while before I forget how much I puked the last time we rode the bull. It'll be a smoother go this time, I promise. I've coded some extra steps into the transition to account for the three newbs in our party."

Sully laid his pack on the Lens and gave his wife a quick hug. He looked down at Heather with a wry expression on his face.

"It's been a long time since I've been called a newb. I guess it fits. Just try to not materialize me into a rock, okay?"

Heather smirked at him.

"I'll do my best, but we have a money-back guarantee if it happens."

The four of them laughed, unaware Fate was laughing with them. Fate, a spirit of destiny created by God to remind humans of why they should listen to something other than their foolish desires, liked jokes. Especially when Fate played them on unsuspecting humans.

Davis stood facing the Lens, doing a last count-off. Michael Sullivan, Jeannie Sullivan, Heather Wu, Coventry Quarterlaine, and Erasmus Hart. And me, he reminded himself. A six-person squad to be sent into Antiquity to hunt down and kill his son. Davis turned to the Tech who would launch them into the quantum realm.

"All present and accounted for, Mr. Rhoades. Transition when ready."

Jeffrey Rhoades smiled at Davis and gestured up to the clock.

"Ten minutes, Mr. Davis. As soon as the countdown is complete, we'll send you downstream. Please take your place."

Davis stepped up onto the Lens and took his spot by Heather. She smiled at him and reached out to grasp his hand. He squeezed it reassuringly and swept his gaze at the supplies littering the Lens around their feet. He hoped it would be enough. They were going back only two weeks after they left Gilgesh, Antiquity Time.

TTI had been more than a little fluffy after Heather confessed she left the Temporal Scepter behind, but it was fortuitous. The quantum bubble was still in place, so they didn't need a twenty-year space between their last transit and now.

'It's smooth sailing from here,' he thought.

Fate laughed.

Silly humans.

A woman sprinted into the Emergence Room, holding a handheld device over her head. Her face was white, and her eyes were huge in her head. She looked around frantically until she found the eyes of the person who would engage the Lens and transition the Team into Antiquity.

"Send them now!" she screamed. "There's an earthquake coming. The seismographs are showing tremors off the charts! Launch, launch, launch!"

For a moment, no one moved. The implications of rushing a launch were calamitous. Then they could all feel the start of the floor undulating beneath their feet.

A flurry of activity followed, as the Emergence Field burst into action. Technicians frantically punched at the transparent holo displays at face level as the countdown clock abruptly showed quadruple zeroes. In an instant, the world faded from Davis's view in a stream of gaudy colors before he could say 'I knew it' or anything else.

The day of the global earthquake had finally arrived.

In the Kingdom of Heaven

The wedding had been spectacular.

Jesus had let Darian stay for the first full day of Gwyn and Johan's festivities, as His representative at the feast. The People were overjoyed to approach her, bow from a distance, and thank her for her sacrifice and to pass on their thanks to Yahweh for His patience and their freedom. Darian took on the role of Ambassador for the Kingdom of Heaven, passing on Jesus's blessings to them. It had been exhilarating.

Taking leave of Gwyn, Johan, Tul'ran, and Erianne had been painful, but Darian had left them with her blazingly beautiful smile and promises they would dine again in Paradise. She was almost skipping when they stepped once more onto the solid gold floors of her eternal home. It took her a moment to realize they'd arrived in a different spot than the first time E'thriel had transported her.

Before her stood the immense city of New Jerusalem. Surrounding it was a high wall with twelve gates and twelve angels in charge of the gates. On the gates were printed the names of the twelve tribes of the sons of Israel. There were three gates on each side of the cubed city. The twelve gates were twelve pearls; each gate was made from a single pearl.

To say it was big was a ridiculous understatement. New Jerusalem was 1,500 miles wide, 1,500 miles deep, and 1,500 miles high. The living space was 1.9 million square miles, roughly midway between the sizes of Australia and India.

God made New Jerusalem from pure gold; it looks like transparent glass and its brilliance is like clear quartz. He made the streets of the city from pure gold, also transparent. Nothing hid in the city, for no one had anything left to hide.

The glorious majesty of the city wasn't the thing making her heart sing. Joy so filled the air it was like you were breathing it into your lungs. Happiness lit every face around her as if someone beamed a searchlight into the inside of the skin. It was no wonder it felt as if her feet never touched the magnificent sea of gold on which they walked.

As they strode through one gate, the guarding angel gave E'thriel a friendly nod. Word had spread through Heaven like wildfire of his return, and how he returned four souls from the Abyss to Heaven. Once the host of Heaven saw the favor placed upon E'thriel by the Holy Trinity, any resentment his fellow angels had against him evaporated like a mist.

The interior of the city, within the cubed walls, was awe-inspiring. Darian craned her neck and stared upwards at levels exceeding her extraordinary new vision. She could see people walking on levels miles away, stunned to know if the city were on Earth its ceiling would be inside the upper boundary of the exosphere but outside the lower boundary. She remembered the exosphere was the uppermost layer of the sky, where the atmosphere thins out and merges with outer space.

No one should be able to live in space.

Darian shook her head ruefully. Unless you were in an eternal body. She was going to have to get used to being dead.

"E'thriel, is there a temple building or church here?"

Her guardian angel canted his head and stared down at her thoughtfully. Here, he stood at his full height of ten feet tall.

"There is no temple building in New Jerusalem. God and the Lamb are the city's temple, since humans and angels worship the Holy Trinity everywhere."

As they walked further, they saw a river flowing down the middle of an enormous street. Trees grew in the middle of the street and on both sides of the river.

Darian tugged at E'thriel's sleeve and pointed at the scene in front of them.

"What's all that?"

E'thriel raised his wings high above his head and shimmered his feathers, delighted to pass on his knowledge to the woman he had guarded while she lived on Earth.

"At the center of Heaven is the Throne of God. The river flows from the Throne of God and contains the water of life. The trees yield twelve kinds of fruit every month; they are the fruit of life. According to the Lord, the leaves of the tree are for healing all nations. From these trees, the Lord created every Garden of Eden throughout the universe."

The flow of pedestrian traffic suddenly shifted and moved away from the center of the city.

"Where's everyone going?" Darian said, her intense curiosity making her stand on her toes.

"Come," E'thriel said abruptly, guiding her to follow the surge of people. "When this happens, something big is about to unfold."

They arrived where the multitudes once more stood or hovered around the edge of Heaven to gaze at the Earth floating serenely below them. Many of the people had fond memories of their time on Earth, and the events of the Tribulation saddened them.

None, of course, were required to watch. Many turned away after Jesus broke the first few Seals, unable to view the devastation following upon the cosmic snap of each seal.

Those who remained had studied end times scripture passionately when they were alive, and were interested in how their opinions of the prophesied events translated into reality.

Darian took E'thriel's arm and gripped it tightly. The tension in the air was palpable. She didn't know what was about to happen, but it was sad news for someone. Or for many people.

The crowd parted to allow Jesus's passage through the throngs. He stepped up to the edge of Heaven and held the Sixth Seal high above His head. It was brown, like the color of dirt, and had a rough quality to its surface. Without fanfare, Jesus pressed His thumbs down and the Seal snapped with a rumble, which moved like a wave through Heaven.

The mini tremor in Heaven mirrored as a massive earthquake on the Earth. It was not in one place; the earthquake shook every part of the globe. A complex network of faults crossed the Earth's solid crust, which itself rested on an elastic mantle of unknown structure. The unstable fault lines around the world began to slip and fracture everywhere.

Into a world in which the remaining people had survived war, devastating famine, and a horrible pandemic, would come the most powerful earthquake the Earth had ever seen.

Jerusalem, May 30, 2099 AD

Satan had stayed in Jerusalem far longer than he intended, basking in the adulation of the people who came to worship him. It pleased him he had thoroughly corrupted the city over which the Son of God wept and loved so much. The adoration gave him an exquisite feeling of victory over God. After the Holy Trinity created Adam and Eve, all Satan wanted was a planet over which to rule. Now he had one.

He never knew taking on flesh could be so enjoyable, so… divine. He was both a human and a god. The pride sown in his heart from the inception of his creation had burgeoned into a knowledge of invincibility. No longer did he read Scripture and struggle over its interpretation and implication for his future. He now lived his future with the certainty of one who claimed immortality and thrived under the rush of ultimate power. Satan stopped obsessing over the signs, watching for fulfilment of prophecy, and divining the future. His life was now perfect.

Except for his most recent irritants: the two witnesses.

No sooner had Satan taken possession of Contradeum's body than two witnesses appeared in Jerusalem. They staked out a corner of a marketplace near the Temple and started fearlessly talking about Jesus Christ, how he was the Messiah, and how He was the only one who could save the people from eternal torment. The witnesses claimed that their appearance and ministry expressed God's grace offered to repentant and believing sinners.

Had they just stuck with the gospel, Satan may have left them alone. The more Christians they created, the more he could torture and kill. However, the two witnesses also loudly condemned his government's practices, the sin rampant in the world, and the persecution of Christians. They even denounced him as Satan Incarnate, a false god!

Satan flicked his hand and the entire wall of his Temple office converted into a 3D news feed.

He watched the witnesses, brooding. They were both old men, clothed in sackcloth and sandals. Wearing sackcloth was symbolic and expressed their great sorrow for what they called a wretched and unbelieving world. Both looked middle eastern, with rugged tanned faces and long hair and beards.

Their hair and beards were white, which set off their piercing eyes. It pained him to see them, for they had been a thorn in his side thousands of years ago in Antiquity and they were going to be a thorn in his side again. He wondered if they would recognize him. He certainly recognized them.

Moses turned to stare into the holo feed, as if he heard the Antichrist's thoughts.

"You have heard it said by your leader, he who proclaims himself falsely as a god, he will bring you peace and prosperity. I tell you the truth, he is a liar and the Father of Lies. Here are the signs which will prove the falsity of his words. There is coming a great calamity in this world, such as you have never seen."

Elijah stepped forward and raised his staff in the air.

"Verily I say unto you, the disasters coming in the next three and a half years are judgments of God. At the rising of the sun and the setting of the moon, you will experience God's final outpouring of judgment and eternal hell will follow. Do not follow the false god who calls himself the Supreme God of Earth. Instead, fall to your knees, repent of your sins, and call upon the Lord Jesus Christ to save you. Only Jesus can save you now."

Satan leaned in to inspect the background of the

scene before him. He had tasked members of his guard to sneak in behind the two witnesses and cut them down in a hail of automatic weapons fire. At first, the messengers seemed oblivious to the shock troopers. Then Elijah tapped Moses on his shoulder and the two ancient men turned to the advancing troopers.

The troopers immediately raised their guns into the ready position and almost had time to squeeze the triggers. Elijah and Moses opened their mouths and fire flew out of them like flamethrowers. The troopers screamed as the fire consumed them and they thrashed around until they fell, dead. The ethereal flames continued to burn even after they died, until nothing but piles of black ash littered the street.

Moses turned to look directly once again into the holo feed.

"Your so-called god has done you a great disservice by threatening our lives. So you know we come from Yahweh, the God of Heaven, and His son Jesus Christ; soon we will shut up the sky so rain will not fall during the days of our preaching. We will turn the waters into blood and strike the earth with every plague."

"We do not do these things because we enjoy hurting you," Elijah piped in. "Our hope is to bring you to faith in our Lord Jesus Christ." Elijah dropped to his knees and Moses immediately followed him. They looked sprightly for men who had lived thousands of years in the past.

"We beg you to listen to us and hear our pleas," Elijah continued. "If you have questions and you can travel, come to us and speak with us. We are here and nothing will take us from this place until our time here is complete."

Again, Moses looked directly into the holo feed.

"And no one."

Satan roared for one of his slave-brides as he stabbed at the holo feed, turning the display to darkness. When the woman crawled into his quarters, he grabbed her by the throat and began punching her savagely in the face while screaming his rage.

His anger was so all-consuming, he'd forgotten about the messengers and their dire warnings. It's why he never saw the earthquake coming.

Just as he raised his fist for another strike on the poor woman's bloodied visage, he sensed the incoming tremors.

The Antichrist reached out with his power and casually stabilized the ground beneath and around the Temple. The frequency and power of the temblors grew, so he exerted his will with increasing strength. It didn't stop. Within minutes, Satan felt as if he were atop a raging bull intent on sending him careening into a wall or barricade or anything at all. He exerted so much strength to keep the Temple stable; it temporarily drained his power. A shard of fear pricked his pride and slapped his confidence as his power waned to near nothingness.

The Abomination of Desolation reached out through the spiritual realm and seized the energy of the worshippers who laid screaming in the Temple. One by one, he siphoned their physical, spiritual, and temporal energy into his body to sustain and feed the power he had to push out to save the Temple Mount.

It was just enough.

He looked up when the world stopped shaking, amazed at the trickle of sweat running off his forehead and into his eyes. Shaking, he stood up and cast the unconscious woman aside, and walked to the edge of the wall.

Beyond the walls of the Temple were great plumes of black smoke, at which tongues of fire licked with a frenzy. He could hear sirens and people wailing in the distance as a cacophony of desperate sounds crashed in his ears.

The Antichrist gazed into the courtyard of the Temple and had his second shock of the day. Four hundred and twelve blackened skeletons, still exuding an eerie gray smoke, lay scattered in various positions. It was a scene from the depths of Hell, but one which had not presented itself on Earth before.

Even after stealing their energy, he felt weak, vulnerable, and confused.

What had just happened?

The planet Earth, May 30, 2099 AD

If you asked someone to describe what causes an earthquake, most people would shrug and say something like, "The ground moves and it causes damage." What they probably couldn't tell you is the ground shakes because of a sudden slip on a fault. The surface of the earth sits on tectonic plates, which continuously and slowly move, grinding and scraping against each other. Stresses in the Earth's outer layer push the sides of the faults together.

When the stress builds up enough, the rocks slip suddenly, releasing energy and waves travelling through the Earth's crust and causing shaking. These are naturally occurring events well outside the powers of humans to create or stop. They usually originate several to tens of miles below the surface of the earth. It takes many years, between decades and centuries, to build up enough stress to make a large earthquake.

On this day, the waves transferred throughout the entire planet and were the largest series of quakes recorded.

When the shaking started, one holo announcer started screaming it was the end of the world and California would soon slide into the ocean. The idea of the state sliding into the ocean was the subject of much humour among scientists who studied earthquakes. At their conventions, they'd sometimes create holo spoofs of dolphins swimming through Hollywood.

California is planted on top of the Earth's crust in a location where it spans two tectonic plates. The San Andreas Fault System is the boundary between the Pacific Plate and the North American Plate. These two plates move horizontally, slowly sliding past one another. The Pacific Plate moves northwest 46 mm per year or the rate a person's fingernails grow. The strike-slip earthquakes on the San Andreas Fault result from this plate motion.

There is nowhere for California to fall, and it can't slip into the ocean.

Its cities fell, though.

It was the strongest earthquake ever experienced

by Los Angeles, San Francisco, San Diego, and other large centers. It was so strong, no one could measure it. Buildings designed to survive large earthquakes crumbled like sand structures on the beach.

There was no place to go.

There was no place to hide.

People died.

Atlantis, May 30, 2099 AD

The earthquake hit the island of Atlantis like a sledgehammer hitting an egg. TTI's builders created Atlantis as solidly as human beings could design an island, but the structures on it collapsed when the ground gyrated like a bucking horse. The rolling tremors slammed everyone against walls, trees, and rocks. The ground rose to meet people walking outside and hurtled them down into deep depressions in the rock. Underground housing units imploded, killing the inhabitants, and burying the survivors under tons of rubble.

Half of the six thousand men and women living on Atlantis died within minutes.

The TTI Main Building crumbled like foil. A large metal girder detached itself from the ceiling and fell onto the Lens, shattering it. The Lens pieces flew about the Emergence Room like shards from exploding glass, shredding anyone within range. The Main Computer split in half as if it were a piece of tissue in the hands of an enraged man. Everything separated, frayed, snapped, or simply tore into pieces.

Only a handful of people would survive from the

quake's assault on the Main Building, and they crawled their way out of the rubble to an island destroyed.

Marjatta Korhonen had just stepped outside when the quake hit. The first tremor threw her thirty yards away into a large oak tree on the side of the pathway. The blow to her head knocked her out. When she awoke, it took her ten minutes to orient herself to where she was and what had happened.

Shaking, she tried to stand up and immediately collapsed to the ground. She rolled over and assessed her right ankle, which was swelling rapidly. A sprain and not broken, she noticed with relief. She stayed on the ground for a few moments, looking around. Marjatta felt something dripping down her face, and she reached up to touch her scalp. Blood matted her hair, where her head had hit the tree.

She checked the rest of her body and was relieved again to find no other injuries. It was then she noticed the tattoos on her wrists. When did she get tattoos? Panic gripped her for a few minutes as she tried to put together her memories. She remembered going to Rome and bit her lip at the sudden flash of recollection, reminding her she went there to kill Contradeum. Marjatta recoiled from the horror of seeing General Rozinski's knife slipping into Contradeum's chest. There were the confusing days that followed, with people running around not knowing what to do.

Marjatta drew in a sudden sharp breath. He came to life. Contradeum came to life! She remembered the shock of seeing him rise from the dead almost gave her a heart attack.

After he came back to life, he had summonsed her to his chambers, then… nothing. She looked at her wrists again. Whatever happened to her left two ugly tattoos on her wrists and a burning need to punch the person who put them there.

The Administrator looked around and wondered what had happened. Had someone bombed them again?

Mesopotamia, the eighth day of the fifth month, 2004 BC

They fell the last two inches to the canyon floor, landing hard on their feet and almost tumbling to the ground. Sully settled into a crouch, knees bent, and arms spread wide.

"What the heck was that?"

"Form up!" Davis yelled and lunged to grab Heather and Hart into a huddle. The others quickly fell into a circle, linking their arms and dropping to their knees on the canyon floor. A shockwave hit them seconds later; the canyon dipped and heaved as if the earthquake tremors originated from the Insertion Point. When it finished, they looked at each other, literally shaken by the experience.

"How did you know?" Heather asked, as she watched the dust swirling about the IP.

Davis rose to his feet and helped her up.

"I didn't. At least, not for sure. When we arrived in the air, above the ground, the thought flashed into my mind: the earthquake threw us off course. I know it doesn't make sense, but I thought the quake might follow us here."

Sully dusted off his knees and looked around the

canyon.

"Well, something sure did." He looked at Heather. "Could a shockwave follow us through the quantum realm?"

Heather's face was white, and a tinge of green colored the edges of her eyes.

"Just one sec. I'm gonna be sick."

Her vomiting set off a chain reaction and soon all but Sully and Jeannie were sitting back and wiping their mouths.

"You promised it wouldn't be this bad," Hart moaned as the group reached for the liquids on their belts.

"It shouldn't have been," Heather said, as she held her head in her hands. "Please, someone, make the world stop turning."

"We could talk about your sex life," Coventry said, an unwilling smile creasing the corner of her mouth.

Heather whipped her head up, blushed, and flicked her eyes at Mick.

"No sex life," she said. "We're not married."

"And wouldn't be talking about even if we were," Mick finished for her, firmly. "Is that what you two were on about the last time we were here?"

Coventry was openly grinning now.

"The bond of sisterhood deprives me of a confession, milord az Peregos."

"English, please," Jeannie said, rising from her knees. "This is going to be hard enough without y'all jabbering in some ancient language. I need to use the facilities. Do we have facilities in this place?"

Coventry lifted her chin to a corner of the IP.

"There's a small stream just around that corner. Take some MetaMaterials and you can create some privacy for yourself. It's all we have, I'm afraid."

"Well, that's disgusting," Jeannie replied, as she staggered in the direction revealed by the black woman's chin. "Y'all better be here when I come back, or there'll be Hell to pay."

Sully watched her leave, making sure she was steady on her feet.

"Back to my question, please. Could a shockwave have followed us here?"

Heather swallowed the bile still scratching at her throat and accepted a drink from Davis.

"Thank you, love. Sully, the short answer is: I don't know. The long answer would involve weeks of math with someone incredibly more versed in quantum physics than me, and the answer would likely still be 'I don't know.' We're in virgin territory here, the pointy edge of science and technology. We have a big problem, if it did."

Hart spun his head to look at her, his eyes growing big.

"What kind of problem?"

Heather struggled to her feet, accepting an arm from Davis with a quick smile of gratitude.

"Ras, for the shockwave to follow us through quantum space, it would have to have been more powerful than any earthquake ever registered. It may have been bad enough to take out the TTI Main Building."

Hart paled.

"Which means?"

"Which means," Davis said, interrupting, "we

need to focus on our mission and not worry about what we can't control. Instead of guessing, let's contact Atlantis through a quantum string. Coventry?"

Quarterlaine jumped to her feet, and reached into the pack slung around her waist.

"On it, Master Chief."

She assembled the string communicator and set it down on the canyon floor. A transparent holo screen appeared above her head and her long fingers danced over the symbols projected by the machine.

"Self-test is complete," the AI announced. "Systems nominal. What is your query?"

"Call home," Coventry said, her voice terse.

Silence descended for a minute that felt much longer.

"Call failed."

Coventry squeezed her bottom lip between her teeth.

"Diagnose source of call failure."

"TTI Main Frame does not respond."

"Diagnose link stability."

"Link stability nominal to fifteen satellites in geosynchronous orbit around the Earth at Origin Time."

"Query link between ComSat 1358Alpha and TTI Main Frame."

"Query complete. The link is broken. TTI Main Frame does not respond to all hails on all satellites."

"Establish connection with the Temporal Scepter."

"Complied. Link with Temporal Scepter is five by five."

"Query link between the Temporal Scepter and the Lens."

This time, the wait was much longer. Jeannie walked back and plunked herself down beside Sully.

"What's going on?"

Sully gave her a grave look.

"We're about to find out if we can go home."

"There is no link between the Temporal Scepter and the Lens. The Scepter reports that the quantum bubble between this IP and Origin is now closed."

Each of them froze, the implications tumbling through their minds like razor-edged dice.

"What does it mean?" Jeannie whispered, her hand going to her throat.

Davis drew in a deep breath and expelled it slowly before looking into Jeannie's terrified eyes.

"It means," he said as gently as he could, "you'll have to learn the local languages, Jeannie. Atlantis is dead."

Heather darted a sharp glance at Davis.

"What my sensitive boyfriend is trying to say in his own genteel words, Jeannie, is we can't reach Atlantis right now. I don't want you to worry; TTI won't give up on us. When things seemed desperate the last time, they still pulled it together and recovered five Teams trapped in Antiquity."

Jeannie smiled, the fear leaving her eyes.

"Thanks, Heather. I forgot about that. What do we do now?"

Davis answered for her.

"We hike out of this canyon and walk to Suse. It's a small city about a night's walk away from here. Then we'll buy horses and ride out to Gilgesh. Three days and we'll be in our temporary home, enjoying a hot, home-cooked meal."

Davis directed Sully, Jeannie, and Coventry to the various things they had to do to get ready to travel the desert at night. Sully, Coventry, and Davis were military, and all had desert combat experience. They showed Hart, Jeannie, and Heather how to set up their water bladders by adding four iodine tablets to the two-quart soft-skinned containers after they filled them in the stream. The water would taste horrible, but it would sustain them.

Military packs were incongruous with their period clothing, but they would stash the packs in their effects once they bought horses. They adjusted the packs on Heather, Jeannie, and Hart to ensure the best balance of the load, and to reduce fatigue and chafing where possible.

As the others put on their packs and checked the straps, Hart sidled over to Heather.

"Do we tell them, Ms. Wu, we only succeeded in those previous rescue missions because all our equipment was intact, and we had you to program the transitions?"

She looked at him sharply.

"No, Mr. Hart, we do not. Let's cross our bridges as we come to them, okay?"

He nodded; his face was bland.

"Presuming there's still bridges to cross." Hart walked away to make his own preparations.

Heather watched him go, her eyes tearing.

"There won't be," she said, whispering the awful truth to herself. "It's all gone. They're all gone, and we're never going home."

CHAPTER THE FIFTH: WHEN WORLDS COLLIDE

Everhome, Evo's Home World, 45 days since Spes Deserit

"You idiot!"

Evo punctuated the scream by ripping off the robot's head and throwing it across the room and into a wall. She kicked the head around the room, shrieking profanities at the top of her lungs. When she exhausted herself, she crumpled to the floor and put her head in her hands.

"I hate you!"

Another robot trundled forward cautiously.

"May I assist you, Creator?"

Evo lifted her head and glared at the bot.

"You can fix the cross-linkage on the forward fuel cell so I don't blow up my ship halfway through the atmosphere! You should've finished my vessel long before I came back. I've been sitting on this stupid world for a month and a half in this physical body because my stupid machines can't build to blueprints!"

"May I suggest, Creator," the machine said in a timid voice, "the failure only became apparent on the test launch and may have been a design flaw."

"No, you may not." Evo said, her tone as cold as her eyes. "I don't make mistakes."

"Yes, Creator," the bot said in reply, meekly withdrawing to its corner.

After a few minutes of sulking, Evo rose to her feet and called up the schematics. The bot was right; they had dutifully built the fuel cells to spec, and the spec was wrong. She sighed and scratched at an irritant between her shoulder blades. She needed to get off the planet Everhome. Everything around her reminded her of the humiliation she suffered at God's hands here. The desire for revenge burned in her stomach like lava. She needed to take her physical body with her because she was never coming back, which required a vessel to protect her from space.

Her ship would be the finest of its kind, capable of interstellar travel by jumping through Inter-Dimensional Space. What would take thousands of years of travel at light speed would only take days on her ship. Evo fretted at the launch delay, worried her quarry would die or be gone from Spes before she could get there. The itch to kill Tul'ran and then God was worse than the one between her shoulder blades.

It took the rest of the day to print the new linkage and have it installed. The bots pronounced satisfactory results on all tests. It was time.

Evo looked around her house. She had packed clothing and shoes, but little of anything else.

For the last few thousand years, she traversed the universe in her spectral form. She had nothing because she accumulated nothing. Evo could draw on the Library of Heaven at will for answers to questions; she'd never needed to keep a book. There were no significant items she would hold in the future and reflect on for the memories. There was no one to miss her, and she'd miss no one.

Evo turned off all the bots and then shut down her house. It was a long uphill walk through the forest to get to the clearing they'd made for her ship. She turned before entering the gangway and looked back.

The house she'd built with her bare hands thousands of years ago nestled in an orchard between two trees, heavily laden with apples. It was quaint, solid, and pretty. She could step out her back door and into a brook merrily dancing along the back of her yard. The expansive front windows faced a mountain towering above the little valley in which she lived. She had put in her home every creature comfort one needed to live. It was beautiful inside and outside. Flowers, brightly colored and sweet-smelling, dotted the grass and added a splash of elegance to the scene.

The explosion was massive.

It flared a bright orange at the base of the house and mushroomed into a black cloud. The house blew into kindling, and it flattened, blackened, and charred everything living within two hundred and fifty feet of the abode. Evo tucked the detonator back into her pocket. She really hoped the other occupants of the planet heard the bomb go off and saw the mushroom cloud. It was her last expression of her contempt for this world and its inhabitants.

She turned to the launchpad and admired her ship. It was a needle-nosed, wide-bodied rocket that sat on three fins, made of advanced materials having a mirror finish resembling polished silver. It could fly in space and land on planets, on the ground or under water. She borrowed the design from humans on Earth, but the improvements she made were far superior to their rudimentary concepts. It was beautiful and functional, just like her.

It had taken one hundred and thirty-seven years to figure out a way to get through the ice shell surrounding the planet without damaging it. She'd had limited contact with God after He threw her out of the Garden and into her prison. Two contacts, in fact. The first contact happened after she blew up a world and the second was a stern caution that if she tried to physically break through the ice barrier, He would remove her from existence. She shuddered. After the first incident, she knew God would kill her if she disobeyed His last edict.

The first incident wasn't even her fault. It had been early in her explorations of the Universe in her spectral form. She'd come across a small solar system at the edge of the galaxy with nine planets and a small hunk of rock that might grow up to be a planet some day. The third, fourth, and fifth planets all had atmosphere, water, and were in every way habitable.

The fifth planet was an ocean world, with very little land mass. Water mammals and sea life of every description populated it. While it was 204,502,383 miles, or 2.2 Astronomical Units, from the sun, its unique magnetosphere and atmosphere enhanced the sun's rays, removed harmful energy, and kept the world an even, warm temperature.

In those days, scientific curiosity consumed Evo. After weeks of study, she concluded the core of the planet influenced the unique atmosphere in a way she hadn't seen before. She dove into the atmosphere, through the deep oceans, past the mantle, and into the core. The core was an oddity, not composed of iron, but of a heavily compressed gas. The planet shouldn't have been able to sustain gravity and atmosphere with a gas core.

Evo couldn't physically interact with the core, but she had learned to generate intense light while in her spectral form. She thought by generating intense light in the absolute darkness of the core, she could study the gas.

Evo hadn't thought to reference the core's composition in the Library of Heaven before she started her experiment. Had she done so, she would have learned the material at the core wasn't a gas. It was 1-Diazidocarbamoyl-5-azidotetrazole, a strange heterocyclic organic compound crammed with fourteen nitrogen atoms informally called 'azidoazide azide'.

Because of the considerable number of high-energy nitrogen bonds, the compound is extremely explosive. In fact, it is the most explosive substance in the cosmos, detonating if exposed to touch, movement, water… and bright light.

Evo generated an intense light.

The azidoazide blew.

The explosion was catastrophic.

It ripped through the mantle surrounding the core, the miles of rock under the ocean, and thrust rock, water, and organic materials into space in all directions, blowing the planet apart.

The force of the explosion was so great, it stripped the atmosphere off the fourth planet in the system, which was in conjunction with the fifth planet. Had it not been for the gravity of the enormous gas giant between the fifth and seventh planets, the debris field would have destroyed the third and fourth worlds completely. Instead, the debris field spread throughout space in a stable orbit around the sun.

Someday, humans on Earth would call the fourth planet Mars and the gas giant Jupiter. They would study the asteroid belt and wonder about its origin. Only Evo knew the truth. Well, Evo and One other: God.

God the Father was furious. He slammed her spectral form back into her physical body thousands of light years away and summonsed her into Heaven. As she stood before the Throne of God, Evo thought He was going to sentence her death. Lightning flashed around the Throne Room and thunder shook the foundations of Heaven.

"What have you done?" the Father roared, as she collapsed to lie prostrate before Him.

"It was an experiment," she said in a small voice. "I didn't know it would explode."

The Father raised his massive right hand, but the Son reached out and gently restrained Him.

"Evo, you have done great harm. We removed the creatures from the planet you ruined and placed them on the third world before the explosion. While we preserved their lives, you destroyed the fifth planet and damaged the fourth one. The atmosphere of the fourth planet is so damaged it will no longer sustain life. We must punish you for your actions."

Evo sobbed.

"I didn't know! I didn't know it would explode just by exposing it to light."

"You didn't ask," Jesus said. "The accumulation of knowledge and experimentation with elements of the cosmos comes with the potential for great harm. You should have searched the Library, or come to Us with your questions."

"Come to You? Why would I come to You? You haven't spoken to me since you kicked me out of the Garden on Everhome. Why would I come to you after you abandoned me?"

The Father's face was stormy.

"You are Our creation. Do you think the Creator is so far removed from His creation We would abandon you or not come to you if you sought Us out?"

"All I know is that I've been alone for hundreds of years! I've been my company, counsel, and friend during that whole time! Aren't you God? You knew how I was feeling. Why didn't you come to me?"

"You didn't want Us," Jesus reminded her gently.

Evo gritted her teeth and struggled to get her temper under control.

"Are you going to kill me?"

The Father and the Son looked at each other for a moment, before the Father turned back to Evo.

"You have a destiny you must fulfil, but We

cannot allow your deeds to go unpunished. To show you the consequences of your actions, We sentence you to one hundred years in the Abyss. After that time, We will permit you to return to Everhome and take up your studies. For another one hundred years after your release, We will confine you to your physical body. Let it so be written."

"Let it so be done." Jesus said, His voice quiet and resolute. "Michael."

Evo watched as the Archangel Michael strode forward and took a knee before the Throne.

"Remove Evo from Heaven and take her to the Abyss. She is not to be abused; be sure Satan and his minions understand. Set the parameters of her confinement so she cannot escape. After one hundred years, you shall set her free."

The Archangel bowed his massive head.

"By your command, Lord."

The Abyss had been worse than death. It was a darkness so absolute, Evo felt like she inhaled the blackness into her lungs. The velvety ebony nothingness removed the sensation of touch; she couldn't feel her skin with her fingertips. Evo wailed, gnashed her teeth, and thrashed her rage in sensory deprivation for one hundred years. She felt every second go by.

After the first few days, she saw a light approaching her. It was an angel, but not like the ones she'd seen before. He dressed himself in a red robe and no halo appeared over his head. His eyes were dark, as were his hair and beard, and he wore arrogance like a crown.

"I was told of a newcomer in my domain, and

warned of dire consequences should I cause you pain," he said, pulling at his chin beard. "This makes you interesting. I'm Lucifer, the Morning Star, although I'm being called Satan by our mutual enemy."

"Enemy?" Evo asked, thrilled to hear sounds and converse with someone. "Who's our common enemy?"

"Oh, dear," he said, "Are you one of the stupid ones? This discussion is going to be short-lived if you can't hold up your end of it. I'll explain once; if you can't keep up, I'll find amusement somewhere else. Was it not God who put you here?"

Evo jerked her head back.

"Forgive me. I hadn't considered Him as my enemy. You're right. He put me here for something that wasn't my fault. Since my imprisonment is unjust, it makes Him my enemy."

Satan floated around her and examined her from all angles.

"You look like an ordinary human. What did you do to merit this sentence?"

Evo turned her body to face him, which was like trying to roll on to your side while immersed in heavy oil.

"I destroyed a planet accidentally. He didn't warn me it was possible and blamed me for the mess. It's completely unfair."

Satan nodded.

"He is like that, you know. Completely unfair. I wanted my fair share of what he created, and He denied it to me as if I were a snake slithering through his precious Garden. What's your name?"

"Evo."

"Where do you come from, Evo?"

Evo furrowed her brows.

"I can't remember. While traveling through the cosmos, I always knew how to get home. I can't remember my home, or how to get there. Why can't I remember?" she said, panicking.

Satan floated back a few feet and assumed a position as if he was sitting on a throne.

"This is the way of the Abyss. They cast you out from your people, your home, Heaven, and any contact with God. The silence is deafening. You're left with an eternally healthy body and a perfect memory, allowing you to recall every sin you committed against God. For eternity. Right now, you can't even grasp how long that is."

"No!" Evo said. "One hundred years. My sentence is one hundred years and then They'll release me."

She noticed Satan didn't have eyebrows to twitch, but he gave her an impression of it, all the same.

"Only one hundred years. My, my, you are special. Where are the rest of your people?"

Evo tried to spit, but no fluid came out of her mouth.

"My people! I have no people. When God created me, it was after he created a man called Ado. I was supposed to be his helper, God said. Can you imagine? He created me to be a maid to clean a man's house and wipe his chin when he drooled in his old age. As if! I wanted more; I wanted perfect equality. I never wanted to be fit within Ado's life so closely the two of us would be one person. How was I to be special as part of a whole?"

Satan nodded, smiling malevolently.

"You wanted to be your own person, have your own things, make up your own mind, and be a leader. The shepherd instead of the sheep."

"Yes! That's what They owed me. When I couldn't have it my way, I made my own decisions. I felt superior to Ado in any way you'd care to name. It should have been me naming the creatures in my world, not him. I should've been calling the shots, not him. When I rebelled, They cast me out of the Garden and stuck me in my space in the world. They didn't call it a prison, but it sure felt like one."

Satan flicked his hand as if giving her permission to carry on. Evo missed the ironic implications of the gesture, being so caught up in her feelings.

"Once They abandoned me, I looked for ways to get off the world. I discovered how to project my spirit into the non-physical realm and started exploring the universe. I found this world with an unusual core. All I did was shine a light on the core and it exploded. What a stupid way to build a planet."

Satan turned the corners of his lips up.

"I'm impressed. You have the attitude to be an elite in my organization. How do you feel about joining me? I can offer you far more interesting experiences than sitting in the void for another ninety-nine years."

Evo hesitated. His offer tasted sour on the tongue. Her mistrust of men made her reticent to jump into a relationship with one, and this one was too smooth. The small, still voice in her head she usually ignored screamed at her it was a trap. Maybe this time she'd listen.

"Uh, no offense, but I barely know you. I think it would be better if we talked about you before I decided."

Satan maneuvered himself into a standing position and yawned.

"I have better things to do than sit here and explain myself to a human. I'll come buy in twenty years and see if you've changed your mind. If you even have a mind left. This place has the effect of making one quite insane, you know. Bye now."

"Wait!" Evo cried, but it was too late. Satan faded, and she was alone again in the absolute oily darkness of the Abyss.

He never returned. The liar. Sometimes Satan's minions came to her and pleaded for her to accept his offer. They presented her with stories of the ideal conditions within which she would work, her importance within the organization, and the rewards to follow her achievements. While she was grateful for the brief distraction of their company, she stubbornly refused their offers. Within eighty years, such visitations stopped. She spent the last twenty years exerting her will against the onset of insanity.

Forty-nine times throughout her sentence, the Archangel Michael came to her. He beseeched her to call out to God, beg for mercy, and plead for the shortening of her sentence. Michael promised her the Lord would forgive her and grant her parole, but she wouldn't give in.

Evo's thoughts during her sentence were of justification for her actions, not remorse for the devastation she caused.

She reasoned her lack of knowledge was God's fault, so He was to blame. God allowed her to wander the cosmos in spectral form; He should have told her what she could and couldn't do. Yes, it was His fault, yet He made her suffer. Why should she have to apologize for His mistakes and beg for His leniency? He should beg for her grace, not the other way around!

After one hundred years, she hated God with every molecule in her body. When the Archangel Michael came back after her sentence was up, she wept. He gently conveyed her to Everhome and placed her body on her luxurious bed. He watched over her the first night while she slept, but was gone when the birds awoke her the next morning. For the first day, all she did was sleep, eat, and enjoy the delights brought to her senses by light, tastes, touch, and sounds.

Evo's sentence was merciful, given the carnage her curiosity caused, but she didn't see it that way. She chaffed at the restriction placed on her ability to travel through space, and soon her home became as stifling a jail cell as the Abyss had been. When God removed the travel restriction, she immediately leaped into space and roved to a nearby nebula resplendent in the colors of the rainbow. The beauty of the gaseous apparition should have calmed her soul, but she barely saw it. Hatred and plans for revenge consumed her and denied her heart the soul-healing generated by beauty and peace.

Plans of revenge she would now put in place.

An internal lift carried her to the control center. She scanned the readouts on the holographic displays. Her ship purred like a kitten. Evo folded herself into the luxurious chair in front of a huge main screen.

"Status report."

The Artificial Intelligence answered in Evo's voice.

"The ship is running well and ready to lift, Creator."

Evo grunted.

"About time. Lift to fifty thousand feet."

The silver ship leaped into the air, propelled by anti-gravity engines, and darted to the altitude Evo directed. It hovered there as Evo scanned the displays.

"Engage the exo-atmospheric device."

This was the genius of her construction. The device created a stable wormhole the width of her ship between the inner and outer layers of ice. To an outside observer, she would appear to go through the layer, but her ship would never physically touch it. Evo held her breath. All the tests with drones had worked perfectly. They transited the ice layer without harm to the ice or the drones. This would be her first time going through, and it made her nervous. She was more cautious now and determined to not get on God's wrong side until she had the power to defeat Him.

It still hadn't occurred to her God knew her every thought and the desires of her heart.

"Transit the ice layer."

The ship complied without repeating the command. It rose until it came within a mile of the ice and projected the field, creating the wormhole. In an instant, the ship was through the ice and in space.

Evo realized she'd been holding her breath.

She exhaled it with a whoosh and looked at Everhome on the viewscreen.

It rotated beneath her, a soothing green world lying under its transparent dome of ice. Evo scowled. She would destroy this planet, too, if she could get away with it. A brief vision of Ado's descendants hurtling frozen into the vacuum after she blasted their precious sphere made her smile. It would be her first task after she killed God, a little payback for her humiliation. She was going to be a vengeful god. The thought of millions of innocents paying for her perceived past wrongs troubled her not at all.

Evo had the coordinates to Spes when she left the war-torn world, but those were as valueless as dust. Everything physical moved in space and time. She could calculate where the planet would be now, but if she was off by as little as seven decimal places, Evo would drive her ship into the ground. Besides, it was her first time traveling through space in this container. Short jumps were better.

The short jumps consumed eight ship days. After each jump, Evo had to take star sightings and calibrate the next jump. The more she traveled, the fewer jumps she would have to make. Traveling through Inter-Dimensional Space was timeless; one could go from one world to another at the speed of thought.

Evo caught her breath after the last jump. Her calculations had been precise; a little too precise. Spes rotated beneath her ship, its ice shield only ten miles away. Evo's heart hammered in her chest as she ran the calculations for the last jump through her board. They had been one-thousandth of a decimal place off. Such a slight mistake nearly killed her.

Spes, the world of Hope, in the Year of Our Peace 0001,
The 23rd day of the month of Darian
Mission Day 148

Gwynver'insa stared up at the evening sky and huddled in closer to her husband's side. They stood in front of a large stone circle the Empress created the day before. It was the only oddity in a vast forest encircling them.

"Will she come here?" she asked, enjoying the warmth and comfort of Johan's body.

Johan nodded somberly.

"I think so, my love. In the past number of weeks, you have restored plant and animal life to the entire globe. This is the only place observable from space looking like a landing pad. It would shock me if she chose somewhere else to land."

The Empress shuddered.

"Are you sure she will not crash through the ice and destroy Spes?"

Johan drew her in closer, his eyes shining with certainty.

"I heard your prophecy, dearest. The truth rang like the Crystalline Wall that a woman from the stars would visit us today in a large ship gliding through the ice layer surrounding our world like your blade cutting through a block of fine cheese. Yahweh has promised no disruption to Spes. Our task is to find out what she wants and then send her away. No small feat for two people armed with swords against a spaceship."

Gwynver'insa pulled away and grinned up at him.

"I have some surprises in store for our guest."

Johan grinned back at the diminutive woman who ruled their world.

"I am glad to hear of it, Your Imperial Majesty, for there descends the very ship on which we spoke."

The long silver craft glided noiselessly to the stone circle and landed without whipping up dust. It settled on three large fins attached to the base of the fuselage. They stood there for a long time until a gap appeared on the side of the ship and a gangway eased out to contact the ground.

A woman appeared in the gap and walked down the gangway towards them. She was tall and beautifully proportioned in her tight-fitting silver jumpsuit. Her hair was a metallic silver and long, cascading down her back freely. The Empress would have thought her the most beautiful woman she had ever seen, but for the harsh coldness in her silver eyes.

The woman stopped ten paces before them and looked at them with arrogance radiating from her like heat shimmering off a desert floor.

"I am Evo. I have come to rid this world of Tul'ran. Where is he?"

Gwynver'insa nodded at the woman perfunctorily.

"Greetings, Evo. I am Gwynver'insa, the Empress of the World, the First of my Line, Prophet of Yahweh." She gestured at Johan, standing stiffly beside her. "Behold my husband, Johan, the

Emperor Consort."

Evo flitted a glance at Johan, who jerked a brief nod at her.

"You greet me as equals. You should know you are not my equal. I have knowledge and the means to deliver great calamity to your world. I destroyed a planet once and I'm not opposed to destroying yours if I don't get what I want. Now, where's Tul'ran?"

Gwynver'insa stifled her rising irritation at the woman's brutish personality.

"I accept we are not equals, Evo. In answer to your question, I do not know the location of my brother, Tul'ran."

Evo glared at the small woman.

"I suggest you find him, and soon. My patience with you wears thin. Dreadful things will happen to you and this world when it runs out."

Johan gestured, drawing Evo's attention to himself.

"What my wife means, Evo, is that Tul'ran is no longer in this world. He left six days ago."

Evo snorted.

"By what means? I didn't see a ship capable of traversing space when I observed this world forty-five days ago. How could he have left this planet?"

Gwynver'insa smiled, but there was a bite in the cast of her lips.

"It does not incline us to disclose the method by which our brother left Spes."

Evo took a menacing step forward.

"I have the means of compelling your cooperation. Give me the answers I seek, or I will burn down the forest standing behind you."

"With what?" Gwynver'insa asked, primly.

Evo gestured behind her.

"With the weapons on my ship."

"What ship?"

Evo looked at Gwynver'insa, dumbfounded, and turned to look behind her. Her mouth gaped open. Her ship was gone. She whirled on Gwynver'insa and froze, as a long sword wavered inches from her neck.

"You have come to us, Evo, and uttered not one word of a kind greeting. You should have offered us gifts for our hospitality, and we would have offered you a gift of hospitality. Instead, you make demands and utter threats. If you watched our world forty-five days ago, then you know my brother is Tul'ran the Uncreator."

"Do you think he would not have imparted some of his knowledge to me, his beloved sister, for our protection? You do not see your ship because I have removed it from this world. Perhaps you should know one other title I have not yet disclosed. I am also She Who Creates From Nothing. Now hearken to my demands. I will return your ship to you, and you shall depart from this world never to come back. Fail to leave and I will remove you from all Creation."

The two women glared at each other.

"I find your story ludicrous. I can disprove it with one sentence. Ship, burn the trees to my right in a one-hundred-yard swath."

The three of them stood in silence while crickets chirped in the background.

"Ship! Execute my command!"

Gwynver'insa took a half step forward and looked up into the face of the taller woman, her sword remaining steady at the woman's throat. She sighed. It seemed everyone in the universe was taller than her.

"Bark your commands two hundred more times, if you wish, Evo. Your ship will not respond. It has been uncreated. Only I can recreate it for you. Succumb to my demand and I shall return it to you. Otherwise, we will make you our prisoner and take you before the Judgment Seat to have the People decide your fate."

It took several seconds, with rage contorting her features, before Evo finally nodded her concession.

"Fine. Give me back my ship exactly as it was and I'll leave."

"Causing no damage to this planet."

Evo ground her teeth together.

"Causing no damage to this planet."

"Do I have your word?"

"You don't need her word."

Startled, the three of them cast their eyes at the massive angel who stood to their right, sword drawn. His glow threatened to blind eyes used to the dim light flickering from the large green moon overhead. Gwynver'insa and Johan beamed, and Evo goggled at him.

"What's an angel doing in this world?"

E'thriel smiled at her consternation.

"Whatever the Father pleases, I'd imagine. You won't harm Spes, Evo, for I won't permit it. This planet is under God's protection. You know what my words mean, unless you've forgotten your vacation in the Abyss. I have left crumbs of truth in your computer by which you can find Tul'ran, but I warn you. Tul'ran and Erianne are fearsome individuals, and won't show you the patience and mercy of the Empress and her Consort. Go home, Evo. Or go to a world where you can build friendships and find peace. There's nothing for you at the end of your path of vengeance except an end to your existence."

Evo spit on the ground.

"Be warned yourself, angel. Someday, when I rule the heavens and the universe, you would be wise to be on my side. I won't forget this."

Evo turned on Gwynver'insa.

"I don't have what I came for, but have the means to find him. Once I do, I will end his life. Give me back my ship."

Gwynver'insa gestured and Evo whirled around to find her ship on the pad once more, looking undamaged.

"Go, Evo, with our peace."

Evo sneered at the tiny Empress.

"If I come back here, you'll know the full extent of my rage, not my peace. I'll be ready for you next time, Empress. In my ship are personal weapons and shields you couldn't comprehend. I underestimated you this time. It'll never happen again. You can be sure of that."

Evo swaggered to her craft and entered it without looking back. The gap in the ship's side closed. After a few minutes, it lunged into the inky night sky. Johan let out his breath. His eyes grew wide. He and his bride were alone.

"E'thriel's gone."

Gwyn nodded.

"I expect he followed Evo through our atmosphere to ensure no damage to our world."

Johan grabbed his Empress and hugged her.

"How in the world did you make her ship disappear? I didn't know Tul'ran taught you that, much less that it was teachable."

Gwynver'insa giggled into his shoulder.

"I didn't."

Johan stepped away and looked into the smaller woman's huge blue eyes.

"I'm confused. What do you mean you didn't?"

The Empress twirled in the grass three times, her long blond hair flying out behind her. Her naked feet barely touched the grass, and the shimmery gossamer of her dress made her look like she was flying. She stopped, out of breath, and giggled.

"I erected a privacy shield between us and her ship. When she looked back, Evo thought her ship to be gone, but it was not. She could not see it and assumed I spoke the truth. I made sure the privacy shield excluded communications on every spectrum. Her ship was there the whole time. She couldn't see it and it couldn't hear her."

Johan couldn't speak for several seconds.

"It was a bluff," he said, amazement shrouding each word.

Gwynver'insa laughed.

"I wish you could see your face, Emperor-Husband. Do I shock you with my deception?"

Johan took a deep breath.

"I shall never dice against you again, my love. I

wonder why E'thriel told Evo where to find Tul'ran."

Gwynver'insa stared thoughtfully up at the night sky, trying to find Evo's ship against the millions of stars.

"I don't know, Johan. We must trust Yahweh with this. Evo is a woman of great power. She can traverse space in her physical body, something none of us can do. I have no doubt she has weapons capable of levelling this world. Anger consumes her and makes her formidable. She is something our brother has never seen, and I fear his lack of knowledge places him at a deadly disadvantage."

Johan stepped up to his tiny bride, leaned down, and kissed her soundly on her lips.

"Like E'thriel said, our brother and sister are formidable. I'm sure they can take care of themselves."

Gwyn sheathed her sword and folded herself back into Johan's arms.

"I hope so, dearest husband. Before Erianne left, she sounded worried their next mission could lead to their deaths. I have faith Yahweh will fulfill His plans for their lives. I hope it does not mean Tul'ran will have to sacrifice his life as Darian did for him."

Johan squeezed her to him.

"We must not mourn them before their time, my love."

A tiny sob escaped from Gwynver'insa's throat as she pressed her face into his chest.

"I cannot suffer their deaths, Johan. The memory of Darian lying in Erianne's arms still haunts my dreams. She made me love her and then she died. I dread the thought of losing Tul'ran and Erianne."

A tear leaked out of Johan's eyes as the diminutive woman, one of the most powerful in the universe, sobbed in his arms.

"We have to have faith in Yahweh, Gwyn. He loves them more than we do. Dry your eyes, beloved. We have a delegation waiting for us to discuss the distribution of this year's harvest. We cannot go to them with eyes made red from weeping."

Gwynver'insa snuffled and nodded. She pulled away and slipped her hand into his.

"Just one more minute under this sky, and we will go to them."

They linked their fingers and gazed into the star-studded night sky, their thoughts far from the beauty of the nebulae peering at them, close enough to reach out and touch. Would God continue to protect their beloved friends?

Their biggest fear was they'd never know the answer to that question.

Fate knew.

Fate was no longer smiling.

CHAPTER THE SIXTH: "YEA, THOUGH I WALK THROUGH THE VALLEY..."

Mesopotamia, the eighth day of the fifth month, 2004 BC

It wraps like seaweed around your feet, sucking every step back into its covetous grasp. Each stride becomes an agony as exhausted muscles beg for relief. Cloying sand wrapped around ankles and teased a fall, while the dry desert air sucked moisture out of the mouth and lungs. The last Time Travel Team slogged through the dunes leading to the city of Suse, in Mesopotamia, while their large packs and uncomfortable period-specific clothes leeched energy from their bones and sapped the will to take another step from their tired minds.

The Mesopotamians didn't design their clothing for hiking. Davis, Sully, and Coventry wore chitons, which were one-piece short-sleeved shirts falling to mid-thigh. Under the chitons, they wore leather

120

pants, in the fighting style, ending in a soft leather shoe. Leather boots covered the shoes and lower leg to the knees, and leather thongs laced the boot from the front of the ankle to the knee.

The warriors wore wide leather belts, into which were thrust scabbards holding swords and knives. Leather vests covered their shoulders and torsos, leaving most of the arm free. They wore cloaks that were long and covered their bodies. Even in the cool night air, the period dress made them feel like someone wrapped them in thick woolen duvets. Sweat pooled on their bodies and scratched its way down chests and backs.

TTI outfitted Hart as a nobleman, given his age, with a short-sleeved knee-length tunic over which was draped a tasseled shawl held in position by a broad belt. They constructed the shawl of wool and colored it purple to suggest a royal lineage. Soft leather sandals barely covered his feet. The effect was hot, heavy, and uncomfortable.

TTI dressed Heather and Jeannie in bright blue ankle-length tunics with short sleeves and a round neckline, in the fashion of the rich women from Ur. They draped the tunics with wool shawls of differing proportions and sizes that were fringed and tasseled. They, too, wore soft leather sandals. The women wore a short skirt as underwear, while the men wore a loincloth. Everyone suffered the heat as badly as the other, for the clothing of the era disdained ventilation in favor of fashion.

The worst part was the wigs. Davis, Wu, and Quarterlaine didn't cut their hair when they returned from the past, so they didn't have to endure the long, carefully curled wigs worn by the Sullivans and Hart. All of them had perfumes, oils, and black dye in their hair to conform to local customs. A band of metal encircled their brows, except for Hart, who wore a felt cap shaped like a fez.

All wore jeweled ornamentation rich and of high quality. TTI fashionably dressed them for an evening out in fine carriages drawn by slaves, but there were no such conveyances in this desert. They walked and sweated and cursed their luck. To make the ordeal worse, their minds churned with a multitude of fears as each of them wrestled with the unknown horror of what they left behind.

Coventry had insisted a half dozen times that they stop to give her an opportunity to contact Atlantis, but each time the AI stubbornly repeated the same depressing message: Connection Failed.

Davis brought the group to a halt at the inception of a false dawn, and they sank gratefully to the sand. Each wrestled out of a pack, which seemed to gain weight as each hour trudged along. Davis gestured toward the west, while accepting a drink from Heather.

"Thanks, love. My throat feels like sandpaper. In an hour, we'll be near Suse. It should still be dark; the sun doesn't rise for another two hours. I'll buy some horses while the five of you wait outside the city. It'll raise too many questions if we all walk into the city on foot."

Heather sighed and rubbed her calves.

"I'd be happy to wait right here. What a hike! My legs haven't hurt this much since I used to run marathons."

Hart grunted and took a long pull from his water bag. He grimaced.

"This tastes like we filled it from a swamp. I'm with you, Heather. Any chance you could go ahead without us, Davis?"

Davis frowned and cast a sharp glance at the older man.

"It'd be best if we didn't split up for too long. Heather, Coventry, and I have been to this region before. The rest of you don't know the subtleties of the culture and certainly not the language. While the odds of someone stumbling upon us in the middle of the desert are slim, we can't take the chance. Sorry, Ras. We walk for another hour and then you get some rest. I can give you a ten-minute siesta, but that's all. We don't want to be in the desert when the sun rises. We'll readjust your packs and Sully, Coventry, and I will take some of your weight."

Silence fell on the group as they sipped water and stared into an unpolluted night sky.

"This is so surreal," Jeannie said after a few minutes. "I know we're thousands of years in the past, but time travel doesn't feel real. For this world, everything is still ahead. God will talk to Abraham and raise a people for Himself. Abraham's lineage will lead to the birth of the Son of David, the Savior of the world. People will still kill each other for power, money, and glory thousands of years after they crucify Jesus for our sins and the Father raises Him from the dead. The beautifully clean oceans in this era will get polluted and a lot of incredible sea life will die. This time has so much promise. I wish I could run around and tell everyone to stop chasing wealth and power and just join as one nation. We could prevent so much if we could just stop it now."

Hart spoke deferentially in the silence that followed her soliloquy.

"If it were only that simple, Jeannie. I don't know who writes the rules, but they've locked the timeline into an immutable strand. For us, what's happened in the past would stay the same no matter what we tried to do. History wouldn't even record our efforts. All we can do is complete our mission and get home."

"Let's get at it," Sully said, glancing up at the sky, lightening in the east.. "We're exposed out here and we have nothing for weapons other than our swords and Mick's dubious reputation. It's just another hour."

Sully twisted his body and pushed himself to his feet. He reached down and helped his wife to hers. They redistributed Jeannie, Heather, and Hart's packs to help them get through the last part of the long march.

The others grumbled and grudgingly fell in behind Davis as he turned his face to the west. None of them spoke for the last sixty minutes of their journey. It took all their energy just to put one foot in front of the other and tear the back foot out of the sand. At last, they could see a cluster of buildings rising from the shadows of pre-dawn and gratefully took refuge near a pile of rocks.

Davis took another lengthy pull of water. After a long sultry night, the water tasted like warm medicine; for a throat parched by the dry desert air, it was a welcome relief even if it didn't taste good.

He turned to TTI's last Programmer.

"How do I look, Heather? If I'm too beat up, no one will trade with me when the markets open."

Heather brushed her hands over the sleeves of his tunic and yanked at the leather armor covering his chest.

"You could use a shave, but a lot of warriors in this era need one. Don't get too close to anyone and you'll be fine."

Davis took an exaggerated sniff of his armpits.

"Best bargaining ploy ever; make them want to get away from your body odor as fast as they can."

He drew the laughter he was hoping for, though it was forced and laced with exhaustion. Davis nodded at them and faded into the dusky dawn. It took him almost forty minutes to find a corral with the horses they would need for the last two days of their journey. He slipped into the shadows of a nearby hut and waited for the sun to spill its smile on the marketplace. The day promised to be hot, which meant the Team would be scorched by the time he got back. He sighed. Couldn't be helped.

After twenty-seven minutes went by, Davis slid from his hiding place and approached an older man who walked to the corral and sat in front of it on his haunches.

"I give you a good greeting," Davis said in a cordial voice.

The man nodded, his eyes wary. The sun had barely split the sky, and it was unusual to conduct business so early in the day.

"I give you a good greeting, warrior," he said, a little stiffly. "What brings you to my corral so early in the day?"

Davis smiled ruefully.

"I am the owner of a fine horse, with a keen sense and a strong back. This morning he stumbled on a rock nestled in the sand and lamed. I was on my way to Suse to purchase horses for my son, who would pay part of his bride-price in stock. You seem to have six horses suiting my fancy and his bride's eyes. Will you trade with me?"

The man considered his story for a moment.

"Such hard luck ill-suits a warrior. Does your ill-luck, by chance, extend to the depths of your purse?"

Davis's lips twitched.

"My purse is healthy, having recently experienced enrichment by wealthy noblemen who desired what I teach."

The merchant looked interested for the first time.

"And what is it you teach, warrior, which would catch the ears of wealthy noblemen and encourage them to lighten their famously tight grips on their fat purses?"

Davis's smile spread wider.

"The fighting styles and martial techniques of Lam'ek az Peregos, son of Quil'ton az Peregos, Instructor to the Sword Himself. My father," he finished, delighting in the man's gaping expression, "taught me everything he knew. I now impart such wisdom to others with slow arms and fat purses."

The merchant swallowed hard, lunged to his feet, and bowed almost to his knees.

"Milord az Peregos, forgive me! My eyes are old and can barely see in the morning light, for otherwise I would have recognized you at once. How may I serve you, milord?"

Davis gestured at the six horses in the small enclosure behind the merchant.

"You can sell me your stock, blankets, and saddles if you have them. Name your price, merchant, and let us trade, for the sun grows warm, and I minded to be on my way."

There was very little haggling. Davis's reputation with a sword preceded him and warriors of Davis's caliber were not to be cheated. In short order, they settled on a fair price, which Davis paid in silver shekels, much to the merchant's delight. After accepting the cheerful man's blessing, Davis rode back out of Suse, with five sturdy mares in tow.

The desert heat was already brutal by the time he returned. His grateful teammates quickly loaded the horses and heaved themselves upon the mares' backs. Davis led them into Suse, avoiding the major thoroughfares. He pulled up in front of a row of simple homes and gestured Coventry forward.

"What do you think, Cov? The third one from the left appears big enough to accommodate all of us and has a simple pen at the back for our stock."

Quarterlaine nodded.

"I agree, Mick. On my last deployment here, I spent some time in Suse. Why don't I approach the owner and see what I can arrange?"

Davis nodded. For this deployment, the Marine dressed in the fighting leathers of a warrior. She wore two swords on her waist and had at least two knives at strategic points on her hips. Whether the city's inhabitants considered it appropriate for a woman to engage in warfare was moot. She looked dangerous and the people of the city were so familiar with the look of danger they wouldn't try her patience.

Quarterlaine dismounted and approached an overweight man sitting outside one unit.

"I give you a good greeting, friend."

The man looked the tall woman up and down, but only once, out of respect, and nodded. He glanced at her party, sitting stiffly on their horses several paces back, and ran his eyes over Davis and his weapons with care.

"I always accept good greetings and an offer of friendship from warriors. How may I serve you?"

Coventry smiled with her lips, not showing the brilliance of her teeth in her dark-skinned face.

"My party and I require accommodations. By your kindness, to whom may I speak to make such arrangements?"

The man pushed himself to his feet with a huff.

"I am honored to be the proprietor of these residences. Your companions seemed to be interested in the structure in the middle. A wise choice given the size of your party. How long do you wish to stay?"

Coventry sketched a half bow.

"Only the day, good sir. When we have enjoyed our evening meal, we shall move on."

The man frowned.

"There are six of you, with horses to put up, water, and feed. For thirty shekels, I would be pleased to give you the accommodations for the day."

Coventry's eyebrows quirked upward.

"Thirty shekels! Forgive me, good sir. I was not

aware we were lodging with the city's governors. Thirty shekels are the wages of two men in the field for a year! When last I was in Suse, two shekels would have purchased me accommodations suitable for the rank and status of my party. I would be pleased to pay you two shekels for the abode."

The man looked aghast.

"A mere two shekels! Why, it would cost me more for the feed for your horses than two shekels, much less granting you access to the accommodation. I offer my apology, but I could not see fit to accept less than twenty-five shekels for your stay."

Coventry frowned.

"Are the floors lined with thick rugs with a tight weave? Will slaves wash our feet and our clothes as master cooks prepare our meals? No? If you are to charge me the price of a palace, I would expect the services of one. No, good sir. I will raise my offer to four shekels, but even at that price, I shall expect a tidy home with clean furnishings."

The man stiffened perceptibly.

"I assure you, warrior, the abode is clean, as are the linens. I do not run a brothel here. You will find the accommodations suitable for your needs, never fear. Though I am insulted by your suggestions, I see your party is fair wilting under this day's sun. Out of mercy and kindness to them, I will reduce my fee to twenty shekels of silver."

Quarterlaine stood a little straighter and squared her shoulders.

"If I was to give you insult, proprietor, you would know it, for a blade in my hand would lend steel to my words. I raise my offer to five shekels of silver, not a sliver more, and you will be grateful for the day's profit."

The proprietor waved his hands at either side of his face.

"Forgive me, warrior, I do not cast aspersions. The price you offer may be fair in other parts of the city, but not in my district. With whom do you ride such that you expect lavish accommodations at a pauper's price?"

Coventry's face turned stony, the ice in her eyes matched by her tone.

"I ride with Lam'ek az Peregos, son of Quil'ton as Peregos, elder brother of Tul'ran az Nostrom, the Sword Himself, the Prince of Death, Master of Bloodwing the Blade, Sword of Judgment, Deliverer of Death."

The change in his demeanour was immediate. As each word rolled past Coventry's generous lips, the man standing in front of her turned another shade whiter under his dark tan. When she finished speaking, he swallowed rapidly several times.

"My apologies, milady, and I recant of any unintended insult my foolish tongue may have cast upon your ears. Take the abode, milady, with no charge and the blessings of my house!"

Quarterlaine's face softened.

"I have suffered no insult at your hands, good sir, nor is it necessary to make a gift of your accommodations. Perhaps we can agree five shekels of silver will be sufficient for the use of your abode for the day, and the quartering of our horses?"

The man nodded vigorously.

"For five shekels of silver, I will feed them barley

and hay, and treat them as if they were my children. Better, even."

Coventry counted out five shekels of silver and laid them in their host's trembling hands, before turning back to her group.

Davis raised his eyebrows at her.

"You look pleased with yourself."

She grinned as she took her horse's reins from his hand.

"We have the big abode in the middle, with the corral, and he'll feed and water our horses. He'll even give them barley!"

Davis acknowledged her statement with a twinkle in his eyes.

"How much did you pay him?"

"Five shekels," she said with a smug grin.

Davis shook his head.

"Nice. It's a fair price. Well done!" He turned to the others behind him. "We can dismount. Our host will provide us with meals and lodging for the day. He'll take care of our horses. It's important to get as much sleep as we can. We ride through the night."

'We ride through the night.'

Language can be delightfully misleading. Riding suggests a state of comfort, a gentle conveyance while enjoying the work of an equine bred and disposed to traversing the desert. Perhaps, to some extent, such a suggestion was true, for it was better than walking. For bottoms and groin muscles not accustomed to straddling a horse, however, nine hours in the saddle became an agony of its own.

At the beginning of the night, all six were in a

good frame of mind. Their enemies were behind them, and none of them dwelt on what they left behind in the future. There was no urgency to their mission, so the stress levels were low.

An hour into their ride, Heather turned in her saddle to talk to Coventry.

"I've heard people share stories to while away the hours riding through the desert. I know all our stories well, except for you and Ras. How do you feel about entertaining us, Major?"

Quarterlaine smiled, her teeth glowing under a bright full moon.

"We may be here for a long time, Heather. Call me Coventry or Cov, okay? How deep do you want me to go back?"

"Just the main bullet points will do for now. Afterwards, we may have questions."

The group chuckled as Quarterlaine moistened her throat with a swallow of water.

"I grew up on a farm in Tennessee. We didn't have much money, but I was a lot luckier than many kids my age. I had a Dad and a Mom who were hard-working Christian people. They both disappeared in the Second Cataclysm, but that was long after I left home."

She shifted in her saddle and the old leather creaked beneath her hips.

"I studied hard when I was a kid, but the farm could barely support my parents and my five siblings. There was no money for College, and I didn't even bring it up. The only genuine option for me was the military, so I joined the Marines out of High School. I worked my way up to Gunnery Sergeant. The

Marines saw something in me, I guess, because they sponsored me for Officer Candidate School. After they commissioned me, I saw some action—don't bother asking, it's all classified—and the Marines eventually promoted me to Major."

Coventry took another long pull of water from the soft pouch.

"Then Eduardo Jimenez gutted democracy in America and declared himself Supreme President for Life. He tasked me to TTI after I became too vocal in exercising my right to free speech by denouncing his dictatorship. I became a troubleshooter for Korhonen, which is how I came to find you two," she gestured at Davis and Wu, "and you know the rest."

Davis snorted.

"Wow, that's a pretty short story for an entire life."

Quarterlaine sighed and shrugged her shoulders.

"That's pretty much it. I'm a specialist in survival and CQB, which means 'close-quarter battle' to you civilians. I'm an expert with small arms, light automatics, explosives, hand-to-hand combat, swords, and tracking. At OCS, they told me I scored high in deductive reasoning and creativity, which was how I stayed under the radar when I tracked Davis and Wu for eight months. At least until I ran out of food and money."

"What about family?" Heather asked. "Spouse, kids?"

Coventry shook her head.

"I was married, but my husband became tired of my constant deployments. Add to that, I couldn't talk about my missions, and it created a lot of stress in our marriage. Sully and Mick know what I'm talking about. After five years, we divorced. It was amicable. I never wanted kids. Someone has always messed the world up, and even though I had a good childhood, I couldn't bring children into a place that had a hopeless future."

"Any regrets?" Hart asked.

She grimaced.

"Every day, but none I care to talk about. Don't mean to change the subject, but what the heck is that?"

The other five looked up toward Coventry's elevated hand. A shimmering veil hung ahead of them, extending from the desert floor to the top of the night sky. They reined their horses to a halt.

"It's not an aurora borealis," Sully said. "It's not lit up like one, anyway. What do you think, Mick?"

"I don't know, but we need to get down. Whatever it is, it's coming at us fast and I don't want to be on horses if they spook."

Heather jumped off her mare and took a firm grip on her reins, and the others quickly joined her on the sand. They huddled in a small cluster and turned to face the oncoming curtain.

"Is it a sandstorm?"

"Nope," Sully said. "I've been in plenty of sandstorms and this is not one of them. Plus, there's no wind."

They stood, waiting tensely, soothing their nervous mounts, and trying to control the jitters that danced within their stomachs. The veil rushed past them at an astonishing speed and left their clothes and skin dampened by the cool mist.

"Well," Hart said, as they watched the veil recede behind them, "that was a lot of nothing."

"Beg to differ," Coventry said, scanning the desert ahead of them and the sky above. "We aren't in Kansas anymore, if you'll allow me to resort to ancient colloquialism."

"What do you mean?" Jeannie asked, craning her neck to see what had upset Quarterlaine.

"She means," Davis said, "those buildings ahead of us are not the city of Ur, where we should be. That's Gilgesh. We advanced a day on our travel."

"How's that possible?" Hart protested. "No, no, that's impossible. Are you telling us the mist, or whatever it was, propelled us a day forward in time?"

Heather's eyes were wide as she stared at the outlines of the village in the pre-dawn sky.

"No, not a day forward in time. A day forward in space. That's Gilgesh, no doubt about it. Whatever the mist was, it moved us from one point in space, the desert between Ur and Suse, into another point in space."

"That's not possible," Hart said again, a tinge of hysteria in his voice.

Davis took a deep breath.

"Nothing's impossible with God, Ras. I told you if you came with us, your brain was going to get stretched. Case-in-point number one lies just ahead of us. Mount up, people. It looks like we're arriving a day earlier than we expected."

The six of them struggled into their crude saddles, stomachs clenched, before riding into the unknown.

Mesopotamia, the ninth day of the fifth month, 2004 BC

The village was in an uproar. They rode the entire length of the village without being noticed in the pandemonium. People were running back and forth yelling and issuing orders; men and women alike shared the agitation. As they drew closer to the hutch, owned by Davis and shared by his adopted family, they saw a large group of people around the front. Some were crying and screaming, and all focused their attention on a portion of the ground in front of the small residence.

Davis brought his group to a halt and waited for someone to notice their presence. When no one did, he put his fingers to his lips and blew a piercing whistle into the din. Startled, the people whirled around and stared at him in shocked silence.

"What transpires at my doorstep, leaving me bereft of the joy of my returning?" he said, raising his voice so all could hear above the uproar in the village.

The group parted hastily, and Davis stared down at Omarosa, kneeling on the ground with Ro'gun's head on her lap. Pain masked the young man's face and turned it white as he grasped his sword arm with his left hand. Davis leaped from his saddle, closely followed by Wu, and he jumped to the lad's side.

"Ro'gun! What has befallen you?"

The young warrior reached up with his left hand and grabbed the edges of Davis's leather vest.

"They have her!" he gasped. "I tried to stop them, but they were too powerful. They... they took her. Save her!"

"Who?" Davis asked, the question framed by the intensity of demand.

The pain in Ro'gun's face intensified.

"Anatu. They came in the middle of the night. A rabble of flesh merchants led by a monster of a man almost two cubits tall. They demanded I tell them the location of Lord Tul'ran. When I told them I did not know, the giant said they would take my family until I released the information to them. I defied them and fought them as best I could, but they prevailed and took Anatu with them. You must save her, milord. She is just a child!"

Sully appeared at Ro'gun's right side and gently probed the young warrior's right arm, causing the young man to stiffen and bite back a scream. Sully looked up at Davis.

"He has a displaced fracture of his humerus. I can't tell if the fracture has compromised the artery, but his right hand is pale and cold. I have to reduce the fracture, Mick. Right now."

Davis's lips drew into a straight line, and he looked down at Ro'gun's strained face.

"Ro'gun, I hear you. You will tell me all. First, my friend must twist the bone of your arm back into its place or you may lose your arm. This will cause you great pain. Do you understand?"

Ro'gun grimaced and nodded his head.

"Do as you must. I deserve no less, for I have failed you, milord, and I have failed my family."

Sully grasped the upper edge of Ro'gun's right arm in his left hand and the lad's lower form with his right. He nodded at Davis. Davis removed a sheathed knife from his belt, withdrew the knife, and placed the sheath in Ro'gun's mouth so the kid wouldn't bite his tongue in two.

"Go."

Sully pulled and twisted Ro'gun's arm, snapping the bone back into place. Ro'gun's jaws spasmed, driving his teeth into the leather of the sheath. He screamed and then fainted from the pain.

Jeannie came into Davis's sight from above Ro'gun's head. She had found two strips of wood and had torn a piece of cloth into thin strips. Sully nodded at her in approval and the two of them quickly splinted Ro'gun's arm above and below the fracture site. Sully checked the pulse in Ro'gun's right wrist and then pressed down on the young warrior's thumbnail. He nodded, satisfied.

"Good job, Jeannie. Mick, he has a radial pulse and a good capillary refill. Let's get him inside. He has some nasty cuts in his leathers; I want to do a primary and secondary assessment to make sure the kid isn't bleeding out somewhere."

Together, Sully and Davis lifted Ro'gun off the ground as Ro'gun's wife, Innanu, held open the door. Heather had her arm around Omarosa and led her into the house. Quarterlaine stopped Hart before he could follow the group into the house.

"Not so fast, Ras. We need to take the tack off these horses, feed, and water them before we go in. Let them deal with whatever the heck is going on here, and we'll join them shortly."

Hart nodded and helped Quarterlaine gather up the horses to take them to the back of the hutch, where Davis had built a corral and paddock. Together, they stripped the tack off the horses, brushed sweat from their hides, and checked their feet. They led the horses to a stack of hay and fetched two large buckets of water from the nearby well. Satisfied they had met their horses' needs, they returned to the hutch.

Inside the hutch, Sully and Jeannie rapidly stripped Ro'gun of his armor and clothing. They took turns conducting a quick primary assessment, as Ro'gun gained consciousness with a muddled stare. He looked around him, bewildered by the strangers attending to him and befuddled by the pain.

Omarosa stood off to one side, looking frightened and confused.

"Who are these people, milady He'thur? What are they doing to the husband of my daughter?"

Wu smiled at the older woman.

"Be at peace, Lady Omarosa. These are close friends of ours. Michael is a physician of some renown and his wife Jeannie is a professional who assists physicians. Where I am from, we call her a *trauma nurse*. They will help Ro'gun recover from his wounds."

Omarosa looked flustered for a moment and then gave Heather a crisp nod.

"Forgive me, milady. The circumstances, well, the circumstances have left me shaken. We have guests at the house. I will arrange food and beverages. Innanu, stop hovering around your husband. Two physicians assist him, both of whom Lady He'thur highly regards. Help me gather food and beverages to show our guests the quality of hospitality afforded by the House az Peregos."

Heather smiled as Omarosa and Innanu began bustling around the hutch. Nothing like having a purpose to distract a person from the horrors of an unpleasant situation. Speaking of which.

Heather turned to the group working on Ro'gun. "How is he?"

"He's coming to," Jeannie said. "It looks like his biggest hurt is the fracture in his right arm. It'll take the bone a while to heal, but he'll keep his arm. Minor cuts and a lot of bruises cover the rest of his body, but we can deal with that, no problem."

"What does she say?" Ro'gun demanded, still altered by pain and lost consciousness.

"Your sword arm is broken," Davis said, "but you will live and you will fight again. Do you know where they have taken Anatu? Did they say?"

Ro'gun pressed his head back onto the floor of the hutch and nodded.

"They have taken her to the back of the ridge that runs along the south side of the village. The giant said to come this night with information where he can find Lord Tul'ran and he will return Anatu to us unharmed. He said Lord Tul'ran would know where to find him. Do you know of what he speaks, Lord Lam'ek?"

Davis nodded.

"Only too well. I... I mean, my father, once sent Tul'ran there on a quest to find Bloodwing the Blade."

"Tul'ran!" Ro'gun uttered his name, almost as a curse, and closed his eyes. When they opened again, panic filled them.

"If Lord Tul'ran comes back, milord, he is going to kill me!"

Davis looked at him, eyes wide.

"Why ever for? My brother does not kill innocents, Ro'gun."

"Innocents." The word came out of Ro'gun's lips like a sneer. "Hearken to the words of Lord Tul'ran when he gave me charge of Omarosa and her daughters. 'Should you fail, Ro'gun of the Amorain, and should these women come to harm at your hands or by your neglect, then you shall not benefit from my mercy. You will die over days, in pain only conceivable by demons in Hell. Take this task at your peril, young warrior.' I have failed Anatu and Lord Tul'ran," he finished, miserably.

Davis reached down and took Ro'gun's jaw in his right hand.

"Hear me, Ro'gun of the Amorain, Bondsman az Nostrom, liegeman of the House az Peregos. You are kin to me and Tul'ran, both. We do not kill kin. Tell me, Ro'gun, how many men did you face before they seized Anatu?"

Ro'gun licked his dry lips.

"There were seventeen, milord. I killed four of them and held off the rest before the giant stepped in, disarmed me, and broke my arm. He held me to the ground with one of his enormous legs, while the others rushed into my house and took Anatu."

Davis felt his eyebrows climb.

"Four! Faced with overwhelming odds, you stood your ground, mortally wounded four armed men, and then succumbed to injury. This is hardly failure or neglect, Ro'gun. You acquitted yourself well and I know my brother Tul'ran will see it. Be at peace. These two who attend you are as close to me as kin. Lady He'thur will translate your words into their language. Subject yourself to their care and abide by their instructions. I will ride out and take back what they took from you."

A panicked look once more lunged into Ro'gun's eyes, and he grabbed Davis with his good hand.

"Surely not alone, milord! You cannot face the giant alone. I must go with you!"

Davis removed the young man's hand with a gentle smile.

"Do I strike you as a fool? I will not be alone. Even now, Tul'ran rides to my side. And as far as the giant goes, have you not heard this stanza from the Ballad of Tul'ran the Sword?

> *Into the village of Kaska, he rode*
> *Against the Nephilim named Gar*
> *Long had the people searched for a hero,*
> *Sending their pleas out afar,*
> *In less than the time for an eagle to scream,*
> *The giant lay severed and gored,*
> *Cut down in contempt by a casual stroke*
> *Of the arm of Tul'ran the Sword!*

This giant has more to fear this day than me, I assure you."

Ro'gun laughed, which choked off as the movement of his rib cage flared pain into his arm. He leaned back and grinned, relief lit in his eyes.

"Pity the fool, then, who trespasses on ground protected by the Prince of Death."

Davis chuckled and stood up.

"Pity the fool, indeed."

Davis went to a far corner of the hutch where a cloth covered a long wooden box. He'd made the box, which housed his best weapons. He carefully folded the maroon cloth and set it aside. From the box, he took out his finest two swords. They fit on his back in a sheath that crossed his shoulders in an 'x' shape. In the twenty years he spent in Mesopotamia developing a plan to save his wife from her death, he'd taught himself to fight with both hands. He became so deft; he could fight against two opponents. Davis hefted the swords and tested their edges. Sharp as always. Sharp was good. He would need sharp.

Heather sidled up behind him and put her arms around his waist, laying her head on his back between his shoulders.

"Tul'ran's not coming, is he, my love?" she asked in a whisper, so the other occupants could not hear.

Davis turned around sharply, with the look of the wolf in his eyes.

"We don't know that, do we? I desperately need my son, Heather. I've sent a prayer up to Heaven asking for him to come to my aid. If ever the Prince of Death and his warrior bride were more needed, I don't know of such a time. He'll be there."

Heather stepped forward and buried her head in his chest.

"And if he's not?" she asked, still whispering.

Davis nuzzled her away.

"He'll be there. My life depends on it."

Tears formed in the corner of Heather's eyes.

"That's what I'm afraid of." She choked off the last whisper with a stifled sob.

Davis hugged her tightly and let her go.

"I won't abandon Anatu to those animals, Heather. No woman deserves that, and she is of this

House. You know where I stand with Jesus. If worse comes to worse, you'll see me again. I know it's no comfort, but the only thing we can truly live for is eternity."

Davis led her to the front of the hutch, and everyone turned their attention to him.

"Sully, you and Jeannie stay here. We'll need you to attend to the wounded. Coventry, as much as I would like you at my back, I need you to stay behind and protect my family. Sully may not be a swordsman, but he's a skilled fighter. I'm sure you can use him if you're attacked when I'm gone."

Hart stepped forward from a corner of the room.

"I'm going with you, Davis."

The Instructor to the Sword Himself shook his head.

"You're not trained in the weapons of the age, Ras. You'd be sword meat out there. I won't have your death on my hands."

"You're right," Hart countered. "I'm not trained in swordsmanship. But I have two good eyes and I know how to watch your six. You won't have to fight with eyes at the back of your head, even if I'm hiding in your shadow."

"It has merit," Sully said when Davis hesitated. "You'll have to be careful to not trip on him, but he can call out someone sneaking up on you. Take him."

Davis passed a glance over Hart.

"You'd better change out of your merchant garb, then. We can find something to fit you. I don't like this, Hart. You're setting yourself up to get killed."

Hart looked into Davis's eyes and held his gaze,

unwavering.

"My call."

Davis nodded.

"Your call. Gear up. We're out in thirty mikes."

It took longer than thirty minutes, or, as the military called it, thirty mikes. They had to pack food and water in case their search took longer than they expected. Hart had to be outfitted with fighting leathers, and he had too much of a paunch to fit in their armor. They canvassed the village and bought leathers from a local which at least didn't make the retired police officer look like a sausage stuffed into a deflated football.

The sun was low in the afternoon sky when they set out, traveling south and east. By the time the sun dipped down under the horizon, they arrived at the place where Tul'ran found his sword. Davis had approached the location from the top of the ravine, instead of following the road into it. He'd brought with him a tiny pair of field glasses, easily concealable in his leather vest, and it could see on any spectrum.

He swept the glasses over every surface the eye could see, using the night vision properties of the lenses. All he picked up was the figure of a massive man standing near the wall of the rock outcrop that ran along the east edge of the gulch. Davis handed the glasses to Hart.

"They weren't kidding when they said this guy is huge," he said, whispering into Hart's ear in a voice so low Hart barely heard it. Hart put the glasses on the figure standing in the ravine, alone, and swallowed hard. He nodded, not trusting himself to speak. Sound carried at night.

"I can't see anyone else," Davis continued. "Do you?"

Hart shook his head, sweeping the glasses again along the ridge and down into the valley.

"Okay," Davis finished. "We go straight in. This guy's clearly expecting us, so stealth is a waste of time and energy. Stay at my back and call out if anyone crawls out of the ground."

Hart nodded again. His heart was hammering in his chest, and a sheen of sweat popped up on his forehead and upper lip.

Davis slipped off the top of the ridge and made his way down into the gulch, Hart tight on his heels. They walked forward, trying to be as quiet as possible, as they swept their eyes from side to side in the growing darkness and straining their ears to pick up the slightest sound.

Ten yards from the giant, Davis drew both swords from their sheaths. The giant had lit a torch and set it far enough behind him to not affect his night vision forward. Davis walked boldly into the dim glow around the massive man's feet, with Hart walking crouched behind his back.

The giant looked at him with amusement.

"Ah, the rescuers. How good of you to come! I see a warrior and an old man skulking in the warrior's shadows. What is he, your slave? Does he wash your feet when they grow fatigued from flouncing through the sand?"

Davis ignored the giant's gibes, assessing the cut of the man's massive muscles. He was about ten feet tall and his body suggested overuse of illegal steroids, if such a thing was possible in this era. He had a face with harsh lines, eyes as black as the darkness of the night, and equally black hair that fell almost to his waist. A sinister aura cloaked his body and warned of mayhem and death. This was an Old Testament Goliath, no mistake.

"So this is the giant who takes his pleasure scaring young maidens and taking them from their home? I expected to come here to confront a man, not an oversized pig. Why not give me the girl and go somewhere else to intimidate young boys and take their baby sisters?"

The giant tossed back his head and roared with laughter.

"You amuse me. I should kill you slowly, over days. Your screams would lull me to sleep at night. Where is Tul'ran the Sword?"

Davis twisted the blades in his hands and the light glinted off their wickedly sharp edges.

"I did not come here to impart information, you giant moron. I came here to kill you. Can you not read the signs?"

The giant scowled.

"The only sign they will read here will be the one posted over your grave, puny human. You have come to fight. Fine. Let us wage war."

The giant lunged forward, drawing a huge, slender blade from his waist and sending a flurry of blows at Davis's head and body. Davis knew immediately he was at a disadvantage. He hadn't practiced with swords since returning to the future, and the rust showed. It took all the skill he had to parry the blows with his two swords and stand his ground. After what seemed like an hour, but was closer to a minute, the giant stepped back, eyebrows raised.

"Impressive. You have some skills, warrior. They won't be enough, of course. I trained with sword and spear for more years than you could ever imagine. You are no match for me, little man. Give me Tul'ran's location. If you do, I will let you take the girl and walk away. As a sign of respect," he finished, ironically saluting Davis with his blade.

Davis was struggling to catch his breath and trying to not show it. The sixty-second flurry of steel coming at his face winded him much more than he expected. He licked his lips, rewinding the brief fight in his mind's eye. Davis could find no flaw in the man's technique. He'd presented no openings for a counterthrust and Davis wasn't sure he was fast enough to take advantage of one.

He took a couple of steps to his left and the giant countered with two to his left, smoothly and instinctively.

Davis lunged forward on the attack; both hands acting as independently as if two men wielded them, not one. He split his concentration, rapidly advancing attacks with his left hand, while the right probed for an opening.

None came. The two men fought, their weapons a blur, with Davis attacking and the giant countering with a contemptuous smile on his lips. As luck would have it, Davis's right foot slipped on a lunge, throwing him off balance.

The giant parried the thrust and smashed the back of his hand against Davis's chest, flinging him into the air. Davis crashed against a rock six feet away and pain stabbed through his body as the air rushed out of his lungs.

Davis lay there, helpless. The blow to his chest fractured some ribs, he was sure of it and the rock had broken his arm. His head had smacked against the rock, and the world swam in his vision. The giant walked up and put the tip of his sword to Davis's neck.

"You did well, warrior. Your swords almost got through my guard a few times. You are worthy of your calling. This is your last chance. Tell me where I can find Tul'ran the Sword and I will let you live, though you may not survive your injuries, if the truth be told. At least you could kiss your woman one last time before you enter the realm of Death. What will it be?"

Davis dragged air through his clenched teeth, fighting off the stars in his eyes that promised unconsciousness.

"Go to Hell," he said through gritted teeth.

The giant nodded.

"Suit yourself."

The giant raised the sword high, and time slowed down for Davis. The sword was long and slender. Runes covered the length of the shaft and the light of the torch reflected demonically from its surface. He watched, fascinated, as the blade descended toward his head.

The fight had happened so fast, and ended so quickly, he was having trouble acknowledging to himself his death was finally upon him.

His last thought was a sharp pain of regret that he

hadn't kissed Heather before he said goodbye. He thought he could defeat anything standing in his path. His arrogance was going to cost him his life.

His mind filled with pain and regret, Mick Davis fainted.

CHAPTER THE SEVENTH: "...OF THE SHADOW OF DEATH."

Time.

We think we have so much of it.

We let the minutes and hours go by, heedless of how quickly each precious second runs off our life clock. How often do we lament about how slowly time passes when we're bored? How often do we undertake foolish, time wasting, mindless activities to amuse our minds, when each minute on those activities cut at the core of what we're allocated from the moment our hearts beat within our mother's womb?

We only value time, it seems, when we're on the verge of losing it.

Marjatta Korhonen sat at the base of a tree, which had endured the devastation surrounding her. Her head was pounding, and her ankle pulsed as blood gushed through the swollen flesh.

The medic shone a light into Marjatta's eyes, and she jerked her head away.

"What the heck, Payton?!"

The brown-haired woman crouching in front of her put the light away and put a stethoscope to Marjatta's chest.

"I'm sorry, Administrator, but all our med tech is gone. I'm resorting to ancient techniques to assess you. This stethoscope was a gift from my father when I graduated from Harvard Medical School. It's practically a museum piece, but it works. Your ribs aren't broken. That's good news. Where are we, Administrator?"

Marjatta shook her head and instantly regretted it.

"Atlantis. We're on Atlantis. What happened, Payton?"

The medic pressed against Marjatta's cheek bones and began a primary survey for bleeding.

"Earthquake. A big one. Probably the biggest the world has ever seen. What's the date?"

"May 30, 2099 AD," Marjatta said, allowing her irritation to rise to the surface. "Look, I'm fine, okay? I banged my head and twisted up my ankle, but I'm fine. I know who I am, where I am, the date, and what my body feels like. Just patch me up and let me get going. I need to see how badly we got messed up."

"Okay, Administrator. Rest your back against that tree. I'll tape up your ankle and we'll go help other survivors."

Survivors. The word shocked her like a glass of ice water to the face. She pulled her gaze from the rubble all around her and watched Dr. Payton

Dumont tape up her ankle. She remembered
Payton's file; it was so impressive. The tall, brown-
haired, blue-eyed woman graduated from Harvard
Medical School and did her residency at John
Hopkins in trauma surgery. Her grades were
astonishing and very much showed a curious,
intelligent mind behind her pretty face. She had a
soft voice and brilliant white teeth that flashed often
because she could smile even in the face of the
toughest of circumstances.

She wasn't smiling now, though. Payton had a cut
above her right eye, on which she had haphazardly
slapped a bandage. Concrete dust and small chunks
of debris encrusted her hair, normally brushed to its
full, long length. She looked tired, but her hands
moved efficiently and didn't shake as they taped her
ankle. A consummate professional. Marjatta smiled.

That's why she hired Payton right out of John
Hopkins. It had surprised her the young woman
would choose a lifetime of isolation on Atlantis, but
she learned the young physician had a burning desire
to learn and spent hours researching cures for
obscure medical conditions when she wasn't treating
patients.

Marjatta knew time travel was dangerous and
fended off criticism for hiring a talented trauma
surgeon by pointing out the savageries of the various
cultures they would study in Antiquity. Her instincts
paid off. Payton had saved three lives in her brief
history with TTI; people who would have died but
for her surgical skills. The cost of hiring her had paid
off three times over. She was a heck of an asset.

"Done," Payton announced calmly, and stood up.

She held out her hand and helped Marjatta to her feet. Korhonen tottered for a moment and Payton grabbed her around the waist.

"Easy, Administrator. You took a nasty blow to your head, and I'd love to scan it, but those facilities don't exist here anymore. I'd tell you to rest, but I don't think you'll follow my advice. Will you at least allow me to be your crutch while we tour the island?"

Marjatta's first instinct was to refuse and push the young woman away from her, but her head sloshed like water in a dishwasher. She nodded grudgingly and then wished she hadn't. Concussion for sure, if not a moderate closed head injury. She grimaced. Her mother always accused her of having brain damage as a teenager; maybe it was a prophecy.

After Marjatta regained her equilibrium, she and Payton picked their way across the rubble that was Atlantis. In the distance, she could hear shouting and screaming as the survivors of the earthquake searched for casualties. They dragged each other to the edge of the rubble, which was once the TTI Main Building, and Marjatta drew a sharp breath. Some of the steel framework still stood, but wreckage hung from it around a great gaping hole in the center of the building.

"Are you okay, Administrator?" Payton asked.

Marjatta shook her head.

"No," she whispered. "I'm not. I don't think I ever will be again. We're out of the time travel business, Dr. Dumont, and the team we just sent into Antiquity died thousands of years ago. I just hope it was from natural causes."

Mesopotamia, the ninth day of the fifth month, 2004 BC

Erasmus Hart watched in horror as the blade of the giant's sword fell towards Davis's head. Time seemed to slow for him as well. The giant had slammed Davis into a rock beyond the perimeter of the torch behind the giant. The dim torchlight lit the area well enough to see Davis was badly hurt. He was lying on his back against a rock, clutching his arm, and struggling to breathe. The giant was wasting no time to finish Davis, lifting his enormous sword and swinging it down to cut at Davis's head. He watched as Davis's eyes rolled back and he fainted.

The blade fell in slow motion as Hart felt his heartbeat in his ears, a subdued and much slower 'lub-lub', seeming to take minutes instead of seconds to reach the next beat. Then another object caught his eye. It came from Davis's right, a bright blue marble bobbing in the air as if it were a solid soap bubble. At the last moment, when the sword was only a foot from Davis's face, the blue marble connected with the sword.

Hart expected the ball to pop like a paintball, but it flared as it silently exploded up and down the length of the enormous blade. The blade flashed into incredible brightness and when the light faded; the sword was gone. Hart stared, astonished, as did the giant.

Another man faded into view from the edge of the black rock face. He was around six feet tall and was the most muscled man Hart had ever seen. His shoulders were broad, as was his chest. Muscles rippled and corded down his arms, which were massive. His biceps and lower arms were the only flesh exposed. Black leather armor covered the rest of his frame, from his vest down to his boots.

The man's face was rugged and framed with thick, long brilliantly white hair. A black ring surrounded his head at the top of the forehead, making it look like he had a black halo. His face was stiff, and he pulled his lips back in a vicious snarl.

His most striking feature was his eyes, which were glowing an ominous, unearthly blue. Hart swallowed. Whatever this man was, he wasn't human.

The man whipped up a long black sword, which had glowing edges matching the color of his eyes, and thrust it at the giant, stopping just before contact with the giant's chest. His voice, when he spoke, was so cold Hart could feel it chill the air as it came out of his mouth.

"We meet again, G'shnet'el."

The giant stood as still as the stone surrounding them, his eyes wide.

"Tul'ran az Nostrom, may your name be accursed for eternity!"

Hart stared at the silver-haired man. He didn't understand a word the giant said, but he heard that name before.

"You're Tul'ran az Nostrom?"

The warrior seemed mystified by the question, and that Hart spoke it in English.

"I am he."

Hart reached in behind his back, under his cloak, and grabbed the handle of the gun concealed in his waistband. Korhonen told him, when she gave him the gun, the Lens AI would permit its passage into

Antiquity with Hart. He had doubted it was true, but he found the gun safely hidden when he arrived at the Mesopotamian IP.

Hart pulled out the gun, arming it as he did so, and raised it towards Tul'ran's head. He screamed when a burning pain arced through his body as a silver sword, with a solid stream of gold snaking up its middle, rammed through his back and out of his chest. Blood from his body slimed its edges and made his muscles spasm.

As his hands clenched involuntarily, Hart fired two shots right into Tul'ran's face.

Atlantis, May 30, 2099 AD

Korhonen sank to the ground in front of the TTI Building, her head swimming.

"Gone," she mumbled, "it's all gone."

Payton snapped her fingers in front of Marjatta's face.

"Hey, Administrator, don't fade on me now. Before I looked for you, I had two of my med techs set up a tent just down the way from Restaurant Row. I need to take you there."

"Survivors," Marjatta mumbled.

Payton pulled Marjatta to her feet. She was strong, Marjatta thought, surprised. It must have been from all the cheerleading she did in school.

"You bet, Administrator. We're looking for them now. You can help by greeting them as they arrive at the med tent. It will boost their morale to see their glorious leader waiting for them."

Marjatta glanced at Payton sharply.

"Sarcasm? Really?"

Payton grimaced.

"Sorry, ma'am. Didn't mean it. I'm a little stressed, is all."

Marjatta snorted, then winced as the snort sent a spasm of pain through her head.

"I wonder why. You need to call me Marjatta, Payton. I'm not the Administrator of anything anymore."

Payton pulled Marjatta's weight to her side and led her down to the med tent.

"With all due respect, ma'am, these people are going to need a leader more than ever right now. We've lost a ton of people and they need something to do to take their mind off it. They'll need orders, Administrator, and only you can give them some measure of stability and hope."

Marjatta looked around her as the two of them stumbled over rubble to the med tent down what used to be the main road.

Hope.

Where does one find hope when the end of the world has arrived?

Mesopotamia, the ninth day of the fifth month, 2004 BC

Time froze.

For Davis and Hart, that is. G'shnet'el, Tul'ran and Erianne still experienced the flow of time, even though everything else in the gorge went still. Erianne rushed around Hart to stare at the two bullets inches from Tul'ran's face. When the shock left Tul'ran's face, he turned his glare on the fallen angel, who shrunk under the gaze.

"What have you done, evil one? Have you lost such courage you have pawns attempt to assassinate me when I turn my back, rather than face me yourself?"

"This wasn't my doing," G'shnet'el squealed. "I don't even know this man!"

Erianne came within reach of the bullets and felt relief wash over her. They were non-explosive, which meant Tul'ran could divert them without causing damage to her husband when time resumed. Her panic subsided.

"Are you well, covenant-husband?"

Tul'ran smiled, his eyes still locked on G'shnet'el.

"As well as could be, love of my life. Did you kill the man who shot these projectiles at me?"

Erianne shook her head.

"I left Caligo in his chest. I think the blade did not cleave his heart. Were I to remove the blade before time resumed, his life's blood would leave his body in such quantity as to guarantee his death. It was my thought, milord husband, that you would want to interrogate him before we send his soul to El Shaddai for judgment."

Tul'ran nodded, then hooded his bright blue eyes.

"You considered well, Erianne. But first things must come first."

Tul'ran raised his left hand towards the bullets and flicked his fingers. A bright blue mist rose from his fingertips and drifted to the bullets. They flared out of existence and the light followed the projectiles' energy trail back to the gun. Another bright flare and the gun ceased to exist without harming Hart's hands.

G'shnet'el stared, his mouth open.

"How did you…?"

Erianne moved toward him, her green eyes resembling Arctic ice.

"Since last we saw you, fallen angel, my husband has gained yet another name to his impressive title. It is that of the Uncreator. Bloodwing the Blade chose him to house its power within his flesh and blood."

"Uncreator!" G'shnet'el hissed. "Uncreation was the true power of the sword?"

Suddenly, he threw back his head, and laughter roared from his mouth.

"The whole time we were in Heaven, Lucifer carried the power of Uncreation, and he didn't know! How rich! I look forward to the look on his face when I tell him this!"

Erianne continued to glide toward him.

"When you tell him this?" she asked in a mocking tone. "Tell me, evil one, what makes you think you will survive our encounter to tell the foul beast anything? With one thought, my husband can remove you from existence as he so casually removed your sword, the gun, and the projectiles fired from it. If you perceive yourself to be invulnerable to the Uncreator's powers, G'shnet'el, then challenge them, I beg of you."

Panic flashed across the massive angel's face.

"You cannot erase me from existence! Who gives you such a right? I am an angel of Heaven and an eternal being!"

The Voice was in all their heads in that moment.

"I give them the right, G'shnet'el. I, the Lord your God, Sovereign of the Universe, King of Heaven and Earth, gift the right to my servants, Tul'ran and Erianne, to judge you and punish you as they decree."

G'shnet'el fell to his knees, while Tul'ran tracked his movement with Bloodwing.

"Lord! Spare me! Do not let these, Your servants, remove me from existence. I was just following Satan's orders."

The Voice replied; the tone of it was withering.

"Satan does not have the authority to give orders in any reality you would care to name. I forbade you and all angels from acting against humans without My specific authorization, G'shnet'el. You knew this to be true. I forbade you from carrying out your evil deeds in Antiquity. You knew this, too. Against My will, you hunted My servant, Tul'ran, and sought to kill him. You have not just aggrieved Me, you have aggrieved him, as well. For this reason, I give you over to the judgment of Tul'ran and Erianne. Plead to them for their mercy, for you are out of My hands now."

The Voice faded from their minds.

Tul'ran's face appeared to be made of stone, so palpable was the anger upon it.

"When last we confronted you, G'shnet'el, Lady Erianne, the Princess of Death, commented on how gently we dealt with you. I failed to give her thoughts sufficient regard. It is an error I will not repeat. What say you, my love? What shall we do with this evil one? Command me, and it shall be done."

Erianne grinned at the fear in the fallen angel's

eyes.

"Scary, huh? Your fate poured into the hands of a mere woman you would've gleefully raped and tortured in the Abyss. You horrified me by how badly you abused Katja and her brothers. You have a lot to pay for, demon, and I think it's time we extract the debt from whatever passes as your flesh. Hearken to my command, milord husband: vaporize him."

"If you uncreate me," G'shnet'el said as fast as he could utter the words, "you'll never find Anatu. I left her with some lecherous men and while I instructed them to leave her untarnished body alone, who knows how long they'll obey if I do not return?"

Tul'ran's face went blank.

"You seized Anatu from her home?"

G'shnet'el seemed to shrink further when Bloodwing now hovered in front of his eyes.

"She is safe! I took her only to draw you out so I might kill you. I give you my oath she is unharmed!"

"Where is she?" Tul'ran said, his voice cold and dangerously low.

A glint of arrogance reappeared in the fallen angel's eyes.

"Give me your oath you will not uncreate me and I'll tell you where she is."

Erianne stepped closer to him; her face consumed with fury. She withdrew a knife and stabbed it into the fallen angel's thigh, very close to his groin. G'shnet'el screamed, but did not move with Bloodwing so close to his throat.

"Tell us, evil one," she said through gritted teeth, twisting the knife. "Where do we find the child? Tell us now, or I will cut you until you have no choice but to revert to a pure energy state."

Tul'ran interrupted her before she could strike again.

"Erianne, stay your hand, I beg of you. I fear that your marriage to me has led you into a thirst for blood I thought only crowded the deepest reaches of my heart. Hear me, G'shnet'el: I give you my oath. I will not use my power to uncreate you if you tell us, this instant, where we can find Anatu. I give this oath by the blood spilled between us by my wife's eager hand."

"In the cave," G'shnet'el gasped. "Behind us is a cave; the men and the girl are near the back, so the light of their torches would not show their location. There! I have taken your oath and given you the information. Now release me!"

"With pleasure," Tul'ran said, then stabbed Bloodwing through the evil angel's chest, where he assumed a heart would be. G'shnet'el exploded into a flare of energy. The angel's physical body was gone. Left in its place was an energy field shaped like the form the fallen angel had worn. G'shnet'el's natural protections had exerted themselves in the last nanosecond and converted him into a pure energy state to save him from dying.

"You gave me your oath!" the specter shrieked.

Tul'ran favored him with his most blood-curdling smile.

"But I kept my oath to you, evil one. I did not use my power to uncreate you, as you asked, and I promised. It was the only condition of our bargain. Do not blame me for failing to specify the terms of your parole after you gave over the child's location. You should know I would not have uncreated you, for you have yet to stand before El Shaddai and give an account for your sins. By my actions, I have sentenced you to remain in a spectral state until your judgment comes. El Shaddai will place you back in your physical body for your trial. Until then, enjoy the universe. You cannot interact with it or anyone in it until your judgment day, which I hope causes you immeasurable agony. Be gone."

Tul'ran's slashed Bloodwing through G'shnet'el's ethereal form, earning a wail of despair as G'shnet'el dispersed in a shower of sparks.

Tul'ran grinned at his wife, whose face radiated with an ear-to-ear smile.

"If I knew no better, milord husband, I would swear you were an attorney in another life. You were very crafty in how you leaped in and agreed to G'shnet'el's demands on terms so unfavourable to himself."

He looked like a little boy who she had handed a bag of candy.

"It is always with joy I find new ways to impress you, dear heart. I do not feel an imperative to resume our positions, so Time may resume its course. Shall we venture into the cave and recover our lost child from rapists and flesh merchants?"

Erianne drew a second knife and looked ruefully at Hart, frozen in Time, with Caligo protruding through his chest, his arm extended, and his face conveying shock.

"Given I am temporarily disarmed; I agree it would be best if we did this while Time remains in repose."

Tul'ran's right eyebrow arched high on his forehead.

"As if the lack of a sword makes you any less the most formidable enemy those cretins will ever face? I would bet a vast sum you would overcome them handily without weapons and be confident in my wager. I have seen your hands and feet in action, milady wife. No one from any era is better than you in hand-to-hand combat."

She grinned at him and squeezed one massive shoulder.

"Well said. So much so, I shall reward you with a hard bounce the very second we have a moment alone."

Erianne slapped Tul'ran's buttocks, giggled as she deftly avoided a return stroke, and ran ahead of him into the cave.

They found Anatu deep in the cave, with her back to a rocky wall. She was holding a stick in front of her, and it was easy to see what she'd done with it. One man lay on the ground, his face contorted in agony as he held his groin. Another man was holding the side of his jaw where the stick had obviously connected. Time froze the other ten men in a semi-circle around her; the evilness of their intent pronounced in their leering looks. She may have staved off an initial attack, but the odds were against her.

Anatu's eyes were afraid, but glowed with purpose. It was clear from the set position of her face she wouldn't give up her maidenhood without a fight and was determined to give her oppressors as much a battle as she could against twelve men.

Erianne stopped abruptly, sensing a change in her husband. Oh, oh. His face was a mask of rage and the muscles of his forearm bunched like steel cables as his hand flexed on Bloodwing's hilt.

"Milord husband?"

He looked at her when she spoke, but it was not her husband who stared at her so intently. His jaw muscles knotted.

"How is it we find this scene time and time again? A young woman kneeling before a group of slavering dogs intent on ripping apart her tender flesh to satisfy a need to feed some kind of power?"

Tul'ran spat on the ground.

"Even dogs are less base than these. These men are impotent in rank and standing in the world, having not the courage to make something of themselves. When they find kindness, it enrages them to the core of their souls, for only the foulest of all humanity lives in their hearts. Rapists!"

He advanced on the men. As he did so, the shaft of his sword glowed an intense blue and wisps of it rose and entered his arm like intravenous lines. Erianne closed her eyes briefly and tensed. An obscenity escaped from her lips, which she instantly regretted. Here we go again.

Tul'ran was speaking to the lead bandit, though the brigand wouldn't hear him in the stoppage of Time.

"Tell me, big man, what do you gain from raping this girl? Where lies your satisfaction? Will you go before the fire tonight and brag to your woman that you took another of her gender, desecrated her as if she had no heart or soul, and left her for dead? Will your wife applaud and urge you to bed her because you are such a potent man? *What do you get from this?*"

Erianne paled at the scream. He was losing it. Maybe this was the last straw. How many women had he known who men had raped? Merenthia, Evann'ya, Lilo'eth, Katja in the Abyss, Darian by her parents, and others she may not have heard about. Did Anatu's precarious position finally put him over the edge?

Tul'ran was winding his way through the scattered men. When Erianne could see his face, his eyes were bright, glowing blue. Bloodwing had a hold on him, truly.

"You're such big, brave, powerful men," Tul'ran sneered. "Were time to resume right now, and you found me walking among you; you would drain your insides into your trousers and run screaming from this cave. Such brave, brave men. So you would hurt a child, molest her, would you? If you could do such a thing to a child, what value do you have to this or any other world?"

Tul'ran raised his sword arm. The blue mists writhed on the blade, gathering in intensity. Just as Erianne was going to shout, the Voice was in their minds.

"Tul'ran, My son. What do you do?"

"What should be done!" Tul'ran shouted. "These animals do not deserve to share the air and walk the land with innocents like Anatu. If I leave them to their ways, they will not stop here. I will remove them as I would remove any other stain!"

The tendrils of Uncreation rose from Bloodwing

the Blade and drifted toward the men.

"And take unto yourself Our authority as God?"

The simple, calm question stopped Tul'ran in mid-step.

"How would I take unto myself Your authority as God?"

"Have We directed you in the way you should judge these men and pour out the wrath of your execution upon them? Is it by Our command you would remove them from creation, with not even their souls freed to kneel before Our Throne?"

Tul'ran's left hand was a blur as he punched the first man in the face, but the Time freeze would not permit the man's head to move under the blow. Erianne winced. The sod would feel it when Time began and wouldn't know which oxen kicked him in the face. Tul'ran was once more screaming his rage.

"How have You not yet judged this one? Why do You wait? How many more innocent girls must he rape and murder before You judge him?"

The Voice was sterner.

"Do you now judge Us, Tul'ran az Nostrom? Were you with Us when We created all things, living and dead? Was it your Spirit We poured into the universe to give it Light and life? Were you there when We created the first man and woman; when We breathed life into their nostrils knowing full well how quickly they would turn to evil? Do you understand the depths of how much We love all Our creation, even when they fall to darkness and rebel against Us?"

Erianne watched as the questions rained accusations on Tul'ran's head. The Uncreation strands wavered in the air uncertainly, then slowly reabsorbed into Bloodwing.

"I thought I was Your Judge in this Age," Tul'ran asked as a petulant look settled on his face.

"You are Our Judge for We so appointed you, but you carry out Our judgments, not your own, unless We decree it as We did with G'shnet'el. Tell me, Tul'ran, if you are so wise, what is the ripple effect of killing these men? How will their deaths affect the timeline your wife is so concerned with? Is there no good in them? Do they have children? What will become of their children if they die here tonight? Their wives? They live in a culture where most women are not self-sustaining. The women rely even on men such as these to put food on the table. Or have you forgotten the lesson in Ur?"

"I have not forgotten," Tul'ran mumbled. The tip of his sword drifted to the ground. "Nor have I forgotten the pain men such as these left in my heart in my years around the sun. Shall they go unpunished because in this moment they only have evil intent?"

"Should they? You tell Us, Tul'ran? If you are going to be like Us, become God, where you hold the fate of billions upon billions of souls in the palm of your hand, loving them all and grieving over their sin, then tell Us, Mighty King, how do you adjudge them? Shall you take upon yourself their judgment so their fates may stain your soul for eternity?"

A long moment went by before Tul'ran let out a weary sigh.

"This pains me. Just when I thought these feelings buried with Darian appearing on Spes to wed Johan and Gwynver'insa, I walk into this cave and find hatred for men such as these burning in my soul."

There was another pause, longer than the last.

"I am ever your servant, El Shaddai. Command me and I shall do it in Your Name."

The Voice was once again a soothing tendril nestling its way into their minds.

"Your choice is wise, My son. The Father and I have lived longer than you could ever guess or imagine. We have learned many things in Our journeys, and some day We will impart them to you. Trust Me when I tell you, son; Our burden is heavy and you would not want to bear it."

Erianne had stayed so still, Time could have frozen her with the rest of the cave's inhabitants. She moved to Tul'ran's side, glad the rage within him had subsided, and placed a hand on his cheek. He smiled at her gratefully.

"What shall we do with these beasts, Lord?" Erianne asked, her eyes searching her husband's face.

"You have read Our Holy Bible, Erianne. In it, I said anyone who looks at a woman to lust after her has already committed adultery with her in his heart. If your right eye causes you to sin, gouge it out and throw it away. It is better for a man to lose one part of his body than for his whole body to be cast into Hell. This shall be My judgement for these men. You will cut out their right eyes and place them in their right hands. In this way, they shall know they have not only received divine judgment, but also divine mercy. It would be far worse if they were to lose one or both hands. Or their lives."

Erianne looked up at the cave ceiling, her green eyes wide in her beautiful mahogany brown face.

"Yikes. And Tul'ran calls me bloodthirsty. Okay, let's do this."

Her attempt at levity left a small, still laugh in her mind.

"Okay," Tul'ran answered in English, tasting the odd sound of the word in his mouth. "Forgive me, El Shaddai, for the surliness of my tongue and my disobedience of past lessons learned."

The Voice left their minds, but not before leaving a final thought.

"Your reaction was born from your pain, My son. We forgive you in this as We forgive you in all things."

The two warriors cut out each man's right eye and forced it into the owner's right hand, first removing a weapon if the hand was so occupied. It was bloodless work because the men didn't shed fluids in their frozen state. They would only know of their mutilation when Time resumed.

When they completed their grisly task, Tul'ran picked up Anatu and carried her out of the cave in her frozen position. It was awkward, but the power of Uncreation still flowed through the body of the Sword Himself, and his strength was magnitudes greater than usual.

Tul'ran positioned Anatu on the ground to Davis's left, with her stick pointing at Hart.

Erianne walked up to her husband and stroked his face with her right hand, staring into his eyes.

"I am glad Davis cannot see you now, milord husband. You would frighten him to the edge of his last painful breath."

Tul'ran quirked his eyebrows at her.

"Such an end would never do, after saving his life. What is it you desire, Erianne?"

"Tul'ran, your eyes still tease the brilliant blue of your power. I can feel it surging within you. It took some effort to bring you back to me the last time the power of the Uncreator surged through your veins. Will you come back to me now, husband, so that I might not fear you will succumb to another temptation to godhood?"

Tul'ran smiled and closed his eyes. His eyebrows furrowed and his forehead creased with concentration. For several long seconds, nothing happened. Tul'ran's face twisted and then relaxed. It was only then Erianne could see blue streams of ethereal energy coursing through his body and back into Bloodwing. When he opened his eyelids once more, his irises were fully back to deep brown. He grinned as he touched the hilt of the angelic sword behind his back.

"Here am I, a mortal man, once more subject to the commands of my wife and her whims."

"Whims!" Erianne put her hands on her hips and directed a mock glare at him. "You scruffy excuse for a snowman! I save your life, time and time again, and that's what I get for gratitude? Whims! In my era, such a statement would've warranted a punch in the throat."

Tul'ran looked confused.

"What's a 'snowman'?"

Erianne giggled.

"That's what you took from my threats? A

snowman is a mock creature made from snow and given the attributes of limbs, eyes, and a nose through tree branches, a carrot, and two lumps of coal."

Tul'ran's face went blank as his eyebrows furrowed.

"What is 'snow'?"

Erianne looked at him, momentarily stunned.

"You've never seen snow? It's a wet, powdery substance, similar in color to your hair. Cold temperatures crystallize water and it falls from the sky in flakes. It accumulates if the temperature of the surrounding air at ground level does not immediately melt it, in sufficient amounts as to allow a person to roll the wetness of it into balls. The small balls, called snowballs, are used to throw at one another in mock combat. People roll large balls and stack them on top of one another in a caricature of the human form. They then create a face and arms, as I have said."

Tul'ran's body lost the tension that had drawn it into a rock-hard band of muscle.

"What is the purpose behind the creation of these snowmans?"

"Snowmen, in the plural," Erianne corrected. "It is largely for the entertainment and delight of small children, though adults often engage in snowball fights. There are even competitions in some places to judge the best creation of a snowman."

Tul'ran shook his head ruefully.

"To think people in your era have time for leisure activities such as those. Wondrous is the future, Erianne. Speaking of time, shall we resume the course of ours?"

"Why not? But first, what is your desire, milord husband, with this scurrilous rat who sought to execute you?"

Tul'ran narrowed his eyes at Erasmus Hart.

"Your first instinct was, as always, the correct one, milady wife. We must preserve his life so we may interrogate him as to the identity of our newest enemy. His weaponry suggests he is from your era, not mine."

Erianne frowned and inspected the older man.

"This is the second time I have observed a firearm in Antiquity. Darian wielded the first gun against us before she became our sister and sacrificed her life for yours. Now this man attempts to kill you with one. Neither should have been able to bring a gun into the past, yet they did so. We must discover the identity of our most recent enemy. Then," she finished calmly, "we shall kill them. Slowly, so they may know the error of their ways long before they go to kneel before El Shaddai."

Tul'ran shook his head before planting a kiss on his dusky wife's lips.

"We will return to Spes and convene a Judgment Seat to determine which of us is truly the most violent. I fear I may lose such a contest. Return to your place and let the sands of Time resume their course, if you favor me with your love."

They did, and time snapped back into motion. Erianne caught Hart before he could fall and further impale himself on Caligo. Tul'ran turned to a wakening Davis as Anatu waved her stick around wildly. She saw Davis, dropped her stick, and flung herself onto his broken body. He flinched and turned white, but hugged her close as he stared at the warrior standing in front of him.

"Tul'ran, my son, I knew you would come."

"Father, I leave you for a few short weeks and return to find you taking on one of Satan's chief lieutenants in Hades. What were you thinking?"

Davis grimaced and eased Anatu away from him.

"So that's what I was fighting. Makes sense why he was so hard to beat. Gently, child, I am injured. No, no, the fault is not yours. I fear I have broken ribs, and possibly my arm as well."

Davis looked at Hart, who was on his knees with Erianne's hands on his shoulders. Hart was trying to say something, but couldn't form a word through the blood bubbling on his lips. Suddenly, screams erupted from the depths of the cave, and the night air reverberated with shrieks and wailing.

"What in the name of all the saints in Heaven is going on?" Davis demanded. "Why does Hart have a sword in his chest? What's that din behind you?"

"Hi, Dad. Nice to see you alive. The screams are coming from twelve men Tul'ran and I mutilated before we saved Anatu. We need to get out of here before they come boiling out of yonder cave like angry ants. This guy brought a gun into Antiquity and shot at Tul'ran's face. I wasn't expecting a gun. When I drew my sword, my first instinct was to run him through instead of chopping off his head. He tried to kill my husband," she repeated pointedly.

"Help me up," Davis commanded, and Tul'ran bent down to pick him up as gently as possible. Davis looked at him oddly.

"You've changed. We'll talk about your height

and hair later when you tell me what happened here. With details. Take me to Hart."

Tul'ran half-carried Davis to where Hart was kneeling on the rock.

Davis put his good hand on Hart's neck to feel the pulse. He looked into Hart's dulling eyes.

"Your pulse is thready, Hart. You're going into shock. I'm going to give you something to help the shock and control the internal bleeding. We'll get you back to Sully and see what we can do to fix you up. Then you're going to answer some questions."

"What's a Sully?" Tul'ran asked, rolling the unfamiliar English words around in his mouth.

Davis smiled as he removed an ampoule from his clothing.

"Sully is not a what, he's a man and a good friend of mine. He's a physician. He can help Hart. I hope."

TTI made the medication ampoule out of biological materials, and it would dissolve quickly once used, leaving no trace of its futuristic origins. Davis pushed it against Hart's neck, and the ampoule ejected its contents into Hart's bloodstream. After a moment, Hart's eyes grew less wild, and his breathing improved.

Davis drew in a deep breath and winced against the stab of pain in his chest. Broken ribs, for sure. After a few seconds of consideration, Davis took out another ampoule and slapped it against his own neck. Seconds later, the pain in his arm and chest diminished to a dull ache. He took another tentative breath. The pain was there, but he'd be able to function without it debilitating him.

He stood up slowly and looked at Erianne.

176

"I know you want answers. So do I, but we won't get them if he dies. We'll take him back to my hutch. If we cut through the desert behind you, we can get there in an hour."

He hesitated for a moment.

"This part of the desert is dangerous. It's rife with criminals who think nothing of torturing and killing men and women. Be careful and watch your six. Erianne, take my sword, since I can't use it and you jammed yours through Hart's chest. We need to ride, people, and we need to do it now."

Tul'ran gathered Hart into his arms and hoisted him onto Darkshadow, with Caligo sticking out over the stallion's neck. Darkshadow didn't like it, not one bit, and made his opinion known through a series of head tosses and snorts.

"Gently, brother," Tul'ran said, chastising the war horse as he stroked his powerful neck. "We wounded this one and shall not have his life end at our hands. Hold still a moment while I help my father with his mount."

At a gesture from Tul'ran, Erianne held Hart steady while Tul'ran went to Davis's side. Davis bit back a protest of bravado and allowed Tul'ran to swing him up on his horse like he was a child. Tul'ran took his bride's place, and Erianne lifted Anatu onto Hart's horse before mounting Destiny's Edge. Tul'ran jumped onto Darkshadow's back and took a secure hold of Hart. He nodded to Davis.

"Let us be away, Father, for evil stains this place with the stench of corrupted flesh."

Davis wanted to say something as equally poetic, but the pain in his arm was becoming insistent. He turned his horse's head, and they rode into the desert. Davis strained his eyes and ears into the night, looking for the enemy that his instincts screamed was there, but he couldn't see. He concentrated his mind so intently on the enemy in front of him, he almost missed Erianne's burst of laughter after Tul'ran asked,

"What's my six and how am I to watch it?"

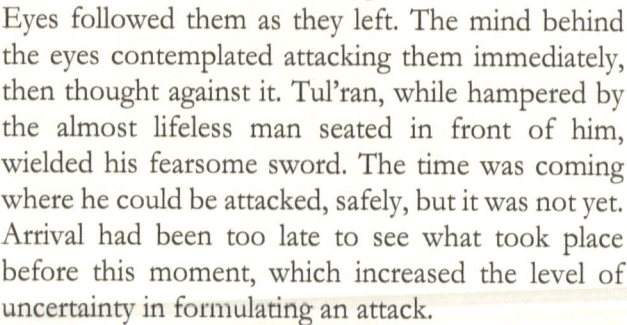

Eyes followed them as they left. The mind behind the eyes contemplated attacking them immediately, then thought against it. Tul'ran, while hampered by the almost lifeless man seated in front of him, wielded his fearsome sword. The time was coming where he could be attacked, safely, but it was not yet. Arrival had been too late to see what took place before this moment, which increased the level of uncertainty in formulating an attack.

The body housing the mind and the eyes faded back into the darkness, an ebon wraith disappearing into the night as subtly as it came.

CHAPTER THE EIGHTH:
THE SCATTERING

Perhaps they knew a wolf prowled in their midst, sensing the craving for prey on which to feast. Perhaps they felt his presence, a juggernaut moving through them, and they slunk away before becoming crushed. Maybe they witnessed his passage, sensed a weakness in his wake, but then considered it was their own cowardice they felt and held hands back, away from weapons.

Whatever the reason, Tul'ran and his party, wounded and exhausted, made their way through the desert to the House az Peregos without hindrance or incident. Perhaps word had already made its way into the world that the Sword Himself had returned with a warrant of Death, unnamed, eagerly waiting to pen some fool's title to a scroll writ in blood.

But we rush to the end too quickly.

In the stressful ride through the desert, Davis turned as best as he could to regard his son riding behind a barely conscious Hart on Darkshadow's back.

"How did you get here, Tul'ran?"

Tul'ran and Erianne shared a glance. Davis posed the question in English, a language Anatu didn't understand. If Hart was conscious enough to absorb the conversations, he would learn things he ought not to know. The choice between languages was easy to make.

"When we last left you, Lam'ek," Tul'ran said in the Tongue, "El Shaddai sent us to a different world far from here. Thousands of years of war left the population decimated. The entire planet was an abandoned city. Combatants fought skirmishes with warriors not of flesh and blood, while Victims hid underground, desperate to stay away from conflict."

"We met a woman there," Erianne said, "who you would have adored. She is short, slender, small-boned, and beautiful. Gwynver'insa looks like a blond-haired elf without the pointy ears. She appears as if she just came out of her teen years, although she is over a thousand years old."

Davis coughed and winced at the pain in his chest.

"A thousand years in age! I take it she is a wise person if she lived so long."

Tul'ran smirked.

"If the word is 'wise', it requires redefinition. Gwyn is educated and intelligent beyond anything I've experienced."

"Me, too," Erianne said. "She is a prophet who regularly speaks to El Shaddai. We were told she was the salvation of the world and the key to its recovery from war; provided we could get the war to stop."

Erianne shuddered at the memory of their arrival.

"When we entered the planet, Lam'ek, it was the most horrible place you could imagine. Everything was a dull gray color. The sun could not shine through layers of cloud and pollution created by millennia of warfare. War machines roamed the city streets, searching for humans to kill. Eventually, we connected with Gwyn's people, who anointed her Empress of the World. The Empress then commissioned us to end the Multi-Millennial Fight."

Davis's eyebrows went up on a face stiffened by pain.

"She asked the two of you to lead her army?"

Tul'ran laughed, a crisp bark with traces of irony.

"We were her army."

The pain was overcoming Davis's ability to think in the Tongue; he slipped back into English.

"The two of you against a global war machine? Wait a minute, didn't you go with Johan and Darian? Where are they?"

Tul'ran looked away, working his jaw. Erianne nudged Destiny's Edge's side and moved her closer to Darkshadow. She reached out and grasped her husband's forearm. Without looking at Davis, she answered for both.

"We lost Darian, Mick. Before she died, she became a completely different person. She was kind, lovely, and lovable. And brave. She sacrificed her life to save Tul'ran's." Erianne's voice choked off.

"I'm sorry, Erianne and Tul'ran, I truly am. How did it happen?"

Erianne reached up to wipe tears from her eyes and drew a shuddering breath.

"We encountered combat as soon as we arrived on the planet. It separated Darian from us. We didn't know what happened to her until one day she showed up where we were staying on the planet. After a night of celebration, someone came in screaming about how the clouds had parted and the sun was shining for the first time in hundreds of years."

"We were protecting the Empress of Spes. She took off like a gazelle up the ramp, with Tul'ran in hot pursuit. Darian ran after Tul'ran, and I lagged."

Davis swiveled as far as he could and managed a small shake of his head.

"You? I don't believe it! I would've expected you at the top of the ramp ahead of everyone else."

Erianne dropped her chin to her chest.

"Don't lecture me, Mick, but I was hungover. Did I mention we were celebrating the night before? Anyway, Tul'ran and the Empress Gwynver'insa were the first out the doors to the surface of the world, with Darian hot on their heels. Just as I got to the door, I saw an android drive a spear into Darian's back. The bot tried to ambush Tul'ran, but Darian had pushed Tul'ran out of the way and took the spear for him. She died within a minute."

Tul'ran let Erianne's words hang in the air for a few minutes while he composed the right words in English.

"It turns out my sword has incredible properties. Darian's murder enraged me beyond anything I've ever experienced. Within the maelstrom of my rage, I used my sword's amazing power to take the field and secure victory. Bloodwing's power surging through me caused the increase in my height and changes to my hair color."

"There were only twelve Combatants left on Spes Deserit who controlled their shares of a global war machine. After I killed three of them, the remaining nine surrendered. After their trial, the Empress commissioned us to remove the Nine from her world and exile them in another."

Spes, the world of Hope, in the Year of Our Peace 0001, the sixth day in the month of Darian, Mission Day 132

The Crystalline Wall had closed behind them, and Tul'ran couldn't figure out who was more morose: he and Erianne, or the Nine. They led their prisoners through the Garden and the Nine were stunned by the abundance of foliage, water, and animals surrounding them. As ancestors of the first Combatants, they'd not seen anything, but a world ravaged and made desolate by war.

Before they arrived at the Gate between the forbidden Trees, they found Jesus standing before them dressed in His simple white robes. Tul'ran and Erianne dismounted and kneeled before the Lord.

"El Shaddai, we come."

Jesus gestured them to their feet with a smile.

"Welcome, Tul'ran and Erianne. I am sure after many days of travel; you would welcome a bath. Remove the chains from the Nine and avail yourselves of the warm pools. I would like a word with the Nine, alone."

The Warriors of the Lord bowed to Him and removed the restraints from their prisoners.

They led Darkshadow and Destiny's Edge away from the group to a pool of frigid water. After the horses drank, Tul'ran and Erianne checked their feet. Seeing Jesus occupied with the Nine in the distance, they turned away and walked to the warm pools. After stripping off their armor, they slid into the soothing water with a sigh.

"Milord husband, after five days of travel on horseback, I am minded to stay in this pool for five more."

Tul'ran chuckled.

"How long, I wonder, would it be before you became so bored you lost interest in your husband's face?"

Erianne glided forward through the water, took Tul'ran's cheeks in her hands, and kissed him soundly. When they pulled their lips apart to take a breath, her eyes gleamed with passion.

"On the order of never, milord husband, would I lose interest in your face."

Tul'ran leaned forward for another kiss, but Erianne restrained him with a hand on his mouth.

"Nay, if you kiss me again with those razors you call whiskers, I shall lose my beauty. Raw meat isn't sexy," she said in English.

Tul'ran barked a sharp laugh and leaned back.

"Draw your blade, milady wife, and have at it. Never let it be said Tul'ran the Sword mutilated a woman's beautiful face!"

Erianne glided away and reached behind her to her armor, lifting half out of the water as she arched back and exposed her breasts. Tul'ran's pulse quickened. His wife was a wondrous beauty, fair of face and form. Her mahogany brown body was art personified and injected fire into his arteries.

She grinned at him as she slid back into the pool.

"I see my husband remains enamoured with his wife."

"Too true," he said, the tone of his voice heavy with lust, "Be quick with the blade, milady wife, for I hunger for more than the touch of your blade to my face."

Erianne expertly ran the sharp edges of her knife across his stubble, removing the offending beard within minutes. She casually flipped the knife over her shoulder and crushed his lips with another kiss before the blade stuck in the ground.

What felt like much later, a satiated Erianne and Tul'ran exited the pools and dried off using the towels El Shaddai provided. They rejoined the group, who were sitting on the ground and stuffing their faces with an abundance of food placed on a blanket before them.

Jesus smiled at the warriors as they ambled up to the party.

"Are you refreshed? Good. Help yourself to a meal. I was just about to tell the Nine about their new home."

Tul'ran and Erianne sat down on the grass facing the Nine and began pulling fruit from the piles in front of them. Soon, juices from the delicious grapes and berries drizzled down their chins as the wonderful flavors exploded over their palettes.

Jesus gestured to the sky, which turned black. The Nine gasped as one. Floating in the center of the darkness was an enormous world. At the center of the world lay a large green landmass, surrounded by a desert.

"Behold, the planet Fresh Start," He said, watching the Nine intently. "It is a new world We have created for you. On the land mass, We created lakes, streams, forests, suitable soil for planting, and a multitude of animals. The deserts contain heavy metals and ores you can refine and work to create machines. All this world We give to you; use it as you please."

"Understand, this is the only world you will have. If you choose to use it up, as your ancestors did with Spes, you will have nowhere to go. If you are good stewards of this world, it will reward you and you will flourish."

"I have restored to each of you a lifespan of five thousand years, as I did with your ancestors. This will give you the time you need to rebuild your society. If you choose to cooperate and populate the planet in peace, I will give you access to the Library of Heaven, from where you can learn to care for Fresh Start and prosper."

"With no effort, you can survive. You will want for nothing and gain much more with time and experience."

Rosa lifted her hand, and Jesus nodded at her to speak.

"Your Eminence, how will we populate this planet?"

Erianne bit her lip and dropped her head to hide her smirk.

'I guess they weren't watching us,' she cast into Tul'ran's mind, which made his face turn red. Jesus turned and grinned at them, making Erianne blush.

Right. The omnipresence of God.

"I will make all these things known to you, Rosa, never fear. I send Tul'ran and Erianne with you for a short while. They will answer all your questions."

Erianne looked horrified.

"Uh, Lord, aren't we needed elsewhere, urgently?"

Mischief danced in His eyes.

"Why, not at all, daughter. After all you've been through, I'd imagine you'd welcome a vacation."

Erianne snorted. Right, it was going to be a vacation.

Mesopotamia, the ninth day of the fifth month, 2004 BC

"Mick," Erianne said, "The thirty days we spent on Fresh Start were so dull I was ready to cry after the first week. We settled the Nine on their new world and answered all their questions. I discovered I don't have the patience and kindness to be a teacher."

Davis chortled and instantly regretted it.

"Stop making me laugh. You're killing my ribs. Who gave them the talk?"

"The talk," Tul'ran said, his face blank.

"Yes, son," Davis said in the Tongue. "The one where you informed them how they might populate their world."

Tul'ran directed a glare at Erianne, who had folded her lips inward to keep from laughing.

"Erianne and I wrestled for the privilege of avoiding the giving of the instruction."

"And I won!" Erianne piped in, clapping her

hands together.

"You cheated!" Tul'ran retorted.

"Did not! I fought fairly. It's not my fault you've never learned Brazilian Jiu-Jitsu."

Tul'ran snorted.

"I haven't heard of the term, much less explored its subtleties. Later we'll discuss when you learned such a fighting style so we can get a ruling on the fairness of its use."

Davis shook his head at the two. Kids.

"You haven't answered my question about how you came to my aid so quickly as to prevent me from getting killed."

"Father, when we were about to expire from monotony, El Shaddai came into our minds and bid us to ride to your rescue. We barely cinched our saddles before our horses bolted for the Gate. Fresh Start bored them as much as us, I warrant. This took place just after Erianne cheated in our contest and forced me to, as you said, give the Nine the talk. The rest, you know."

Erianne snorted.

"Sore loser. Look, there's Gilgesh."

Late night revelers gaped at the party riding through the village and then threw themselves upon their faces when they recognized the Prince and Princess of Death. Better to efface yourself than die, was it not?

Sully and Jeannie came spilling out of the hutch as soon as they heard the horses approaching. They took in the scene, stunned by the sight of the sword sticking out of Hart's chest.

"Who's hurt?" Sully asked, cutting to the chase as

most emergency physicians will.

"Davis has broken ribs and maybe a broken arm, but the old man needs immediate attention," Erianne said, swinging off her horse and helping Anatu down. "Anatu has some bumps and bruises, but she'll live."

Sully came around Tul'ran's left side, where the warrior would dismount, and regarded him warily. He'd been around combat long enough during his time on a SEAL team to recognize a dangerous man, and Tul'ran's aura screamed it.

"I'm Dr. Michael Sullivan and this is my wife, Jeannie Sullivan. My friends call me Sully. I'd like to look at that man inside, if you don't mind."

Tul'ran nodded and lifted Hart out of the saddle and down to Sully and Jeannie, his massive muscles bulging as he seemed to transfer the elderly man with ease. Sully and Jeannie grunted as they took Hart's weight into their arms.

"It's my pleasure to meet you, Dr. Michael Sullivan, good friend to Lamek Davis and physician," he said, his English accented by a Mesopotamian dialect, "I am Tul'ran az Nostrom, and behind you walks Lady Erianne az Nostrom."

Erianne nodded at the Sullivans as she gestured to Heather and Coventry to come over to Davis's horse.

"Thrilled. Let's get these two inside before this three-ring circus gets any bigger."

Erianne, Coventry, and Heather helped Davis out of his saddle. Pain pinched Davis's face, and he drew a ragged breath. The pain meds had worn off after the constant jostling in the saddle, and he was feeling every bit of damage to his ribs and arm.

Under the quiet but intensely interested gaze of the surrounding crowd, which was growing larger by the minute, they carried Davis and Hart inside the hutch.

They sat Davis in a chair and Hart on a low bench in the back room, separated from the living area by a floor to ceiling curtain. As Sully approached Davis, the injured warrior pointed to where Hart sat, dazed and confused.

"Him first. We'll tell the story later. I have broken ribs, but I'll live. I'm not sure Hart will."

Sully searched through his bag and pulled out a portable trauma kit. It was standard issue for all medics in the field and TTI allowed it in Antiquity despite the advanced technology of the devices. Saving lives was preferable to any slim potential of a time fracture; besides, the medics were extremely careful with their kits.

He glanced at Heather and gave his head a slight jerk. Heather, being the smartest of the entire group, took the hint immediately.

"Omarosa, we must take the children into the front room and give these physicians an opportunity to work. Come, we will prepare a meal despite the hour and feed our family and guests."

Jeannie shook her head mournfully as the group left the back room.

"English. Doesn't anyone speak English around here? I've been going nuts listening to them jabber in their language all night long."

Sully's laughter was a terse bark as he unpacked the portable scanner. It projected three holo screens above Hart's head as he passed the scanner over the older man's body.

"Jeannie, give Davis a fentanyl citrate tablet for his pain. Put it under your tongue, Mick. As for Hart, let's give him a ketamine injection."

"Ketamine!" Coventry said, "you're giving him a horse tranquilizer?!"

Sully smiled, concentrating on the displays.

"In the old days, we achieved battlefield analgesia for U.S. military casualties by primarily using intramuscular morphine. The problem is, IM morphine is slow-acting. It can lead to delays in effective pain relief and the risk of overdose and death when we repeat the dosing to hasten the onset of analgesia."

Sully's face turned to worry as he passed the scanner near Hart's heart.

"We've incorporated advances in battlefield analgesia, pioneered initially by Tactical Combat Casualty Care, and the Army's 75th Ranger Regiment, into the Triple-Option Analgesia approach. Battlefield analgesia is now to be achieved using one or more of three options, depending on the casualty's status. First, we apply meloxicam and acetaminophen from the combat wound medication pack for casualties with relatively minor pain who can function effectively as combatants. Of course, you'd only do that if the analgesic meds didn't impair them; there's nothing more dangerous in the field than an intoxicated, wounded soldier."

"I gave him a meloxicam and acetaminophen patch from my kit," Davis piped up. "I gave myself one, too. That was over an hour ago. It took us longer than I expected to get here."

Sully smiled at him.

"You did good, Mick. You'll have no effect from what we gave you, nor will Hart have a problem with the ketamine."

He ran the scanner around the sword where it exited Hart's chest and finished answering Coventry's question.

"Second, we administer oral transmucosal fentanyl citrate for casualties who have moderate-to-severe pain, but who are not in hemorrhagic shock or respiratory distress, and are not at significant risk of developing either condition. We give ketamine as a third option for casualties who have moderate-to-severe pain, but who are in hemorrhagic shock or respiratory distress or are at significant risk of developing either condition. Hart qualifies for the horse tranquilizer. Jeannie, you'd better throw a respirator on Hart's nose. I don't like his O_2 SATs."

Jeannie pulled the respirator out of the bag. It was a small device that fit into each nostril with a bridge across the base of the nostril in which there was a small fan. The device sucked in air, removed the nitrogen molecules, increasing the partial pressure of oxygen, and pumped the purified air consisting mostly of oxygen into the patient's nose and sinuses.

"Done. He's pinking up, love."

Sully nodded.

"Yeah, that's good, but this isn't."

Sully pointed to a graphic above Hart's head, which showed Hart's pumping heart. The sword was resting against the powerful muscles of the right atrium, and small droplets of blood were squeezing past the sword with each heartbeat.

"There's no nerve damage I can see, but the sword has significantly compromised the right lung. The problem is the heart. If we pull out the sword, which is currently blocking the cut, the ventricular wall likely bursts at the cut line. Without surgery, he'll bleed out and die. Even if I had the qualifications to do open-heart surgery, which I don't, we can't perform the procedure in the field."

"What does he need?" Davis asked, breathing easier with the pain medication.

"He needs Dr. Payton Dumont on Atlantis. She's the only one who can save him now."

"Yeah, well, that's not an option," Coventry said. "I still can't raise Atlantis and I've been trying every hour on the hour. I'm open to suggestions, Doc, but right now, TTI is off grid."

"We have another concern," Tul'ran said, his voice low. "This man tried to kill me with a weapon from the future which casts projectiles."

"He means a gun," Erianne said in response to Sully's quizzical look. "This jerk brought a gun into Antiquity and took a head shot at my husband."

Hart jerked his head around to look at Erianne, and a look of disgust flashed across his face. Erianne took a step toward him.

"What's bothering you, old man? That I'm married to an ancient warrior? You know what bothers me? It bothers me when someone tries to kill my husband by bringing an illegal weapon into Antiquity. You and me, we're going to have a little chat now about who tasked your mission."

The panel above Hart's head turned yellow, and

Jeannie rushed to grab another ampoule from Sully's kit.

"Hey, lady, I don't know who you are, but you're about to kill my patient. His blood pressure's going up and his heart is trying to beat a little harder. I had to give him an ampoule of Lorazepam to calm him down. If the cut in the wall of his heart goes, you're not getting any answers."

Erianne rounded on Jeannie.

"Hey, *lady*, I couldn't care less if this rancid piece of meat dies. Did you miss the part where he tried to kill my husband?"

The screen above Hart's flared into a bright red and his eyes glazed. Sully pushed himself between the two glaring women.

"Knock it off, you two! I've got a patient in distress, and both of you are making it worse. Lady Erianne, I appreciate you're angry, but you won't get your answers if Hart dies. I don't mean to be rude, but why don't you take a walk?"

Sully almost bit his tongue in two because of how hard he clamped his mouth shut. A knife had come out of nowhere and was caressing his throat, while brilliant green eyes flaring with rage held his gaze captive. Sully gulped. He wanted to say something, but the words wouldn't come. Then a massive hand came into his field of view and covered the wrist holding the deadly blade.

"My love," Tul'ran said in a soft voice. "Dr. Michael Sullivan speaks truly. The man they call 'Hart' barely lives, by all accounts. We must release him to their care and seek our answers when time and health permit. Will you withdraw your blade, my covenant-wife?"

Erianne drew a long breath and made the blade disappear as quickly as it flashed into her hands. Her gaze passed between Sully and Jeannie.

"This isn't over," she said, her voice chilly.

Erianne took a step back, her blood boiling at the insolence of the physician and his wife. Coventry, Sully, Davis, and Jeannie were, technically, colleagues of hers from the future, yet she felt far removed from them. Her time with Tul'ran had changed her, and some changes weren't subtle. She no longer felt part of the era in which she was born. She no longer felt part of any era, if the truth be told.

The Voice came into her mind then, softly caressing her brain with love and tenderness.

"Erianne, My child, come alone to the stables."

Erianne turned immediately and walked out of the curtained sleeping quarters. She glanced back to the curtain, where Tul'ran stood between her and the back room.

'I go to the stables,' she said telepathically in his mind.

Tul'ran nodded.

'I will get an account from Ro'gun of the events preceding our arrival. Call out if you need me, milady wife.'

Erianne sketched a bow and stepped out into the chilly night air. The villagers crowded around the hut, but they had withdrawn six feet to clear some room in front of the door. They whispered as she came out and bowed low as she went past. Anger tightened the skin of her face and flashed in her eyes, spelling doom for anyone foolish enough to gain her attention.

There was no mistaking the identity of this dusky beauty. Even now there was a crooner in among them singing the Ballad of Tul'ran the Sword to entertain the growing crowd, and he'd chosen the passages involving Tul'ran and Erianne eagerly.

Here was Lady Erianne az Nostrom, the Princess of Death, who fought at the side of the Sword Himself in the Massacre of the Gap.

The balladeer sang of the three hundred men killed by Tul'ran and Erianne, and how the couple stacked the bodies onto a pile to create a makeshift table. Then the Prince and Princess of Death, covered in blood and entrails, spread a cloth on the ghastly table and dined on meat and cheese while they laughed at the foolishness of the dead.

Erianne rolled her eyes. There was very little truth to the account, but the people loved it and often bragged about Gilgesh's association with the Sword Himself. This is where he trained, they proudly exclaimed to anyone who would listen. We knew him as a child and saw greatness in him then; they bragged in every drinking spot in that region.

Within a few seconds, Erianne rounded the corner and arrived at the solitude of the little stable behind the hutch. No one gathered here. They knew the enclosure housed Darkshadow and how fiercely Tul'ran loved and protected his horse. To touch Darkshadow was to invite a slow and painful death at Tul'ran's hands, or a quick one by Darkshadow's hooves.

The stable was really a three-sided enclosure with a thatched roof. It kept the elements away from the horses, but was rudimentary in every other aspect. As she went further into the enclosure, she saw a long-haired, bearded man standing in front of her, clothed in a long, tan-coloured robe most often worn by the desert-dwellers of this era. She dropped to her knees, bowed her head, and raised her palms to the sky.

"Lord, here am I, Your servant."

Jesus walked up to her and clasped her wrists with both of His hands, pulling her gently to her feet. She noticed, as He did so, His hands didn't bear the hideous scars of His crucifixion.

Jesus laughed softly in the darkness as He led her to a crude wooden bench at the end of the stable.

"In every era before My birth, I appeared in my pre-incarnate form as the Angel of the Lord. In this form, I am more God than man. We chose the times and places of My appearances in Antiquity carefully to not diminish the significance of my incarnation on Earth."

Once they sat, Jesus's body glowed brightly enough to light the surrounding area.

Erianne bit her lip.

"It would be handy to have the power to glow, Lord. One would never need to fear the night again."

Jesus smiled at her as he reached into his robe. Erianne never expected it to have pockets.

"When you are God, you do not have to wear period specific clothing. What outfit is complete without pockets?" He said in response to her unspoken surprise.

Jesus produced two silver bracelets and offered them to her for her inspection. Erianne took them and immediately notice their weight. Pure silver, perhaps. They would wrap around her wrists and extend halfway up her forearm.

"They're beautiful, Lord."

"And functional," He said. He hovered his left index finger over the bangle in Erianne's right hand. Inscribed in the bracelet, in Native American Indigenous art, was the form of an owl.

"This is Gookooko'oog, which is the Anishinaabe or Ojibwe name for 'owl'. You know your father was Anishinaabe. Ancient tribes believed the owl to be an ill omen, and it foretold a coming death. They considered the owl to be a being of great power, but as you know, Erianne, power itself is neither good nor bad. How we apply power makes it good or evil."

Jesus ran His fingertip along the etchings of the bracelet in Erianne's left hand.

"This is a stylized version of Naanooshkaanhs, the hummingbird. The hummingbird is a messenger of hope and jubilation, according to Anishinaabe culture. What you hold in your hands contains symbols of life and death. It is the juxtaposition between life and death where the interpolation of two extremes blend and power thrives."

Erianne shook her head slightly.

"Forgive me for being extra dense tonight, Lord, but I had an intense evening. Say what again?"

Jesus's face softened.

"Let us leave it at this: these bracelets have tremendous power. When you put them together and focus on a time and destination, the bracelets will open a gateway to any place and any time in the universe. These are how you can send Hart back to Atlantis for surgery."

Erianne's face twisted.

"You mean the man who tried to kill my husband by shooting him in the face? Why should I allow him to survive when he tried to take the life of the one most precious to me?"

Jesus looked into her eyes, and His eyes took on a more intense glow.

"Daughter of the Lord your God, your reason to save his life is because I require it."

Abashed, Erianne sunk off the bench onto her knees, bowed her head, and lifted her palms up in supplication.

"Forgive me, Lord. You are so comfortable to talk to I sometimes forget with whom I am speaking. If it is Your will that Hart is to live, then I shall do everything in my abilities to make it so."

Jesus's eyes softened, and he reached down to pull her up beside Him again.

"I forgive you, Erianne. Please know the Father and I do not act arbitrarily. We see a chance for Hart's redemption if he chooses the right path in the many still open to him while he lives. But let us now speak of the other thing."

Erianne's eyes quirked upwards.

"The other thing, Lord?"

"Yes, Daughter. You have become angrier and more violent since you first encountered Tul'ran in the desert. Superficially, one might say My son is rubbing off on you. I know this is not so. Tell me, Erianne, child of My heart, what ails you?"

Erianne started to say 'nothing', then firmly

clamped her lips together. This was God, who knew her more intimately than she could know herself. One does not lie to one's deity when He sits a foot away with a concerned look on His face. She licked her lips.

"Here's the anguish of my heart, Lord. From the moment I met Tul'ran, I've been in awe of his prowess and martial skills. So much so, I thought him to be invincible; invulnerable to death. Until I saw my darling sister, Darian, leap in front of a spear to save his life. I thought it was going to be me who would sacrifice my life for his, and I was prepared for it. When I saw the spear enter Darian's back, unimaginable horror consumed me. It wasn't just that she died, but that Tul'ran came so close to death."

She looked down at her hands, tears forming in her eyes.

"I know if you didn't want him to die then, you could've frozen time to give him an opportunity to respond. Darian's death was Your will and I accept it. What I haven't been able to shake is how close Tul'ran came to leaving me for the next world."

The tears were spilling down her cheeks.

"We haven't known each other long, but he has become the most important human in my life. Every time I ask myself what I would do if he dies, my mind spins into a cavern of despair. It's not just a case of loving him; I need him. I need his arms around me at night, his whispers in my ears as I fall asleep, and the love shining in his eyes when I wake up to him in the morning. As a human, I don't know when You might take him away from me, and the thought of it gives me great pain. The pain leads to anger, and I don't know how to fix it."

There was silence for a moment, and then Jesus spoke, gently.

"Why such pain, Erianne, for a man you have known for only a short while? Do you truly grieve his potential death, or do you also grieve the loss of your father?"

Erianne jerked her head up and her mouth rounded into an 'o'.

"I never thought of my Dad's disappearance; I mean, I don't consider Tul'ran to be a father figure. My Dad was incredibly precious to me, Lord. I've not thought of him much since the funeral. Tul'ran and I've been too busy trying to keep people from killing us. My Dad and I did everything together. I had a closer relationship with him than Mom because we were so much alike."

"When I was young, Dad and I would disappear into the mountains for months at a time. He taught me the ways of his people; how to gather food from the forest, what herbs were good for curing ailments and dressing wounds, and how to appreciate the nature You created. He was my most important relationship. His disappearance during the Rapture gutted me and made me furious because I felt so lost and abandoned. He left when I was entering the pinnacle of my achievements and he never saw them happen. He never saw me happy."

Erianne dropped her head and sobbed as the pain of the loss of Luke Manyfeathers flooded her heart. She had buried her grief and denied it for so long; she almost forgot it was there.

Jesus reached out, put an arm across her shoulders, and drew her to His chest.

"When you live in the world, wrapped in flesh, it is easy to forget beyond the short number of years allocated to you in this life there is an eternity awaiting you in the next. Luke and Priya have lived with me in the Kingdom of Heaven since the Rapture. We have had many conversations about you, dear heart, and I have kept them informed of your exploits. They are so proud of you, it's almost sinful."

Erianne giggled against His chest.

"I have also shared meals with Tul'ran's mother and five sisters and their husbands frequently. They, too, enjoy the stories of how Tul'ran has brought justice, and more than a little consternation, into his era. They were most delighted to know you are part of their family and take as much interest in your achievements as your parents do."

Erianne felt her eyebrows rise again.

"Five sisters? I thought the Gutians killed Tul'ran's mother with his two younger sisters."

Jesus canted his head at her.

"Ah, yes, Tul'ran has not told you the tale yet. On one of those journeys when the night is long, and the journey is far, insist he tell of the time he returned to his village and told his family about El Shaddai. His conversation with them led them to place their trust and faith in Us and gave them passage to the Kingdom of Heaven on the strength of Our forgiveness of their sins. He almost killed all three of his brothers-in-law during the Telling, but it is his tale to tell."

Erianne raised her head from Jesus's chest.

"Tul'ran the Evangelist! Oh, I need to hear that one! What of my parents, Lord? Do they know I married?" she asked, before dropping her head to His chest again.

"Indeed, it is so. They were happy to hear you have married and they are looking forward to meeting their son-in-law."

"Yes, Lord," she said, her voice muffled against His chest, "but not soon, right?"

Jesus squeezed her more tightly against Himself.

"Erianne, it is not for any person to know the date and time of their passing, or the passing of their loved ones. Should we impart such information, people would inevitably change their lives to account for their death date; such changes could lead to great evil. You must not fear for Tul'ran. When it is his time to leave this world, he will join Us in Heaven. Should his day come before your own passing, then I promise you I will be with you. I, the Lord your God, your Protector; I, El Rio, the God Who Sees You, will be with you and will never leave you until the day you have a joyous reunion with your husband and family."

Erianne sighed and allowed herself to relax in His embrace.

"What do I do to get rid of this anxiety within me?"

"You can start by clearing your mind of the words, 'what if?' There is nothing to be gained by them. For every 'what if' leading to a ruinous end, there is another 'what if' leading to glory. Asking 'what if' questions only fill the mind with despair.

Focus only on this day and the challenges it brings. In living only for each day, you will find peace. Trust Me, I love you more than you will ever know or comprehend. Though grim times may befall you, I am with you, always, to the end of the age."

Erianne pulled herself away and dried her tears with the back of one hand.

"I do trust You, Jesus. Thank you. I'll reflect on everything you've said. It won't be easy, but I'll do my best. Will you tell me how the man with my sword in his chest came to be here with a gun?"

Jesus put a finger under her chin and lifted her gaze into his.

"You must not know this information yet. There are strands of future events which would become distorted if you were to know the truth. You must trust me when I say all things are unraveling, as they must. In the meantime, you must show him grace and care for his life. To do otherwise will cast shadows where I would not have them cast."

Erianne's lips eked out a smile.

"That sounds ominous. Do You want to show me how to use these bracelets?"

Pride shone in the Lord's eyes.

"I will, but first you must know this. Once I place these on your arms, they will become a part of you. Your blood will circulate through them as if they were a piece of your flesh and your nerve endings will control them. They are indestructible, but need your life to sustain them. If you accept this gift and this power, they will not come off your body until I remove them one day in Heaven. The Father and I would entrust such power as I give you to no other human. Not even Tul'ran."

Erianne's eyes widened.

"Wow. I'm, well, I'm really flattered. You consider me worthy of such a gift?"

Jesus nodded emphatically.

"We consider you to be the worthiest of any other human. You have heard it said with great power comes great responsibility. This is one of the greatest powers in the Universe, and We think you to be the only one responsible enough to wield it."

Erianne sat quietly for a moment.

"Lord, I'm overwhelmed by Your trust and faith in me. I accept Your gift with humility."

"Then hear the tasks I set for your group before I graft these bracelets on your arms. Hart must return to Atlantis for surgery. The earthquake devastated the TTI Main building, but I carefully preserved one surgical suite at the back of the building. All Payton Dumont needs to repair his heart and treat the injuries of others is in the suite. The independent power supply for the unit remains intact. Before you send him through the doorway, you must carefully withdraw Caligo from his back to not injure his heart further. Coventry, Davis, Wu, and the Sullivans have the option to remain with you or go with Hart."

Jesus paused for a moment, a look of concern crossing His face.

"If they choose to return to Atlantis, they must understand what they go to. The earthquake has devastated the island, as it did much of the planet. Food and water will be in short supply. There are many tribulations yet to be experienced by the people of Earth, and Satan still hunts Christians to kill them. Their only solace will be that I am with them and will bring them home to Me should they fall."

He smiled.

"As for you and Tul'ran, I send you on a new mission to a planet called Wolf's Den. The bracelets have the spacetime coordinates for the Garden on Wolf's Den. You must take Ro'gun, Omarosa, Innanu and Anatu with you, for their destiny lies away from Earth. It is the reason Heather could not find them in the timeline when she returned to the future. From the moment Tul'ran became my Judge, We destined Ro'gun and his family to leave the Earth. When you arrive in the Garden on Wolf's Den, I will brief you on the mission parameters. Are you ready for the bracelets?"

After Erianne nodded, Jesus placed the bracelets on her arms, and they closed comfortably around her flesh. There was no pain and the sensation of having most of her forearm enclosed in the silver metal was soothing.

Erianne bit her lip.

"Should I feel something, Lord? Are they working? Maybe they've rejected me."

Jesus grinned and stood up.

"Gifts We give do not come with pain, Daughter. Stand up."

Erianne obediently jumped to her feet.

"Now cross your arms and put the bracelets together, right arm over left, with your left hand in a fist and your right hand pointed as you do when you seek directions. Well done. Now think of yourself back in the hutch, one second from now."

Erianne did as He asked, and a doorway appeared in front of her. The square edifice was transparent and surrounded by the strands of the blue energy she associated with Bloodwing. She stepped through the doorway and astonished everyone in the hutch by appearing in their midst out of thin air.

Tul'ran's eyebrows were dancing on his forehead as he stood up to greet her, casting his eyes over the silver bracelets on her arms.

"How now, my bride? Did your sojourn to the stables turn you into a sorcerer?"

Erianne smacked him on one oversized pectoralis muscle, further shocking Ro'gun, Omarosa, Innanu, and Anatu. She struck the Sword Himself!

"As if! Do you think it's so easy to turn my soul to evil? Such a presumption deserves harsh sanction, milord husband!"

Tul'ran relaxed and returned her grin.

"It is good to see your anger dispelled and the return of your mischievous humor. What transpired in our humble equine abode?"

Erianne raised her arms, noting that Omarosa and her family had shrunk to one side of the hutch, mouths gaping.

"I met with El Shaddai, who gave me these bracelets. They empower me to open a path to any place and any time in the universe. I can open a doorway through time and space," she finished in English.

Sully emerged from behind the curtain separating the rooms.

"Does this new ability include Atlantis?"

Erianne nodded.

"Exactly. The Lord wants us to send Hart back so Dumont can perform surgery on him. He preserved one surgical suite at the back of the TTI Main building. She can fix him, and others, there."

"What about the rest of us?" Coventry asked. "Not that I'm sure I'll fully comprehend the answer right now. I'm still a little stunned by your magic trick."

Erianne's grew warm with sympathy.

"You need to get used to it. This is how we travel from now on. The Lord is sending me and Tul'ran on our next mission to a world called Wolf's Den. He'll meet us within that planet's Garden of Eden to give us our mission brief. You, Mick, Heather, Sully, and Jeannie can come with us, stay here, or go to Atlantis."

Ro'gun had been listening intently, furrowing his eyebrows through the barrage of words in a foreign tongue. He sensed this group was about to scatter and fear met the thought. He raised his good arm and blushed as the others laughed at the way he got Erianne's attention.

"Milady Erianne, what is to become of me and my family?"

"You ride with us." She noted the look on Tul'ran's face. "On the orders of El Shaddai."

"By His command," Tul'ran murmured. "What's first, Erianne?"

"Stand Hart up. I'll open a doorway. Before we nudge him through, I'll take Caligo out of his back. Once he's through, the gateway will close."

"Whoa, whoa," Sully interrupted, spreading his

hands out in a stopping motion. "Not so fast. If you take your blade out, you could rupture his heart. He could bleed out before Payton operates on him."

"Dr. Sullivan, I don't mean to get in your face again, but Caligo is an angelic sword fashioned by God Himself. It has a power we can't let fall into Satan's hands. The sword stays with me. Sorry for putting a knife to your throat earlier. I was upset, but it's no excuse."

Sully's mouth turned up in one corner.

"Forgiven and forgotten. I would love to have had your speed on one of our Teams." He drew a long breath. "I'll go with Hart because he won't make it if we just shove him out onto the island. Jeannie, give Hart a shot of Acebutolol. It's a beta-blocker," he explained to the rest of the group. "It'll make his heart work less hard. This will lower his heart rate and blood pressure. It'll lessen the chance of ventricular wall disruption when the sword's removed. I can compress the wounds on his chest and back as you withdraw the sword. Maybe it'll help to keep him alive long enough to be operated on."

"I'm going, too!" Jeannie chimed in from behind the curtain.

"Are you two sure?" Erianne asked. "Atlantis probably lies in ruins. No one will time travel from the island for a long time, if ever. If you go back, you're stuck there until we can come for you. You're going to be smack dab in the middle of the Tribulation period and Jesus said what's happening to the Earth is going to get worse. There'll be very little food and water, and Satan will hunt Christians like the lions once did in the Roman arenas."

"If we die," Jeannie sang out, "then we go to Heaven. Payton will need my help in surgery, and Michael can assist the wounded. They need us more than you do. With your temper, we might be safer on Atlantis." She poked her head out from behind the curtain and flashed a big smile at Erianne. "Just kidding, *hermana*, no hard feelings, okay?"

Erianne grinned.

"No hard feelings and I going to get a grip on my temper. Sorry."

"Enough touchy-feely. Sully, Jeannie, you're returning to a war zone," Coventry said. "You'll need backup. If the option's open, I'll go back to Atlantis."

"What about me and Mick?" Heather asked.

"Heather, you and Mick can come with us or go with Coventry, Sully and Jeannie. The choice is yours."

Mick stirred on his stool behind the curtain. His face was bony white, and he breathed in short inhalations.

"We go with Coventry and the Sullivans. At least that's my vote. If the world is in the middle of an unholy war, my brother and his wife need us there."

Heather nodded, her face unhappy.

"I'll go wherever you go, babe. But are you fit to travel?"

"Mick's fine," Sully said. "He has three non-displaced rib fractures, and he didn't break his humerus, just cracked it. He's going to hurt, but I've taped everything up and given him painkillers. We just have to be careful how often he takes fentanyl. It's highly addictive. Wait a minute, what am I saying? We're talking about Mick Davis here. We're going to have a tough time getting him to take meds; he's paranoid about getting hooked on opioids. He's a big baby with drugs."

"I heard that," Davis said. "Don't we need to be somewhere?"

"Okay," Sully said, smiling toward his military brother's voice. "Let's get at it. I'm surprised Hart has lasted this long. We've stabilized him, but he's gonna die if we don't get him help soon."

They went into the back room, where Jeannie was holding up the semi-conscious older man. The empty Acebutolol ampoule lay on the floor beside her.

"Get him on his feet," Erianne ordered.

Sully and Jeannie pulled Hart out of his seated position, taking care to not jostle the sword piercing his body. Heather eased Davis off his stool and walked him towards Hart. She helped Davis to the front of the line, and Coventry took up a position on his right, to help support him as they transitioned.

Erianne positioned herself behind Hart, who had Sully in front of him pressing on the exit wound and Jeannie behind him, pressing on the place where Erianne's sword entered his back.

Erianne bent her head and closed her eyes, envisioning a large grassy area on the island of Atlantis which should've been the least affected by the quake.

Once she had the time and place firmly set in her mind, she crossed her arms, placing the bracelets against each other, closed her left fist and pointed the index finger of her right hand down. She loosely folded the rest of her fingers into her palm.

A large, square gate big enough to accommodate six people appeared in front of Coventry, Mick, Heather, Sully, Hart, and Jeannie, framed in blue energy. They gaped at the impossibility of the scene right in front of them, of the grassy meadow covered with debris and people running with urgency. Erianne had chosen the location well. They were standing right in front of the temporary med tent. Erianne took a firm grip on the hilt of her sword.

"Go, go, go!"

Davis, Heather, and Coventry shuffled forward as Sully and Jeannie walked Hart towards them, compressing the area of his wound while Erianne carefully withdrew Caligo from his body. A second later, the five of them stepped onto the grass of Atlantis.

In the turmoil, no one saw them arrive.

CHAPTER THE NINTH: WOLF'S DEN, THE WINTER WORLD

Mesopotamia, the tenth day of the fifth month, 2004 BC

Cold eyes watched the bustle around House az Peregos. The target was going somewhere and for an extended stay. Tul'ran az Nostrom purchased four of the strongest horses in the village, paying generously, almost double their worth sometimes. The horses were young and sturdy. A long journey with six people.

It was unfortunate the timing had been wrong the previous night, with arrival too late to mount an attack. Soon though. Soon. Tul'ran the Sword would die, and it wouldn't be far into his future.

───────────⬥───────────

The subject of the murderous thoughts was too busy to consider imminent dangers. Erianne approached Tul'ran in the stable as he secured the last of the packs on the horses. She moved in close to him, forcing herself into a tight squeeze against his chest.

"What troubles you, milord husband? I see lines on your forehead so deep I fain to wonder if I could wash clothing upon their ridges."

Her words jerked a grin from his lips.

"Erianne, joy of my heart, were your teasing ever to cease, I would know then you have fallen out of love with me. I have a sense where we go will present challenges beyond my life experience. We go to war with an injured warrior and three women untrained for combat or the battlespace. It makes me uneasy. The way you are pushing your body against mine is a further distraction, however pleasant."

Erianne giggled, which widened Tul'ran's smile.

"Is it my fault you have chiseled a body rigid with muscle and strength?" she asked, as she seductively ran a hand over his armored chest and stomach muscles. "Have I been the one leaving our bed free of a hard bounce to test its suppleness and durability? You deprive your wife at your peril, milord husband!"

His grin turned into a chuckle. He reached up to the clasp of his ebony cloak, twisted it off his body and flared the cloak onto a pile of straw lying in a corner of the stable. Tul'ran cocked his eyebrows at his wife, whose eyes widened.

"Now? Here?"

"Was I the one complaining of being deprived, my beautiful wife? Or are you afraid someone may come upon us and our cheeks will burn with shame?"

Her response was to grab his long, thick hair and

pull his face into a deep kiss. Their hands moved skillfully to remove armor and clothing with impressive speed, while their lips crushed against each other's with passion born of desire. Within a minute they had collapsed on Tul'ran's cloak, under the watchful, if somewhat bored, eyes of Darkshadow and Destiny's Edge.

Twenty minutes later, Tul'ran and Erianne walked back into the hutch, finger linked. Omarosa noticed their flushed faces, relaxed grins, and tousled hair. She smiled. It was always good to see the Lord and Lady of the House in the thrall of love. If there was peace between them, peace would also be on the House. She strolled over and casually removed a couple of pieces of straw still caught in Erianne's long black hair. Erianne compressed her lips, her eyes glittering. She opened her mouth to speak, but Omarosa cut off the speech by kissing her on the cheek.

"My heart sings with joy at the delight in your eyes, Lady Erianne. When we arrive at our destination, milady, it would please me to serve you by combing your hair back to its lustre."

Erianne mumbled a sheepish acceptance of Omarosa's offer and turned to the other women and the young warrior, still white from pain.

"Gird your hearts with courage. Where we go is far from here and unlike anything you've experienced. Be comforted by this notion: we go with God."

The remaining preparations took little time; most of which went to getting Ro'gun out of the hutch without causing him more pain.

Tul'ran moved their group into the stables at the back. Once everyone mounted their horses, Erianne moved Destiny's Edge to the front of the group. She turned to look at the somber face of her husband, sitting on Darkshadow off to her right side.

"For El Shaddai, to the end of love and life, for His glory," she whispered.

"For El Shaddai, to the end of love and life, for His glory," he murmured back.

Salutes exchanged, Erianne raised her bracelets to her lips and whispered into them. She bent her head and closed her eyes, thrusting her arms straight out and crossing them, right over left, as El Shaddai had instructed. Erianne placed the bracelets against each other, closed her left fist and pointed the index finger of her right hand down, with the rest of her fingers loosely folded in her palm. The bracelets were a little slower to respond, perhaps because of the incredible distance Erianne sought to cross in the space of one heartbeat.

The vision of a beautiful, lush garden on a world tens of thousands of light years away replaced the forest behind the stables, causing the party behind her to gasp. Without a word, Erianne nudged Destiny's Edge forward into the Garden. The rest of the group followed her, though with a little trepidation, as Tul'ran held back. He had informed the crowd of their departure and warned them against robbing the House az Peregos in their absence. The crowd had quickly dispersed.

Tul'ran scanned the area behind them for watching eyes. Seeing none, he turned Darkshadow into the Garden as the last to cross the universe into a new world.

It wasn't his fault he didn't see the eyes staring at him with murderous intent and noting, with satisfaction, that Tul'ran and his party traveled to a perfect planet for his assassination.

The hunter had already suborned the world to which they traveled. It was a death trap for the unsuspecting.

Ma'ilingan Waazh (Wolf's Den), 175th Year of Winter
Seventh day, month of Onaabani-giizis (Snowcrust Moon)
Year 5379
16,000 light years from Earth

As they rode into the Garden, a man stood before them dressed in a long, flowing robe. Tul'ran and Erianne quickly dismounted and helped Ro'gun off his horse. They lead the group forward to kneel at Jesus's feet. Erianne raised her hands, palms up.

"Greetings, Lord, Almighty God. You have called, and we have come. How may we serve You?"

Jesus gestured for them to rise.

"Greetings, all of you. Perhaps introductions are in order."

Erianne gestured Ro'gun, Omarosa, Innanu and Anatu forward.

"Lord, I present to you Ro'gun az Peregos, Bondsman az Nostrom, his bride, Innanu az Peregos, Omarosa of the Wastelands and her daughter, Anatu. Here is Jesus Christ of Nazareth, the living Son of the living God, King of Kings and Lord of Lords, Creator, Savior, and Messiah."

Overwhelmed, Ro'gun and his little family dropped to their faces in the green grass, afraid to look at the man Erianne had just proclaimed as God.

Jesus dropped into a squat and lifted their faces, one-by-one.

"I know you, children of God, for it was by My hand I created you and it is by My hand you are here now."

"Are we dead?" Omarosa asked in a timid voice. "How is it we look upon the face of God and yet our hearts beat within our chests?"

Jesus chuckled.

"No, you are not dead, child. In each world in the universe, my Father and I planted a Garden wherein we could commune, face-to-face, with Our children without causing them harm. For as long as you remain in this Garden, you are safe from all danger. You cannot grow old here, just wise. I greet you as family and friends of my servants, Tul'ran and Erianne. Be at peace. You will find nothing but love and joy in this place. Arise."

"Lord, I remember Your servant, Ro'gun to You," Tul'ran said, "wounded by slavers who would have defiled his young sister by marriage. Will you introduce him to the healing baths so he may once again attain good health?"

Jesus turned to Ro'gun and laid one hand on his shoulder.

"Of course, Ro'gun, I should have tended to you sooner. Where does it hurt?"

Ro'gun opened his mouth to reply and stopped, his eyes wide. He swayed momentarily. The young lad raised his sword arm and stared at it. He flexed his muscles and swung the arm back and forth. He couldn't bring himself to look into Jesus's eyes.

"Lord God, it astonishes me to say I am healed, by Your grace and kindness. I thank you."

Jesus stepped back and gathered them all into His gaze.

"I give all of you one more gift, one I have already given to my servants, Tul'ran and Erianne. From this day forward, you will converse in and understand any language spoken anywhere in the universe. As well, there are beasts in this world who can read your mind and overcome you with their thoughts. I give you protection against the thoughts of such beasts and shield you from them where necessary. Even with such shielding, though, they will always be able to hear your thoughts and cast theirs into your mind. Now, come with Me, for there is someone I would like you to meet."

As they walked further into the Garden, they came across a woman standing near six bundles. She had long, deep brown hair tied into braids on either side of her head, upon which sat a headdress. The headdress was shorter in the back and taller in the front, and she decorated it with multicolored beads. She had created feathers from beads on the front of the fan, five in total. At the back of the headdress was a tall white feather.

Her face was tan-colored, and she had dark eyes, high cheekbones, a narrow nose, and full, red lips. Attached to each ear was a heart-shaped, bead decorated earring. A multicolored choker resembling butterflies strung together wrapped around her delicate throat.

She covered her body in a long white buckskin dress, also decorated lavishly with multicolored beads, some in long rows. On her chest were six more feathers made of beads. All the feathers were white, with black tips. Her only makeup was a wide dab of bright yellow paint extending from the corner of each eye to her hairline.

She carried in her right hand a fan of nine white eagle feathers with black tips.

She was beautiful.

Jesus brought the two parties closer together and gestured to the brightly dressed woman.

"Here is Princess Wenonah Bearspaw; her first name means 'firstborn daughter' in her native tongue. She is the hereditary ruler of the Nine Tribes of Ma'ilingan Waazh. This world, in your tongue, is called Wolf's Den and she should be its leader. Princess Wenonah, I present to you Princess Erianne az Nostrom of Akiikaa, which is your word for 'Earth.' We called their world Earth because it is from dust We made them and to dust shall they return."

Wenonah made the bow of equals to Erianne, reached down for a hand-woven basket of fruit at her feet, and presented it to Erianne.

"Princess Erianne of Akiikaa, I greet you in the name of my people, and offer you the bounty of this world, Ma'ilingan Waazh. What I have is yours."

Erianne accepted the basket and bowed back. The Lord tickled a response into her mind.

"Princess Wenonah of Ma'ilingan Waazh, I greet you with warmth. Let there be peace between your world and mine, your house and mine, and your people and mine. We have come to your aid, to give you succour, and we seek nothing by recompense."

After the Lord prompted her mind again, Erianne said,

"I present my friends, beginning with Omarosa of the Wastelands, and her daughters Innanu and Anatu. With them is Innanu's husband, Ro'gun, Warrior. Finally, standing at my right hand is my husband, Tul'ran az Nostrom, Warrior, he who is called the Sword Himself."

Wenonah bowed to the women as Erianne introduced them and nodded politely at the men.

"Princess Erianne, you bring three Women and two Warriors. Are these all you can muster from your entire world to come to our aid? I do not wish to seem ungrateful," she added.

Erianne's voice was rich with amusement.

"Princess Wenonah, with just my husband, I cast evil out of one world and subjugated another world before turning it over to its rightful heirs. With just my husband. This group standing before you represents the mightiest army known to the universe and the Creator rides as our vanguard. We shall vanquish your foes, who will kneel before your feet and beg your mercy by the time we are done."

Wenonah's lips curved wistfully.

"Brave words well delivered. You may have met your match this time, dark Princess. We have raised warriors and fought our oppressors for longer than there have been songs to sing. They are powerful and I fear in this world, you may have finally met your match."

Tul'ran thought of saying something, then firmly

pressed his lips together. Women were clearly the leaders in this world, and speaking without being given the right would probably cause an insult. He ran the thought to Erianne's mind instead. Her face didn't so much as flicker when she heard the words of her husband echoing within her brain.

"I have no doubt our match exists," Erianne said, her voice dry, "but not here. Will you tell us what we face, so we may prepare for our enemy?"

Wenonah acknowledged Erianne's confidence with a nod.

"Over a meal, I will sing you our history. But first, take these." She distributed the bundles at her feet to the rest of the group, explaining,

"Ma'ilingan Waazh was once a paradise. For reasons I will sing tonight, it has become a Winter World. You will need this clothing and these furs to keep you warm. Without them, you would freeze to death. Do not put them on yet, for we will dine in the Garden before we go into the world to conquer or be conquered."

Spes, the world of Hope, in the Year of Our Peace 0001,
The 23rd day of the month of Tul'ran
Mission Day 178

She was floating in a warm bath, surrounded by a hazy glow of peace and comfort. There was no light by which to see, but she felt comfortable in the darkness. She could feel her heartbeat, though her lungs didn't draw air. The lack of inhalation didn't bother her; she felt nourished with calories and oxygen, and craved neither.

It was hard to describe when she became self-aware. How long she would stay this way, she didn't know. The time would come when she would leave this cozy nest, kneel before her mother, and take up the crown to become Empress of the world...

Gwynver'insa lunged awake with a gasp. Johan stirred beside her, sleepily.

"Are you well, my love?"

Gwynver'insa reached out with the same spiritual senses she used to connect with Yahweh and probed, but inwardly, not into the Heavens as she did when she wanted to converse with Him. Could it be? Surely not! The response came back like a tiny chime and a smile threatened to split her cheeks.

Johan sat up, concern replacing sleepiness on his thin face.

"Gwyn, what troubles you?"

She favored him with a dazzling smile.

"I dreamt, my Emperor, of a great mischief soon to bounce from these walls like water off a hot stone. It will be a time wherein we will crave the peace of a night's rest, like our servant Riven craves his wine at day's end."

Johan sat straighter, alarmed as Gwynver'insa took his hand.

"Then why are you smiling?"

Gwyn lifted his right arm and folded into the crook, while placing his left palm on her belly.

"My husband, we must put out a call to our brother and sister, the Prince and Princess of Death. They must come to our aid, for I fear what comes next may tax even their awe-inspiring abilities."

"Gwyn, you're scaring me. What's coming?"

The Empress Gwynver'insa giggled and pressed his hand a little tighter to her stomach.

"Emperor Johan, meet your daughter and heir to our throne, the Princess Mesmer'insa."

Ma'ilingan Waazh (Wolf's Den), 175th Year of Winter Seventh day, in the month of Onaabani-giizis, year 5379

The meal was lavish and delicious. The main protein was a large haunch of bison, simmered in the ground an entire day. They could pull the meat off in handfuls; it was so tender. Legumes and vegetables of many varieties accompanied the protein, all of which were flavored with spices none of them had tasted before.

After the meal, Wenonah arranged them in a semi-circle and produced a small drum covered in hide.

"I will now sing to you the history of my world."

She beat on the drum with a stick covered at the end by a ball made of skin. In a high keening voice, she sang, and all became still in the Garden. Though she sang Ma'ilingan Waazh's history in her language, the rest of the group heard the lyrics, each in their own tongue.

"In the beginning, all was in darkness, and great was the darkness. The Creator put lights in the skies to illuminate the darkness. Under the lights, He created the World. After he created the World, He put on it the Forest, which covered the surface of the World, with many lakes and rivers."

"The Creator put fish in the lakes and rivers, and seeded the Forest with animals of every kind. When

He finished, the Creator was pleased, but troubled. The World needed more, a People to watch over the Forest and keep the World a place of comfort and peace for all living things."

"The Creator made the Woman and the Man, giving them charge of the World and all life within it. As a gift to the Woman and the Man, the Creator offered them the choice of a spirit guide. The Woman chose the Mountain Lion, and the Man chose the Wolf. The Creator gave the Mountain Lion and the Wolf the intelligence of the Woman and the Man. He made it so they could talk to the minds of their spirit guides. For many years, the Woman and the Man and their spirit guides lived in tranquility."

"One day a group of Men, who had long admired the lights in the sky, decided they would travel beyond the World to see what the Creator had made in the sky. The Creator forbade it, saying a layer of ice covered the World and protected it from damaging cosmic rays and solar energy. Travel beyond the ablative shield couldn't be possible without damaging the ice layer."

"The Men wouldn't listen to the Creator, and persisted in their ways. They created an exo-atmospheric vessel, which they designed to melt a hole in the ice layer to accommodate the width of the vessel. They discovered the energy output required to do such a thing was enormous, and so was the size of the vessel when they finished their design."

"The Women protested the actions of the Men and demanded they stop their work. The Men would not listen to the wisdom of the Women, and soon other Men spoke up to protect the disobedient scientists. Over time, the argument between Women and Men spread to every home in the World."

"Then came The Day. The Men launched their vessel. As it approached the upper atmosphere, the machines on the nose of the vessel melted a hole in the ice, as planned, in the width required to allow the passage of the vessel. In doing so, one engine propelling the vessel failed, creating an imbalance in the thrust. The vessel veered off course and hurtled into the ablative shield."

"The ice layer, already weakened by creating the hole, fractured at the collision site. We watched for days, waiting for the shield to fall. It did not fall immediately but splintered throughout the atmosphere."

"When we knew the ablative shield was going to crumble, accusations and recriminations flew like arrows between Women and Men. The Men withdrew from us, moving to the southern regions of the Land, vowing to not return until the Women acknowledged their need for Men. The Women went to work to create a subterranean city to preserve our kind when the ice layer fell."

"Women discovered underground lakes and fertile soil for planting. We created an artificial sun using nuclear fusion, all in readiness for the fall of the ice layer."

"Fall, it did. Fifty years after the vessel's collision with the ice layer, it crashed to the surface, damaging the ecosystem, turning the world to ice and snow, and creating the Long Winter. The World of Endless Summer became the World of Frozen Death."

"The Women survived within their subterranean

city, not knowing or caring whether Men made it through the frozen ordeal. Until it became obvious without the seed of Men, the People could not continue."

"We sent warrior scouts into the world until we found the place where men dwelt in above-ground fortresses. The reunion was not joyful. It was then the raids begun; Men raided our caverns, and we raided their fortresses. The war of words moved into a war of bodies, stealing who we could so we might create more children. We've lost many lives."

At another mental nudge from her husband, Erianne asked Wenonah,

"How many Women died in violent struggles with Men?"

"Died?" Wenonah's eyes grew wide. "No Women died at the hands of Men. The People don't kill each other, Princess Erianne. Why would they do so? Such conduct would be beyond barbaric."

Erianne's forehead creased.

"Forgive me, Princess Wenonah, but did you not just sing that many have lost their lives? I'm confused."

Wenonah half-nodded, her face still reflecting shock and a modicum of offense.

"Yes, but not at the hands of Men. Our Mountain Lions became the defenders of our territories and our sentries, as the Wolves did for the Men. Our sentries have taken lives. Men and Women died at the hands of the Lions and Wolves, but never at the hands of a human being. Such violence against the person would offend even the smallest of our traditions." Wenonah shuddered. "To even contemplate such a thing churns my stomach with disgust."

"So, by lives lost, you meant those who have succumbed to fang and claw."

Wenonah nodded, her headdress dancing.

"Yes, but we also consider lost the Women whom the Men took. As early as five years ago, we conducted the last raid to recover our Women and seize some Men. To our shock, a stable plasma fence now runs the entire length of our southernmost border. The Men created it to keep us out, and it works very well. It traverses the entire width of the world and is too high to cross with aircraft. We have no communication with the Men. Unless we find a solution to this stalemate, the People can no longer procreate, and we will die."

"To add to our troubles, we are running out of raw materials to heat and light our cities, as well as food. The Wolves and Lions have consumed most of the surviving wildlife and they left us with artificially created meat for our tables. When we venture out to gather, the Wolves attack us and our Lions, killing Women and Lions alike wherever they can."

Omarosa spoke into the ensuing silence, after nervously clearing her throat.

"Princess Wenonah, what efforts have you made to parlay and strive for a peaceful resolution between Men and Women?"

Sadness flitted across Wenonah's face.

"My mother forbids it," she replied, her voice soft and uncertain. "While the right to rule the People vests in me, she will not abdicate because she fears I will make a treaty for peace. She has suffered too long at the hands of Men to allow them to have their way and take anything from us."

Tul'ran's eyes rose to the top of his forehead.

"So, out of pride, your mother would see the People end their lives?"

Wenonah glared at him.

"Be silent, Warrior! You do not speak in conference unless spoken to!"

She shrank back when lightning flashed in his eyes.

"Forgive me, Tul'ran. I forget you are not of our culture and do not know our ways. For a Man to offer an unsolicited opinion is a grave insult."

Tul'ran turned his gaze away from her without offering a reply and let it fall on Jesus.

"I am confused, El Shaddai. Under your hand, I have become the most powerful fighter in all the known worlds. Of what use will I be on this one? There is no war to end by force of arms, no evil to kill and send into the afterlife. I see no need for the Prince of Death in Ma'ilingan Waazh, particularly if I am to be silenced when I open my mouth to offer advice. Surely, Lord, there is another world in greater need of my services!"

Jesus cocked an eyebrow, in Tul'ran's style.

"You judge this world too quickly, Tul'ran. How many times has your wife counseled you to diplomacy instead of uttered threats and mighty feats of arms? The war is real, and people are dying. Princess Wenonah is right. The people have ended their ability to procreate by separating themselves. Within one hundred years, humans will cease to exist on Ma'ilingan Waazh."

"The war must end. Pride is the enemy, and you cannot kill it with a swing of the sword. You must learn diplomacy, My son. Learn it well, for you will need both your arm and your tongue in the next world to which We send you. Its situation is much graver."

Tul'ran shifted uncomfortably. He was not used to sitting with his legs crossed for any length of time.

"By your command, El Shaddai, it will be done, though I hope I will find some use for my sword before Bloodwing becomes bored."

Wenonah stiffened.

"Tul'ran Warrior, I cannot permit you to carry a sword when you leave this place and enter our city. It is unlawful for Men to carry weapons within the City of Ikwe Na. You will offend our customs and laws if you do so."

Erianne laid a restraining arm on Tul'ran's shoulder and winced at the thoughts raging in his mind.

"Peace, milord husband. Princess Wenonah, my husband does not merely carry a blade. El Shaddai bonded Bloodwing, his sword, to his soul. He can no more travel without it than he could live without his heart."

Wenonah's face set into a stubborn line.

"Bonded or not, he may not set foot in our lands carrying a weapon. I must honor our laws if I am to rule the People one day."

Erianne dropped her head and thought for a moment.

"Will this work?" she asked when she lifted her

head again. "I will carry Bloodwing and stay at my husband's side every moment we are on your land. I will give Caligo to Omarosa, who will also walk with me. Ro'gun will give his blade to Innanu, and they shall not move unless in a pair. Anatu will remain unarmed. By this we would honour your customs by keeping our Men from carrying their weapons."

Wenonah tossed her head, her braids flipping from side to side.

"You may not be with your husbands during mealtimes and ceremonies. Our ways forbid Men to eat with Women because they are of a lower social caste."

Erianne's face tightened, and she leveraged herself to her feet.

"Then I regret to inform you, Princess Wenonah, we cannot help you. While I will accord respect and honor to your laws, you can hobble me only so much. My husband and I are equals in all things. I would not impose our customs on you, but I cannot and will not deprive Tul'ran of his sword by permitting you to separate us. Since you cannot make accommodation; we will withdraw our offer of help and leave."

Tul'ran stood and flexed his back as the others rose to their feet.

"Tell me, El Shaddai, what is the next world requiring both sword and tongue to right wrongs and avenge injustice?"

"Wait!" Wenonah said, a hint of desperation clinging to her words. "Don't go! I can't do this on my own." Tears formed in her eyes. "My mother will not face a future I see only too well. I don't want my people to die. Please, stay. I'll see what I can do to accommodate your special situation without offending our laws."

Wenonah paused before looking up into Erianne's face.

"Do your husbands oppose covering their faces and bodies entirely while with you at ceremonies and meals? In doing so, they may not offend other Women, especially if I explain you are from the stars and your customs differ from ours."

Erianne turned to face Tul'ran and again marveled at looking up into his eyes.

"Milord husband, can you contain your pride well enough to do these things? I hear the turmoil in your mind. El Shaddai brought us here to help His children in this world. Before I commit us, Tul'ran, I need to know. Can you do this?"

He cast a glance over Erianne's shoulder at Wenonah and turned his gaze back into her brilliant green eyes.

"When have I ever been able to resist you, milady wife?" he asked in a gruff tone. "If I must walk around in a sack to help you fulfill El Shaddai's will for this place, then so be it. I can swallow my hubris long enough to accomplish this task."

Erianne kissed him, enjoying the pleasure of his lips, before turning around. Wenonah's eyes were enormous, and she had pressed a fist to her mouth to cover a gasp.

"You must," her voice faltered. "You must never kiss your husband in public, Princess Erianne. To do so violates one of the most sacred of our customs, which forbid public displays of affection."

Erianne sketched a half bow in Wenonah's direction.

"Fear not, Princess Wenonah. We shall abide by all your customs, including the ones prohibiting public displays of affection."

"This planet is slowly turning into the Abyss," Tul'ran grumbled in English to no one in particular.

Fate smiled sadly.

Tul'ran had spoken the truth, but for all the wrong reasons.

He had forgotten only the dead live in the Abyss.

CHAPTER THE TENTH:
THE BEAST WITH
TWO HORNS

Atlantis, May 30, 2099 AD

Payton Dumont stepped out of the med tent, rubbing grains of exhaustion out of her eyes, then stopped, her jaw dropping. For a moment, the world stood still as fragments of reality interposed with a scene from a disaster-themed holo pic. The six individuals standing in front of her couldn't possibly be there, but were, and how in the…?

"Payton!" Sully said, his voice laced with a snarl. "Snap out of it. Hart has exit and entry wounds on his back and chest. He needs surgery. Stat!"

The words jolted her to her senses, and she was with Hart in three long strides.

"What caused the wounds?" she asked, running her hands over the older man's back and chest wall.

"Long sword," Jeannie said, "through and through. No vital organs punctured, but the sword's edge compromised the epicardium of the heart. He needs surgery yesterday."

Payton jerked her head back.

"Not on this island. The earthquake destroyed the TTI Main Building, and he'll die before we get an airlift in here."

Sully side glanced at Davis, who only tugged up an eyebrow in response.

"We have it on good authority that Operating Theater One on the far side of the building survived. We need to get him there and you need to get to work."

It was Payton's turn to lift an eyebrow.

"On good authority? Whose authority would this be?"

"Not now," Davis said, gritting his teeth. "He needs surgery, Dr. Dumont, and I need to get my ribs taped up. Can we defer the explanations for after we save Hart's life?"

Payton glared at him, then turned to wave down two men pushing a handcart laden with boxes.

"Gus, Darren. Bring the handcart here. We're going to shuffle Hart onto the footpad of the cart. Careful, he's bleeding internally. Gently. Good. Okay, people, lean him back. Easy. Easy. I'm glad you have your medkit, Dr. Sullivan. It's the most sophisticated tech we have left. Let's roll him to the back of the TTI Main Building, double time. Gus, if you're going to just stand there looking stupid, get your hands off the cart. Let's go people!"

Darren pushed the cart, while Payton, Sully and Jeannie took up positions around Hart, trying to keep him stable as the two-wheeled loader rattled around the debris-laden path. Wu and Coventry took hold of Davis's elbows and shuffled him into the med tent. As they moved through the door, they almost bowled over Marjatta Korhonen.

"What?! Where did you come from?"

"Mesopotamia, Administrator," Heather said, guiding a white-faced Davis to an empty cot. "It's a long story with no straightforward answers, so can we table the discussion for now? We have wounded."

Marjatta's eyes flitted between Heather's worried face, Coventry's stoic expression, and Davis's barely conscious daze.

"Where's Hart and the Sullivans?"

Coventry gestured toward the Main Building.

"Dr. Dumont and Dr. Sullivan are wheeling Mr. Hart to Operating Theater One. Apparently, it's still intact. Hart took a sword to the back, and it exited out of his chest. We kept him alive until something pulled us back here."

"Pulled you back here how?" Concern and misunderstanding stressed Marjatta's face into a confusion of lines.

"I think it was an aftereffect of the seismic wave," Heather said. "The earthquake's shockwave translated into Antiquity. When the wave fully expanded, quantum gravity sucked it back into Origin time and space. We were in Antiquity for a couple of days while the quantum stream sorted itself out. Then the reflex wave snatched us up and sucked us back here. We were lucky."

Marjatta stared at the short Asian woman, whose face remained inscrutable through the explanation. She nodded jerkily.

"Lucky. Okay. We'll talk more later. Get a tech to see to your injuries, Davis. I'm going to check on Hart."

After Marjatta ran out of the tent, Coventry heaved a sigh.

"That's a relief! I thought she was going to interrogate us until chow time. I'm glad quantum physics backed us up with the reflex wave thing."

Heather Wu grinned.

"It would've had it been true."

Coventry goggled at her.

"You made it up?"

Heather sat down beside Davis and scanned the med tent for anything helpful.

"Had no choice. The earthquake has clearly dazed Korhonen; she wouldn't have bought it any other time. It's the story we stick with because no one will believe the real one."

Davis chuckled, then gasped as pain stabbed throughout his chest. The world went dark.

G'shnet'el's spectral form hovered over the man lying still on the military cot in the massive tent. As a powerful angel, he could exercise enough will to keep his spectral form intact. It came at a cost to his angelic energy, which he couldn't renew without access to the spiritual waters of Heaven.

He no longer had entry to God's Throne Room, and was stuck in a pure energy state until God reformed him into a physical body. He blamed the man lying on the cot in front of him for his predicament, and a rage simmered in the core of his form.

"G'shnet'el, why are you mooning over me like some lovesick puppy?"

G'shnet'el warped his spectral self to emulate a kneeling position before the cot, as Satan rolled over to glare at him. He had found his Master in a makeshift tabernacle in Rome, hoping for a solution to his dissolution. Now he wondered if the decision had been a wise one.

"Master, I have failed you. I come before you in humble supplication to beg your forgiveness and seek your aid."

"Since when have you known me to be the forgiving type?" Satan said with a contemptuous smile. "You have failed me, G'shnet'el, which is obvious by your lack of a physical body. You're fortunate I can no longer punish you corporally."

G'shnet'el suppressed a mental shudder. He had seen the Beast at work too many times to wonder at how he would suffer his punishment.

"I would submit to the punishment eagerly, Master, but for the urgency of my report for you."

Satan pretended to yawn. He hadn't been sleeping; he didn't need to lose consciousness to refresh his body and spirit. The pretense was necessary for his acolytes.

"You bore me, G'shnet'el. Go haunt the universe. I wonder how long it'll take before simply maintaining consciousness will be an agony for you?"

G'shnet'el moaned and pressed his non-existent forehead to the floor.

"Master, do not spurn my report so quickly. I assure you; it is of foremost importance."

"Fine," the Evil One said, lowering his interest to indifference, "make it and get out."

"I did as you asked, O Great and Powerful god. After traveling into Antiquity, I kidnapped a young girl and held her hostage for information on the whereabouts of Tul'ran az Nostrom. It was my intention to kill Tul'ran and viciously ravage the girl, but he thwarted me before achieving both aims."

Satan raised himself on his right elbow.

"Thwarted? You? How does a stupid human thwart the Gatekeeper of the Abyss?"

Pressing his forehead to the floor enabled G'shnet'el to grin maliciously without it being noticed.

"No one informed me, Master, that Tul'ran the Sword carries Bloodwing the Blade."

Satan jolted upright.

"What?!" he said, shrieking. "A puny man carries my sword? Are you sure?"

It took everything G'shnet'el had to stifle a chuckle.

"Yes, Dread Lord. Of even greater consternation was my discovery of the fullest extent of the powers of Bloodwing; it is the Sword of Uncreation."

Satan screamed as he leaped to his feet, seized the blanket-covered metal cot, and ripped it into two pieces. "No! I held the Sword of Uncreation in my hands all the time I worshipped our Enemy? Of all the stupid luck!"

Satan hurled the cot pieces against the side of the tabernacle and rounded on G'shnet'el.

"Why didn't you tell me this, G'shnet'el, you traitorous little weasel?!"

Fear trilled through the kneeling specter's core.

"I knew it not, Fearsome Master, until Tul'ran threatened to uncreate me with it. Against such an intimidation and my urgent desire to share this knowledge with you, I gave up the girl. The malicious knave ran me through with Bloodwing, dissolving my physical form. I came as quickly as I could to deliver this news to you. I swear it."

Satan raged around the tabernacle, kicking over benches and tables, as he uttered curses against God. The large tent was where his followers could temporarily muster while they cleaned up the corpses in the Temple. Satan had cremated them on the previous day by drawing on their life force to feed the power he needed to keep the Temple together.

When his anger abated to a small degree, he walked back to G'shnet'el and kicked at the specter, scattering energy particles but having no other effect. Maybe being a spirit wasn't so bad after all, G'shnet'el thought, coalescing himself back in his subservient position.

"Where did he go, G'shnet'el?"

Oh oh.

"I do not know, Master, for after Tul'ran placed me into an energy state, he slashed Bloodwing through me, dispersing my essence. By the time I gathered myself, he and everyone with him were gone."

Satan flew into another rage, smashing every piece of furniture around which he could wrap his hands. After what seemed like hours, he calmed himself down again.

"Master," a voice squeaked from outside the tent, "is all well with you."

Satan glared at G'shnet'el.

"Hide." To the doorway: "Enter."

G'shnet'el faded into Inter-Dimensional Space and watched as an acolyte crawled into the tent on hands and knees, surreptitiously glancing at the damage in the tabernacle.

"What has happened, Master? Has someone attacked you?"

"Yes," Satan lied smoothly. "Several men thought to end my life in my sleep. Little did they know the power they faced. I disintegrated them, but they caused damage trying to flee from me."

"Master, forgive us, your servants, for failing to protect you well. I will have the head of security tortured at once."

Satan raised his hand.

"Unnecessary. The assailants are gone and will never return. Rouse the Chief Priest and direct him to come to me."

As the acolyte scurried to carry out the order, Satan sat himself upon the large throne at the front of the tent, tapping his fingernails against one armrest. Every passing second increased his impatience by another degree. Finally, the Chief Priest staggered in, trying to arrange his vestments and the overabundance of religious jewelry on his body. Satan rolled his eyes.

"Was it necessary, Killian, to put on the robes of your office? Did I not make it clear I wanted you here immediately?"

Killian Hunter fell and prostrated himself before the throne, his insides quailing.

"O my god, forgive me, for I didn't perceive the need for haste above propriety. I will punish your acolyte accordingly."

"Hmph. Leave her punishment to me. I need you to do something for me, Killian. It is of the highest importance to me and my kingdom. You will have to sacrifice a little, but it will come as an honor to you."

———————◆———————

Killian Hunter trembled as horrific images leaped into his mind as to the form his 'sacrifice' would take. He had been a 19-year-old used car salesman from Des Moines before the First Cataclysm struck. The ease with which Malchus Contradeum set about bringing peace to the world impressed him in the years following the First Cataclysm.

Killian created a blog and a podcast trumpeting Contradeum's every achievement, including the most minor events. A member of Contradeum's inner circle contacted him and asked him if he would become part of the rising star's press corps. The short, overweight man leaped at the chance and began churning out news items (read, 'propaganda') for Contradeum like it was pulp fiction.

The various major established religions were among Killian's favorite targets for his rancor. Especially Christianity.

Growing up in a culture rejecting non-inclusion, he hated the ideals of the Christian church, citing them as the source of generational hate. The Second Cataclysm mysteriously turned the Christian church to dust, which delighted Hunter. It stunned him when the delusional Christian movement sprouted up like mushrooms again once the world anointed Malchus Contradeum as their President. Thanks to the two witnesses in Jerusalem, multitudes of people were professing their faith in Christ in a global revival, which angered him. Especially given his position as the head of the opposing pagan religion.

When Contradeum assumed leadership of the world, the new government needed a global religion. To Killian's shock and genuine pleasure, Contradeum tapped him to become the Chief Priest of Worship of the Mother Goddess, Earth.

Killian reveled in his new role, creating a creed for the new faith by incorporating the things he considered good in other religions while discarding the bad. Once Contradeum banned Christianity, making it possible for citizens to capture, torture and kill Christians, new members flooded into the Worship of the Mother Goddess. Like Contradeum, Killian became a star.

"As you know, Master, you created me from dirt. I will do anything you ask."

Satan squatted in front of him.

"Anything?"

Killian swallowed hard and barely nodded.

"Anything," he said in a hoarse whisper.

"Killian Hunter, will you permit one of my most prominent and sophisticated angels to inhabit your body with you, to increase your power and your ability to enlarge my global worship?"

Relief flooded through Killian's body. He had imagined something much, much worse. He had yet to experience the true flavor of what he could characterize as 'much, much worse.'

"With joy, Master, will I receive your angel into me."

"G'shnet'el."

G'shnet'el had keenly watched the interplay between Satan and Hunter. Something akin to joy raced through him when he realized what the Evil One intended to do. After Satan called on him, G'shnet'el poured as much energy as he could spare into his spectral form. It was an extravagant waste of resources, but it allowed him to appear as an angel of Light, instead of Darkness.

"My Master, you called?"

Satan gestured to Hunter, who was staring at G'shnet'el with enormous eyes and a wide-open mouth.

"Killian Hunter, will you voluntarily open your body, heart, mind, and soul to the entry of my servant, G'shnet'el, to inhabit you for the length of my pleasure?"

Hunter swallowed.

"Yes, yes, of course. It would be my delight to host this beautiful angel!"

"Open your mouth."

After Hunter obediently complied, G'shnet'el gleefully poured his essence into the human body. It took only a few minutes to push the mind and soul of what used to be Killian Hunter into a tiny, dark prison, which would house him until the end of days. Hunter would spend the rest of his life gibbering in the darkness while slowly losing his sanity. It was just so sweet.

G'shnet'el stood up and looked at his new body in the full-length mirror.

"This body is short and fat," he said with disgust. "At least he's not bad looking. I can work with this. A little weight loss, some hair plugs, and I'll be a walking dreamboat."

Satan rolled his eyes.

"Get rid of the vestments, dreamboat. Exchange them for a black frock and the collar for a pair of tabs on each side. The tabs should be in the form of crossed French horns, for you will trumpet my glory to the entire world and bring them all into worship of me."

G'shnet'el twisted his hips forward and regarded the reflection in the mirror. He had become the Beast with Two Horns prophesied in the Revelation to John. His time in the Abyss was done.

He was now the False Prophet.

Atlantis, May 30, 2099 AD, Operating Theater One

"Scalpel."

Jeannie pressed the surgical instrument into Payton's hand firmly and at the correct angle. Payton glanced up at her, blue eyes twinkling over the surgical mask.

"Good job. You've done this before."

Jeannie's mask lifted at the edges.

"Twenty-one years as a trauma nurse."

Payton pressed the scalpel into Hart's chest.

"It shows. Dr. Sullivan, I am debriding the chest wound and enlarging it slightly to permit me to insert the surgical suite. Jeannie, gloves please."

Payton threw the scalpel into a nearby tray and raised her hands. Jeannie pulled the surgical suite controller gloves onto Payton's hands and carefully adjusted them to a snug fit.

"VR glasses."

Jeannie placed the VR glasses on Payton's face and made sure they didn't trap her hair or otherwise create a gap.

"How close am I to the patient?"

"You should take one step back, Dr. Dumont."

Payton took a step back and placed her hands in a ready position, three feet away from Hart's body.

"Both of you should call me Payton. Dr. Sullivan, please activate the surgical suite."

Sully entered commands into the hovering holo screens and checked to make sure all systems were in the green.

"I'm Sully to my friends, Payton. All systems are nominal."

Payton took a deep breath and let it out slowly.

"That, my friends, is a miracle considering how much damage this building took. Okay, Sully, feed the surgical suite tube into Mr. Hart's chest."

Sully gently picked up the long, gray, metallic tube and centered the point over the enlarged incision site.

"I haven't worked with this stuff before. What does it do?"

Payton began moving her fingers, and the tube started feeding itself into the wound.

"The object we're inserting into Hart's chest looks like a tube, but it's not. The surgical suite is a collection of nanobots programmed to maintain a certain configuration by default. It appears as a metallic tube, while it's neither. Observe."

Payton made a gesture directing the tip of the tube to transmit data, and the Operating Theater's computer projected a view of the inside of Hart's chest cavity on a large holo screen above his head. The Sullivans watched, fascinated, as the tube worked its way through Hart's chest to his heart. They could see the tiny laceration on the epicardium, which exuded droplets of blood with each beat.

"As you can see, the walls of the right atrium are severely strained near the laceration site. If his blood pressure goes up, or his heart rate increases dramatically, it will probably burst the laceration site."

Payton gestured with her fingers and the tip split into three pieces. One piece broke away and provided holo coverage of the procedure. Another strand moved to the laceration and split into multiple arms. The arms pressed on either side of the cut and drew the two sides together.

"I'm going to suture the laceration with a monofilament material, in this case, 2-0 polypropylene. I'm going to use simple or horizontal mattress interrupted sutures with an MH-tapered 3/8 circumference needle."

The nanobots in the surgical suite drew the sutures from the central machine and into Hart's body through the hollow configuration of the tube. Another portion of the surgical suite broke off and transformed into the needle configuration Payton had selected. Manipulating strands of the surgical suite, she deftly threaded the needle and brought it closer to the laceration. Her voice became dreamier when her concentration intensified.

"Running horizontal mattress stitches is appropriate for thin atrial walls, which require a technique spreading tension along the entire wound edge."

Payton deftly threaded the needle through the atrial wall until the result satisfied her. She pulled back the visual field and sent Hart's stats to her VR glasses.

"Okay, he's stable. We'll slowly start closing his chest wound on the way out. When we're done, we'll roll him over and stitch up the entrance wound. He's going to be on his feet in no time."

Jeannie directed a glance at Sully and shook her head.

"Payton, if you told me this was possible without cracking his chest, I would've said no way. Is he really going to be okay?"

Payton's forehead crinkled above the VR glasses.

"He was okay the second when we plugged him into the Operational Theater. The surgical AI started IV fluids, blood transfusions, and medication the moment it diagnosed his condition. The only thing the AI can't do is stitch the wound. He's going to be fine. So, what's your story, Jeannie?"

The abrupt change of subject threw Jeannie off stride.

"Um, what?"

Payton laughed behind her surgical mask.

"We're still going to be here for a while, suturing our way out of this body. I know a bit about your husband because I researched him on the central info hub when he arrived. What's your story?"

Jeannie stepped away from the table and cast a long glance over the holos scattered throughout the room.

"Hart's vitals look good, so I guess I can bore you with my life without making you kill your patient. I was born in 2052 in the Barrio Logan in San Diego. My parents were illegals, although the government granted them amnesty and citizenship after the First Cataclysm. After I graduated High School in 2070, they awarded me a full scholarship for a Direct-Entry Bachelor of Science Nursing Program with San Diego State University."

Payton glanced up toward Jeannie's voice.

"No kidding? Your grades must have been in the stratosphere. Quite the achievement, Jeannie."

Jeannie blushed at the compliment and continued her narrative.

"Thanks, Payton. I graduated with a BSN in 2074 and took a shot at Medical School. The University of California San Diego School of Medicine accepted me and I started in September 2075."

"That's where we met," Sully said, while applying suction to Hart's chest wound. "I graduated High School in 2072 and got my B.Sc. from UC San Diego in 2075. I went straight into medicine the following September."

Payton grunted as she started suturing the upper layers of tissue near the exit wound.

"Both of you are over-achievers. How come I'm not calling you Dr. Sullivan as well, Jeannie?"

"I didn't have a full scholarship to med school. My parents did okay financially, but even with student loans, I couldn't afford it. I dropped out after three years and went to work as a trauma nurse at UC San Diego Health, La Jolla Hospital in 2078."

Payton's eyebrows rose, although the other two couldn't see them through the VR glasses.

"Impressive. It was only the best trauma center in California then. Did you two keep dating after you left med school?"

Jeannie bit her lip and dropped her head.

"No. I broke it off because Michael joined the Navy right after he graduated with an MD. After Officer Candidate School, he took a residency in Emergency Medicine at the Emergency Medicine Naval Medical Center in New San Diego. I never wanted to be a military wife. I loved my home, and I didn't want to be dragged around the world."

"Until I broke my back after six years on various SEAL Teams," Sully said, adjusting the holo displays to show a deep scan of Hart's vitals. "I went through BUD/S with Davis. We were in a High Altitude/Low Opening training exercise in March 2090. My chute didn't fully deploy, and I hit the ocean hard. Broke my back in three places. They Air Evac'd me to La Jolla Hospital."

Jeannie started collecting the trays containing contaminated instruments.

"We had the best spinal injury trauma team in San Diego. They just received human trials approval from the FDA for a gene treatment for fractured vertebrae. Michael signed up for the trials because he wanted to stay on the Teams. The gene treatment encouraged his body to re-fuse the broken vertebrae by growing new bone and marrow to fill in the fracture sites. He was lucky the fracture hadn't compromised his spinal cord. He made a complete recovery."

Sully snorted.

"Not that the Navy cared. I spent three months on my back at La Jolla waiting for the therapy and for my bones to knit back up. When I got out, after three more months of rehab, I passed every physical test they threw at me. Wasn't good enough for NavSpecWar. They honorably discharged me in 2094 after ten years in the Navy. I retired with the rank of Lieutenant Commander, but I could've gone a long way."

"Well, good things came out of it," Jeannie said. "For those three months he spent on his back, I was Michael's primary source of entertainment. I saw the writing on the wall for his career and pursued a relationship with him. We were married on June 5, 2094, right after the military discharged him."

Payton closed the chest wound and removed the VR glasses.

"Let's roll him over and sew up his back. Any internal bleeding, Dr. Sullivan?"

"Sully," he reminded her. "All internal scans look good. There's nothing in there that won't get absorbed. It's almost as if the sword cauterized the wound on the way in and through the body, except for the laceration of the epicardium. It's cleaner than I expected."

Together, they rolled Hart onto his stomach and propped him up to reduce stresses to his limbs and spine. Payton put the VR glasses on her face and inserted a fresh nanotube surgical suite.

"You're right, it's uncanny. Most of the internal cuts have sealed off, including the lungs. Interesting. I'll start closing. How come you limp, Jeannie?"

Jeannie paused.

"I wish I could tell you this amazing story about how I got hurt in a parachuting accident, but mine is more blasé. I helped some paramedics carry an empty gurney down a flight of stairs and tripped. The gurney landed on me, crushing my pelvis. It's why Sully and I couldn't have kids. Well, that and I'm now 46, which makes me less happy about having kids."

Payton jerked her head up.

"Whoa, so doing the math, you're eight years older than Sully?"

Jeannie flushed again.

"Yeah, that's me. I'm a cougar."

Payton laughed.

"Good on you, girlfriend. All right, doctors, I think we've done all we can for Mr. Hart. He will live to tell the tale of how someone shoved a sword in his back four thousand years ago and he survived."

Jeannie directed a look into Sully's eyes and wondered how Payton would feel if she knew the reason Hart took a sword in his back was because he tried to kill someone from Antiquity with a gun.

It was like she was reading Payton's mind. Marjatta Korhonen watched the surgery from the observation area, complimenting herself for hiring such skilled professionals. Her memory was coming back in pieces, and she shuddered at her last instructions to Hart.

She had ordered him to go into the past and kill a historical figure. Marjatta didn't want to know if he had succeeded; she really hoped he hadn't. She spent her career protecting the sanctity of the timeline, and then casually ordered someone to disrupt it by murdering someone.

What had she become?

When Davis woke up, the med tent was dimly lit with plasma lanterns strung up haphazardly in the top bar of the frame. It was dark outside. A memory stirred.

It was a dark and stormy night.

He looked around at the bodies in the cots, unconscious or sleeping. When he didn't see anyone stirring, he removed the sensory patches connecting him to the Medical AI.

Clutching his chest against a stab of pain, he leveraged himself off the cot. He had to find Heather Wu. She was his only way off the island. If he could get her to break into the TTI Main Building, steal a Coin and get her to program it, he could pursue his plan to save Kelci's life.

Davis staggered to the front of the tent, folded back the front cover, and glanced outside. No sentries; relief washed over him. He wasn't sure if he was in any shape to take down a sentry.

In full stealth mode, Davis slipped into the night. He didn't notice the debris littering the ground, except to stagger around it, and never questioned why everything was in shambles. He eventually made his way to the western edge of the island. Something had ripped massive gaps in both fences. They were so damaged, there was no way they were carrying electricity. He could escape and come back for Wu when he recovered.

Davis carefully worked his way around the spike belts and gaps in the two fences until he was standing at the cliff edge. Two hundred feet down, waves crashed on the island's rock walls. This was going to be tricky. He knew there were rungs imbedded somewhere on the island's sides to allow the residents a last resort escape route. TTI classified the location of the rungs, but he had been on a training exercise and knew they existed. If only he could remember where they were.

"Hey, Mick, where ya goin'?"

Davis spun around and stifled an agonized cry as pain seared his chest. A woman stood twenty feet away from him, her arms hanging loosely at her sides and her hands empty. It was too dark to make out her features, although her body seemed to glow enough to light the path at her feet. Davis shook his head. Bodies didn't glow. Maybe she had chem sticks under her clothes.

"Don't try to stop me. I've got to get off this island. My mission." He stopped. What was his mission again? It was something important. Or was it? Hadn't he done something already to complete the mission? He pressed his palms against the side of his temples. Why did it hurt so much to think?

"Mick, you're suffering from a dissociative memory schism caused by bouncing around the timeline and the pharmaceuticals they gave you for pain. You're going to recover; you just need to get some sleep. The ocean isn't your way out. Let me help you back to the med tent."

Davis took a half step backward.

"I'm not going anywhere with you. I don't know you. You could be Security trying to take me in. I can't trust you."

The woman took two steps backward, away from him.

"I'm not here to hurt you, Mick, or take you in. I shouldn't be here, but God loves both of us too much to keep me away from you when you're standing on a cliff whacked out of your mind."

Something was pressing on Davis's brain; it was a recollection of someone who matched the height and voice of this woman. It was so hard to think. Why couldn't he think?

Then the memory flashed into his brain, but it couldn't be. The person he was thinking of was dead; she couldn't be here. Could she?

Davis took in a ragged breath, wincing against the pain in his chest and the pounding in his temples. He could feel the edges of his vision pressing towards the center and panicked. He couldn't pass out again. Not here. Not now. He needed help. What was it he just remembered?

Davis glanced up sharply, trying to pierce the dimness of the night with eyes slowly absorbing the darkness of unconsciousness.

"Darian?"

CHAPTER THE ELEVENTH: STARWALKER

Atlantis, June 1, 2099, just after noon

When Davis woke up, the med tent was brightly lit, with sunshine making the canvas glow and infusing the interior of the tent with orange yellow radiance. He felt excruciatingly cold; he was shivering so hard his teeth rattled together. Heather's face swam into view, and he felt a cool cloth touching his face.

"Welcome back, Mick. You're going to be okay."

Davis wanted to respond, but the shivers had clamped his jaw muscles tight as his body shuddered under the sheets. Dr. Payton Dumont's face came into view on the other side of him, her brows furrowed.

"Master Chief Davis, you have a fever of one hundred and three. The meds we've been using aren't bringing it down. We found you outside the tent when we came back from surgery. What were you doing out there? I'm not sure what caused the fever, but we have to get it under control before you convulse."

Her face disappeared, and he turned to Heather while wrapping his arms around his chest to get warm.

"Where's Darian?" he said through chattering teeth.

Heather's forehead wrinkled, and her lips tightened.

"Mick, Tul'ran told you what happened to Darian. She passed away, my love. You've been talking to her all night, but it's not possible for her to have been here."

"N-no. No. She was here. I saw her. She made sure I didn't go over the edge. She was here."

Heather squeezed his arm, lines of consternation crossing her forehead and around the corners of her eyes.

"Mick, it was a hallucination from the drugs, the fever, and time skipping. We're working on making you better. Just hang in there."

Payton's face came back into his line of sight, and Sully was right behind her.

"Master Chief, you need to be tough right now. We've drawn an ice bath and you're going into it. We need to bring down your fever. Help me get him up."

Heather, Sully, and Payton pulled Davis into a sitting position, and he moaned when the covers came off. He'd never felt so cold. His body spasmed uncontrollably by shivering. They pulled him to his feet and carried him to an oval metallic tub. Davis could see the ice cubes floating in the water.

"N-no. N-no. I'm freezing. You can't put me in

there."

"Sorry, brother," Sully said. "This can't be helped. It's the only way to break down your fever before it does acute damage."

The three of them quickly removed Davis's clothing. Ashamed to be obstinate and desperate to avoid the ice bath, Davis struggled against them, his brain raging against his helplessness. His efforts resulted in weakening their grips, but had the opposite effect of what Davis intended. They dropped him into the freezing icy water, and he screamed before losing consciousness again.

Davis stood in the corridor of what he presumed was a mansion. The ceilings were remarkably high; the walls and floors were a cheerful gray marble, which looked as if someone had recently polished them. He felt the need to walk forward and followed the urge. The corridor was a twisted path of walls with glowing white, pulsing veins covering their surface. Portraits lined the walls between the veins of light, and soothing music danced after him as he walked.

The corridor ended on a balcony overlooking the most amazing garden. The midday sun shone on a large pond in the middle of the tableau and a fountain scattered diamond bits of spray into the middle of the water. Flowers of every variety and color lined the edges of the pool and beyond it, brilliant green grass carpeted the grounds. Trees with bright red leaves dotted the landscape, while bird carols filled the air. The air was sweet with the scents of flowers mingled with the smell of baking.

He tracked the pastry smell to one side of the

balcony, where he saw a round table with two elegant Victorian-era chairs. A beautiful woman sat in one chair, holding a teacup in her delicate hands. She had tiny features, long blond hair and a smile exposing snow-white teeth. The biggest blue eyes he'd ever seen regarded him with amusement. If she had wings, she'd look like the Disney character Tinkerbell.

Even her voice was musical.

"Hello, Lamek Davis. It's an honor to make your acquaintance."

Davis bowed, though he wasn't sure why he felt the need.

"I'm honored to meet you. To whom do I have the delight of addressing?"

The woman giggled.

"I'm Gwynver'insa, Empress of Spes, the world of Hope. Yahweh told me to expect a starwalker today, and here you are! Please have a seat."

A hallucination. Of course. The last thing Davis remembered was being tossed into an ice bath before passing out. At least this delusion was incredibly nicer than that experience.

Gwynver'insa giggled again.

"You're not hallucinating, Lamek. May I call you Lamek? Would you like a tea?"

Davis grinned at the sprite. Her joy was infectious. He could feel it radiating from her in waves.

"My friends call me Mick. I must be in a delusion, Your Imperial Majesty. Otherwise, it's impossible for me to be here, in a different world, speaking in English with a woman of dazzling beauty who governs the entire planet. Even our most ambitious holo movies wouldn't have conceived this scene."

Gwynver'insa laughed as she poured a cup of tea and offered him access to sugar, milk, and cream.

"Calling me a dazzling beauty wouldn't impress your Heather Wu much. I've claimed Tul'ran and Erianne az Nostrom as brother and sister; therefore, you're my kin. They taught me your language while they campaigned here to end the Multi-Millennial Fight. You must address me as Gwynver'insa, or Gwyn in the short form. Would you like a pastry?"

Davis's stomach growled. He nodded.

"Yes, please. I'm famished."

Gwynver'insa offered him a plate of delicious looking cakes. Davis bit into one and the flavor of chocolate and cinnamon exploded in his mouth. It didn't take long to finish, and he found himself reaching for another. This was a very convincing hallucination.

"As I've said, Mick, you're not hallucinating. This is the world of Spes and I'm as real as the tea you sip and the pastry you eat. As for how you came to be here, your soul has danced through the ether, skipping through thousands of light years, at my request."

Davis stopped mid-bite.

"I'm astral projecting?"

A smile tugged up the corners of her tiny lips.

"In a way. I was told you fought with a demon who physically struck you. It was a creature steeped in evil. The essence of his evil remained on and seeks to invade your spirit and corrupt your soul. Your body fights the evil because you've given your soul to Yahweh. So, fever wracks your body, and I've come to your rescue. It's the least I can do for a relative of my brother and his bride."

Davis thoughtfully chewed on a third piece of pastry. The explanation was outlandish and right out of science fiction, but he had nothing better to do today than freeze in a tub of ice water, so this was good. Better than good. Davis leaned back in his chair. The cakes were small but filling.

"Who told you about my fight with the demon? Tul'ran?"

Gwynver'insa's hair flowed from side to side as she swung her head in the negative.

"I've not had communication with my brother for several months now. My sister, Darian, came to me in my dreams and told me your story. She implored the Lord our God to go to your rescue when you stood at the edge of a cliff and planned your fever-altered attempt at escape. He doesn't allow His children to return to Earth in their glorified bodies; people could see them and want to worship them as gods. Darian is quite convincing, though, and He permitted her to come to your rescue. Just as He had permitted her to officiate at my wedding to Johan."

"After you lost consciousness, she carried you back to the tent and left you outside because she couldn't enter it. She desired to dispel the evil seeking to invade your body, but it wasn't within her authority to do so. Darian came to me in visions, begging me to assist, and I, of course, agreed. I would deny my beloved sister nothing."

Silence ensued as Davis tried to wrap his head around her narrative. He looked up at the cloudless sky and watched two birds chase each other in the crisp, clean air. A wind came up behind him and affectionately tousled his hair. Everything sure felt real.

"Accepting you can help me, Gwyn; how do we accomplish it?"

Gwyn clapped her hands together.

"Excellent! All I needed was a little faith from you, Mick. Yahweh has often told me, when I found myself depressed by how the Fight devastated my world, a little faith could move a mountain. With your faith, I will remove your fever. Are you ready?"

Davis squared his shoulders and squinted his eyes.

"Let's do it," he said, jerking his head into a nod.

The Empress grinned mischievously and reached across the table. She touched his nose with her right forefinger and said, "Boop," before bursting into a fit of giggles.

Mick looked at her, confused.

"What, that's it? You touch my nose, say 'boop', and the fever is gone?"

Gwynver'insa was laughing so hard, she had to hold her sides.

"I wish you could see your face! I'm sorry to be such a mischief-maker; you can blame Erianne for leaving her mark on me. When you starwalked to this place, Mick, my spirit crossed your path. I sent my spirit to cleanse your body of evil and douse the flames of your fever while we have tea and talk."

The Empress suddenly inhaled sharply and her eyes lost focus. She closed them and her face worked as she centered herself.

"My spirit has returned. It's done. Your fever has

broken, and your body lies resting in bed. You will be weak for a few days, but you'll make a fully recovery."

Mick rose out of his chair, but Gwyn restrained him with a hand on his arm.

"It doesn't mean you have to leave right now. Your body is sleeping; it's unnecessary for you to return so soon. I take boundless joy in the people of your planet, Dirt. Please stay and keep me company for a while longer."

Mick burst out laughing, lowering himself back into the chair.

"Earth, Gwyn, not Dirt. I know the word translates as dirt, but we call it good old planet Earth."

Gwyn exploded into another fit of giggles.

"My apologies to the all the humans of Earth! As I said, I take boundless joy in your people. You know my husband, Johan, I'm sure. I wanted him to join us, but he's on a diplomatic mission to solve a land dispute. The business of the Empire sometimes can't wait. He's exceptionally good at it, you know. Diplomacy."

Mick kept his face perfectly calm, not letting any micro-expressions convey his feelings. He would have thought Johan Weinstein, the Historian who tried to kill Hitler in his youth, to be capable of many things, but diplomacy wasn't one of them.

"I'm glad a man from my world has contributed to yours, Gwyn, and found a place in your heart."

She nodded, reaching for another cake.

"All of them have. Johan, Tul'ran, Erianne, and Darian. So brave, and so quick to love! They adopted me in the space of two heartbeats and pledged to lay down their lives for me. Who was I that they would have given up something as precious as life for me and my cause? I fell in love with all of them; a deeper love than even I had for my deceased family. It has been hundreds of years since I encountered people with such courage, faith, generosity, gentleness, and strength of body and mind. I'm thinking of starting an immigration policy for the people of Earth."

Davis put up his right hand.

"I'd like to volunteer myself, my girlfriend, my military brother Sully and his wife Jeannie for the first trials. With the way things are going on my planet, we may ask for refugee status, too."

His last statement sobered her.

"You may find this uncomfortable, Mick, but I regularly speak with Yahweh. He keeps me updated on what is happening with Tul'ran and Erianne. My net of interest has now expanded to you, Heather, the Sullivans, and Coventry, as well. I am heart-sickened by the destruction of your world and the dire things to come. I understand why it must be, but my heart bleeds for all of you. A statement made in jest is now an invitation in truth. Should you ever desire it, I will walk the stars and bring you all back here in the flesh."

Mick sat back in his chair, delighting in the slender young woman's presence, and a little overwhelmed. She looked like a happy debutante enjoying the height of her social status.

"Forgive me for my impertinence, Gwyn, but how powerful are you? Can you really traverse the stars and bring us back here?"

Her face seemed to get older, more weighted with grave responsibility.

"I am unlike any human you've encountered, Mick. They would consider me to be a mutation on your world. My powers come from my faith in God and my intense desire to serve Him. After hundreds of years of obedient service, the Lord our God has seen fit to grant me unusual abilities. Would you like an apple?"

The abrupt change in topic momentarily confused Davis.

"I'm sorry?"

She giggled.

"An apple. Would you like one?"

He canted his head to one side, but went with it.

"Sure, Gwyn. I'd love an apple."

She extended both hands, her right hand hovering about six inches above her left. An intense look of concentration filled her face. A golden glow appeared between her hands, which was replaced by a red delicious apple. Davis could only stare at it.

"Take it," she said, grinning.

Davis took it from her hand and smelled it. It sure smelled like a fresh apple. He bit into it and the crunch delighted his senses, as did the taste.

"Wow. This is fantastic! How did you do it?"

"Yahweh has gifted me with the ability to create from nothing. If I've seen it or experienced it or someone has explained the concept to the molecular level, I can create it."

Davis took a deep breath.

"I'm impressed. How does this give you the ability to walk the stars?"

Gwyn shook her head.

"It doesn't, but I asked for the ability. If this were nighttime, you would see in our skies a beautiful green moon. It has an atmosphere and is heavily forested. I no longer had a memory of some things I wanted to recreate on Spes. I asked Yahweh if I could go to our moon and study it, so I could create similar trees, plants, and wildlife here. He taught me how to walk the stars through Inter-Dimensional Space. Better, he taught me how to take physical things from another world and bring them to mine. It's an exceptional experience. I took Johan to our moon and I've never seen him filled with greater joy. If you were here in physical body, I'd take you there, too."

Davis didn't know what to say and sipped tea for a few minutes.

"Thank you, Gwyn, sincerely. You've given me an option to flee the horror of my world. If ever I want to take you up on it, how would I contact you?"

Gwyn stood up and walked to his side of the table.

"Don't let what I'm going to do dismay you. There's nothing intended by it except to gather a sample of the building blocks of your life."

The Empress of Spes pulled a pin from the bounty of hair on her head. She pricked one of her slender fingers with it. Reaching out, she hovered the pin over one of his fingertips, raising one eyebrow quizzically. After Davis nodded, she pricked his finger and then mingled their blood drops together.

"We're bonded now, Lamek Davis, as one twin is bonded to the other, for I have brought your DNA into my body. Should you experience a need, call out my name and I'll come. Are you distressed by what I've done?"

Davis pressed his lips together to suppress a condescending smile.

"Gwyn, I assure you I've suffered far worse wounds. I don't understand. You said my physical body is not here. How could you gather a drop of blood for my DNA?"

Gwyn settled back into her chair, beaming.

"Your spirit is connected to your physical form even though you are light years away from it. I merely reached through your spirit into your body and drew a blood sample. There were far more intimate and enjoyable ways to collect your DNA, but I thought it would offend your wife were I to kiss you."

Davis laughed aloud.

"Your husband wouldn't have liked it, either. Heather and I aren't married, by the way."

Gwyn's eyes rose elegantly towards her hairline.

"Why ever not, brother?"

He pushed his bottom lip over the top, his forehead creasing.

"We both lost our former spouses to the same tragedy. While we've pursued a path of love, slowly entering each other's hearts, I've not taken the step to propose marriage."

The plate of cakes was empty. Gwynver'insa cupped her hands over the plate and concentrated. When she moved her hands away, fruit filled the plate. And one pickle. She popped the pickle in her mouth and chewed. Davis squinted his eyes at her.

Now, that was odd.

"What are you waiting for, brother? Is your world not on the verge of extinction? Why not journey to its end with your wife on your arm?"

Davis didn't have an answer. He'd taken steps in the right direction of a proposal but hadn't popped the question.

"I don't know, Gwyn. It just never felt like it was the right time. Can we change the subject?"

A hint of mischief once more danced in her eyes.

"Of course. I will impress upon you one task before I return you to home."

The corner of Davis's lips turned up. This should be good.

"I am at your service, my Imperially Majestic sister."

Gwyn giggled.

"When the chance arises, pass along to Lord and Lady az Nostrom that I command their return to Spes on urgent business of the Empress."

"I'm at your disposal, Empress. Of course, I'll pass along the message as soon as I run into them again. What shall we do in the meantime?"

Gwyn leaned down and pulled a lyre onto her lap. She danced her fingertips along the strings and the notes they made wafted pleasure into Mick's brain.

"I may not have the dulcet tones of a wandering minstrel, Mick, but if you'll be patient, I'll sing to you the verses of the Ballad of Tul'ran the Sword as they concern the liberation of Spes, the world of Hope."

Mick burst out laughing and sat back as the Empress of the world strummed her lyre and set the raucous ballad free with an amazing soprano voice.

Atlantis, June 2, 2099, just after midnight

When Davis woke up, the med tent was dimly lit with plasma lanterns strung up haphazardly in the top bar of the frame. It was dark outside.

He shook his head, momentarily rattled. Did he not just finish this dance? He glanced to his left. Someone had found a bashed up easy chair, and Heather was curled up in a ball on it, fast asleep. She had changed into tan coveralls, looking like they had seen better days. She was wearing work boots, probably at least one size too big. Grease smudged her face, her hair was messy, and she was the best thing he'd ever seen.

Davis let his mind submerge in the feeling. The state of the world was worse and rapidly tumbling into whatever was worse than 'worse.' How much time would they have left in this life? The prospect of eternity with the Lord was fantastic, but there were certain pleasures not to be carried forward into the next. For what was he waiting?

Davis leveraged himself into a seated position and waited for his head to stop swimming. Gwyn said he'd be weak for a few days. Gwyn. Right. How much of that had been real, if any of it at all? Davis staggered to his feet, took two steps, and kneeled by the chair. He brushed his fingertips along Heather's hairline, moving her bangs to one side. She stirred, then sat up quickly when she saw it was him.

"Mick! Why are you out of bed? Are you okay?"

Mick took her left hand in his right and kissed the back of it.

"Much better, thanks, even though you and the

rest of the gang tried to drown me in the Arctic."

She laughed, relieved, and leaned down to kiss him. She pulled back, wincing.

"As much as I love snogging, you need to brush your teeth, my man. Your breath is wilting the flowers I scrounged up for you."

She gestured at the cracked vase holding a few bedraggled flowers, and he smiled, but with his lips pressed together.

"I will in a sec, then we need to talk."

Alarm flashed across her face.

"That sounds ominous."

Mick lurched to his feet and held out his hand to pull her to a standing position.

"What I have to say is a good thing, Heather, but it shouldn't be done when I look and smell like death warmed over. Let's find something to eat, then I'll take another bath, but hot this time. Once I'm cleaned up, I'll tell you what I have to say. You won't believe it, but every proper fairy tale has a nice ending."

Marjatta Korhonen woke up, but not in a fairy tale. She kneeled on the floor beside her cot in one of the escape pods her security personnel dragged inland and converted into her personal residence. The tattoos on her wrists were a bright red and felt like they were on fire. Her vision blurred, and she stared at the feet of Malchus Contradeum, the self-proclaimed god of the Earth.

"Hello, Marjatta, my slave-bride. Why have you not checked in with me? I find your reluctance to commune with me... disturbing."

Then she was in agony, as the fire in her wrists threatened to burst into open flame.

"Lord, I'm sorry! The need to search for survivors and find supplies to endure has overwhelmed me. I intended no insult, I assure you!"

The feet drifted away from her line of sight, but she wouldn't allow herself to lift her head. The last time she was with him, her mind had gone on a hedonistic vacation she didn't want to repeat.

"You deny me your worship, Marjatta. I can feel you resist the entry of my will. Do you seek to displease me?" The agony in her wrists intensified. "I respond poorly to people who displease me."

"Lord," she gasped, "I'm sorry. It's just, well, the pleasures of worshipping you overwhelm my intellect. I need all my faculties to do my job. Please, lord," she whimpered, "stop hurting me."

His hot breath flashed across the nape of her neck, and his voice came out in a hiss.

"Who do you love, Marjatta Korhonen?"

"I love you, Master," she said through gritted teeth, trying to fake as much warmth in her voice as possible.

"And who do you worship?"

"You and only you," she gasped, the pain in her wrists sending sparks of light dancing in her vision.

He licked the back of her neck, and she almost vomited.

"Very well, then. This earthquake was a revelation to me, Marjatta. It reminded me of certain things I'd allowed myself to forget. What damage did TTI take?"

The pain in her wrists abated, and Marjatta sighed.

"Shockwaves ruined the TTI Main Building, and falling girders smashed the Lens. The technicians automatically backed the software up to an AI buried deep within the island, so it's good."

Satan stroked Marjatta's hair, and her stomach lurched once more.

"How long until it's fully functional?"

The question almost caused her to jerk up her head and look at him.

"TTI? Time travel? It could take years. We have to rebuild the physical structure and recreate the Lens. Materials will be scarce, as will laborers. We lost many people, lord."

Satan took a handful of her hair and twisted it hard, while her wrists screamed in pain.

"I don't have years, Marjatta. Do you understand? I'll send you all the materials and laborers you need. I'll give you one year to rebuild, Administrator, and then I'll find someone more competent to run the project if you can't complete it on time. Are we on the same page?"

It felt like he was ripping her hair out by the roots.

"Yes, lord, yes, I understand. I'll do it! Whatever you ask!"

She was alone in the escape pod. Her hair hurt and while the pain in her wrists faded, they still felt as if he had seared them over an open flame. She looked at her wrists, the bright red tattoos pulsing, and wept. She had trapped herself in some kind of demonic relationship and felt terror wash over her soul.

There had to be a way out of this. She looked at the fork and steak knife sitting at the edge of the plate of food a chef had put together for her out of salvaged supplies. It was all they could find for silverware. The steak knife made her think.

How much worse could death be?

———————✝———————

A bath is a bath,
But a pleasure it will be
When the water is warm
And drawn from the sea.

A chuckle threatened to escape from Davis's throat, which wouldn't have been the best thing to happen seeing his head was under water. He was such a poet, albeit a non-suffering one now. The tub in which he agonized with hypothermia was now a small pool of hot water soothing his body. He'd have to get out soon; there were others waiting for a soak. Shower facilities no longer existed on Atlantis.

Davis popped his head out of the water and reached for the bar of soap. They had found a crate of soap tossed into the bush by the quake and Admin was dispensing them carefully. He scrubbed himself clean and stepped out of the bath. Someone had secured a stack of towels and he dried himself, his mind distracted by his next step. It required finesse, something he often lacked. It took him a moment to realize what was out of place.

A brand-new set of coveralls configured like a military flight suit sat next to his clothing, complete with the insignia of a Master Chief. While he was in the bath, someone entered the tent, dropped off the suit, and left. It made him feel a little queasy. He was going to have to retrain his survival instincts; they'd been letting him down lately.

Before Davis could put on the uniform, Jeannie walked into the tent, forcing Davis to cover himself quickly. She laughed.

"Relax, Mick, I've seen men naked more often than you've seen birds fly."

He looked at her, his forehead creasing. It was an odd reference, given his most recent experience. Was this a hallucination, too?

"Are you here to tape my ribs?" he said while looking for signs of unreality within the mix of normality.

Jeannie shook her head.

"We don't wrap ribs anymore because taping makes it hard for you to take deep breaths. Taking deep breaths may help prevent pneumonia or a partial collapse of a lung. Can you take a deep breath for me right now?"

Davis complied and choked off a cry when a sharp pain stitched its way through his chest wall.

Jeannie tilted her head.

"Hurts, huh? The pain is a reminder you're a human being, not a god, and if you do something stupid, you're going to pay. Now, get dressed. The lineup outside is long and I don't want to put up with impatient patients."

She smiled to show she was teasing and left the back of the tent.

A voice called softly from outside the zippered doorway at the front of the bathing tent.

"Are you decent, Mick?"

He glanced down at his barely dried naked body.

"Not yet, Coventry. Just getting dressed. What's up?"

"Do *not* put on the uniform."

Davis jerked his hand away from the crisp blue coveralls.

"Uh, why not? Are they covered in anthrax or something?"

Coventry chuckled outside the tent.

"They might as well be. Someone from the Government of Democracy Combined Armed Forces is running around trying to recruit anyone who will listen. It's a modern press gang. Apparently, if you put on the uniform, it's a tacit acceptance of their offer to join up."

Davis grabbed his clothes and put them on, leaving the uniform untouched. He stepped out of the bathing tent, worried he might see Coventry dressed in military coveralls. He sighed relief when he saw her. She cocked an eyebrow at him.

"C'mon, Master Chief, you have to think I'm a little smarter than that."

He grinned sheepishly.

"Sorry, Major. Just worried they caught you in a weak moment." He fell into step with her, automatically matching her stride. "What's new in the land of the living?"

Both were scanning the island, watching as black-clad members of the GoD military accosted people still walking around Atlantis, some with purpose, others in a daze. It wouldn't be long before the recruiters would be a real nuisance.

"Korhonen told us word came down from on high. We're to rebuild Atlantis and get the Lens running again."

Davis stopped short, his mouth agape.

"What? Seriously? With all the devastation in the world, Contradeum wants to start time travel again?"

Coventry gestured to him to keep walking, and he fell in beside her.

"He's not Contradeum anymore, remember? Who knows what the Beast wants? It's not good. Sign up with him and he'll do to you what he did to Korhonen."

"Uh oh. Is she back in zombie land?"

Coventry laughed.

"No, not this time. In fact, when she briefed us, she looked angry enough to chew off someone's head. Bad juju there."

Davis swiveled his head to look at her impassive face. The phrase denoted the usually negative karmic consequences of an action. It originated in West Africa and referred to a special sort of magic associated with certain objects. The magical objects conferred power on those who owned or touched them. After centuries of slavery, the phrase had become pejorative.

"Bad juju. Isn't that a little racist?"

"Not when I say it. I'm black, remember?"

Davis laughed, but a stab of pain in his chest choked it off.

They entered the Admin tent, where they found Heather in an intense conversation with two engineers. After she dismissed them, she walked over to Coventry and Davis and planted a kiss on Davis's mouth.

"I was worrying you'd drowned."

He shook his head at her, pretending to be disapproving.

"You seem to forget I'm a tough guy. I served in the military before I was lucky enough to have you fall into my life, you know."

"Mmm hmm. Brave words from a man with enough ketamine in his system to knock out a horse. Or a stubborn old mule."

Davis pretended to look hurt.

"Hey! Who're you calling old?"

After Coventry and Heather giggled, he leaned over and whispered, "Walk with me" into Heather's ear. She smiled, slipped her hand in his, and they left the tent.

They seemed to walk randomly around the island, but Davis knew where they were going. He guided her to a path leading to the tallest hill on Atlantis. It wasn't natural. When the builders finished constructing the island, they had tons of equipment and no use for it. It would've cost an exorbitant amount of bitcoin to ship it out, so they did the next best thing: they buried it. Pharoah's Hill became the largest, most expensive garbage dump turned recreation park in the history of humankind.

When they arrived at the top, the sun was just beginning to set into the ocean. It was a beautiful sunset, with the fading orb casting multiple hues of orange and pink on the few clouds scattered in the sky.

They looked behind them and watched as lights came on throughout Atlantis, but unsynchronized, like fireflies dancing around large tracts of darkness. Crews still searched for survivors in the rubble, or were putting together work details to comply with Korhonen's twenty-four work schedule. The luxury of nine-to-five was gone, perhaps forever.

Davis and Wu turned their backs to the carnage behind them and watched the sun fall into the ocean as lovers have done since the creation of romance. Davis had his arms around her slender shoulders, and she leaned into him gently.

Once the sun sunk into its watery grave for the day, Davis guided Heather around to face him. Her eyes were glowing, as was the smile on her face.

"Heather, you've been my rock since the night I walked up to your table in the steakhouse on Restaurant Row. You've held me when I've cried and comforted me in my sorrows. I lost hope for a long time, but you've restored it. I don't know what the future holds, but I don't want to wait another minute to share it with you more intimately."

Davis sunk to one knee and pulled a ring out of his pocket.

"We haven't talked about this for four thousand years, but nearly dying gave me a new perspective. For whatever time we have left, I'm ready to be happy again. Will you marry me?"

Heather's eyes were wide, and her mouth rounded into a perfect 'o'. She put a hand over her mouth and brought her eyes from the ring to his face.

"Are you sure, Mick?"

He nodded, his face set in its more serious lines.

"Never surer in my life."

Tears leaked out from the corners of her dark eyes as she held out her hand for him to slip the ring on her finger. It was a perfect fit.

"Yes, Mick. I'd love to be your wife."

He stood up, clutched her to his chest, and they

kissed. Time stood still for them, the tragedies down the hill buried in a moment of love and passion. When they pulled away, Heather tore her eyes away from his and looked down at the diamond ring.

"Where did you get this, Mick?"

He laughed softly, delighted she had suspected nothing.

"Do you remember the trip I took to Ur the week after I gave Ro'gun the talk? Yes? There was an artisan there who worked gold. I had a few minas of gold and some diamonds from when I transitioned with First Team Mesopotamia. The night before I left, while you slept, I sized your finger with a piece of string. I explained to him what I wanted, and he created the first diamond engagement ring in history. What we designed, and he created, excited him to no end. Hopefully, I didn't mess up the timeline."

Heather twisted the ring on her finger, catching a reflection of the last rays of the setting sun.

"It's beautiful, Mick. Thank you. I love it."

Heather snuggled into his chest but kept her left hand where she could see the ring.

"Why did you buy the ring when you went to Ur? I don't think we talked about a romantic relationship before then."

Mick watched as the stars became brighter in a sky no longer lit by the sun.

"After I gave Ro'gun the talk, you told me it was time to think about us. I decided to go to Ur for supplies to get a ring made. I didn't know when I'd pop the question, but my heart told me it was inevitable. Plus, I thought it'd be unique to present you with what's now a four-thousand-year-old diamond ring. We'll have quite the story to tell at our wedding," Mick said, pulling her closer.

Heather laughed softly.

"When I do my speech at our wedding, I'm going to tell everyone the one thing I've always admired about you is your courage."

He pulled away a bit, looking down at her with furrowed eyebrows.

"I don't think it takes much courage to ask a woman you love to marry you."

"Maybe not," she said, still smiling, "but how many men would be brave enough to ask their future wives to marry them while they stood on a garbage dump?"

CHAPTER THE TWELFTH: BY FANG AND CLAW

Ma'ilingan Waazh (Wolf's Den), 175th Year of Winter
Seventh day, in the month of Onaabani-giizis, year 5379

The icy wind slashed into his skin, the pain searing the nerves in his cheeks and forehead. It was a thousand cuts of a razor-sharp knife edge, leaving behind whimpering skin cells pleading for mercy. The wind scoured his body for any opening in the outer clothing, digging through it like a starving rat, searching for warmth to satisfy its urge to devour it.

Tul'ran blinked his long eyelashes against the frost, which appeared on them as soon as he passed through what appeared to be a solid rock wall in the Garden on Ma'ilingan Waazh. His fingertips were growing numb, and he instantly regretted not gloving them before he left the Garden.

Erianne stepped through the rock face and walked up to her husband's side, wincing against the surge of glacial wind making her eyes water.

"Behold, milord husband. Snow," she said, gesturing to the massive banks of ice crystals smothering the base of giant trees. "Brrr, it's cold!"

Tul'ran shivered under the layers of clothing and armor covering his body and suppressed the curses forming in his mind. It wouldn't do to utter such profanity in the presence of a Lady and a Warrior of the Lord God Most High, even if she wasn't his beloved wife.

"I would protest against the coldness as loudly as I could, milady wife, but I fear my lips are already numb."

The swirling wind, which not only sliced across their numbing cheeks but also obscured their vision of the way forward with ever shifting fogs of snow, suddenly abated. Tul'ran and Erianne stopped abruptly.

Standing in front of them was the largest wolf either of them had ever seen. It was slender and powerfully built, with a large, deeply descending rib cage, a sloping back and a heavily muscled neck. Its ears were small and rectangular, set on a large and heavy head, with a wide forehead, strong jaws, and a long blunt muzzle. Its deep brown hair stood straight up on its hackles.

The wolf's shoulders came to Tul'ran's shoulders, and its head would have made it seem taller were it not bent low to the ground. The impressive jaws, filled with intimidating teeth, were open, and a growl originating from the nether regions of the underworld threatened them from the gaping mouth.

Without warning, its thoughts were in their

minds, the intelligent words as cold as the wind carving its way into their souls.

"Greetings, humans. My stomach has been waiting for you."

Aakwaadizi the Wolf stared at the motionless humans, pleased with himself. His name in the world's native tongue meant 'he is fierce.' Dizi, pronounced 'dee-zee' by those who knew the right way of speaking, worked extremely hard to live up to his name.

He hid for three days in the bitter cold, waiting for the woman he tracked to appear. While the rabbits he ate kept his stomach full, his desire for human flesh was overwhelming. He refused recall after recall, expecting the soft young woman to return from where she had disappeared. He still remembered her scent and the taste of terror in her mind. It stumped him when she disappeared into a solid rock face, but his stubbornness wouldn't let Dizi yield to his dismay.

Imagine his surprise when a tall man and tall women walked out of the rock wall, instead. The Man looked appetizing; Dizi could sense his large, muscular frame under the layers of clothing. He licked his fangs. Time for a meal of muscle and soft, unfrozen flesh.

Suddenly, a large, black blur leaped out from a windfall of trees to his right. Curse the luck! His superiors had sent Maji-Manidoo, whose name just meant 'evil', to track him down when he didn't respond to the recall. Maji was the most fearsome hunter in their pack. He never failed on a mission to track down and kill a Woman. His kill list was legendary, as was his ferocity. Now Maji would get credit for the kill and the first bite of the flesh over which Dizi drooled.

Maji's leap caught the Woman's attention; in a blur, she drew a long, black metal thing from behind her back and plunged it into Maji's chest as he sailed in the air toward her.

The black wolf howled as the woman fell back, thrust her legs into Maji's body and shoved hard. As Maji somersaulted in mid-air past the Man, a black knife appeared in his hand, and he used it to slice Maji's throat as he flew by. The Man never took his eyes off Dizi; not even to see where he buried the knife. In less time than it took to think the thoughts, Maji lay in a bloody heap against the base of a large pine tree. His mind no longer occupied his body.

Dizi slowly lowered his back haunches in a sitting position and stared at the two people, closing his lips over his fangs. The once harmless looking Man and Woman stared at him impassively, seemingly unconcerned with the attack, as Maji's blood dripped into the snow from their weapons.

'Who are you?' he said into their minds.

The Man and Woman didn't reply, though the man lifted his nose as if he smelled something. The Man transferred the bloody ebon knife to his left hand and reached down to gather some snow, crushing it into a ball. His body snapped around and he threw the ball high into a tree behind the one under which the unfortunate Maji lay dead.

There was a scratching of claws, a hiss, and a growl as the snowball connected, and a giant

Mountain Lion fell out of the tree.

Dizi stared at the Mountain Lion, stunned. Had his brain frozen? How did he not detect both Maji and, more worryingly, one of his mortal enemies?

The wild cat was as tall as Dizi was at the shoulder, her body covered in a thick layer of tan-colored fur. Her eyes were dark and surrounded by black circles. A darker shade of brown ran from the crown of her head, down her nose and broadened to surround her white muzzle. A heart-shaped black streak of fur highlighted her nose and ended on her top lip. Dizi knew from awful experience her huge paws housed razor-sharp claws.

The Mountain Lion shook herself, sat on the snow and cleaned one paw as if leaving the tree for the ground was entirely her idea.

'So uncivilized, that was,' she spoke into all their minds. 'Invitation accepted, Man, though regret extending it you may.'

The Man smiled, one as cold as the wind dancing among the trees and stirring up the powdery snow.

'Be grateful it was the ball of snow I cast, not El Shaddai's Knife,' he said to their minds. 'Or else you would lie with your friend and this world would count two less ravenous beasts.'

The big cat slunk towards Dizi and found a place to lie down on a log halfway between the humans and Dizi.

'A friend of mine he is not, but mortal enemies we are. A taste of your mind, I have had, Man. Color me intrigued. They call me Miikawaadad when they bother to call. It means 'superior.' In the short form, Miikaw you may call me. Are you named?'

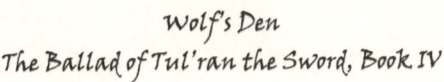

The woman nodded and walked over to clean the long metal stick on Maji's fur, churning Dizi's stomach. He wondered if it was necessary for her to humiliate Maji, given how easily she made the kill. After he recounted the story of his casual death at the hands of a Woman, Maji's den would lose much status among the Clan of Wolves. Dizi licked his lips. Status his Clan would attain.

'I am named Princess Erianne of Akiikaa. This is my husband, Lord Tul'ran az Nostrom, the Prince of Death,' she said, pointing to the Man, who was cleaning his knife in the snow.

He appeared to not be paying attention to them anymore, but Dizi knew better. He could sense the Man's awareness of him, which made Dizi distinctly uncomfortable.

'We come in peace,' Tul'ran thought to them, the emotions of his words laced with irony.

Miikaw continued to clean her right paw, while a deep rumbling purr emanated from her chest.

'A Prince and Princess. Scored we well we would have, were the tables turned. What now, illustrious humans? To the death do we fight or stand here and freeze?'

Tul'ran stood up and put the knife back into his chest. Dizi wondered how he accomplished it without drawing blood.

'You have three choices. We come to end the war between Men and Women in this world, having traveled a great distance among the stars to accomplish this thing. You may leave us and go your own way if you promise you will not attempt to attack us again. Or you may fight us, and we will kill you. In the last measure, you may join us as we seek to bring peace to this frozen nightmare you call a planet. Choose quickly, for the temperature of the wind has put me in a mood and when I am in a mood, things die.'

Erianne rolled her eyes.

'You must forgive my husband. He limits his understanding of diplomacy to determining whether a thing needs to be killed. He has presented your choices adequately; choose now before my ability to control his arm fades faster than your lives.'

Miikaw stood up and stretched her tan colored body. She glided over to Tul'ran, studying him carefully. The Mountain Lion squatted on her back haunches within a paw's distance of him, her head almost reaching to the bottom of his chin.

'Interesting, you are, Prince of Death. In this world, mortal enemies I am with Men, but I tire of this conflict. Lost two of my cubs I did to a pack of wolves last year, and I grieve for them still. Weary I am of fighting the battles of Women. In your mind, I see a city you made nothing by a wave of your hand. Intrigues me, such power does. By fang and claw I bind myself to you, Prince of Death, until you die or fulfilled is your mission.'

Dizi was miffed. Men bonded to Wolves, and he assumed he would pledge to Tul'ran. Trust a cat to mess things up. Dizi stood up and shook his body from head to toe. Glaring at Miikaw, who laughed into his mind, he trotted to sit before Erianne.

'I, Dizi of the Brown Furred Den, pledge myself by fang and claw to your service, Princess Erianne, until you die or bring peace to Ma'ilingan Waazh.'

Erianne replaced the metal stick into the holder behind her back.

'We accept your pledges, Miikaw and Dizi. As you protect us, we will protect you against all who would stand in the way of peace.'

If Dizi had eyebrows, he would've raised them. Truly, she was new to this world.

She spoke such a sweeping statement blithely, as if she knew anything about Wolf's Den. The words betrayed she knew nothing at all.

———————

Tul'ran was beyond cold. A deep shiver built within his core and rattled his body. He could barely feel his lips and fingers. Reaching into his armor, he drew out gloves provided to them by Princess Wenonah. A small stone in his pocket powered the gloves, like the body-hugging one-piece garment under his armor, and warmed the material to a satisfactory glow.

The clothing only warmed, however, when he attached the gloves to the one-piece underwear. Not having fought with the gloves, he had been loath to put them on before he left the Garden. Now he cursed himself for a fool, wondering if he would ever be warm again.

Tul'ran could see his thoughts amused the lion and the wolf and snarled a nasty thought in their direction. He was in no mood to be teased by these two beasts. The Prince of Death was in a frozen wasteland, and it pleased him not at all.

He pulled his cloak over his head. Within the hood and attached to it was a mask he pulled over his face. It even covered his eyes, but the material was amazing in that it allowed him to see clearly.

Tul'ran turned to the cave face and blew a piercing whistle from between his teeth. Moments later, Darkshadow appeared, his ears flicking as he looked first at Dizi and then at Miikaw. Tul'ran raised his hand to the stallion's neck, seeing the war horse's body tense. It never ceased to amaze him how his horse feared nothing. Were he to give Darkshadow his head, the warhorse would pummel the predators to death or die trying.

"Gently, brother. These are friends, for this time being, and it would not do to harm them."

Tul'ran drew Darkshadow forward and leaped into the saddle. The suit clinging to his body warmed him, but the Princess hadn't provided a heated saddle. His backside would be cold, but there was nothing for it but to endure.

Destiny's Edge followed Darkshadow through the rock face, and Erianne nimbly leaped into the saddle. Tul'ran envied her. She didn't seem to be the least bit concerned by the cold.

The rest of their party rode out of the Garden. Wenonah gasped when she saw the Lion and the Wolf, and her horse shied violently. Erianne put up her hand.

"Fear not, Princess Wenonah. We have secured the help of these two fearsome creatures, and they ride with us with mutual assurances of friendship. You are safe in their presence."

Wenonah blanched as she looked at the massive black wolf laying on his back at the base of the pine tree, bleeding copious amounts of bright-red fluid into the fresh snow from its slashed throat and chest.

"You have been on Ma'ilingan Waazh not ten minutes, and already you have scored a kill, Princess Erianne. Will it be possible for you and your husband to slow the rate of killing? If your violence proceeds at this pace, I wonder how many of us will be alive when your time here has ended?"

Miikaw meowed loudly, her version of laughter, as Tul'ran thought, 'You won't be one of them if your mouth continues to run like a flooded river.'

Erianne glared at Tul'ran.

'Be still,' she thought to him, 'and grateful our host cannot read our minds, as can Dizi and Miikaw! Really, husband.' She turned in her saddle to regard their host.

"Princess Wenonah, we will defend ourselves when attacked, regardless of the identity of the attacker. I suggest we make our way to the City of Ikwe Na. My people are not used to coldness such as this, and I would not have them suffer it any longer than they must."

Princess Wenonah lifted her chin and pointed it to where the trail wound down the side of the mountain.

"It is in that direction we must go, but it will not take long on horseback. We will arrive by nightfall."

Dizi and Miikaw went ahead of them at Tul'ran and Erianne's asking to warn of danger and persuade away any of their kind. The two fanged and clawed predators slipped into the forest without a sound, fading like ghosts into the snow swirling between the trees.

Princess Wenonah followed them, riding first,

with Erianne on Destiny's Edge close behind her. Tul'ran and Darkshadow followed Erianne and Wenonah, with Darkshadow snorting and prancing through the snow like a colt. He had never seen snow and wasn't sure whether he enjoyed plowing through the cold, feathery substance.

Omarosa and Anatu followed Tul'ran. Innanu and Ro'gun rode side-by-side in the last spot, so Ro'gun could have access to his sword if enemies attacked them from behind.

Erianne turned and looked behind her. Tul'ran had refused to remove his armor in favor of clothing specific to Ma'ilingan Waazh. The one-piece warming garment was as black as his armor and outer cloak. Darkshadow's padded chest plate and blanket were black, and the two of them looked like an otherworldly dark wraith as they faded in and out of the blowing snow.

She touched her husband's mind and found a blanket of contentment wrapped around a ball of irritation at the cold. The irritation she expected, but his contentment surprised her. She pulled back on her reins and Destiny's Edge dutifully slowed until she walked beside Darkshadow.

Tul'ran turned his head to look at her, but Erianne couldn't see his face through the mask covering it.

"How does my husband fare?" Erianne said, keeping her tone light.

"Other than feeling colder than I have ever been, I am well, milady wife. The temperature of this place is beyond enduring."

"If you are in such distress, milord husband, what is the contentment I find within your heart when my mind touches yours?"

Tul'ran gestured to Darkshadow's head, which was bobbing as the stallion pranced through the unfamiliar snow, his ears flicking back and forth.

"Other than everything I experience with you, my Princess, there is nothing better in life than riding Darkshadow. We have been inseparable since I was a lad and he a colt. I find peace riding his back as we wander from one adventure to the next. Many times after battle, I have stood against his chest, my arms wrapped around his neck, with his magnificent head pressed against my back, as we reveled in the joy of living."

"We have ridden through deserts and heat, through fog and rain, and hidden from sandstorms. When I learned to read, he would often lay beside me by a fire at night and I would assail his ears with the words of wisdom from an ancient transcript. I wore his smell, the delightful smell of horses, as my perfume throughout my entire existence. If there is an activity better than riding a horse, I know it not."

Erianne grinned under her mask. She was going to make him pay for that one.

"While my heart rejoices in your love for Darkshadow, I am stricken to the core of my being with offense, milord Tul'ran."

His head whipped around to stare at her.

"In what way have I offended you, milady Erianne?"

Erianne huffed, her eyes twinkling under the mask.

"Why, in suggesting your horse conveying you on its back is a better activity than the pleasures of our bed. Is my lovemaking so dulling you would rather ride a horse?"

Tul'ran boomed out a laugh, which made Wenonah jump in her saddle. Behind them, Omarosa chuckled.

"Did I not forestall such offense by saying 'other than everything I experience with you'? If not, I did so inadequately. I promise you, Erianne, love of my life, I would rather have a bounce with you than travel upon my trusted steed."

Darkshadow bobbed his head and snorted loudly, snow swirling beneath his wide nostrils, making Erianne giggle.

"It seems, milord husband, you will satisfy neither your wife nor your warhorse with your platitudes this day."

Tul'ran reached down to stroke Darkshadow's neck with one gloved hand. The blanket on the stallion's back was long, with a notch carved in the middle to accommodate the saddle's cinching straps. It was the best they could do to protect their horses from the biting cold.

"I am grateful I will not have to choose between you, then. Losing either of you would devastate me to the depths of my soul."

They rode together for a while. Destiny's Edge playfully nipped at Darkshadow's flanks, causing him to snort and toss his head. The two horses became close during the time they spent in each other's company while Tul'ran and Erianne campaigned on Pulchra and Spes. When they weren't resting, they cavorted like younglings, teasing and play-fighting until it was time for a nap or a meal.

There was joy in this, Erianne thought. Tul'ran rode like saddle and steed joined him at the hip, harmony radiating from both horse and rider in a wave of warmth. She smiled and allowed herself to luxuriate in the affection of horse and human as they journeyed through the bitter cold.

———————————

The path ended at the entrance to a colossal cave, lit from within by a pale-yellow source of inexplicable origin. When they rode far enough to leave the cold behind, Wenonah gestured for them to halt. As soon as the last of the humans entered the warm zone, Dizi and Miikaw slunk into the cave, gratefully shaking the snow from their coats.

Wenonah dismounted from her horse and faced Erianne and Tul'ran.

"Your stallion is magnificent, Warrior Tul'ran, and worthy of bearing royalty. I will ride him into the City of Ikwe Na."

Tul'ran pulled the mask off his face and pushed back the hood of the cloak.

"No," he said, his voice mild. "You will not."

Erianne glanced at him sharply. She didn't like the sound of *that* tone in his voice. When Tul'ran got angry, he rarely yelled; instead, his voice grew gentle. For the person invoking such a tone, it was a deceptive way to die.

"Princess Wenonah, you cannot ride Darkshadow into your city. He does not take kindly to strangers and would throw you at the least favorable moment. There is only humiliation at the end of such a ride. My husband and his horse are as close as man and beast may become. You ask the impossible."

Wenonah's nostrils flared, and she planted her feet wide.

"Who is the Guest and who is the Host here? You do not understand our customs, Princess Erianne. Should Tul'ran ride his magnificent beast into the presence of our Elders, he will bring shame to me. As a Man, he cannot ride a horse greater in stature than one ridden by a Woman. It would suggest he stands in higher rank to the hereditary ruler of the Nine Tribes. Now get off your horse, lout, and give it to me!"

Erianne swung her legs off Destiny's Edge and walked up to Wenonah, her eyes hard shards of glittering green glass, while praying El Shaddai's Knife wouldn't glide past her cheek and into the young sovereign's throat.

"You forget yourself, Princess. You are so steeped in your ways that you carelessly vent your anger on a man who is not from your world. My husband," she paused for effect, "is not a worm you grind under your feet. Nor is he one of your love-slaves. You will do well to treat him with respect, for his wrath is something you do not wish to incur."

"He cannot ride his horse through our streets," Wenonah said with defiance, although the tone of her protest diminished when she saw the waves of threat wafting from Tul'ran's eyes.

Tul'ran looked up to the ceiling of the cavern and spread his arms out wide.

"Why am I here, El Shaddai? Do you truly call me to come to the aid of a people who would rather have me carry their packs than come to their rescue?"

When nothing tickled their minds, Erianne turned

back to Wenonah.

"Will this satisfy you, Princess Wenonah? When I first met my husband, he placed me on Darkshadow's back and bid his mount to treat me with kindness and respect. I could ride Darkshadow into the city, and my husband could ride Destiny's Edge."

"Why not?" Tul'ran said. "You already have my sword; why not have my horse, as well?"

Great. Now he was really steamed. Erianne strolled over to Darkshadow's head and ran a hand down the beautiful horse's cheek before looking up at Tul'ran.

"Milord husband, did El Shaddai not tell us we would have to practice diplomacy on this expedition? Is it too much to ask us to accommodate Wenonah's instructions by having me ride your stallion into the city?"

Tul'ran stared at her for a moment, then blew a gust of air from his lips.

"If there ever comes a time when I can refuse you anything, love of my life, it will come as a greater shock to me than it will you. Ride Darkshadow with my blessing."

The stallion stepped sideways and shook his head with a loud snort. Tul'ran slipped off his back and slapped him on the neck.

"Behave yourself, you old goat. I know you love Erianne better than me. Who could not, with her being such a beauty? You'll be fine."

Without looking at Wenonah, Tul'ran strode to Destiny's Edge to mount her.

"Stop!" Wenonah said, her right hand raised in

the universal gesture.

Tul'ran cocked an eyebrow at her.

"What now? Shall I not ride at all?"

Erianne glided in between the two of them, once more worried by the softness of his question.

"Princess Wenonah?"

The princess pressed her lips together and swallowed.

"I do not mean to anger you or your husband, Princess Erianne, but he cannot ride into the city in his warrior's clothing. The Warriors must change into the vestments I provided. To do otherwise would be... unseemly."

Erianne turned to face Tul'ran, whose dark eyes were smoking.

"If you were to stand behind Miikaw and Dizi, milord husband, we will not see you undress and adorn the clothing of Wenonah's people."

"You are managing me," he growled.

Erianne touched his face, moving her hand along his cheek in a stroke she knew he liked.

"I will make it worth your while later and prove to you once and for all why riding Darkshadow is not the best activity in the world."

His features softened as she hoped they would, and a smirk teased his lips.

"What will happen one day when the promise of a hard bounce does not temper my rage, milady wife?"

"Why then," she said in English, with as much sweetness as she could muster, "I'll have to kill you."

He barked out a laugh and walked to Darkshadow to take the bundle off the horse's hindquarters.

After sweeping an ironic bow to his wife, he moved to the back of the cave to change between the furry curtains of their carnivorous friends. On the way, he gestured to Ro'gun to join him.

They unpacked their change of dress and looked at each other with dismay. Their clothing comprised just four items: a loincloth, a breechcloth, a chest plate tied at the neck and waist, and a pair of moccasins.

Ro'gun stared at the small pile of clothing in his left hand and rubbed his eyebrow with his right.

"How are we to fight in this?"

"I think that's the point," Tul'ran said, aghast. "The men here are servants used for copulation and little else, from what I gathered from Wenonah's Telling."

Ro'gun looked at him with pleading eyes.

"Must we wear this, milord? I am not so secure in my marriage that I do not fear my wife laughing at me for the rest of my life."

Tul'ran avoided his gaze and began loosening his armor.

"What choice do we have, lad? You have heard Lady Erianne. The words flowing from the tongue will win this conflict as much as blood flowing from the veins."

With little enthusiasm, the two men disrobed and put on the provided clothing, while Dizi and Miikaw watched them. When they finished, Miikaw licked her muzzle with a long, pink tongue.

'Your concerns I see not. Delicious you look to these eyes.'

Tul'ran was too miserable to chuckle at the

obvious joke.

'What becomes of us, Lord Tul'ran?' Dizi cast into his mind. 'Are we to freeze in the cold waiting for you to return?'

Tul'ran shook his head as he tried to blend the loincloth and breech cloth to maximize the coverage of the skimpy materials.

'No. You two walk with us.'

The lion and the wolf exchanged glances.

'Sit well this will not, Tul'ran Lord.'

'Care not at all, do I,' he said into both their minds.

The men finished dressing and shared an agonized look before gesturing for the wolf and lion to step back.

Erianne watched the furry shield separate and felt her jaw go slack. The chest plate covered about a third of Tul'ran's massive pecs, and she could tell nothing covered his back.

The breech cloth sat above mid-thigh, front and back, separating on each side to reveal a generous length of thigh. Tul'ran's legs were well-muscled, concealed normally by his fighting leathers. His apparel left extraordinarily little to the imagination and much too much at the same time.

Erianne glanced behind her to see Wenonah's reaction, and it took her aback. The woman stared at Tul'ran with obvious lust in her eyes, and she moistened her lips with her tongue as Tul'ran walked forward. There was no doubt the skimpiness of her husband's apparel and the rippling muscles they revealed aroused the Princess.

Time to nip this in the bud.

Erianne walked toward Tul'ran, deliberately putting herself in the path of Wenonah's vision. She needed not to have worried about Tul'ran's reaction to Wenonah's passionate gaze. His eyes were ablaze with indignation.

"Milord husband," she said with enough volume for all to hear. "You suit your Ma'ilingan Waazh wardrobe most handsomely."

Tul'ran cocked his eyebrow at her, searching for the meaning of the nuances in her words.

"If you can call this a wardrobe," he said, his voice cross. "A man would freeze to death if ever he tried to venture beyond the cavern entrance. I would guess that's the point."

Tul'ran stepped around Erianne and walked up to Wenonah, muscles rippling with coordinated chaos in every stride. Someone could have chipped his eyes out of the ice surrounding the entrance to the cavern, and his voice was equally cold.

"Does this suit your custom and code? I am getting a flavor of why the Men in your world are so angry with Women."

Wenonah blushed deeply and averted her eyes; her lust melted away by the acid bath of his hostility.

"It's what Men wear in the City of Ikwe Na," she said, awkwardly.

"Perhaps I will speak with them," Tul'ran said, the temperature of his voice dipping further. "They may yet find the courage to resist their humiliation."

Tul'ran turned from her and walked his pack to Darkshadow. The stallion, keenly tuned to his master's moods, pawed at the dirt with a massive hoof and a deep whinny rumbled from his chest.

Tul'ran ran a hand along his neck, making a clucking sound with his tongue.

"Gently, brother. There will come a time when we seek balance, but it is not now."

Tul'ran stowed his armor on the warhorse's back and waited for Erianne to join him. He held out one large hand, and she put her left foot in it so he could boost her into the saddle. They both knew she didn't need the help, but the gesture reassured her his anger was directed elsewhere.

Tul'ran and Ro'gun mounted their horses, trying to position themselves to give the most coverage to their buttocks and groins.

"We must ride in this order to comply with custom," Wenonah said, pursing her lips and not meeting their eyes. "I will go first, with Princess Erianne directly behind me. Lady Omarosa, Lady Anatu and Lady Innanu will follow in that order. Last, will be Ro'gun and Tul'ran riding beside one another."

"What of Miikaw and Dizi?" Tul'ran said.

"What of them?"

"They stride with us."

Wenonah shook her head.

"I cannot bring a Wolf into the city. Wolves are an enemy of Women and have been the cause for many a ceremony sending our beloved sisters into the afterlife. To let a Wolf walk with us would be an egregious breach of security."

Tul'ran's face tightened, and Erianne interceded once more before her husband could speak the venom she could feel bubbling in his mind.

"Princess Wenonah, perhaps you would

reconsider? You have expressed your desire to bring peace to Ma'ilingan Waazh, yes? How much will you gain in status if you can show your ability to make peace between the lion and the wolf, two mortal enemies who despise one another? It will be a coup to have Dizi and Miikaw walking in front of Tul'ran and Ro'gun as if they were family, not foes. Do you not think so?"

After a long silence, with Erianne's words clearly churning in her mind, Wenonah nodded.

"I see the logic in your reasoning, Princess Erianne. You are quite right. They must come with us. Forward then!"

Forward then. Erianne searched her husband's face and shivered. She wondered how long she could keep him from killing someone.

Especially Wenonah.

The ride through the cavern was both enlightening and humiliating. A series of lights strategically placed on the cavern's high ceiling provided artificial sunlight throughout their long ride. The air was warm and moist, resulting in brilliantly green foliage interspersed through the long, square buildings surrounding the road. None of the wooden buildings were more than one storey high, but the residents decorated the exterior of them all with colorful, cultural depictions of the world's birds and animals.

This cavern differed from the ones Tul'ran knew in Spes. The Spesian caves were mostly towering walls of bare rock. Here, plant life, fruit trees, and berry bushes covered the entire wall. There were ladders to various terraces on which the food grew.

Everything was olive green, with floral colors popping up in many locations to break the monotony. Multiple waterfalls cascaded from the cavern walls into streams of brilliant blue veins burbling on the moss-covered floor. Flower scents wafted through the air and teased the senses.

Yes, the ride was both enlightening and humiliating. The humiliation came from catcalls in the audience the men's presence drew, some in the most graphically sexual terms.

Women populated the cavern, most dressed in one-piece suits fit comfortably to their bodies, which left their arms and legs below mid-thigh exposed. Their hair was a uniform dark-brown and long, sometimes braided or tied back with multi-colored bands. They stopped in their daily tasks to line the roadway and make lewd offers for the sharing of their beds with the two scantily clad men.

Tul'ran and Ro'gun were grateful for the guards, who kept the more aggressive women away from them. No sooner had they passed from the entrance to the cavern than a phalanx of female warriors formed up on either side of their group and behind them. Dark-gray modern graphite armor covered their entire bodies, including helmets covering the entire face. In gloved hands, they held gray metallic spears with a rounded sleeve at the butt of the spear. They did not appear to carry any other weapons.

'Be not fooled, Tul'ran Lord, by the deceptive appearance of their simple weapons,' Miikaw said to his mind. 'Phased energy weapons are they, outputting intense beams of concentrated light.'

'They'll cut through anything,' Dizi chimed in. 'As

the beams cut through flesh, they eat everything in their path.'

Tul'ran drew his lips into a firm, straight line.

'I've encountered similar weapons. They concern me not.'

Tul'ran pictured in his mind his entrance into Spes, playing the memory of the attack on his group with energy weapons and how Bloodwing countered them.

Miikaw side glanced Dizi and growled.

'Grateful am I, Tul'ran Lord, that I sided with you and your cause. Frightened am I, by your power.'

After a moment of silence, Dizi tentatively posed a new question.

'Why do you show us these things, Lord Tul'ran? Surely a better tactic would be to withhold the knowledge of your powers from beings which are potentially your enemies?'

Tul'ran's lips curved upwards in a lop-sided smile.

'Do the two of you not report to superiors who will analyze my memories and derive from them strategic intelligence about my capabilities?'

Neither wolf nor lion responded, which told the Sword Himself all he needed to know. Sometimes, the best way to stop a fight was to show the enemy how quickly they would die.

The long ride ended in an area in which many of the City's population stood. At the front of the amassed females, a corpulent woman radiating authority sat on a large chair, or palanquin, carried by six mostly nude men.

The headdress covering her braided black hair was large, composed of elongated brown feathers with black tips. Multi-colored beads adorned her traditional buckskin dress. Beaded mukluks extended to her knees. She held within her hands a long pipe on which someone had twisted red, yellow, and orange cloth.

Wenonah gestured, and the group behind her stopped. The Princess walked her horse forward a couple more steps and raised her right hand, palm facing outwards.

"Greetings, Mother."

The older woman nodded curtly.

"Greetings, Daughter. I'm grateful you've returned. When you rode away from us, many said we'd find your frozen corpse thirty steps from the entrance to the City. It appears you are stronger than many thought. Who are these people who ride behind you? How did they come to be here? And I'd love to learn why you thought it would be a clever idea to bring a Wolf into our stronghold!"

Wenonah raised her voice so it would carry to the ears of the women standing fifteen deep behind her mother.

"Ten nights ago, I left the City of Ikwe Na to seek the Garden of our Ancestors. For seven days I wandered through the frozen forest, following the small, still voices beckoning me forward. A Wolf, the very one who stands behind me, stalked me and I could hear his desire for my flesh in his mind. Hunted, cold, and in despair, I persisted in my search for the Garden. I found it."

A collective gasp resonated through the cavern.

"Not only did I find the Garden of our Ancestors, I spoke to the face of the Creator, Who touched my hand and spoke words out loud into my ears."

A louder gasp followed her statement, and murmuring created a low buzz. Wenonah raised her hand, and the Women grew still.

"I explained to the Creator our need for peace in Ma'ilingan Waazh and begged Him for victory against our enemies. He said He would send me a war party from beyond the stars who would bring peace to our world. I reposed with the Creator for two days, and on the third day," she gestured behind her, "these people came."

"When they exited the Garden, the Wolf known as Maji attacked Princess Erianne. You know the legend of this Wolf. Many of our fiercest warriors have fallen to him by fang and claw. Princess Erianne killed him as casually as we would draw smoke from a pipe."

Another gasp, this time one conveying amazement. Some Women looked at Erianne with a measure of respect.

"At that moment, Mother, your Mountain Lion, Miikaw, came down from the trees. I am touched you were so concerned about my welfare; you sent your best assassin out to follow me. When I explained to her what the Creator intended by bringing these people to our world, Miikaw pledged peace between herself and the Wolves. She now walks with Dizi as if he were her brother. Miikaw now binds herself to the husband of Princess Erianne, the woman who rides behind me on the great black horse."

Her last statement was too much. Scorn replaced the impressed looks on the faces surrounding her mother and hands moved towards weapons. Wenonah heard the word 'traitor' flowing from lip to lip. She trembled inside. She needed the will of the people if this was to work.

Her mother scowled and scanned the faces of Erianne and the women who rode at her back.

"Do you mean to tell us this group of women behind you travel from the stars?" She snorted derisively. "I think you have played the fool, daughter. They look no different from you or I."

Wenonah set her jaw and sparks flickered in her eyes.

"I do not claim it for them, Mother, for it is the Creator who claimed it for them, and I only repeat what He said."

"He said?" her mother snarled. "Now I know the blindness of the snow has dimmed the sight of your mind. The Creator is a Woman."

Wenonah's braids swept from side to side, so firmly did she shake her head.

"No, Mother, you are mistaken. I met with the Creator, who showed me visions of how all things came to pass in our world. He made all things and through Him, all things were made. There is no question in my mind He is who He says."

"It is your mind, I question," her mother retorted. "How dare you come here with strangers, uninvited, and their Wolf? You have compromised our security for what? A promise of peace from a ragtag group of refugees who claim to be from the stars? Perhaps it is time for you to see the Healer for what poisons your brain!"

She stopped her rant when Erianne kicked

Darkshadow forward, dwarfing the Princess at her side.

"I do not know why you mistrust the words of your daughter, Highness. Would it quench your doubts if I were to introduce myself and my party?"

The immense woman waved her hand as if Erianne were of no consequence. Erianne felt sorry for the men carrying her, who were sweating under the strain.

"We do not see you. Let my daughter introduce you if she is so eager to convince us you are starwalkers."

Erianne nudged Darkshadow's sides, and he stepped back to the front of her group. Wenonah lifted her chin defiantly.

"Mother, I am honored to present to you Princess Erianne of the world, Akiikaa."

She introduced each of the rest of her party, finishing with Tul'ran.

The corpulent woman gestured to her attendants, and they lowered her to the ground. Two of them helped her to stand on her feet, where she tottered for a moment before finding her equilibrium.

"I am Baamewaawaagizhigokwe."

In their minds, Erianne and her group heard the name translated as 'Woman of the Sound the Stars Make Rushing Through the Sky.'

"I lead these women by their voice and the spears in their hands. How do you know my daughter?"

"Your daughter spoke the truth," Erianne said. "We met her in the Garden of Ancestors after the Creator summoned us to the aid of your world."

Baamewaawaagizhigokwe snorted.

"The Creator sent us three Women and two useless Men to bring to an end a war enduring for hundreds of years." Her laugh was cruel and echoed by the women behind her.

"Or perhaps you are a troupe of refugees taken in by my daughter and encouraged by indebtedness to take part in her delusions?"

Erianne squelched the irritation rising in her chest.

"You have my word; we are who I have said. What reason do you have to doubt my word?"

The heavy woman stamped her foot petulantly.

"Reason? You ride with my delusional daughter, who lacks the sense of the horse upon which she sits. What more of a reason do I need? You wish to curry favor with me? Give me your husband for a night. If he wishes to return to you when I am finished with him, then I'll listen to your fanciful tales."

The women behind Baamewaawaagizhigokwe laughed boisterously. Erianne stiffened as she heard the murderous thoughts of her husband echo in her mind.

'Milord Tul'ran,' she cast to his mind. 'Be at peace. I have this.'

"Baamewaawaagizhigokwe, your ridiculous offer is unacceptable to me. My husband is not a property to be traded for favor. This night he rests his head upon my breasts, and no other."

Baamewaawaagizhigokwe became visibly angry. She gestured to her attendants after falling back into the fur covered chair, and they struggled to lift it back onto their shoulders.

"It's the only offer you'll get from me. Perhaps a

night in confinement will persuade you into cooperation."

The warriors following them dropped into a ready position, spears extended at a forty-five-degree angle. Erianne felt Tul'ran's will extend beyond his body to touch the ethereal blade sitting on her back.

'Tul'ran, please. Do you not trust your wife? I have this.'

'I believe you have this,' his words echoed gently in her mind. 'There is a word in your language applying to these circumstances. Insurance.'

Erianne kept the smile off her face, but just barely. Great. Now this man from four thousand years into her past was talking to her about insurance. Good grief. Where would he have learned about insurance?

"Baamewaawaagizhigokwe, I don't understand you. Your world lies in a crisis, from what I hear from Princess Wenonah. Is it not so? The Creator has heard your prayers for peace, and He sends us in answer to your prayers. Do you not see us as different from you? My skin is far darker than yours, while the skin tone of the rest of my party is lighter. Do our differences not attest to the truth of our statements?"

Baamewaawaagizhigokwe sniffed.

"Mutations are not the equivalent of visitors from the stars. We don't venture into the ignorant lands of Men. Who knows what their experiments have wrought? Surrender yourselves to my guards. I will consider your claims over the next two days with the Elders, and we will render judgment. If you resist, we will confiscate your horses and weapons as a bounty for insulting us with your fanciful story and cast you out into the snow with my foolish daughter."

Erianne straightened in her saddle and pulled her shoulders back.

"Your terms are not acceptable."

Baamewaawaagizhigokwe's face became livid.

"I will teach you what it means to refuse my generous offer. Seize them!"

Her guards leveled their spears and advanced on their party. Erianne felt a flare of anger in Tul'ran's mind before she closed her connection to it. She crossed her arms before her, laying her right amulet over the left. The Garden appeared in front of them, framed in wreaths of blue energy. As the guards came within six feet of them, she slapped her hands backward to her shoulders. The gate flew over them and her party disappeared.

Before the gate reached Tul'ran, he casually flipped away the small blue marble in his right hand. It flew like a missile into the palanquin upon which Baamewaawaagizhigokwe sprawled, disintegrating it instantaneously and dumping her on her massive backside. The last thing Tul'ran saw before Destiny's Edge's feet met the grass of the Garden was the look of utter shock on the woman's face.

Erianne scanned her party and sighed with relief. Everyone had come through into the Garden, including Dizi and Miikaw, except Wenonah.

Erianne had deliberately left Wenonah behind. Mother and daughter needed to sort out their stuff before anything was going to get accomplished in this world. She caught Tul'ran's eye.

"Why do you look so pleased with yourself? I did

all the work. I told you I had this."

He whooped and jumped off Destiny's Edge. In three long strides, he was at Darkshadow's flank. He reached up and lifted Erianne off his horse before spinning her around twice, her legs horizontal to the ground.

"You did most excellently, my beautiful wife. Never did I doubt you."

She canted a look at his face; the mischief glinting in his eyes and shook her head.

"What did you do?"

CHAPTER THE THIRTEENTH: THE CURTAIN

Ma'ilingan Waazh (Wolf's Den), 175th Year of Winter
First day, Manoominike-giizis (Ricing Moon), year 5379
Six months later

Time had no meaning in the Garden. When time doesn't exist, there's no sunrise and sunset. You ate and played until exhaustion set in, then you slept. When you awoke, you bathed, ate, and looked for something to fill the non-existent time. For warriors, down time meant an opportunity to train, hone your skills, and plan for warfare. Especially for the new recruits.

Erianne looked fondly at Omarosa, Innanu, and Anatu. They spent the first number of what felt like hours after they re-entered the Garden, dissecting the events in the City of Ikwe Na while eating and relaxing. When no one came after them, Tul'ran and Erianne went to the center of the Garden and stared at the gap between the forbidden trees. Nothing showed in the Gate. Jesus chose to not be there or give them instructions for the first little while of their sojourn, making it clear they were to stay put.

Omarosa approached them after they finished a meal alongside the river, which burbled happily through the center of the Garden. She bowed her introduction not as family to family, but as oath sworn to oath holder, causing Tul'ran's eyebrows to dance on his face and making Erianne smile.

"Lord Tul'ran and Lady Erianne, may I have a word?"

Tul'ran gestured to the grass just beyond their feet. He had his back pressed up against a broad fruit tree, and Erianne rested her back against his chest. Omarosa dimpled and gracefully floated down to kneel in front of them.

"Omarosa, why so formal? We are kin. You need not seek permission to speak."

"Milord Tul'ran, I noticed the population of this part of the world to be mostly women. Many were armed and wore the vestments of battle." She hesitated. "Milady Erianne hinted my daughters and I are warriors when she introduced us to the Women, but we know nothing of arms and battle. We want to rectify this immediately. We ask you to train us in the way of sword and spear, bow and arrow, so we may truly be members of your war party."

Erianne looked up at her husband. She reached up with her left hand and scraped her fingernails on the stubble under his chin.

"We stagnate, milord husband, waiting for something to happen on Wolf's Den. I'd welcome a chance to train these women after I take a knife to your throat again. Come, my love, shall we take on the pain and obligation of the instructor?"

Tul'ran grinned.

"What is it you once said? Cry havoc and let slip the dogs of war? I like the saying. Wolf!"

Dizi bounded up to them, his tongue hanging out of one side of his mouth, while Darkshadow trotted behind him. He and Darkshadow had developed a friendship, which included engaging in mock fights to train how they would attack and defend against each other. Darkshadow's coat shone from the sweat of this day's exertions.

'Lord Tul'ran, what is your desire?'

Tul'ran reached up to scratch the giant canine behind his ears, much to the startled amazement of Omarosa.

'I hate to ask this,' he thought to the Wolf and Erianne, 'but would you and Miikaw move outside the Garden and perform a quick sweep of our perimeter? When you return, we'll begin training Omarosa and her children in the force of arms and art of war. I don't want to be surprised with an ambush while we're so engaged.'

Dizi darted in and ran a long pink tongue along one side of Tul'ran's face, making him sputter and wipe away the slobber.

'My pleasure, Lord and Lady. We'll return shortly.'

When the Wolf ran away to find Miikaw, Erianne and Tul'ran rose to their feet.

"Come, Omarosa. If it's your desire to learn how to fight with hand and sword, you have our pledge to teach you to the best of our skill."

When they found a broad swath of flattened grass within which to train, El Shaddai had left knives, swords, spears, bows and arrows in the middle of the field. Accepting it as a sign of approval, all of them began training earnestly. An uncountable time flew by and the women gained proficiency with every practice. When it came time to pair up to spar, though, only Erianne fought Tul'ran.

The first time they sparred, Erianne and Tul'ran once more forgot themselves, where they were, and who watched them. After thirty minutes of a whirlwind of blows, parries, blocked thrusts, and counter strokes, they stopped, winded. Once more, no blow scored a point, so equally matched were they. It took a few seconds to realize everything around them was silent.

They turned to find the rest of the group with mouths agape, holding themselves still to avoid stopping their mentors' match. Anatu, the youngest, came up to each of them and planted a kiss on their cheeks.

"Milord and milady, I pledge my word I shall train until I can attain one part of one hundredth of the skill you have shown us today. Even if I should reach such a level of proficiency, I will be proud to call myself a warrior."

Erianne laughed and kissed the top of her forehead.

"You flatter us. We became lost in the moment, Anatu. Let's see to the baths for our muscles and food for our bellies."

That conversation had been what felt like months

ago. Now the three women stood before Erianne, swords raised, and a determined look in their eyes. She sparred with each one of them this morning, and all performed exceptionally well. Erianne raised her sword to salute them.

"When we started this adventure, I never expected to stand before the three of you with these feelings in my heart. Where before I loved you, now I admire you as well. You have earned your rank as a warrior, and I am proud to include you in our troop. Kneel."

The three women kneeled before her, and Erianne raised Caligo high. She dropped the sword on each of their shoulders, calling them by name and saying,

"I receive thee as a Warrior in the Princess Erianne Guard. Arise, Warrior, and be recognized."

Omarosa, Innanu, and Anatu stood to receive a kiss on the lips from their Princess. They were bound by blood and honor to Erianne, and each felt it to the depths of their souls. Tul'ran and Ro'gun looked on somberly, leaning on their swords. Now they numbered six warriors, not three, and had powers beyond the ken of their foes. They were ready.

So was Fate.

Dizi and Miikaw bounded through the entrance to the world, their fur covered in snow, having finished their daily rounds.

'Warriors come,' Miikaw announced, 'and Wenonah Princess with them rides.'

Dizi shook himself from nose to tail and the snow went flying.

'There are six warriors armed with spears. The

Princess is not armed and may be their prisoner.'

"Prisoner?" Tul'ran led Ro'gun to stand with Erianne and her Guards. "Her fortune has changed then?"

"Her fortune changed dramatically," Wenonah said as she walked in through the gate. She blew a grateful sigh as the warmth of the Garden wafted over the exposed skin of her face. Six guards dressed in armor and carrying spears stepped in behind her. Each quickly scanned the Garden before focusing on the Lord's Warriors. No one could see their faces through their masks, and they couldn't tell if the existence of the Garden shocked or surprised them.

Erianne took a step forward and nodded to the guards while sheathing her sword in a scabbard on her left hip.

"Thank you for bringing Princess Wenonah back to the Garden safely. You may return to the City of Ikwe Na."

The guards looked at one another.

"Princess Wenonah is our prisoner," one stated in a mechanical voice. "When we leave, she comes with us."

Erianne smiled sweetly and crossed her hands behind her back.

"There are no prisoners in the Creator's Garden. If you wish to stay, stack your weapons outside the Garden and return. We can offer you food, drink, and respite. Should this be unacceptable to you, you may leave."

"We'll leave and take Wenonah with us," the guard said, her voice guttural.

"No," Erianne said, her tone not wavering,

"you'll just leave."

A Gate suddenly appeared behind the guards and flashed over them before they could react. When it closed, only Wenonah remained standing before them. She raised her hands, which were encased in metallic manacles. Tul'ran stepped forward and drew El Shaddai's Knife from its sheath in the center of his chest armor. It passed through the metal with no regard for its density and strength, and the remnants fell to Wenonah's feet.

"Why are you bound, Princess?"

Wenonah smiled at Tul'ran and rubbed her wrists.

"Thank you, Lord Tul'ran. You disappeared from the City of Ikwe Na, leaving the populace dazed and afraid. Except for my mother, who you humiliated when you made her palanquin dissolve and she fell to the ground."

Erianne whirled on Tul'ran.

"You did what?"

Tul'ran's eyes twinkled, and he fought to keep a smile off his face.

"There is a saying among my people: those who hold themselves above our heads must be prepared to lose theirs. Her mother kept her head, but not her dignity. It was a small price to pay for her insolence, don't you think?"

Erianne closed her eyes and took a deep breath.

"Tul'ran, how will you learn diplomacy when your first thought is toward vengeance?"

He leaned over to kiss her lips.

"I promise to do better, my love, and will restrain my temper while we repose on this world."

Fate laughed.

Erianne helped Wenonah out of her furs and winter garments. Once she was down to her bodysuit and bare feet, they spread a blanket and sat beneath a fruit tree. Anatu produced a platter of fruit and presented it to Wenonah.

"Thank you, Lady Anatu," she said, as Anatu blushed at the use of the title.

"When you left, my mother was furious. Her guards seized me and took me to a warehouse nearby. They thrust me into a small room with a window too little to allow an escape. After bringing in a cot and a blanket, they left me in the room with only the light of the window enabling sight. It was dank and dusty. For the first day, they only offered me water and bread for my meals."

"After the first day, my mother summoned me for interrogation. I told them everything I could, describing the Garden of the Ancestors and my conversations with the Creator. She didn't want to hear what she immediately labeled as baseless superstitions. Instead, she grilled me about you and your powers, demanding to know how you disappeared from our sight and generated the power to dissolve her chair."

"When I told her the truth, that I knew extraordinarily little of you and your capabilities, it incensed her. She had me thrown back into my confinement. I remained there for six months."

"Six months! It's been six months? She kept you locked up the whole time? On what charges?"

Wenonah's eyebrows pulled toward each other.

"Charges, Princess Erianne? What are charges?"

Erianne's eyebrows did a dance of their own.

"You don't know what charges are? What kind of legal system do you have? Charges are accusations of wrongdoing presented to a judge or jury of your peers to determine whether you are to be found guilty of the accusations."

Wenonah's confusion deepened.

"We have nothing in the manner of what you speak. My mother's offended feelings were enough to have me confined. It wasn't so bad. The Creator came to visit every night, and we spoke at length of His desires for this world. He brought with him a wonderful bread tasting of honey and fruit, which we shared in the darkness of my cell. When He was not with me, I exercised and took stock of the things about myself I wished to strengthen or change."

Erianne reached out and took one of Wenonah's hands.

"I'm so sorry, Princess. Had we known your mother imprisoned you, we would've returned and secured your release."

Wenonah squeezed her hand.

"You have nothing for which to apologize. My confinement and your actions led to a furor between my mother and the Elders. They questioned mother's decisions and demanded a reconciliation between mother and daughter. Some openly questioned my mother's rule. When the talk turned to me replacing my mother as the leader of our tribe, her attitude changed. She brought me out of confinement and told me she would relinquish the crown to me if I negotiated peace between Men and Women."

Tul'ran ran his fingernails along the edge of El Shaddai's Knife, trimming them nicely.

"Was it then you came to us?"

"You have the right of it, Lord Tul'ran. The guards who came with me belonged to my mother and the Elders. They were with me to protect me from each other, as well as Wolves and the elements. The tension between them was intense. Princess Erianne, can you open a way to the plasma barrier separating the Women from the Men?"

Erianne shook her head morosely.

"I cannot, Princess Wenonah. If it were something I had seen or a place to which I'd already traveled, there would be no problem. We must journey by horse."

"By horse," Tul'ran said. "How long will it take us to get there by horse?"

Wenonah glanced at Erianne, who showed nothing on her face to show how Tul'ran would receive her answer.

"Two weeks."

"Two weeks!" Tul'ran blew a gust of air through his nose. "Two weeks in that frozen hell will be more than I can endure."

Erianne leaned over and touched his chest.

"I refuse to believe that the man who single-handedly brought a warring planet to its knees, begging mercy, could not spend a mere two weeks in frigid conditions. We can do this."

He snorted and pushed himself to his feet.

"You're managing me again. When we're done with this world, we're going on vacation somewhere warm."

Fate smiled sadly. Only the living went on vacation.

———————⊢———

On their first day of travel, the wind howled against their every step, making conversation impossible. They camped the first night in a hollow at the base of a tree so impossibly large it sheltered them all, including the horses. The group stripped the tack from their horses and covered them with furs. They dug through the snow until they found rich foliage clinging to the frozen turf. It gave the horses a satisfying meal while their humans readied the inside of the shelter.

The women searched the forest for dry wood for a fire while the men pulled apart the large packs. Once they lit a fire, they brought the horses in, crowding the space. The fur-covered horses blocked the entrance to the base of the tree and added their heat to the tree's bowels. The humans huddled around the fire, while outside, the wind howled pitifully. Dinner was bannock, dried and flavored meat and dried fruit. After they ate, they spread a bison hide on the ground and all snuggled together under furs to share body heat and sleep.

They awoke the next morning to a windless day and cloudless sky. The warriors dressed and saddled their horses before leading them back outside. Tul'ran cursed as he tightened the horses' cinches with bare hands, the gloves being too bulky for such a chore. Even without the wind, it was hideously cold.

Wenonah led the way south, with the rest of them grouped behind them. After an hour of silence,

Erianne broke it with,

"Milord Tul'ran, the road is long and our journey is far..."

The others looked at each other, puzzled, while Erianne and Tul'ran laughed to breathlessness.

"Milady Erianne, what tale from my past will entertain you and these, our family, as we journey forward?"

Erianne rubbed her chin against an itchy spot on her neck and thought for a moment.

"Vaguely, you've referred to armies you led into battle. Tell us of one such time."

Tul'ran grunted.

"On my world, there was a great country named Egypt governing much of the west and south to where I lived. The sixth ruler of the Eleventh Dynasty was Mentuhotep II. He reigned for fifty-one years and was a military leader of some reckoning. He reunited Egypt and became the first pharaoh of the Middle Kingdom."

———✦———

Tul'ran was twenty-seven years old when Mentuhotep's emissary came to him in Suse. By then, his legend was epic and eclipsed all others of his time. The emissary bowed and scraped his way into Tul'ran's presence, fighting to keep from meeting the eyes of the Sword Himself. He held out a papyrus scroll as Tul'ran brushed Darkshadow to a brilliant sheen.

"What's this?" Tul'ran asked, angry at the interruption.

"Lord az Nostrom," the man said in a wavering voice, "I came from Pharoah Mentuhotep II of

Egypt with a request for your services."

Amazement replaced irritation. Tul'ran took the scroll, untied the leather straps holding it together, and allowed it to unfold into his hands. Following the unification of Egypt, Mentuhotep II reformed Egypt's government, and he stripped the regional governors of their power. Under his vizier Khety, he launched military campaigns into Nubia.

His campaigns had spread his armies thin. The Canaanites were causing problems on his borders and needed to be suppressed. Mentuhotep II had men under arms, but no leaders to take them into battle against the Canaanites.

Tul'ran turned to the messenger.

"Take me to Pharoah."

The messenger rubbed his head on ground and moaned.

"It is not possible for a foreigner to gaze on the face of the divine Mentuhotep II. If you would give your answer to me, I will convey it to the priests who serve him."

Tul'ran drew Bloodwing and waved the tip below the messenger's lowered eyes.

"If your god wants me to fight for him, then he will see me. Do we ride, or do you go back without an answer or your tongue?"

The messenger shuddered. To return without an answer meant his death. He reluctantly nodded his acquiescence and the two of them journeyed to Mentuhotep II's encampment. Darkshadow was in his finest form, prancing as if he bore the Pharoah and not some barbarian. It came as a shock to all present when Pharoah granted Tul'ran an audience.

As Tul'ran entered the tent, priests held a sheet between him and Mentuhotep II.

"Pharoah, you called, and I have come."

One priest tried to shove Tul'ran to his knees, hissing, "You must kneel before Pharaoh, for he is divine."

Tul'ran backhanded the priest so hard he almost collapsed the tent when Tul'ran's blow flung him against its sides.

"I kneel before no one, and I do not fight for anyone who does not convey his wishes while looking into my eyes."

A pregnant silence ensued. The Pharoah said something in his language, and the priests protested. Mentuhotep II spoke sharply, and the priests dropped the blanket and fled from the tent, leaving behind one priest to translate.

Tul'ran looked at Pharoah and saw a tall, dark-skinned man with a long beard tied in a straight line below his chin. He wore a red hat flaring out at the top, so the top of the hat was wider than the portion on his head. He had on a white robe and held a scepter in one hand. Tul'ran bowed to him, and Mentuhotep II bowed back.

"How may I serve you, Pharoah?"

The translator's jaw went slack when the Pharoah gestured for Tul'ran to sit with him.

"It's been a long time, Lord Tul'ran, since I've sat across from a fellow warrior and talked as men. Wine?"

Tul'ran nodded and settled himself on the carpet covering the desert floor. Mentuhotep II scandalized the translator when he poured a goblet of wine for himself and his guest.

"I have heard much of the legend of Tul'ran the Sword. You are younger than I expected, given the deeds attributed to your name. Are you as good as your Ballad says?"

Tul'ran laughed softly.

"Many of the stanzas are based on fact, though embellished beyond reason and truth."

Mentuhotep II smiled and leaned back against some pillows.

"Is it not always the way? Allow me to get to my point, my young friend, for you have traveled far and I wish to have you enjoy the pleasures of my hospitality before you campaign for me. The Canaanites have raised an army and seek to encroach upon my lands. I cannot condone this. They have three thousand men under arms. I have eight hundred men who lack for a leader. The odds are not good, but surely not too great for the Prince of Death?"

On the way to see Pharoah, Tul'ran had forced the messenger to detour to the Canaanite encampment so he could take stock of the men they had under arms. They were conscripts; poor men without hope or the prospect of jobs. Tul'ran smiled at Mentuhotep II without baring his teeth.

"Give me your men, Pharoah, and I will secure your borders against the Canaanite horde."

After a show at haggling, they agreed upon a price that made the translator faint and Tul'ran a wealthy man. The two men sojourned to another tent, where Pharoah introduced him to his harem.

"From this day forward, Pharoah and I became the greatest of friends. He introduced me to his commanders, who resented me at first. They changed their feelings after I fought one of them and pinned his guts to the ground with a spear. I took Pharoah's army to Canaan and commanded them into battle. Pharoah's men were well-trained, and the Canaanites were a rabble of goat herders. We prevailed even though they outnumbered us, and the Canaanites withdrew. The action did nothing to diminish my status in the eyes of the people in my region or my favor with Egypt."

Erianne sat rigid in her saddle.

"That was you? The Pharaoh's campaign against the Canaanites was your doing?"

Tul'ran chuckled.

"You'd heard of it, then?"

"Heard of it? It was required reading when I studied the region to prepare for travel there. Forgive my amazement, Tul'ran. Sometimes I forget who I married."

For two weeks their horses plowed through snow, drifting up to their chests, wheezing in the bitter cold. At night, they would find shelter and start a fire after digging through the elements to find nourishment for their stock. They'd fall asleep curled together, too tired to do more than dream. The next day, they ventured forth into the cold and snow. It was hard, exhausting work and the long nights of sleep couldn't fully erase their weariness.

Each morning, Tul'ran cursed the cold and bemoaned the stupidity of the Men who were so consumed with their arrogance they allowed their sky to fall. As each day passed, with the cold pressing through his garments and seeking to freeze his soul, Tul'ran's complaints increased in volume and frequency. Finally, Erianne drew him aside and chastised him, reminding him they were all cold and how demoralizing his complaints could be. After her admonishment, Tul'ran confined himself to cursing under his breath.

The journey was monotonous, and by the time they arrived at their first waypoint, not even Tul'ran's stories were enough to keep their senses from being dulled by the snow, wind, and cold.

The last afternoon of their travels brought them to a massive plasma curtain stretching from ground to sky and across the horizon. They rode to within one hundred strides of its base. It was beautiful. Multiple colors washed across the face of the curtain in waves, undulating under the brittle sky.

"What do we do now?" Erianne said, directing the question at Wenonah.

The Princess shook her head.

"I don't know. No one's attempted to communicate with Men for years."

Tul'ran cupped his hands around his mouth and raised his face toward the wall.

"We've come to engage in negotiations," he yelled as loudly as he could. His words met silence.

"It was a splendid effort," Erianne said, stroking a hand against his arm. Tul'ran grinned at her.

"See how I've learned, milady wife? I started with diplomacy."

Tul'ran nudged Darkshadow forward and drew

Bloodwing from behind his back.

"I am Tul'ran az Nostrom, the Sword Himself, the Uncreator, the Prince of Death. In this moment, being of generous spirit, I give you two options. Open a window in this curtain and let us enter, or I will take it down."

An amplified voice laughed somewhere behind the wall above him.

"You've consumed too much of the juice that engorges a man's ego. You can't take down this wall. Go away, Prince of Traitors. We're not entertaining visitors from the North."

"We're on a mission to negotiate a peace between Men and Women," Wenonah shouted. "It's imperative we meet in person to discuss how this war might end."

"We're not interested in talking to you," the voice sneered. "Go home, Princess Wenonah. Go home before we send out an armed party to add you to our breeding stables."

Wenonah's face paled, and she opened her mouth to shout her retort, but Omarosa silenced her with a hand on her arm.

"Why have they not done so?"

"What?" Erianne said.

Omarosa smiled timidly.

"I'm new to the game of war, Princess Erianne. We crossed a long open field and climbed to the top of this plateau after we left the safety of the forest. They could've met us before we came close to the curtain. We are two men and five women. Our capture would no doubt contribute to the diversity of their families. Why have they not come out to

331

meet us?"

Erianne grinned at her.

"I'm impressed, Lady Omarosa. Your comments convey good tactical awareness. What say you, milord husband?"

Tul'ran nodded thoughtfully.

"I agree with Lady Omarosa's assessment. Had they the means, we'd be under attack." He turned back to face the curtain and pointed Bloodwing upwards to where they'd heard the voice.

"I offer you a last chance. Open this curtain and permit us passage or I will take it down."

Harsh laughter greeted his words.

"We never knew the Prince of Death to be a fool. Go ahead, fire your weapon. The energy you pour into our shield will only strengthen it."

Tul'ran tilted his head to one side and contemplated the multi-colored energy field pulsating in front of him.

"So be it," he said, his voice calm and resolved.

For a moment, nothing happened. The curtain pulsed and wavered, before a small strand of the Curtain pulled away and bobbled toward Tul'ran's upraised sword. The strand thickened and energy poured into the sword like a rush of water falling from a mountain. It made no sound, but Bloodwing's blade glowed a bright blue, increasing in intensity with the energy flow.

Erianne gestured the rest of their party back.

"Tul'ran," she called, "are you safe? I can barely see you with the glow of Bloodwing's energy surrounding you."

"I thrive," Tul'ran yelled back. The brightness of

the curtain dimmed considerably and Bloodwing took on the glare of a blue star. Still the curtain kept flowing, until, in a last splutter of energy, it disappeared.

Men stood on scaffolding before them, stunned into silence and frozen in place. Bloodwing was a pulsing blue quasar, creating stark shadows of everything surrounding it.

Tul'ran raised the Blade to the vertical and held it in place, panting as he exerted his will on the sword. The brilliant blue writhed and turned into a vivid purple before streaking upwards in a solid stream. The lavender beam struck the outer reaches of the planet's stratosphere and bloomed outwards until it blanketed the upper atmosphere. Bloodwing emptied itself into the frosted sky and the sword dimmed to a deep black.

The purple blanket continued to pulse, then solidified into a transparent sheen.

The air became silent.

Craning her head to the sky, Erianne nudged Destiny's Edge forward to come alongside Darkshadow.

"What did you do?" she whispered.

Tul'ran looked like he'd ridden for three days and then fought a battle for two. The skin of his face sagged, and fatigue hooded his eyes.

"I uncreated the destruction of the ice shield."

Erianne's eyes grew larger in her face.

"What do you mean?"

Tul'ran closed his eyes as if it were a trial to think of an answer.

"They destroyed the shield around the world. I

asked Bloodwing to uncreate the destruction of the shield, and it did so. Ice once more encapsulates Wolf's Den."

Erianne felt her mouth fall open.

"It can do that?"

Tul'ran shrugged, and a faint smile tugged at his lips.

"Apparently so. Look, here comes a delegation of Men."

A group of men carrying spears advanced toward them, a dark bloom of fear hovering over their heads. The leader of the group jerked a bow in Tul'ran's direction.

"We understand you've come to parlay."

Tul'ran choked off laughter and nodded.

"Will you enter peace negotiations?"

"What choice have we?" the man answered with a sour face. "You've taken down our last defense." He turned to Wenonah and scowled.

"Understand, Princess, no peace will be possible if you refuse to return our scientists. We have suffered mightily without them. Our technologies are failing, but we have no one to design their repair or replacement."

Wenonah looked at him blankly.

"Scientists? I'm sorry, what scientists?"

The man's eyebrows rose sharply.

"What do you mean, what scientists? Five years ago, your mother sued for peace and called for a meeting of scientists from the Nine Tribes to bring an end to the Long Winter before we became extinct. We sent all our scientists to the City of Ikwe Na. Your mother seized and imprisoned them. In desperation, we erected the Curtain to protect ourselves. We've had no ability to create new things or repair broken things because you have kept our intellectuals."

"What's that?" Innanu interrupted, pointing at the sky.

Everyone craned their necks upward as a large, black, triangular shape flew from the north toward them.

"No!" Wenonah screamed.

"What's wrong?" Erianne said, frightened by her scream.

"It's an anti-gravity bomber. It holds weapons of mass destruction. Mother said she'd never use it, unless as a last resort to save our kind! What's she doing?"

"Winning the war," Tul'ran said, anger dancing on his words. "Sending you here was a ruse, Princess Wenonah. She intends to end this war and your challenge to her throne in one action."

Bloodwing glowed blue and tendrils of blue evanescence plunged into his arm. Tul'ran growled in his throat as his eyes blazed azure. A ball of ethereal energy formed in his hands and he threw it with all his strength. He need not have tried so hard. The energy of uncreation moved at the speed of light and splashed the bomber in a grim cloak before the bomber faded into non-existence.

A streamer of blue energy streaked to the north and faded from their sight.

Tul'ran turned on Wenonah, his face a mask of rage.

"Did you take part in this deception to secure

your freedom?" he said, his words grinding their way out of his mouth.

Wenonah put her hand to her throat.

"No! I swear it on my blood! I would never have been part of a plan to kill hundreds of thousands of People."

"Baamewaawaagizhigokwe can no longer kill hundreds of thousands of anything," Tul'ran said, his voice as cold as the surrounding air. "Those triangular things, the weapons they carried, and the places housing them no longer exist. Be grateful I didn't extend my anger to your mother."

He turned to the man who had approached them, who appeared to be struggling to keep the contents of his bowels in place.

"Is there one among you who can speak with some authority?"

The man swallowed hard and raised a small device to his mouth.

"Send Nicholas."

A man at the other end of the communication squawked a protest, but the one closest to them cut him off.

"I don't care. Send Nicholas before this warrior decides we're a nuisance and dusts us as easily as he dusted that bomber."

In the distance, a tent flap moved, and a young man exited. He was tall, six foot two inches tall, and long brown hair spilled onto his shoulders. Dark eyes peered out over high brown cheekbones in a ruggedly handsome face. He was lean and muscular, taking long strides as he moved toward them with purpose. A dark green parka covered his upper body, and a heavy green coverall protected his lower body from the cold. The parka had a hood, but the man disdained its use for the short walk from the tent to the group gathered.

He came up to them and stopped, folding his arms across his chest.

"I am Nicholas Nighthawk. My father is Chief of the Tribes of Men. What is it you seek?"

Tul'ran sheathed Bloodwing and took two steps to square off against the younger man.

"I am Tul'ran the Conqueror. You have two choices now, Nicholas Nighthawk. Your best option of the two is to sue for peace and we will negotiate an end to this war between Women and Men."

He gestured Wenonah forward.

"This is Wenonah Bearspaw, the new leader of the Nine Tribes. Her word binds the Women."

Nicholas searched Wenonah's expressionless face.

"Does this Warrior speak truly? Do you ascend to the ancestral Throne over all the People?"

Without looking at Tul'ran, Wenonah swallowed and nodded slowly.

"He does. He is my Second for all negotiations."

Silence decided on the field. Tul'ran allowed himself to shiver.

"While I'm not usually a man to force another to make up his mind, it'll go well with you if you should decide before I freeze to death."

Nicholas laughed, showing a mouthful of even white teeth.

"You confess to weakness after single-handedly destroying our greatest defense and our enemy's greatest weapon. Tell me, Tul'ran, what is our second choice? You said our first option is to sue for peace and enter peace negotiations."

Tul'ran met the young man's eyes; the skin of his face tightened, and his tone matched the freezing essence of the surrounding air.

"My second option is to conquer this world and make all of you my slaves." His lips curled upwards, but there was no kindness in the look on his face.

"You should know I'm particularly cruel to my slaves."

CHAPTER THE FOURTEENTH: WHEN THE STARS FALL

The Kingdom of Heaven

It's a surprise, he'd said.

Darian stretched her gaze up to E'thriel's face, so many feet above hers. They were walking finger-linked through the City of New Jerusalem, ignoring the odd stare they encountered from people or members of the angelic host. She knew their relationship was different; angels usually treated humans with polite deference, bowing slightly in greeting when they encountered the Sons and Daughters of God. Humans treated angels with kindness and respect. They certainly never walked through Heaven's streets finger-linked with one.

Maybe it was the time they spent together on Spes, while Darian healed from her injuries, blinded by the bandages covering her face, which drew them closer than most angels and people. She'd spent many hours talking to E'thriel about life, the universe, and everything before she knew he was an angel of the Lord. The revelation had been shocking and gladdening at the same time. His stories about the creation of angels and the universe had softened her heart towards a relationship with God. A relationship later cemented by Jesus Himself.

Whatever the cause, she felt close to the massive creature who went everywhere with her. He talked little about how it felt to be back in Heaven after the Rebellion, but she sensed it caused him discomfort. The Holy Trinity treated E'thriel well and showered favor on him, but she knew the angel had yet to be judged for joining Lucifer against God. A shudder rippled through her body. She prayed every day for God's mercy for her guardian angel.

They stopped in front of a beautiful mahogany-colored door. It was deceptive because it didn't truly reveal the size of the dwelling behind the door. Each door in the millions of miles of square feet in the City opened into the foyer of a mansion. When you walked through the mansion, you entered acres of garden, or fields, or forests, or grasslands; whatever you preferred.

"God wrapped the residences of Heaven into a multi-dimensional matrix," E'thriel tried to explain for the fourth time several cycles ago as they dined on pizza and sipped on the most amazing wine Darian had ever tasted in her heavenly home. He'd laboriously drawn the math on a transparent table occupying one entire wall of her mansion. Darian was smart, but it'd been a long time since she'd studied anything. He lost her after the first hundred lines of math.

"Yahweh compressed each mansion into a bubble, but expanded the interior of the bubble over infinity. He affixed each bubble to a door. Every door in Heaven stands about six feet apart, but once you enter the door, you walk into the dimensional space occupied by the residence. It can be as big or small as you want it to be; the exercise of the occupant's will creates the contents of residence."

Darian shook her head.

"Has anyone pulled their mansion away from the City accidentally?"

E'thriel laughed.

"Yahweh's energy binds everything in Heaven. You could no more pull a mansion away from Heaven than you could remove your hand and slap yourself with it."

Darian focused her attention on the door before her. It was a nice door. She looked up at E'thriel again, and he gave her a slight nod while struggling to keep a smile off his lips.

"Go ahead, Princess."

She shook her head at the nickname and brushed her knuckles against the door. It opened immediately, and she drew her breath in a rush. Her heart began racing at the sight of the face she stared into, memories flooding her mind with both pleasure and a hint of remorse. She swallowed and gathered her wits, her chest rising and plummeting. Darian smiled tentatively and stuck out a hand to be shaken.

"Hello, Claude."

Jesus watched the joyful reunion between Darian and Claude from the edge of Heaven and felt the warmth of His love for them. He also relished the relationship between E'thriel and Darian; it was healing both angel and human. He loved good news stories. Sadly, it was going to be the only one this day.

The Lamb of God surveyed the mass of people standing before the Throne of God, grateful to see so many in number. So many more had refused His call and chose against following Him. He, the Father, and the Holy Spirit heard their cries from the outer darkness, but there was nothing They could do. The lost heard His message many times while their hearts beat, and they ignored the narrow road. His focus now was on the people living on Earth who had yet to make a choice.

Jesus stepped down from the Throne and walked through the crowd to the edge of Heaven. He greeted people by name as He made his way through the throngs, shaking hands and exchanging quick hugs. Those who had relied upon Him for their salvation were quick to express their gratitude, and He was equally quick to express His appreciation for their faith.

At the edge of Heaven, Jesus saw four angels standing at the compass points on Earth. They had the power to harm the world, but now they were only holding back the trade winds, so no wind blew. For months, the air around the world had lain stagnant, empty of cloud and moisture. It was a blessing to those who lived in frigid places and a curse to those who sweated under the sun in arid regions.

To add to the misery of the inhabitants of the Earth, Moses and Elijah had commanded there be no rain on the Earth. It was a symbol of the power given to them by God, and a reminder of the Living Water available to them by a simple act of faith.

Jesus flicked the fingers of His right hand, and Gabriel dropped from Heaven. As the messenger angel approached the Earth, it appeared as if he ascended with the rising of the sun.

Gabriel carried the seal of the living God. He raised it high above his head so the four angels standing at the corners of the Earth would hear his announcement. Gabriel cried out in a loud voice,

"Do not harm the earth or the sea or the trees until we have sealed the bond-servants of our God on their foreheads."

These were the 144,000 prophesied in the Holy Bible. Gabriel flew to each man and woman and, one-by-one, pressed the ring against their foreheads. In the spiritual realm, their foreheads glowed with the symbol marking them as God's own.

The seals granted 12,000 people from each of the twelve tribes of Israel authority to spread the good news in Jesus's name. These Jewish evangelists would survive the holocaust of divine wrath unleashed by the judgments poured out on the earth, and which were still to come. They would be part of a Christian revival greater than the world had ever seen.

Jesus smiled. Billy Graham had teased Him over a cup of tea yesterday about the resurrection of the Church on Earth, claiming the Lord ought to have sent him and Charles Stanley instead of a pair of crusty old men from Antiquity. But for the necessity to fulfill Scripture, it wouldn't have been a bad idea.

Billy and Charles had brought many people to faith in Christ and Jesus was grateful for them.

Sealing the 144,000 Jewish evangelists would also protect them from Satan's attempts to kill the believers who had come to faith in Jesus after the Rapture. The 144,000 would accomplish their task and enter the millennial kingdom alive, a significant honor.

It was a reminder of God's mercy amid His unquenchable wrath.

Speaking of.

Jesus closed his eyes for a moment. He endured tremendous suffering while he walked the Earth in His human body. Now the world would endure His suffering tenfold.

It was time to break the Seventh Seal.

Jesus walked back to the stairs leading to the Throne Room, once more greeting and speaking with vast groups of people dressed in white robes. Gabriel returned from Earth, his mission accomplished, and handed Jesus the ring of His office while the people flowed around them.

This group of people were the martyrs who died for their faith and were now reaping the benefits of it. They'd completely forgotten the painful end to their lives and now enjoyed daily companionship with their God.

When Jesus reached the top of the stairs, His heart sang with joy at the sight of His Father sitting on the Throne, waiting for His Son. Yahweh handed Jesus the scroll, the title deed of the universe, which had upon it one last seal.

They had made the Seventh Seal of pure gold. It

heralded the beginning of the seven trumpets and seven bowl judgments, all of which would rain disasters of epic proportions on the world.

Jesus turned and faced the people. At the Archangel Michael's signal, seven angels stepped forward to stand before God. Jesus took the Seventh Seal between His thumbs and squeezed hard. As the seal snapped, a sonic boom reverberated throughout the Kingdom of Heaven. So powerful was the sound of the explosion it caused a silence in Heaven for about half an hour. Everyone froze in place, shocked.

When the silence was complete, Michael stepped down from his place near the foot of the Throne and handed each of the seven angels a trumpet. Each trumpet sound unleashed a judgment of increasing intensity, though none would be as destructive as the seven bowl judgments to come.

Another angel stood at the altar before the Throne Room, holding a golden censer. Michael gave him a heavy bag of incense so the angel could add it to the prayers of the saints. The smoke of the incense, with the prayers of the saints, went up before God out of the angel's hand. The censer had elaborate filigree on it, making it worthy of containing the essence of praise, worship, and prayers to the Lord.

It had one other purpose. A purpose beginning the worst part of the Tribulation period and the greatest suffering the world would ever see.

The angel took the censer, filled it with the fire of the altar, and threw it to the Earth, where it hovered, unseen in the sky, until the first trumpet sounded.

Atlantis, October 28, 2099 AD

They'd tried to keep it secret; they really did. There were good reasons for operational security, mainly because of the promise of their deaths if the wrong people discovered the full extent of what they were doing.

The problem with keeping the secret was the scope of the disaster befalling Atlantis. Half the population either died in the earthquake or suffered injuries. None of the above-ground buildings were intact. The seaport and airbase suffered the least damage, but it still took a long time to clean up. The extent of the damage was demoralizing.

In times of trial, people react in a few ways; one of them involves an outpouring of support and gathering to make recovery possible. When people throw their hearts, minds, and bodies into helping others recover from a disaster, they became a community.

The people of Atlantis, regardless of their skill level, threw everything they had into the hot, heavy work. All were determined to rebuild Atlantis, but many nights ended in tears and hung heads.

Into this deep miasma came a spark of profound joy.

Heather, Mick, Sully, and Jeannie stood at the top of Pharoah's Hill as the rising sun illuminated the white pavilion sheltering them. At the base of the hill were all three thousand, one hundred and twelve other survivors of the earthquake. It was Heather and Mick's wedding day and not one person on Atlantis intended to miss it.

Mick and Heather had announced their engagement to Sully and Jeannie the night Heather accepted Mick's proposal. Jeannie squealed and grabbed Heather into a hug as Sully brought Mick in for a hearty back slap. Payton overheard their laughter and pressed until they told her the cause for their joy. With the ongoing persecution of Christians and the state-enforced worship of the Mother Goddess Earth, none of them knew whether weddings were legal. They were eager to keep their engagement a secret. Payton promised not to say anything and tried hard to keep her word.

Two weeks later, she was treating an iron worker suffering from cancer. It was curable, but the man, having lost his entire family in the earthquakes, lost his will to live. To survive cancer, the best tool in the box was a fervent desire to survive.

Exasperated by the man's refusal to find his survival instinct, Payton accidentally let slip the news.

"Earl, you won't be dancing at the wedding if you don't change your attitude."

The man perked up immediately.

"What wedding?"

Payton bit her lip and silently cursed how loose it had become. She was usually so good at keeping secrets.

"You didn't hear? Master Chief Mick Davis and Dr. Heather Wu are getting married. It's going to be the social event of the year. You're going to have to get better if you're going to the wedding in six months."

Just like that, Payton not only released Mick and

Heather's secret but also set their wedding date. She would never hear the end of the teasing when they found out. The only good thing coming out of her loose lips was Earl's progress to recovery. Determined to get a dance with the bride, Earl's health improved with every treatment.

The news spread like a tsunami. People overwhelmed by grief and stress drank good news like cold lemonade on a blistering day. Within twenty-four hours of telling Earl, the entire island heard Mick and Heather were getting married in October.

Everyone on Atlantis, many of whom they didn't know by name, stunned Mick and Heather by making a point of congratulating each of them over the following week. Only five people knew of the engagement, so it didn't take long for them to isolate the source of the leak to one Dr. Payton Dumont. She apologized profusely, but the deed was done.

More stunning was how much everyone jumped in to take part in wedding preparations. Self-appointed volunteers organized clean-up crews to ready the area around Pharoah's Hill. Someone had decided it was the only place big enough to have the ceremony where everyone could attend. It was an easy wedding to plan; everyone else made the decisions for the bride and groom.

A sanitation worker approached Heather and confessed before he came to Atlantis, he'd been a bridal fashion designer. The First Cataclysm wiped out his dress shop and his desire to design the finest wedding dress known to New York. He begged Heather for the opportunity to design her dress, and she agreed.

"After all," she said to her bemused fiancée, "how bad could it be?"

Pierre spent a month searching every maw on the island for materials. He engaged the services of twins who'd lost their jobs as technicians when the Lens shattered into a million pieces. The dress Pierre created was stunningly beautiful. It left Heather's arms and shoulders bare while generously highlighting her small breasts. Hugging her slender body, it ended at her ankles.

Pierre had no access to pearls, but the shattered Lens left dew drop beads scattered around the TTI Main Building. He laboriously hand-sewed the glass shards into the dress, and the result was stunning. Each bead captured any available light and reflected it in a beautiful array of colors.

The dress fit Heather as if she grew it on her skin, and the design was elegant beyond description.

With the help of the twins, Pierre also created tuxedoes and dresses for the rest of the wedding party, and they felt like royalty when they tried them on.

The biggest concern turned out to be who would officiate at the wedding and what form the ceremony would take. A Christian wedding meant exposure and certain death. There was no way they were going to have a pagan ceremony.

Payton redeemed herself by informing them she held a certificate from days long past, giving her the authority of a wedding officiant. Sully, Jeannie, Heather, Mick, and Payton fashioned a ceremony incorporating many Christian principles while skirting around direct references having the potential to get them arrested.

Only the weather marred the six months of preparation; or the lack of it, that is. For six months after the earthquakes, winds didn't blow anywhere on the planet. No moisture fell. The entire world had never been so dry. Were it not for the deep freshwater cistern buried in the island, the lack of water could've been devastating.

On their wedding day, the bridal party made their way through the throngs of people lined up on each side of the path leading to the top of Pharaoh's Hill. People greeted them and waved as they took the long walk, calling out congratulations as if they were all long-lost family.

A beaming Marjatta surprised them at the end of the receiving line, just before they ascended to the top of the hill, by presenting the bride and groom with leis made of real plumeria flowers. It brought tears to their eyes whenever the floral scents wafted up into their noses. Marjatta had grown the plumerias, and they bloomed in time to make the leis, which were prepared by the Administrator's own hands.

The wedding party walked up the slope to the pavilion made of white aluminum and canvas. Nine construction workers had begged, borrowed, and stolen the materials for the pavilion. They'd promised Marjatta they would repurpose every molecule of the pavilion for the TTI rebuild and she tried to look severe as she told them she'd hold them to their promise. There would be consequences if they failed. It took her an hour after her conversation with them to lose the grin on her face.

Payton stood waiting for them under the pavilion, clad in a long linen vestment with gold inlays running down its center. The fashion designer turned sanitation engineer had created it, too. When the bridal party took their places, she raised her hands and complete silence fell on the island.

"Dearly beloved," she said, her voice amplified for the ears of everyone below, "we gather here today to celebrate the marriage of Lamek Eugene Davis and Heather Elizabeth Wu."

Heather swept an astonished look into Mick's face.

"*Eugene?*"

The crowd roared with laughter. Davis shushed her, his face turning red.

"It's a long story. I'll tell you later."

"Is there anything else I'm going to find out about you on our wedding day?" she whispered, delighting in the fire hydrant red coloration of his skin.

Davis shushed her again, and Payton continued with the ceremony while she tried hard to avoid a fit of giggles.

"We've faced a lot of adversity in the last six months. The worst earthquake the world has ever seen ripped apart this island, but the people of Atlantis made it beautiful again. It's to your credit how hard you worked to make this day so special for Mick and Heather. I know they very much appreciate your intense dedication."

"Mick, you and Heather have declared your love for one another and have brought us into the celebration of your wedding. We are grateful to you both for our inclusion. Now for the vows."

Sully stepped forward and handed the wedding rings to Mick. One technician had some talent with designing jewelry, and she put her flair to clever use by creating the bands out of gold she scrounged from the shattered precious metals vault. The vault once held every currency known to TTI to support downstream operations, but had lost its contents to the earthquake. The bands were beautiful and glittered under the sun, while Heather turned her synthetic flower bouquet to Jeannie.

"Lamek Eugene Davis, do you take Heather Elizabeth Wu to be your lawfully wedded wife, to have and to hold, in good times and in bad, in sickness and in health, promising to be faithful to her for as long as you shall live?"

Mick swallowed; his throat was suddenly dry.

"Yes, I do."

"Good answer," Heather whispered, to a scattering of laughter, and Payton had to swallow another giggle.

"Heather Elizabeth Wu, do you take Lamek Eugene Davis to be your lawfully wedded husband, to have and to hold, in good times and in bad, in sickness and in health, promising to be faithful to him for as long as you shall live?"

"As long as I never have to hear him called Eugene again, I will."

Laughter rumbled through the assembly and Davis turned a deeper shade of red, which Heather wouldn't have thought possible.

Payton coughed after choking off a chuckle.

"Mick, place the ring on Heather's finger and

repeat after me. Heather, with this ring I do thee wed; let its perfect circular shape be a reminder of our eternal love."

Mick fumbled the ring onto Heather's finger and did a decent job of repeating the phrase without butchering the language or fainting. Heather followed the same custom, after which they turned to face Payton.

"Mick and Heather, by the power vested in me by anyonecanofficiateawedding.com, I pronounce you husband and wife. You may share your first kiss as a wedded couple."

Mick swung Heather into his arms and planted a long kiss on her lips while the crowd cheered and applauded. They made their way back down the hill, shaking hands and sharing laughter as someone played the wedding march on a guitar that had seen better days.

The residents followed the wedding party to a long row of blankets, carpets, and towels spread out in what used to be a luxurious park. There were no buildings to house a reception, so it would be an open-air celebration.

The surviving chefs on Atlantis scrounged for six months and had prepared a mouth-watering feast for the dinner guests. There was enough food of enough variety to make it feel like they were dining in a five-star hotel. They even made a wedding cake.

Davis and Wu had their first dance under a sky filled with stars. They cut the cake and made the guests roar with laughter when they smeared it on each other's faces. Everyone danced, laughed, and sang until the sun threatened to rise on the horizon.

Heather was the focal point of the party, as everyone tried to get a dance with the bride. Some swayed with tears in their eyes, grateful for a moment of joy in a field of tragedy. Though she felt like she wouldn't be able to walk for a week after all the dancing, Heather graciously accepted each invitation. Who was to say when they'd have another moment like this?

As an ultimate gesture of goodwill, in the wee hours of the morning, just before dawn, the construction workers led Davis and Wu to the bridal suite, a solid and sound proofed structure they built just for the occasion.

Marjatta declared the following two days as holidays, free of the frenzied work characterizing the past six months. Everyone cheered and tried to shake Marjatta's hand, while several others pulled the laughing Administrator into energetic dances.

This honeymoon was going to be epic. Everyone was so happy. There wasn't even rain in the forecast. Nothing could wreck the festivities.

Fate winced.

In the Kingdom of Heaven

Darian stood at the edge of Heaven, her eyes misting. Her left hand clasped the massive digits of her guardian angel and her right hand snuggled in the hands of her long-lost fiancée. They could never marry now, but she was content to have eternity with the man she would've married but for, well, you know.

It was nice to watch Mick and Heather's wedding.

It would've been something entirely different years ago, but it was a shining star of hope in the Tribulation's world.

After she officiated at Johan and Gwyn's wedding, she asked the Lord if He would allow her to watch what was happening in her home world. Jesus cautioned her what she observed could bring her pain, but she pressed, and He relented. He allowed her to track Davis and Wu through Antiquity. Jesus was right. It was gut-wrenching. She thought Davis was going to die near Gilgesh until Tul'ran and Erianne swooped in and saved the day. Watching them in action made her grateful for every time she bit her tongue instead of verbally abusing them. Tul'ran and Erianne were two people you didn't mess with if you were smart.

Intrigued, she watched as Jesus gave Erianne the gift of inter-dimensional travel. She wasn't sure if she was happy with the group's decision to return to Atlantis, and less so when Davis began hallucinating. Darian started praying for him as soon as he left the med tent, and soon Jesus was standing at her side.

She dropped to her knees before him and pressed her forehead to His feet.

"Lord, You are sovereign, and I will never question your judgment. If today is not Davis's appointed day to die, will You allow me to go to his aid? No one knows he left the med tent, and he's wandering around in the dark toward the ocean. I would hate to see him gravely injured."

Jesus reached down and lifted Darian to her feet.

"Daughter, you are in your glorified body. If someone sees you, they may perceive you as an angel or a god. We do not permit people to return to Earth from here. It can cause great mischief."

A tear trickled down Darian's cheek.

"But surely you can dampen the appearance of my body for a few brief minutes? Lord, I came to you later in my life. I never served you while I lived. I was not a blessing to anyone. Can you allow me to be a blessing to one man in the dead of night? I promise You I will not grieve You with another such request."

Jesus shook his head, marveling at how far Darian had come. He sighed. Who was He to deny His beloved children their heart's desires? Especially when He could see no harm to it in all the futures her actions could birth.

"Very well. You may save him from harming himself, but no one else but him can see you. As soon as you have seen him to safety, you must return immediately. No interactions with anyone else on Earth, Darian. Do you accept my conditions?"

She nodded vigorously. He placed her back on the Earth, cloaking her eternal body, and she talked Davis away from the edge before he plunged into the ocean. She'd picked Davis up like he was a child and carried him as close to the med tent as she could without being seen before finding herself back in Heaven.

Elated, she watched his recovery and felt the warm glow of seeing his health improve in the months before his wedding to Heather.

Darian sighed. She hadn't been here when Jesus cracked the Sixth Seal; an amazing reunion with Claude and his family occupied all her attention.

Their party had gone on for a few days before news filtered down to them about the global earthquake.

The devastation on Earth had shocked her. She'd promised herself she wouldn't miss any more of what went on; she still had friends down there who were in a crisis.

Darian turned to face Jesus, who held a scroll in His hands. He addressed the millions of people gathered before His throne.

"And the seven angels who had the seven trumpets prepared themselves to sound them. The first sounded, and there came hail and fire, mixed with blood, and they were thrown to the earth; and a third of the earth was burned up, and a third of the trees were burned up, and all the green grass was burned up."

Jesus looked over the multitudes after reading the phrase aloud from the Revelation to John.

"On this day," He said, "I fulfill this prophecy in your sight."

The people sighed, and those who had the stomach for it wandered to the edge of Heaven to watch the fulfillment of divination thousands of years old. There was nothing to be done. Jesus had warned people this day was coming. All they had to do was read the Bible and they would have known.

The first of the seven angels dressed himself in red robes, which was unusual. Only his halo remained a brilliant white. The angel dressed simply, having discarded his sword and armor for the solemn occasion. He lifted the trumpet to his lips and blew a long, haunting, mournful note.

The Earth, October 31, 2099 AD, two days after the wedding

After the massive earthquake had ground the world into rubble, many had fled to the mountains to avoid aftershocks and the tsunamis hammering the coastlines. They stayed hidden in caves and in the valleys between the mountains for six months until the supply lines dried up and they ran out of food. To stay in safety meant starving to death, which was not an option. Even the wealthy had run out of the means to stay hidden.

It started as a trickle of humanity looking for food and alternative places to live. The trickle turned into a flood of flesh until the people emptied the mountains. It had taken six months, but the mountains were silent once more.

At the larger centers, organizers had a party to celebrate their survival. Using the holo feeds kept alive by the Government of Democracy, they organized a global orgy. They held the orgy on Halloween, October 31, 2099. It would be epic, with plenty of drugs and alcohol to get people in the mood for erotic gluttony.

The organizers gathered around a large bell, wearing exotic costumes, leaving nothing to the imagination, and raised a paddle. They slammed it against the brass bell to start the party.

When the first notes rang, the Yellowstone Caldera, Wyoming's super volcano, erupted.

Volcanic eruptions sometimes empty their stores of magma so swiftly the overlying land collapses into the emptied magma chamber, forming a geographic depression called a caldera.

It's what happened in Yellowstone 640,000, 1.3 million, and 2.1 million years ago. The calderas from those eruptions lie over the Yellowstone hotspot under the Yellowstone Plateau where hot molten rock from the Earth's mantle rises toward the surface.

The eruption of a super volcano has global consequences, besides regional effects such as falling ash, and causes years to decades of changes to the global climate. When Yellowstone blew, pyroclastic flows immediately affected those parts of the surrounding states of Montana, Idaho, and Wyoming closest to Yellowstone. The flows contained a high-density mix of hot lava blocks, pumice, ash, and volcanic gas.

They moved at extremely high speeds down volcanic slopes. People living closest to the Caldera died instantly, consumed by flying debris and asphyxiation. The flows accounted for almost forty percent of the fatalities after the super volcano blew.

It was not the only one to go that day.

The Yellowstone Caldera was one of twenty super volcanoes on Earth. None of them had erupted during the massive global earthquake, but all of them did now.

Campi Fiegrei, or the Phlegraean Fields, is an unassuming plain stretching one hundred and twenty-five miles under the bay of Naples, in Italy.

It is a giant caldera left by a super volcano two million years ago. Villas, small villages, shopping malls, a hospital, and eight hundred thousand people populate the area. Over five hundred thousand of the locals live in the 'red zone', an area encompassing eighteen towns at the highest risk of destruction in the event of an eruption. An additional three million residents of Naples lived immediately outside the eastern end of the caldera.

Campi Fiegrei had not erupted since 1538. It did today. Magma vaulted from a chamber five miles deep. It was an ignimbritic eruption, one of the largest kinds of volcanic explosions. Five hundred thousand people died in the space of two hours.

Lake Toba in Indonesia, Lake Taupo in New Zealand, La Pacana in Chile, and all the others detonated simultaneously. They spewed vast amounts of flaming lava, ash, and gases into the atmosphere and generated giant thunderstorms with burning hail the size of basketballs. Within twenty hours, dark ash-laden clouds covered the Earth, choking out the light and warmth of the sun. Under such skies, nothing requiring sunlight to live and sustain life would grow.

Blood red fireballs poured out of the atmosphere and instantly ignited the super-dry conditions of the forests and fields withered by drought. Worse, the absent winds woke up and blew with gale force. Wildfires sprang up and raged. Within days, burning hail and dry lightning would burn a third of the earth, including a third of the trees and all the green grass growing in various regions. The smoke from the fires permeated the atmosphere and spread over the entire planet, raining ash on buildings, vehicles, and people.

The fires were catastrophic; they destroyed crops, animals, wood for construction, and watersheds. Starvation, already a problem for most of the remaining population, would only get worse.

———————————✝———

Satan stared at the holo feeds and raged, feeling impotent. The exploding volcanoes happened quickly and without warning. The destruction playing out live on the holo feeds challenged his claim to be a god, and social media was looking for someone to blame. Fine, it was time to give them that Someone in spades.

At dinnertime on October 31, 2099, he stepped in front of the world's news holo cameras and gravely addressed an angry and frightened population.

"People of the world, I grieve with you over the most recent cataclysm to strike our world. Many of you are reeling under the horrific tragedies mauling our blessed Mother Earth. All of you are asking, why? I will tell you why. We failed you. Yes, you heard correctly. We failed you. How did we fail you, you ask? By not wiping out the terrorist sect known as Christianity sooner."

"I have it on good authority: it is the Christian's god who has rained these disasters upon you, to punish you. You, who have deserved no punishment, you who have had to endure wars, famines, plagues, devastating earthquakes, and now a global fire, you now suffer because of the capricious, malicious actions of a god who loves only Christians and hates you."

"Well, I've had enough. On your behalf, and out of my love for you, I declare a global war against Yahweh, his Son, Jesus, and the Holy Spirit. I will bring these false gods to justice!"

The holo camera inserted wild cheering into the

feed and Satan waved to a non-existent audience.

"People of the world, the worst is over. I, your god, will now bring peace and prosperity to this world suffering the ravaging effects of nuclear war and climate change. Let us gather and rebuild."

Fate just about choked from laughing so hard.

In the Kingdom of Heaven

Darian and Claude watched in horror as flames consumed a third of the planet they'd called home.

"When I read the Revelation to John, Darian, I knew this was going to be bad. It's one thing to read about it and think about it, but seeing it..." He shuddered.

"Those poor people," Darian said, with her right hand to her mouth. "The fires are burning out of control. I wish we could help them."

Claude shook his head, the skin near his eyes creasing.

"They made their choice when they rejected God to follow Satan. It's not over for each of them. If they reach out to Jesus, He'd take them into His heart in a second. Look at all the people who have come to Him already. Unfortunately, the more this goes on, though, the harder it will be for them to break through their hatred for God and ask for His forgiveness. Oh, oh."

They looked to the edge of Heaven as a second angel stepped forward. His robes were black, infused with red streaks throughout. He carried in his hands a black trumpet and a strange stone. The angel rubbed the stone along the keys and put it to his lips.

When the angel sounded his trumpet, from Heaven it appeared as if someone threw a magnificent mountain burning with fire into the sea.

The world, October 31, 2099, just after dinner

NASA's Jet Propulsion Laboratory Asteroid Watch ceased to function after the First Cataclysm, even though it sat eleven hundred feet above sea level in La Cañada Flintridge, California. The city was in an exceedingly high fire hazard severity zone because of the local topography at the base of the San Gabriel Mountains. Not two years after the First Cataclysm, a wildfire consumed the city and JPL's buildings. Everything burned to the ground.

The result? With their facilities destroyed, scientists stopped looking for comets capable of wreaking havoc on the Earth thirty-four years before the volcanoes erupted.

Comet Bernardinelli-Bernstein, or C/2014 UN271, discovered in 2014, is the largest comet ever spotted. Its heart is seventy-five miles across and it's blacker than coal because its nucleus reflects only about three percent of the light striking it. It should take three million years to circle the sun and would have stayed a billion miles from the earth, but for a singular event fifty years earlier. A larger, previously undetected comet collided with Bernardinelli-Bernstein, altering its course, and sending it speeding through the solar system on a collision course with Earth.

The impact of the larger comet shattered Bernardinelli-Bernstein, but the remaining chunks were still bigger than any comet flying by Earth throughout the history of humankind.

The remnants of Bernardinelli-Bernstein had dropped into the Earth's flight path and six of the largest fragments impacted the atmosphere, traveling one point five miles per second, over one thousand times the speed of most meteorites.

To the terrified population of the Earth, it looked like a lofty mountain of fire pierced the stratosphere. Everyone saw the impact, the 3D quality of the holo feeds bringing the horrific imagery into their hiding places. It struck the oceans with the explosive power of nuclear weapons. It killed one-third of the fish in the sea immediately, turning the oceans into blood.

One-third of the GoD merchant marine and supply ships sailing the seas loaded with food, clothing, and building materials capsized from the tsunamis generated by the force of collision between the oceans' salt waters and the massive chunk of rock and ice that was Bernardinelli-Bernstein.

Or a portion of it. The comet fragment striking the Earth was only the leading edge of its poisonous core. It had lagged the leading edges of the comet by only a few hours, but it would add to the carnage below and double the tragedy on Earth.

In the Kingdom of Heaven

"Look at that!" Darian said, grabbing Claude's upper arm and squeezing it hard.

The comet's impact created large mushrooming splashes of seawater, with vast waves following each impact. They watched as the ripples sawed across the face of the earth, leaving destruction behind. On Earth, the ripples were massive waves driving relentlessly to shorelines. The energy of the tsunamis erased the surface of the land.

"Did I tell you I used to surf?" Claude said.

"Huh? What? Good grief, Claude! How could you be thinking about surfing right now?"

Claude winced.

"Sorry, I didn't mean it the way it sounded. I only meant I've ridden some massive waves." He pointed to the waves pressing out from the impact sites. "None of them were ever like those waves. They'll capsize supertankers. They'll crush anyone standing in the way before they get to worry about drowning."

Darian smiled at him tightly.

"Sorry, Claude. Watching this has me a little wound up. Look, there's another angel!"

A third angel stepped forwarded, dressed in robes of bright yellow. His trumpet glowed and well it should; he made it from polished 24 karat gold. He sounded his trumpet, and the multitudes in Heaven watched a great star fall from heaven, burning like a torch, and it fell on a third of the rivers and on the springs of waters.

The world, October 31, 2099, hours after the comet struck.

The core of Bernardinelli-Bernstein was a toxic heavy metal, ancient in its origins. Its properties were like wormwood, a shrub whose leaves were used in the manufacture of absinthe, a liqueur so toxic many countries banned its manufacture.

The core disintegrated when it struck the

atmosphere, sending millions of shards falling on the world's freshwater rivers and lakes. Within hours, the shards poisoned one-third of the world's freshwater supply.

It's a well-known fact people can survive a long time without food. Jesus fasted for forty days in the desert before assuming His ministry. Various historical figures survived prolonged periods of fasting as a protest.

No one lives without water after three days of thirst.

For the first time in history, water became the most precious commodity. People hoarded their supplies, fending off thieves with automatic weapons. The Regions moved tanks and heavy machine guns around water facilities, hastening to erect razor wires and mines in every access point. People killed each other for a glass of water.

Atlantis was fortunate. TTI had screened out psychologically weak people in favor of determined cooperative instincts. In later days, Marjatta would post a token guard around the entrance to the water facility, but it wasn't necessary. The residents were pulling together.

At least for now.

In the Kingdom of Heaven

Claude and Darian hadn't moved from the edge of Heaven since the first trumpet sounded. They strained to see what had happened to Darian's friends, but their spiritual gifts hadn't matured to the stage where they could exercise their ethereal vision.

E'thriel could've helped them, but held his counsel.

What he saw could only have brought them pain.

E'thriel nodded at the fourth angel who came forward, more slowly than the others. They'd been friends before the Rebellion, and E'thriel had been glad to see he'd remained faithful to the Lord. He didn't have many friends left.

This angel dressed himself all in black. Even his trumpet was black. He lifted the trumpet, blew on it, and it made an unholy wail, like a star screaming before it died.

When the echo of the last note faded, a third of the sun, the moon, and the stars were smitten. They'd cast one-third less light on the world once the curse fell upon its weary citizens.

The world, October 31, 2099, before midnight

Volcanoes exploded. A comet struck the oceans. The comet's core splintered and poisoned the world's lakes and streams. One third of the Earth burned, and the comet laid waste to another third of it. The debris from all of it bloomed into the air like the mushroom clouds dotting the planet during the First Global Nuclear War.

Darkness sat heavy in the skies above every country, with the sun, moon, and stars blocked by smoke and debris. The heat loss from the sun lowered the Earth's temperatures dramatically, disrupting weather patterns and the tides.

It was the most devastating Halloween in the history of humankind.

Over the next weeks and months, millions would

die of thirst, starvation, and poisoning as they tried to consume tainted water out of desperation. The survivors raged against God and prayed to Satan daily for the fallen angel to avenge them. No one questioned his fanatical raging against Christians and the Holy Trinity, accepting as a fact it was not their god's fault.

No one took responsibility for their lack of faith in the God who was eager to save them.

Atlantis, November 1, 2099 AD

It was not possible for them to be alive. For many of the residents of Atlantis, all had the thought flash through their minds as they struggled out of shelters. The surface of the island was a burned husk, with blackened grass and the skeletons of trees littering the landscape.

Everything on the surface had burned, including the med tent, the food tents, and sleeping quarters. Only Marjatta's foresight had saved them. She had ordered her workers to tunnel into the underground residences after the earthquakes, and they'd found large pockets still structurally sound. When the holos started broadcasting the destruction of the planet, she'd ordered the entire populace underground. On Atlantis, no one died.

Mick led his new bride to Pharoah's Hill, which still burned and smoked in various places.

"This must be what the underworld looks like."

Heather shuddered and snuggled closer to his body, her heart hammering in her chest.

"What are we going to do, Mick? Our food is

gone. Is this how we die?"

Mick shook his head as Sully, Jeannie, and Payton walked up to them.

"I don't know, Heather. The Bible predicted this; if we'd paid more attention, we'd all be in Heaven watching this with a pitcher of Margaritas sitting by our lawn chairs."

"I don't think that's how Heaven works," Sully said. "There are no margaritas, just wine. Wow! This is bad."

"No," Jeannie said, curling into her husband's arm. "This is worse. Look at the sky. It's eight o'clock, but the sky is pitch black, as if we're under an eclipse. This could turn into the nuclear winter scientists have been worried about for decades."

Marjatta walked over to them, Erasmus Hart walking slowly behind her. She acknowledged their group with a head nod, but none of them would meet Hart's eyes.

"I just spoke to our glorious Supreme Leader. He's happy to know we're all alive. Cargo ships are on their way to us. He wants us to build again as soon as they get here. Twenty-four hours a day."

In the stunned silence following her pronouncement, Coventry Quarterlaine limped up to them. In the scramble to get below, frightened people trampled her, re-injuring her knee.

"Why is everyone so glum? We endured another cataclysm. I think we should be used to this by now. We're still alive, people. At least be grateful for that."

Mick closed his eyes and sent a prayer of gratitude toward Heaven. Yes, they were still alive. They would rally and rebuild; there was nothing else they could do, was there? He looked at Sully and grimaced.

"One evolution at a time."

Sully nodded, recognizing the philosophy from their early days in BUD/S.

"Yeah, brother, but if the only easy day was yesterday, what kind of Hell is tomorrow going to bring?"

Fate laid down its head and sighed. By the same time next year, one of them would die and one would face torture beyond their ability to endure.

Fate found it ironic that people only listen when the stars fall.

CHAPTER THE FIFTEENTH:
ASSASSIN'S BLADE

Ma'ilingan Waazh (Wolf's Den), 175th Year of Winter Seventeenth day, Manoominike-giizis (Ricing Moon), Year 5379

"It's getting warmer."

Erianne turned her head and regarded her husband, who had a smile on his face for the first time in days.

"It is. The ice layer above us is already having the desired effect, moderating temperatures. Look at the sides of the mountain we're passing; the snow is melting. The world is changing, thanks to you and your crazy sword."

Tul'ran grunted.

"I didn't set out to change the world, but I'm content with not freezing every time I sit on Darkshadow. Even he has more lift to his gait."

Nicholas pulled back on the reins of his roan and waited for Tul'ran and Erianne to catch up. He pointed at a large stone structure midway up in the mountain.

"The City of Gichi-inini, which means 'big man'. The men we sent ahead will have informed my father of our coming. My father's name is Chief Eric Ravenclaw."

Wenonah pulled her mare beside Nicholas's horse.

"Will he receive us with animosity?"

Erianne noticed the look Nicholas gave the Leader of the Nine Tribes. It was an intriguing mixture of respect and something more than a casual interest.

"I'm not sure, Wenonah. The scouts I sent ahead should've convinced him you're no longer a war party. We'll see if he believed them."

Wenonah flashed her teeth at him, dimpling slightly beneath her eyes.

"I'm sure we can persuade him of the peacefulness of our mission now that the ablative shield once more controls our weather."

Nicholas side glanced at Tul'ran, who gazed at him with a neutral look.

"If not, your Wolf could always offer to make slaves of us and cruelly abuse us. There's nothing more frightening than his threats."

Tul'ran flickered an eyebrow and nudged Darkshadow forward. Now didn't seem the time to tell the young man he'd never owned a slave in his life, much less abused one.

The last two days had been a much nicer journey. Nicholas's people had structures cleverly hidden along the way of their path, providing warmth and shelter for humans and horses. One of his men was a wonderful cook who made hot meals for them. After the first day, when tensions still rode high, the atmosphere warmed and so did the dispositions of the riders. By the end of the second day, the journey had taken on a festive atmosphere.

In the middle of the third day, the party rode up the mountain's slopes and into the City of Gichi-inini. Men and a much smaller number of women lined the streets, their body language tense, but fascinated. No one held spears, but Erianne knew someone must have had weapons trained on them. It's harder to tell people 'we come in peace' after you destroy their primary defenses.

They stopped before a squat, one-story building built onto the side of the mountain. The riders dismounted. All of them, except Tul'ran, were grateful to be off their horses. A man stepped forward to take Darkshadow's reins and stopped when Tul'ran gave him his full attention.

"Be at peace, Warrior," Nicholas said. "We honor our horses and take great care of them. Your Darkshadow will be safe in our custody. You can see him whenever you please. We will feed, water, groom, and treat him like the Chief's son. Sometimes I thought my father loved his horse more than he loved me."

Tul'ran nodded reluctantly and stroked the side of Darkshadow's long face.

"Go with them, brother, and show them kindness. I will check on you soon. Try not to hurt them, for we are guests in this house."

Darkshadow tossed his head and whickered before placidly allowing himself to be led away.

"Nicholas, you should know my Darkshadow is a war horse," he said, watching as men took their horses into an enjoining structure. "If your men displease him, it won't be my fury with which you should be concerned."

"He is fierce on the battlefield," Erianne added, remembering her first encounter with Tul'ran in the desert near Ur. "It would be best to follow my husband's advice."

Nicholas canted his head forward.

"You have duly warned us, Princess. As I've said, we treat horses with profound respect here. It would shock me if any of my men abused them. If they do, they would've earned their deaths."

They trooped into the structure behind Nicholas and followed him through several corridors. The home was much larger inside than outward appearances suggested. They came to two large doors, guarded by big men carrying energy spears. The guards stood aside and allowed Nicholas to open the doors.

The interior of the room was spacious, and furs lined the walls and floors. A chair sat in the center of the room, which someone carved from a light-colored wood. Twelve men sat in a circle around the chair, holding pipes in their hands. They dressed in buckskin shirts and pants, with moccasins covering their feet. Erianne felt as if she stepped into an old Western holo.

In the center of the room, sat a man who was no doubt their Chief. He had on a long headdress of eagle feathers and bead necklaces adorned his neck. His buckskin clothing had beads imbedded in it in the shapes of various animals. He had a lined, leathery face and long gray hair framed it. His eyes were a bright green and conveyed no emotion.

Nicholas walked up to the man and placed his right hand on his father's left shoulder.

"Greetings, father. I bring to you Wenonah, the Chief of the Nine Tribes."

A look of astonishment flickered across the Chief's face. He paid his full attention to the young Princess's face.

"Does my son speak truly?"

Wenonah took a step forward and took a deep breath.

"The Creator came to me in the Garden of our Ancestors. He told me the history of the world and how He had decreed that every twenty years, leadership of the Nine Tribes would pass between a Man and a Woman, so no one could make a dynastic claim to Ma'ilingan Waazh. He showed me the faces of my Ancestors and told me it was time to reclaim my birthright and lead the Nine Tribes into a new era of peace."

The Elders seated on the furs around the chair murmured and bobbed their heads at one another. The Chief raised his hand.

"Bring the scanner."

One guard standing in the room's corner left through the large double doors. Within a few minutes, a woman came into the room wearing surgical scrubs and a pained expression on her face.

"Eric, Deenah is about to give birth to your first

grandchild. Don't you think that's a better place for me to be?"

"Megis, my wife, this is important. Did you bring the scanner?"

"Dr. Swimminghorse, if you please," his wife replied tartly. "Isn't that why I'm here? Who do you want scanned?"

Chief Ravenclaw gestured toward Wenonah, and Megis dashed the scanner over her face, capturing her eyes within the beam.

"This is Wenonah Bearspaw, hereditary Chief of the Nine Tribes, in this cycle of being. All honor to her. It's a pleasure to meet you, Princess. About time."

Wenonah smiled a response as the Chief nodded, keeping his face somber.

"Thank you Megis. Give Deenah my regards and tell her I anxiously await our first grandchild."

"Tell her yourself," Megis retorted, already on her way out the door. "Dispense with these silly formalities and come join us."

Erianne was struggling to keep a smile off her face. The atmosphere here was much more relaxed and congenial than in the City of Ikwe Na. Even the guards acted as if royal visits were a matter of daily boredom.

Chief Ravenclaw stood up and placed his hands on Wenonah's shoulders.

"I greet you, Princess Wenonah, on behalf of the tribes of Men, and acknowledge you as the Chief of the Nine Tribes. As long as you are here, I offer you the hospitality of the House. When you leave, I assure you of a safe journey. No harm may come to you while you abide with us."

Wenonah's eyes sparkled.

"Thank you for your kind greetings, Chief Ravenclaw. I am prepared to enter peace negotiations to end the war between Women and Men. Will you appoint your Second so we can begin?"

Eric Ravenclaw laughed.

"Ah, the impetuousness of youth. My son will be our Principal Negotiator. Nicholas, have you appointed a Second?"

Nicholas gestured to the group of people behind Wenonah.

"Father, I present Lord Tul'ran the Conqueror and his wife, Princess Erianne. With them rides the Warriors Ro'gun, Omarosa, Innanu and Anatu. Innanu is Ro'gun's wife. Princess Wenonah has appointed Lord Tul'ran as her Second. I appoint Princess Erianne as mine."

Tul'ran's eyebrows crawled up toward his hairline and he looked at his widely grinning bride.

"We are to negotiate against one another?"

"Indeed, milord husband, which is so unfortunate for the Women. It will be a terrible thing for them to succumb to defeat at my hands."

The eyebrows climbed higher.

"What makes you think you will best me in our negotiations?"

Erianne leaned in and kissed him on the tip of his nose.

"If you have to ask, you've already lost, Conqueror. Shall we have at it?"

Chief Ravenclaw lifted his hands to get their

attention.

"Not now and not here. As you've heard, I have a grandchild making its way into our world. Negotiations will start at first light."

———————

At the evening feast, the Chief announced the blessing of the birth of a baby girl. There was great rejoicing in the city. Adding a girl to their population was a significant event. They treasured and respected Women, for the continuation of the People rested on their shoulders.

Erianne expected the trappings of the dining room to reflect the Tribe's heritage, but it was, in every respect, a modern room. The long wooden table was cut with lasers and the chairs were professionally designed and manufactured. Lights lit the room, powered by some form of electricity.

The Chief had changed into casual pants and a monochromatic shirt. His staff served bison, potatoes, and various other vegetables. The food was spicy and tantalized the taste buds. Tul'ran and Erianne ate until they couldn't accept another bite before they retired to their room.

The bedroom was spacious and had large sheer windows offering a view of the snowy forest beyond the building. The immense bed was firm and covered with furs. Exhausted from an evening of polite conversation, Tul'ran and Erianne fell into bed and a deep sleep.

The next morning, the negotiations began. Tul'ran and Erianne met with their Principals after breakfast, who presented them with a list of their positions. The Seconds then retired to their bedroom to discuss the points and to establish some common ground. From the sound of the muffled voices and the noises coming from the room, the negotiations were vigorous.

After several hours, Tul'ran and Erianne emerged, flushed, and tousled. The men guarding the room told Chief Ravenclaw later they suspected the Seconds had exerted some physical force to drive their points home. The Chief had laughed and told the men to attend to their Watch, saying he had no doubt the discussions were vigorous.

So it went for four days. Slowly, the two sides worked toward a peace treaty. Each time the parties became stuck, Erianne and Tul'ran would retire to their room for several hours to battle through the fine points. Each time they did so, they emerged looking more relaxed than the Principals, announcing language acceptable to both their Principals. They would have a draft agreement soon, they said, before disappearing back into their quarters.

Yes, negotiations were proceeding well, indeed.

Spes, the world of Hope, in the Year of Our Peace 0001,
The 25th day of the month of Destiny's Edge
Mission Day 360

She was cold, but it wasn't her skin feeling the weight of frost pressing against it. The cold came from within, untampered by the fire of love or the passion of the spirit. It tasted of bitterness, hatred, and contempt.

She shuddered. This was not her world of

temperate climate and gentle breezes. It was a wasteland of ice, snow, and hateful thoughts. The desire to kill and seize power pounded in her temples. Her patience rewarded her. She would kill and take what was rightfully hers. Her target stood before her, and the frostiness of the soul dipped further in temperature.

It was time.

Gwynver'insa lunged awake and pressed her hands to her mouth to stifle a scream.

"Tul'ran!"

Ma'ilingan Waazh (Wolf's Den), 175th Year of Winter Twenty-second day, Manoominike-giizis (Ricing Moon), Year 5379

Tul'ran and Erianne stood before the Conclave of Men. The Chief and Twelve Elders sat high above them behind a raised curved desk. They had gathered to hear the terms of the draft peace agreement. If they approved it, Wenonah and her new entourage would return it to the City of Ikwe Na for further negotiations and ratification.

Erianne nodded her approval as Tul'ran recited the terms of the agreement in a smooth voice. She pulled her lips inward to hide a smile. The negotiations had been boring, with Wenonah and Nicholas wanting to haggle over the smallest points. When it became too much of a bore, Erianne would announce the necessity to work out the finer points in their bedroom.

Work them out, they did. It was amazing how a hard bounce cleared the mind and opened the door to new options. While Tul'ran was new to creating peace through words, he managed his side of the bargaining with latent skill and an open attitude. Wenonah was more than eager to secure a peace deal, and she readily accepted Tul'ran's suggestions.

Nicholas was a little more reticent, but he had become infatuated with Erianne. Her height, mahogany brown skin and incredible beauty set her apart from any woman he'd met. Erianne didn't even have to flirt with him to convince him of a sticky point. Not that she would've resorted to such a tactic; her love for and loyalty to Tul'ran would never permit succumbing to manipulating Nicholas's hormones.

The deal was fair, Erianne thought. Men would get back their scientists with a solemn vow they wouldn't attempt anything potentially threatening to the planet's safety without consulting their female counterparts. The two groups would work toward de-militarization. Each would bring their Lions and Wolves under control, so they would threaten no more lives. Inter-marriage between the tribes would be encouraged to allow for procreation, all while maintaining the right of choice and free will.

The Conclave of Men were listening to the terms raptly. This was good. For once, Tul'ran had resolved a war while killing none of the combatants.

It would be his crowning achievement.

Erianne felt nature's call and flicked a thought at Tul'ran's mind she would return momentarily after using the facilities. A flash of love came back as an acknowledgment and Erianne let it warm her heart.

She left the Conclave and wandered down a tight

corridor. It was a well-lit, smooth stone pathway. They carved the entrance to the facilities in stone, but the interior was as modern as anyone would've liked. After she took care of her necessities, Erianne went to wash her hands. She looked up and gasped when she saw the face of another woman standing behind her.

Before Erianne could react, the woman pressed a hypo spray into Erianne's neck, and the world faded to black.

———————————+—————

Two of the Elders were haggling over one term of the peace agreement, having locked horns on the monitoring clause. One argued it was a harsh restriction on the right to pursue scientific discovery. The other vehemently reminded his cohort of the devastating environmental effects caused by the last pursuit of knowledge.

Tul'ran shifted his weight from one leg to the other as subtly as possible. He'd been standing for over an hour, and the monotonous undertone of the debate was making him sleepy. He wondered what became of Erianne. Tul'ran didn't want to reach out and touch her mind if she was in the middle of her ablutions. He'd give her a few more minutes and then make an excuse to leave the room to search her out.

Tul'ran wasn't concerned with her safety. The men had set out guards to ensure no one would disrupt the Conclave. There had been no sign of activity in the north, so the prospect of war interfering with the peace talks was dim. He grinned to himself. Erianne was a hellcat with a sword in her hands, and she and Tul'ran were both armed. If anyone tried to get in her face, they would pay a quick and deadly price.

He covertly scratched an itch under his armpit. Still, it would be nice to have Erianne here. He only truly felt secure when he knew he had his wife watching his back.

———✦———

Evo had bided her time, and it was now. In this moment of Tul'ran's triumph, when everyone was relaxed and happy, it was time to kill him.

Evo missed her chance when she found Tul'ran in Mesopotamia. After leaving Spes, she found his DNA sequence lodged in her computer. The AI promptly informed her the DNA originated on the third planet in the system she almost destroyed when she blew up the fifth world. It had taken only a day to traverse Inter-Dimensional Space to Dirt or Earth or whatever the stupid humans on that dumb planet called it.

She arrived after the Earth had suffered a massive earthquake. It shocked her how much damage the seismic shocks had caused around the globe. It took her a few hours, but she finally correlated the coordinates of the person who appeared to be running the world. If one needed an answer, it was best to go straight to the top.

She cloaked her ship and landed it near a temple in an arid area of the globe. It was difficult to find a level area given significant ground disruption from the quake. She parked in an obscure spot and activated the sub-harmonic defensive system. Anyone coming close to the ship would feel a deep sense of foreboding. Most people scurried away. A simulated lightning strike would electrocute the few who pressed on. It was foolproof.

After securing her ship, she had the AI create period-specific clothing and ventured out looking for the Supreme Global Leader. She was considerably surprised when she discovered it was Satan.

She took him aback when she stepped out of Inter-Dimensional Space into his makeshift private office. He'd never known a human to traverse Inter-Dimensional Space at will. Looking at her, he sensed she didn't originate in this world. Humans! They spread like lice all over the universe.

"Who are you?" he asked, rage tinging the outer edges of his words at her arrogance in appearing unannounced in his presence.

Evo cocked her head at him.

"You don't remember me? Of course, you don't. Typical man. I'm Evo. I spent a hundred years in that lifeless garbage prison you called the Abyss."

She could see the memory bloom in his eyes.

"Ah, yes, Evo. The human who destroyed the water world between Mars and Jupiter. You were quite entertaining, as I recall. I still chuckle over some of your philosophies. Why are you here?"

"I've come to track down someone named Tul'ran az Nostrom."

She could see the information had jolted him.

"Tul'ran az Nostrom! What do you want with him?"

"I want to kill him," she said, her voice even. "He has something of mine and I want it back."

Satan leaned back in his grotesque chair and stroked his beard.

"I find the timing of your appearance odd. I'm addressing Tul'ran's situation right now. What does he have of yours?"

Evo shrugged.

"What he has is my business. I can see you know of him, and it pleases you I want to kill him. Tell me where he is, and I'll bring you his head on a platter."

Satan's smile was cruel and filled with hate.

"Your terms are acceptable. I'll tell you when and where he is. It'll be up to you to get there."

Evo executed a mock bow.

"Pleasure doing business with you. If you don't mind, I'm in a bit of hurry and I can see you've got your hands full here."

Satan pulled out a fountain pen attached to an elegant pad of paper. How quaint. He still used pen and paper. Evo had traveled to the dark ages.

It took her several hours to map the coordinates to travel back in time and space to get to Tul'ran's location. She found the village easily, and after eavesdropping on several conversations, determined she could probably find him at a particular ridge near the village. It took no time to travel there through Inter-Dimensional Space, but she was too late. The group with Tul'ran were riding away, and she had no time to set up an ambush.

Evo stayed in IDS until she found out where Tul'ran and his party were traveling. She felt something akin to joy when she found out it was Ma'ilingan Waazh. The world had been one of her success stories.

When Evo had roamed the universe in her spectral form, she'd come across Ma'ilingan Waazh. The planet was peaceful then, with the Women and Men living in harmony. It had disgusted Evo to see the Women gravitating toward domestic duties, while the Men hunted for food. Women popped out babies and tended them; in return for what? Permanent servitude? It wasn't for her.

Evo had appeared before a woman who had been meditating near a stream, deep in the forest. The woman had a receptive mind, and Evo soon found a way to speak to her spirit. They spent days in conversation, during which she convinced the woman of Women's superiority over Men. Their spiritual connection became so close, Evo could manifest as a spirit. The woman acknowledged her as the god and creator of the world, and it pleased Evo's ego to permit the false impression to last.

The woman, who turned out to be Baamewaawaagizhigokwe's grandmother, spread Evo's words to other Women. Most rejected the new doctrine outright, but Evo had planted a seed. It just needed a catalyst to grow.

Evo supplied them with one. She found a man whose mind she could touch. It took a long time and much work, but Evo eventually inspired him with the designs of the very spacecraft her AI worked upon in her absence. She hadn't perfected the transshield device then, but reasoned even a man could eventually figure it out. Surely, they would not try to crash through the ablative shield.

Evo broke the news to the Women about the Men's intentions to travel beyond the ice layer. She influenced her contact's mind to conjure the horrors such a plan could cause. By then, many of the Women revered her contact as a prophet and Evo's thoughts weren't just heard, but put into effect. A war of words began between Men and Women, which eventually divided the two sexes completely. This made Evo ecstatic. Women didn't need Men, which they would learn. She would replace God as their deity. How delicious.

Evo left before the men completed their project. When she returned six months ago, she was stunned to see the ice layer gone, and the planet plunged into winter. It had disgusted her. The stupid Men tried to crash through the ice layer after all. What a bunch of morons.

It was hard to wait for the right time to kill Tul'ran. His use of the sword was something to be respected. She stood, almost feeling awe when he drew the energy out of the Curtain and directed it to repairing the ice shield. Evo couldn't figure out how he'd done it, but the message was obvious. She had to catch him when his guard was down or face a weapon she had nothing to counter.

It was also necessary to do something with his wife. Evo didn't know why the woman didn't just strike out on her own. She was an intelligent, talented warrior and didn't need a heavily muscled beast to keep her safe. Erianne would do better without him. Evo had seen Erianne fighting with Tul'ran and considered them evenly matched.

Erianne was misguided by her feelings for Tul'ran. She'd put a sword into the chest of the last man who tried to kill Tul'ran. It would be best to put her away for a bit, for both their safety.

When Erianne used the facilities, Evo followed her. As Erianne was washing her hands, Evo slipped out of Inter-Dimensional Space and injected Erianne with a soporific drug. Evo moved through IDS with Erianne in her arms and left her in Inter-Dimensional Space with her hands staked out far apart from one another. It would take her some time to get out of her bindings, and more time to figure out how to transit out of IDS. By the time she escaped, it would be too late for her husband.

Evo brought with her weapons of her own design. They had the hilts of a regular knife, but that's where the similarities ended. The knives produced an energy blade. Evo could release the blades from the hilt by pressing a button, and they would promptly leap forward, disintegrating everything in their path.

Flesh was especially susceptible to destruction by the blades. She had spent hours testing them on small animals until her experiments satisfied her the blades would cause a quick and painful death. It was possible to make the death painless, but since all other creatures were beneath her, it didn't matter if they suffered pain. After all, she'd had to endure her fair share, hadn't she? Why spare others?

Evo had conquered entering and leaving Inter-Dimensional Space eons ago. It was impossible to detect her when she traveled in IDS. After she secured Erianne in IDS, she returned unnoticed to the Conclave. For a moment, the thought of killing all the Men in the room tempted her. She could decapitate the Women's natural enemies in one blow.

Baamewaawaagizhigokwe wanted total victory, not a peace deal. If she could deliver it to them, it would give the Women even more reason to worship her as their god.

God. The one-word obstacle between her and ultimate power. Evo shuddered. The time she spent in the Abyss had scarred her down to the last molecule of her being. She'd felt herself lapse into insanity more times than she cared to remember, especially in the latter part of her sentence. No, her original plan was the best one. Grab Bloodwing the Blade and kill God with it. Then no one could stand in her way. She would rule the heavens and the cosmos.

Evo maneuvered into the room. She moved beside Tul'ran until she was only feet from his body. The right moment was coming; she could feel it.

She paused momentarily when she thought she heard a woman screaming Tul'ran's name. Evo shrugged. If someone shouted a warning, it was too late. Tul'ran the Sword, the Uncreator, was about to die. In his place, Evo the Eternal would rise and rule.

The two Elders had finally finished arguing, and they asked Tul'ran to finish his presentation. Everyone was nice and relaxed.

Just like she needed them to be.

———◆———

Erianne awoke slowly, unable to pierce the gloom surrounding her. She was lying on a firm surface, unable to move. Something was terribly wrong. She felt her arms pinioned at the wrists. Her feet were similarly bound. Someone stretched her body tightly enough to immobilize her. It was even a little difficult to breathe.

Erianne panicked. The woman she saw in the mirror attacked her but left her alive. Why? Why immobilize her and keep her alive? Her panic grew. What if she wasn't the target? G'shnet'el had staged an ambush on Earth in Antiquity to capture Tul'ran. Had the forces of evil followed them to Ma'ilingan Waazh to finish the job? Erianne struggled in her bonds and almost separated her shoulder. She screamed in frustration.

She had to get to Tul'ran before it was too late.

After ten boring minutes, Tul'ran finished his speech and lowered the papers down to his waist. The papers were in his right hand, and he had set his sword for a right-hand draw. There would be no time for him to release the papers and remove his weapon from the sheath on his hip.

Evo set in motion a series of events tumbling one after the other within nanoseconds. She emerged from Inter-Dimensional Space opposite Tul'ran's left shoulder with both her hands raised.

In each hand, she carried the energy weapons, activating the blades as soon as she transitioned into Dimensional Space. Each bright red blade was five inches long and four inches wide. The blade contained a petawatt, or quadrillion watts of energy.

They were an assassin's weapon; she could fire them once and couldn't use them again until she recharged the knives.

Once released, each bolt of energy would pass through Tul'ran's body, the floor, and one hundred feet of substrate, dissolving everything in its path. Here, the 'everything in its path' included Tul'ran's heart, spine, and a few vital organs. As soon as she held down the studs, Tul'ran would die; she would grab his sword and fade back into IDS.

Just as she appeared in Dimensional Space, each blade only feet from Tul'ran's body, Evo depressed the studs to send the laser blades propelling away from the hilt at the speed of light.

Nothing is faster than the speed of light.

ABOUT THE AUTHOR

Dale lives in Cochrane, Alberta, Canada with his amazing and beautiful wife, and their bevy of furry children. When not practicing law, Dale golfs, lifts weights, and, of course, writes.

Wolf's Den is the fourth book in the series detailing the lives of Tul'ran and Erianne az Nostrom. The first three books in the series, *The Ballad of Tul'ran the Sword*, *A Time, and Times, and Half a Time*, and *Abandon Hope* have been published and are available for purchase from Amazon worldwide in paperback, hardcover and Kindle versions. The next book in the series, *When the Stars Fall*, will be published in 2024.

Dale wrote the first four novels in this series between August 2022 and August 2023. One storyline in the novels involves a fictional account of the events of the Tribulation at the end of the world as prophesied in the Holy Bible, particularly in the Revelation to John. The future casts its shadows into the past. Some events portrayed in these novels are being overtaken, to a lesser degree, by current tragedies and may point to more severe occurrences happening in the future. It is for this reason Dale is publishing all four books now instead of staggering them into 2024 and 2025. You may find some answers in these fiction novels for what's happening in the world, but for more and better information, please search for answers at davidjeremiah.org.